SERIAL KILLER SUPPORT GROUP

SERIAL KILLER SUPPORT GROUP

A NOVEL

SARATOGA SCHAEFER

NEW YORK

This is a work of fiction. All of the names, characters, organizations, places and events portrayed in this novel are either products of the author's imagination or are used fictitiously. Any resemblance to real or actual events, locales, or persons, living or dead, is entirely coincidental.

Copyright © 2025 by Saratoga Schaefer

All rights reserved.

Published in the United States by Crooked Lane Books, an imprint of The Quick Brown Fox & Company LLC.

Crooked Lane Books and its logo are trademarks of The Quick Brown Fox & Company LLC.

Library of Congress Catalog-in-Publication data available upon request.

ISBN (hardcover): 979-8-89242-077-8
ISBN (paperback): 979-8-89242-230-7
ISBN (ebook): 979-8-89242-078-5

Cover design by Heather VenHuizen

Printed in the United States.

www.crookedlanebooks.com

Crooked Lane Books
34 West 27th St., 10th Floor
New York, NY 10001

First Edition: March 2025

10 9 8 7 6 5 4 3 2 1

For Bella, as a little treat.

And if you gaze for long into an abyss, the abyss gazes also into you.

–Friedrich Nietzsche

Support Group Rules:

1. No outside contact.
2. No identifying information.
3. No in-fighting.
4. No re-entry.
5. No communication with the police.

Those who break *any* of these rules will be killed.

CHAPTER

1

IT BARELY LOOKED like a frog, if Cyra was being honest. Simply constructed and only a few inches tall, it was made up of two round balls stuck together. No webbed feet, no long tongue. The pale green glaze and the giant white eyes bugging out of its small head were the only indicators that the clay object was supposed to be a frog. Handmade, obviously. It was sitting near the edge of the desk, crouched behind the lamp.

Cyra stared hard at the lumpy frog approximation, meeting its blank gaze, trying to keep her hands from shaking and her teeth from chattering. The precinct wasn't cold; the chill was coming from her bones, brought on by the detective's news.

The man seated across the desk from Cyra cleared his throat, noticing her sudden stillness. "Ms. Griffin?"

Cyra reluctantly drew her focus away from the frog. Something Detective Bellows's kid made in art class, no doubt. Garbage to anyone else, but important enough to him that he brought it into work and stuck it on his desk. "It's Cyra."

"Of course. Cyra." Bellows pronounced her name wrong even though she had just said it. "Did you hear what I said?"

Sigh-ra, not Seer-ra, she wanted to snap, but she had to choose her battles.

"Yes, I heard you. What else?"

"Sorry? I'm not sure what you mean," the detective replied, expression wary.

"I mean, you can't say you think my sister was a victim of a serial killer and not give me any more information," Cyra said. Her voice was steady, and she could feel the googly eyes of the clay frog watching her cheeks, as if it was wondering where her tears were.

Mind your business, she thought at the frog.

Bellows blinked at her from across his desk, which was covered in manila file folders, a beat-up old laptop, and three framed photos of a young boy being practically smothered by a woman with a cloud of black hair. The rest of the precinct hummed around them, drowning out their conversation so that it camouflaged itself among the other tragedies happening concurrently.

Cyra's hands were clasped tightly around the backpack on her lap, clutching it like it was a life raft, the only thing keeping her afloat in an upside-down sea. The zipper was pressing uncomfortably into her inner arm, but she didn't move to adjust herself.

Detective Bellows's throat worked, and he frowned slightly. "This is an open investigation. Frankly, I shouldn't have even told you that, but your little friend down in Records begged me to give you something, so that's why we're even here talking right now. You need to understand that we're doing everything in our power to find your sister's killer. Let us do our jobs."

Cyra wanted to scream, but she swallowed it like she had been swallowing all her rage since she received the call on September 25 at 2:06 PM that severed her heart. "It's been well over a month." Cyra said instead, pleased with how calm her voice sounded. She resisted the urge to get into another staring contest with the clay frog on the desk and met Bellows's eye instead. "There has to be more. If there's not . . ."

Detective Bellows seemed to understand what she was saying. "The case won't go cold." His voice softened, his irritation leaking away. "I can't imagine what you're going through. But as I told you last week, just because we don't have a lot of physical evidence doesn't mean we can't solve this. I can't share everything with you to preserve the investigation, but there are some ... similarities in your sister's murder that I think are pointing us in a promising direction."

"Such as?"

"I just said I can't share them." Some of the irritation returned to the detective's voice as he shot her an admonishing look.

"Was it how many times she was hit on the head?" Cyra asked. "It was a lot, right? But she would have died from the second strike. The rest was overkill. Right? Or did you find what they killed her with? The first cop I spoke to said they thought it was a rock."

Bellows looked a little green. He almost matched the frog. "That's your sister you're talking about."

Cyra leaned forward, her eyes intent. "Did you know we shared a birthday? We were both born on January 12th. Same day, five years apart. Do you know how annoying it was when we were kids? To have to share our birthday? Get joint gifts, joint parties? God, I hated it. You know what I would wish for when we blew out the candles on the cake we shared every year?" Cyra swallowed and clasped the backpack tighter against her body. "I would wish for my own birthday. I would wish that I didn't have to share with Mira anymore." Bellows looked as if he would like to be anywhere else in the world, and he suddenly couldn't make eye contact with her. "This will be the first year I'll have my own birthday. And every year after this I have to live with knowing I wished for this."

"You didn't wish for this," Bellows intoned. "No one would have wished for this."

"I need to know what happened," Cyra said. "I need to know who killed her. What's the pattern you're talking about? Was it a signature? A calling card?"

"I can't discuss this with you any further," Bellows repeated, reddish-blonde brows drawing together. "Please. Stop asking."

That means yes, Cyra thought. *There was something about Mira's body that must be connected to other victims.*

"If this is the work of a serial killer, why can't you catch them?" Cyra asked instead.

"These things take time," Bellows insisted. "Trust me, we're doing all we can. But this isn't a case that can be solved overnight." The man slumped in his seat, ruffling his ginger hair, the roots of which were starting to gray, and stared at Cyra. "I won't give up on your sister, OK? I won't lie to you; this might take a while. But we're going to get him."

Cyra tried to imagine this detective sprinting down a dark alley, feet pounding, beard twitching as he chased a perp, and couldn't. She knew, from their first meeting, on that terrible day, that he had a family. He had used them as a way to try to bond with her: "I would lose my mind if anything ever happened to my son." But all it had really done was show her that the man had priorities in his life that had nothing to do with her sister.

Maybe she could trust the NYPD to do their jobs. But maybe she couldn't. And maybe she didn't want to sit around and wait years for them to arrest someone. Besides, that outcome wasn't what she wanted anyway.

"Ms. Griffin? Cyra? Are you OK?" Bellows was leaning forward now, perhaps noticing the expression that settled over Cyra's face as she thought of the pricey switchblade she recently purchased that was tucked away under her pillow back home. She pretended she bought it for self-defense after Mira's death, but at night Cyra would clutch the knife and picture a faceless killer. She would imagine the blade plunging into his chest over and over.

"I'm fine," Cyra said, standing abruptly. "Thanks for meeting with me."

Bellows scrambled to his feet as he cleared his throat again. "Of course. But . . . in the future . . . let me contact you when we have information, OK? It'll be faster if we can work without interruptions."

Cyra understood. *Leave us alone, let us get on with it so we can do the bare minimum, and then label this a cold case and get on with our lives.*

"Will do."

"I can walk you out . . ." Bellows trailed off, his voice questioning.

"Not necessary."

Relief blossomed on the detective's face as he nodded. "We'll be in touch, Cyra. Soon, I hope."

Cyra made an effort to not roll her eyes, inclined her head toward him in what she hoped looked like a display of gratitude, and then pivoted, swinging her backpack around so it settled on her shoulders as she walked into the lobby of the precinct.

"Cyra!"

She turned to her left to watch Eli rush toward her; he must have been hovering near the stairs, waiting for her to emerge. Cyra tried to arrange her face in a way that would look welcoming—she owed him, after all. Eli worked in Records, a job he mostly hated because it was boring archival and data entry work, but whatever tiny influence he had on the force paid off. He was able to get Cyra this meeting with Bellows after the detective started ducking her frequent and occasionally demanding calls. Cyra waited for Eli to get abreast of her, and then she started moving again.

"How'd it go?" Eli jogged to keep up as Cyra kept striding toward the front of the police station. Eli *looked* like he worked in records—short curly hair, thick glasses, a pert, upturned nose, and a wardrobe that seemed to consist mostly of flannels.

"All he'll tell me is that they think it might be connected to a serial killer."

"Whoa, really? That's . . . horrific." Eli had stopped for a moment at Cyra's words, struck, but now hurried to catch up with her. "They're gonna get him then. If there are other victims. Don't worry, Cyra, we're going to get this asshole."

"They're moving too slow," Cyra replied, reaching the exit and pounding down the concrete steps into the chilly fall air. "And there are twenty-five to fifty active serial killers in the United States at any given time, did you know that? And New York City has the highest population of people. It would make sense if there are multiple killers here, but when's the last time you heard of cops catching a serial killer in the city?"

"Cyra . . ."

"They're going too slow," she repeated, Eli trailing her down the sidewalk now.

"Cyra!"

She stopped. People streamed around her, some giving the two of them dirty looks for clogging the congested sidewalk. There was an event at Barclays Center today, and the avenue was more crowded than it was the last time Cyra had shown up, unannounced, to hassle Bellows for more information. The cream brick building of the precinct loomed, looking down at the two of them with reproval.

Cyra turned to Eli, who was shivering in his plaid flannel and skinny jeans. "What do you want, Eli? I gotta get back to Queens."

"When was the last time you slept?" Eli asked.

"Last night," Cyra lied.

"Not according to Izzie."

"How would she know?"

Eli sighed. "She got in touch with Bea the other day. We're worried about you."

"Your girlfriend is keeping tabs on me by hitting up my ex?"

"Someone has to," Eli said, exasperated. "Your dad is out of his mind with grief, and Mira wouldn't want you to go on like this. We all have to stick together. Mira needs us to be a united front."

Mira didn't need anything anymore. Didn't Eli get that?

"I haven't seen Bea in weeks. She wouldn't know if I was sleeping either. I'm fine, Eli." Cyra tried to inhale deeply, but something was stuck in her lungs, preventing her from taking anything other than shallow breaths. Her eyes ached with exhaustion, but every time she tried to lie down, images swarmed her mind: Mira, bleeding, sightless eyes, sprawled near the boathouse in Prospect Park. Images Cyra had never seen, only heard about. Images that were bloated and exaggerated by her ruthless imagination.

She had put a framed photo of Mira beside her bed, one of her sister's self-portraits, in the hopes that she could fixate on that version of her instead. The photo was staged in the dark, as Mira's work often was, but her face was lit up by the warm flicker from a beautiful candelabra, and she was smiling softly. Mira had their father's Irish features—flaxen hair, slightly curled, smooth skin, a long, thin nose, and huge, green eyes. Cyra, on the other hand, was darker, shorter, sturdier than Mira. To her disappointment, Cyra inherited her mother's face. She tried to wear her glasses as often as she could, to give her face a slightly different shape. Even so, sometimes she'd flinch to see herself in a passing mirror, thinking she was Grace Griffin, the woman who left them.

But looking at Mira's self-portrait in her apartment every day wasn't working. That version of Mira was never the one that showed up in Cyra's dreams.

"I need to find this guy, Eli," Cyra finally said. "I know Izzie was Mira's best friend, but I'm the older sister. It's my job to do this." She paused, looking up at the crisp blue sky, thinking of what she'd done for Mira in the past. "The cops are limited; they can't break any laws. But I'd do anything to find the truth. I just wish I had something to go on."

Eli's eyes widened. "I get it. OK, listen. I might be able to help you. Come over to our apartment tonight. Seven?"

Cyra was intrigued, even though it meant she'd have to trek back to Brooklyn in just a few hours. "OK. Seven."

Eli gave her shoulder a squeeze, and he disappeared back inside the precinct.

Only then did Cyra unfurl her left hand, revealing the little clay frog she'd swiped from Bellows's desk. She slipped the frog into her backpack and melted away into the crowd.

"We're so glad you could make it! I feel like I haven't seen you in a while," Izzie said, handing Cyra a chilled can of flavored seltzer. Her voice was chipper, almost forced, an obvious effort to be normal. "Did you ever end up watching the Potomac season finale? That lady is a piece of work . . ."

Cyra took the dripping can, dropped her bag to the floor, and flopped down on to the velvet sofa. "The what?" she replied absently, popping the top of the seltzer, watching it fizz.

"The Real Housewives!" Izzie said, darting back to the kitchen area to grab her own seltzer, Eli trailing behind her with a bag of veggie chips. "Potomac's your favorite, right?"

"Oh," Cyra said, looking up from her drink, fighting a wave of confusion, carefully pasting a small smile on her face and trying to inject brightness in her voice she didn't feel. Did Izzie really expect Cyra to care about stuff like that anymore? "Yeah, sure."

Eli opened the bag of chips and passed it around, as Izzie started chattering about the show Cyra hadn't bothered to see or think about in over a month. She stared down at the ridged chips, their greasy, salty smell coating the inside of her nose. A pulse of irritation shot through her. What the hell were they doing talking about reality TV and eating snacks? Eli promised her help. That was why she was here. She put the bag of chips down on the coffee table.

"Eli," Cyra said, barely noticing Izzie's chirp of annoyance as she interrupted her midsentence. "You said you had something about Mira's murder."

The apartment went dead silent. Izzie's mouth snapped shut, and Eli flushed. Cyra realized she was still wearing the impression of a smile on her face, which perhaps explained her companions' aghast expressions. Her lips flattened, and she swallowed.

"Are you OK?" Eli asked.

"I'm fine," Cyra replied. "I just need to know what you know."

"It's . . . You say it so casually," Izzie whispered.

"What?"

"Her . . . her murder," Izzie said. "You say it so calmly."

This wasn't the first time they'd had this conversation. But Cyra was too busy trying to figure out what happened to Mira; she didn't have time to constantly perform the emotions other people thought she should be expressing after a shocking and sudden death.

What she wanted to say was, "Sorry I don't burst into tears every time my sister's name is mentioned. Sorry I'm not exhibiting grief in the way that is most comfortable for you."

"Please, Eli, I've had a long day," she said instead.

"Yes, Eli, do tell," Izzie added, rounding on her boyfriend with knitted brows. "What does she mean? You know something about what happened?"

"We need more snacks," Eli muttered, turning back to the kitchen.

"I'll get them," Izzie snapped, scooting in front of him. "You talk."

"Well," Eli said, looking anywhere but Cyra's face. "OK, so Bellows told you they think this might have been the work of a serial killer. But what he didn't tell you is that there's chatter about a . . . a meeting. A weekly meeting. For serial killers."

"A *what*?" Izzie shouted as she returned to the living area, placing a bowl of peanuts on the coffee table. "Please tell me you're joking, Eli."

"I'm not. It's a serial killer support group."

Cyra ignored the snacks and scooted forward on the velvet couch, fingers wrapping around the bottom of the cushion she sat on, staring at Eli, who was now crammed into the armchair next to the loveseat.

Izzie and Eli lived in a six-hundred square foot apartment in Park Slope they paid a ridiculous amount of money for considering Eli's sad government salary and Izzie's kindergarten teacher one. But Izzie had wanted to live within walking distance of PS 321, where she taught, and both of them fit in seamlessly with the growing hipster crowd despite Izzie being from Michigan and Eli from Wisconsin. It wasn't far from where Mira had lived in Dumbo either. Cyra, on the other hand, lived in a crappy studio in Jamaica, Queens, and had to take an hour-and-a-half train ride whenever she had wanted to visit her sister.

"Explain, please," Cyra demanded, her focus on Eli only, even as Izzie puttered around nervously, digging different things out of their fridge, hoping to tempt her best friend's sister into eating something.

Eli seemed to steel himself. "I'm not supposed to know about this, so neither of you can tell anyone else. Not even your dad, Cyra."

There was no worry there. Cyra had only spoken to her father twice since Mira's death. Holton Griffin had been inconsolable during both conversations, barely functioning, barely listening, gripping his bottle so tightly his knuckles seemed permanently stained white. Her father had already been a house of cards due to his love of whiskey; he fell apart instantly and spectacularly after Mira's death. Leaving Cyra to manage everything—the cops, the stray reporters, Mira's friends, extended family who heard the news. She had to arrange her little sister's funeral alone.

Their father was struck down by his grief, and Cyra, knowing that Mira was his favorite, let him have his despair.

At first, Cyra's own pain was minor. Like someone had pinched her heart with small fingers. Not pleasant, but bearable. Except the fingers never let go. Discomfort that goes on for too long soon blooms into full agony. The pinching began to feel like a vice. When weeks went by and the fingers kept ahold of her heart, twisting, it was a relief when the pain became so intense that she finally went numb.

"How'd you find out about this if you're not supposed to know?" Izzie asked, finally coming to sit next to Cyra on the loveseat, her brown eyes narrowed, her tan cheeks paling in anticipation of her partner's words. "This better not be something that could get you fired." By the look on Eli's face, it was exactly that, and Izzie's frown deepened. "Eli, no!"

"My job is so boring, Iz," Eli complained. "Sometimes I do some . . . light reading."

"*Light reading*?" Izzie repeated.

"Sometimes I access files for interesting cases," Eli said sheepishly.

"And then you put them back where they belong, right?" Izzie demanded. "You would never bring them into this apartment, correct?"

Eli's face flushed, and Izzie's face shuttered dark.

"Get to the important part," Cyra said impatiently, trying to reign in her agitation.

"OK, OK, so about a year ago I was reading this file that was sent over from the cybercrimes department. I guess they sent it to all NYPD precincts because, well . . ."

"Spit it out, please," Cyra snapped. Her hands were wet; she was squeezing the seltzer can, sloshing fizzy water over her knuckles and down her wrists.

"There are rumors of a serial killer support group that meets somewhere in the NYC area," Eli said, his words all rushing together at once. "The FBI found talk of it on the dark web. It seems to be local to New York; they meet weekly, there's a code word on an encrypted forum, and it's obviously very, very secretive."

"Why haven't they shut it down?" Izzie asked, her voice pitched higher than it normally was. She inched a little closer to Cyra on the couch.

"Well, first, they can't confirm it actually exists. The report notes that it could be a hoax or a couple of incels messing around. Especially because none of the Feds have been able to prove it's real; every time they use the password, they struggle to make contact. From what I understand, there's a . . . gatekeeper or something on the forum. You have to send photographic proof of your . . . kills. The Feds have doctored some images and tried to trick their way in, but whoever is monitoring the group never bites. Maybe they know the photos are fake, somehow. I don't know. And I guess most of the force is skeptical because . . . you know . . . serial killer support group? Come on, it sounds like a hacky movie plot."

"But you think it could be real," Cyra stated. "And so do the Feds if they keep trying to access it."

"Well, if this group *is* real, the forum is the only evidence of it. If they get cybercrimes to shut the forum down, the freaks will go someplace else, and they'll lose them all together. I guess they're just trying to keep an eye on it."

"And they think the group meets in person?" Cyra asked.

"I guess so? It's unclear."

"Seems dangerous. The in-person meeting, I mean. And odd. Aren't serial killers supposed to be loners? I bet it's a virtual thing."

"I don't know, Cy. Like I said, it's probably fake."

Cyra's mind was racing faster than she could keep up. Something was unfurling like a rug before her, leading her into a dark hallway, foreboding but also enthralling.

"Well, maybe it's a good thing these people are trying to get help?" Izzie suggested. "They are trying not to kill, right? Maybe they can be rehabilitated."

Eli let out a disbelieving laugh. "Oh, Iz, no. It's not like an AA group or something. It's not to stop them from killing. It's to *encourage* them. It's a 'safe space' to share."

All the remaining color drained from Izzie's face, and she buried her head in her hands. A sheet of her dark hair fell over her shoulders, closing her off like a curtain in a theater.

But Cyra sat ramrod straight, blood rushing to her face. "I need to see this file."

"Hell no," Eli said immediately. "I could get fired just for telling you this."

"You said you wanted to help," Cyra accused. "Why tell me this then?"

"Yes," Izzie asked, emerging from her hair to stare daggers at her boyfriend. "Why the hell would you tell us this?"

Eli said nothing for a moment, just stared down at the sage green carpet.

"Because there's a chance Mira's killer is in this group, if it really exists," Cyra finally said. "Did the file say how many people participate?"

"No. No info about who, how many, where they meet, nothing."

"But they have the dark web forum, and the password." Cyra stared at Eli, willing him to look her in the eye. He compromised by staring at her throat.

"Yes."

"Eli, no," Izzie said.

"What makes you think you'll get any further than the literal FBI could?" Eli asked, crossing his arms and leaning back in the chair, suddenly reticent. "It's not like you can send them a photo of a dead body either, Cyra."

"They're the law," Cyra said. "I'm not. And I'm a bit more motivated than they are. She was my sister. I don't care about following any rules." At the word "rules," Eli flinched and looked away. "Let me at least try. You wouldn't have said anything if you didn't anticipate this outcome."

"No," Izzie protested again. "It's insane! It's too dangerous!"

Eli twisted his hands together like he was trying to wring a decision from his fingers. The apartment seemed to go quiet as he sat there, thinking. Then his shoulders sagged, and he looked up at her.

Cyra didn't bother to hope. She already knew.

"OK," Eli whispered. "I can get you on the site. I can get you the passcode. But that's it. Then you're on your own."

"That's all I need."

"What do you know about the dark web?"

"Um . . ."

Eli grimaced. "Yeah, thought so. I know a little bit, some stuff I've picked up from work. I'll write down the instructions for you. Follow them exactly."

Cyra nodded. "Thanks."

"And you tell me right away if anyone makes contact with you. And you definitely don't do anything stupid like ask to meet up with anyone."

"Are you both out of your fucking minds?" Izzie shrieked.

Eli rocketed to his feet, moved around the crowded coffee table, and pulled his girlfriend up. "Give us a minute, Cyra." They moved toward the kitchen and pressed up against the sink as they whispered furiously.

Cyra kept herself rigid, but out of politeness pretended to scroll through her phone even though she could hear every word; it was a small apartment after all, and Izzie had trouble controlling her voice when she was upset.

"You're going to get her killed," came Izzie's harsh whisper. "Then both of them will be gone. And why didn't you tell me any of this?"

"Relax, she's not going to get anywhere," Eli replied, his voice softer than hers. "She probably needs this. To help with healing, with closure. She can't do what the FBI can't, OK?"

"And you didn't clue me in because . . . ?" Izzie's voice was pointed, tinged with hurt.

"Come on, Iz, not now."

Cyra tuned them out. Izzie would fold, latching on to the reasonable expectation that of course, Cyra, a marketing coordinator for an upscale nursing home, would never be able to infiltrate a secret, possibly fake, support group for the most dangerous people in the city.

But Cyra felt like everything she'd ever been through had been leading to this. Her mother leaving, everything she did to protect Mira in the past, even the mixed-martial-arts classes Cyra had taken for five years—it was all for this, and she hadn't even known it. Her sister was dead. Her father had gone off the deep end. Her girlfriend had left, unable to handle the tragedy. And yet, Cyra was ready.

Izzie didn't know that Cyra had cut her hours and was now only working part-time, barely enough to survive on. She didn't know that after talking to Bellows earlier, Cyra went online and ordered six books about serial killers for research. She didn't know that Cyra had been watching knife fighting tutorials online since Mira's murder in order to better defend herself while she hunted for her sister's killer. She didn't know that Cyra had pulled away from all her friends and family, claiming she needed time to process.

What Cyra told Bellows was true—she resented sharing a birthday with Mira, but it didn't change the fact that her entire life had revolved around keeping Mira safe.

Now it was different.

Mira was gone, and Cyra's morals were gone with her. The world was gray; everything was detached and meaningless. Cyra never broke down after Mira's death. Never cried. Never screamed. Cyra just started planning, determined to find who killed her sister and why.

She floated away from her body and returned empty and hungry.

And now, finally, was something to feed her.

CHAPTER

2

Truthfully, it was reprehensible, but Cyra didn't have the luxury of caring about that.

Doris Mathers was a nice woman. Her mind wasn't all there at the end, but she always smiled gummily at Cyra whenever she walked past her room. When Doris first arrived at the nursing home, Cyra had bonded with her over their shared appreciation for sea glass. Cyra sometimes wore a pendant Mira gave her, and Doris noticed, showing Cyra the jars of cloudy, color-coordinated sea glass scattered around her room.

But the sad reality of working at a nursing home was that residents died. Frequently. When Macy, the nurse on shift, caught Cyra in the hall a few days after her meeting with Bellows and quietly let her know Doris passed away an hour earlier, Cyra waited for sadness to flood in.

It didn't. All she felt was the familiar numbness that crept inside her after Mira's death. The same numbness she felt on occasions in the past. It used to scare her, this yawning, disconnected sensation, but now it was a relief.

"I know you two chatted occasionally," Macy said, squeezing Cyra's arm. Why did people always think death meant they could touch you? "I'm sorry. If you want to take a break . . ."

"Is she still in her room?"

"Oh, um, yes. There's some paperwork that still needs to be filled."

"I'd like to go say goodbye," Cyra said, aware of her disturbing lack of grief. In its place, opportunity, screaming at her to hurry before the chance slipped away. But for Macy's sake, Cyra sagged forward, squinting her eyes like she was trying not to cry. "You know, pay my respects."

"Of course. You know her room. We'll be by to move her shortly." Macy gave Cyra a brave smile, and Cyra tried to mimic it, wondering if she was pulling it off.

In Doris's room, Cyra tried not to think too hard about what she was doing; posing next to the woman's body as it cooled in a snug space filled with sea glass. Cyra angled her phone above her head, making sure both her stoic, slack face and Doris's still body were in the frame. Cyra tapped the screen, taking a selfie with the dead woman.

A shudder fluttered through Cyra's body. Morally, it was fucked up. She should hate herself, but even that seemed to require too much energy. The same way feeling Bea's hands on her body or Izzie's hugs after Mira's death required too much energy. It was easier to succumb to the numbness.

"Sorry," Cyra whispered to the woman's body, wishing she meant it.

Doris would have understood. Or maybe she wouldn't. Either way, it didn't matter; Doris was dead, and there was no changing that. It was easier to accept that instead of wailing, putting on a show for her coworkers.

Her whole life, Cyra felt like people expected more from her. Larger reactions, stronger emotions. When one of her past partners cheated on her, Cyra simply threw the belongings left in her apartment in the trash, blocked him, and never looked back. Mira encouraged her to tell him off, get revenge, do *something*, but Cyra didn't care.

The person Cyra loved the most was Mira, and when she died, all the feelings Cyra was constantly asked to have became inconsequential. It was far easier to disappear behind nothingness. Why sit in the stagnant pain of grief and loss if she could be unfeeling instead?

No, she wasn't reacting to her sister's death in a "normal" way, but it was a way that allowed her to keep going, to do whatever needed to be done to get justice.

Besides, Cyra's ability to disconnect had protected Mira in the past.

When Cyra was in her junior year at community college, Mira, still in high school, started dating PJ Longfellow. Cyra hadn't liked him right away—why was a senior interested in dating her sophomore sister? There was only one possible reason, and it made Cyra's teeth clench.

Cyra lived at home while she got her marketing degree at Duchess—it was only seven minutes from their house in Poughkeepsie, and it was affordable. Which meant she was around to see the bruises start to pop up on her sister's collarbone and shoulders. She saw how Mira's bubbly exterior grew quieter, how her clothing changed to more muted, conservative looks. Mira denied anything was wrong, so Cyra tried to talk to their father about it on one of the rare times he was home and not working at a construction site or out with some new woman who would last three weeks.

"Oh, honey," Holton Griffin said, his hands running across his rugged cheeks as if he was too tired to deal with the conversation. "I know it's hard for you."

"What?" Cyra replied, thinking that was an odd response.

"I know you two are very different," he continued, a tumbler of whiskey in his hands as he watched the Mets, his attention drifting between her and the game. "But jealousy isn't a productive emotion. PJ is good for Mira. I worked with his dad for a bit last year, he's a good man. You'll find yourself a nice guy if you stop focusing on your little sister's life and live your own."

He had said the words casually, calmly, like they barely mattered, but they sang through the air like arrows and hit Cyra's heart, one after another. Her father knew Cyra dated boys and girls, but he didn't care enough to even remember that. Her mouth dried up and her response along with it.

How could she say that he was placing too much trust in a sixteen-year-old girl because that was easier than actually parenting her? He'd never listen to Cyra. She looked too much like her mother. Mira, the mirror image of their father, only had to ask, and she got whatever she wanted, even if they couldn't afford it. Of course he would be blinded by Mira's own denial. Of course he wouldn't trust Cyra, the daughter who wore the face of the woman who broke him.

The few times PJ came over for dinner, Cyra stared daggers at him, wanting him to feel her hatred, but he barely seemed to notice she existed. Cyra always looked at his hands, scouring them for signs of defensive scratches or red knuckles. She never saw anything, only the tacky class ring he wore on his left hand. It was brassy and featured a cut ruby, but you rarely got to see it because PJ liked to wear the gem on the inside of his finger, an odd choice that Mira said allowed him to "feel beauty in the palm of his hand at all times."

Cyra threw up in her mouth a little bit when her sister told her that.

As the relationship continued, unsure of what to do, how to make Mira see the truth in what was happening to her, Cyra felt paralyzed and powerless.

Until one day Mira came home with a scarf wrapped around her neck. Cyra slipped behind her in the hallway and watched as Mira removed it in her room, revealing angry red marks around her slender pale throat.

"Mira!"

Her sister whipped around, a look of guilt passing across her face as she scrambled to put the scarf back on. Cyra didn't let her; she raced into the room and pulled Mira's hands away from her neck, horror building in her chest.

At the center of Mira's throat was the faint imprint of a ring. The sharp indents of a gem could be seen pressed into her sister's delicate skin. Which would only happen if someone was wearing a ring on the inside of their hand.

Cyra turned and ran to her car, Mira following her and begging her to stop. But Cyra couldn't. Mira didn't have anyone else—their mother was gone; their father was oblivious. She had to protect her sister. It was her job.

Mira threw herself into the backseat before Cyra took off. As she drove, a strange calmness descended over Cyra, a disconnect from her body that crept in when she wasn't looking. Cyra found PJ in the front yard, practicing spirals, shirtless in the warm May afternoon. PJ was a whole head taller than Cyra, petite as she was, but it didn't matter. She leapt from the car and drove her body into him, knocking him to the lawn.

"You ever, *ever* put your hands on my sister again, I'll . . . I'll . . . make sure it's the last thing you do," Cyra said, voice cold and hollow.

Mira sat in the backseat of the car, pressed up against the window, crying silently. PJ looked up at Cyra from the grass, eyes wide.

Cyra didn't regret what she did to PJ, but something broke between her and Mira that day. A seed of resentment was planted. Cyra ruined Mira's first relationship—and Mira had never been able to accept or discuss the abuse she suffered. The sisters made up, remained close, moved to the city together, but Cyra felt tendrils of Mira's anger, her suspicion, touch her over the years.

Especially when Mira took the photo. The one of Cyra that went viral.

Cyra looked down at Doris, eyes half closed, face wrinkled and waxy. The room smelled of mothballs and lemon-scented air freshener.

Cry. Do something. Don't just stand there like a sociopath, Cyra snipped at herself. But she couldn't draw upon an emotion she didn't feel.

Instead, she grabbed one of the many jars filled with sea glass from the bedside table and slipped it into her pocket. She left the room, and Doris, behind.

That night, Cyra sat at her computer in her cramped studio apartment with Eli's notes scribbled on torn-out journal pages in front of her. Following his instructions, she made sure her webcam and microphone accesses were blocked, covered her camera with tape, and closed all her other applications before opening the dark web browser Eli told her to use, a network that would bounce her encrypted traffic through random nodes, making it difficult to track. Eli mentioned she would need to "rinse" her web identity every half hour and after the session, which would wipe away any traces of her existence.

The link below is for the forum, Eli had written. *It's what they call an onion address—not searchable via standard browsers.*

Holding her breath, Cyra typed the address in, glancing down at the notes to eye the password needed to access the forum and the supposed gatekeeper.

Eli described the site as a forum, but in reality, it looked more like an old school chatroom. The page was blank save for a pixelated icon of a skull. When Cyra clicked it, a chatbox appeared.

Anonyme0220: *Can women join?*
Unbear0237: *Passcode?*
Anonyme0220: *Parasitic.*
Unbear0237: *How can I help you?*
Anonyme0220: *Is it for men only?*
Unbear0237: *. . . No. But you'd be the only one.*
Anonyme0220: *Good.*
Unbear0237: *We need more information.*

Anonyme0220: *And I need confirmation that you are who you say you are.*
Unbear0237: *That's not how this works. There are steps to this process. We need more from you first. A photo. Of a recent mark.*
Anonyme0220: *[untitled.jpg]*
Anonyme0220: *Hello? Still there? It's been ten minutes.*
Unbear0237: *So you* are *a woman. Interesting.*
Anonyme0220: *I told you. Now what?*
Unbear0237: *How do you do it?*
Anonyme0220: *Shots of air. Where I work. Old people die at hospitals all the time. It's easy if you're careful. And I'm very careful.*
Anonyme0220: *Hello?*
Unbear0237: *I'm going to inbox you an address. You are to go there. Alone. Something will be waiting for you. You must dispose of it. If you do anything else, tell anyone else, we will know. Return here when it's done. Further instructions will follow.*
Anonyme0220: *How do I know this isn't a trap?*
Anonyme0220: *Hello?*
Anonyme0220: *Hello??*
<Unbear0237 has logged off.>

Cyra knew it was stupid.

She figured the chances of this being a set up or of her getting immediately murdered were high, but she didn't have much of a choice. It wasn't like she could ask for a police escort, and she needed to do this. It was her only lead.

As she prepared to leave her apartment, a hum started deep in her bones, a familiar sensation. Her breathing got short and ragged, and her armpits began to sweat profusely. A queasy feeling flooded her stomach.

"No," Cyra said, clenching her hands. "Not now."

A panic attack was a terrible sign. This was her first one since Mira's death, and Cyra needed her wits about her for what she was about to do. Dealing with panic attacks for years meant Cyra learned a few tricks for squashing them before they could ramp up. If she acted fast, she could prevent this one before it picked up steam.

Cyra rushed to the corner of the apartment that held her tiny kitchen and ripped open the freezer door, sticking her head inside and taking large gulps of the icy air that blasted out. Her body slowed down, settled into the prickling cold, her lungs burning but working as she inhaled frigid air that would travel into her chest and pack away all the emotions rising to the surface.

As she was breathing, feeling the wisps of the baby panic attack subside, she wondered if any of the serial killers she was trying to track down would be excited to think of her head sitting in a freezer.

Cyra pulled away and shut the freezer door, feeling the even and calm bump of her heart under her fingers. She'd managed to stave off the panic attack with the cold and deep exhales, but she had to get going now, before she could think too much about what she was doing.

She left the apartment, hurrying down her building's stairs and bursting out into the chilly night. Cyra's switchblade was in her back pocket, her clothing was loose and nondescript, and she wore her prescription sunglasses and a baseball cap, looking like an undercover celebrity even though it was after midnight. Unsure of what she would face at the coordinates but tipped off by the gatekeeper's use of the word "dispose" in their chat, Cyra brought gloves and garbage bags in her backpack.

The address the group's gatekeeper messaged her ended up being coordinates, sent with terse instructions: *Monday night. Arrive at 1:10 AM exactly. Look behind the dumpster on the north side of the lot. It will be there. Make it disappear. Go alone. Tell no one.*

Cyra took the N to Astoria Boulevard and walked the extra mile to a tiny abandoned parking lot not far from LaGuardia Airport. A chewed-up chain link fence surrounded the lot, but there were gaps where the links had split apart, and Cyra was able to slip through, stepping on overgrown weeds pushing their way through the cracked pavement. This block was dark, the streetlights dim or out altogether. It was quiet, empty—an industrial area that turned into a dead zone at night. The lot itself was swathed in shadows, backlit by the pinpricks of light from apartment buildings blocks away.

As Cyra slowly moved deeper into the lot, looking for the looming shape of the dumpster at the north end, her hands were shaky. She couldn't stop the sweat from pooling under her arms despite the chill in the air, but her nerves originated from anticipation rather than dread—was she finally getting somewhere?

She could barely see with the sunglasses still covering her eyes, but she didn't dare remove them, nor did she chance using a flashlight. She didn't want anyone driving by catching a glimpse of her. She was squinting by the time she got to the dumpster, heart racing, fists tight. Taking a deep breath, she peered around the edge.

At first, she couldn't see anything, which was good. She had been steeling herself for a body. She didn't want to imagine what she would end up doing in that situation. What choice she might make, and how quickly she would make it.

Crouching lower, Cyra finally spotted it, nestled deeper in the shadows. A duffle bag.

She didn't dare touch it with her bare hands. Glancing once over her shoulder to make sure she was still alone in the lot, Cyra pulled on a pair of black rubber gloves from her backpack and gingerly drew the duffle bag toward her by the strap. Out from the shadow of the dumpster, there was just enough light to allow Cyra to unzip the bag, glancing inside.

"Ah, shit," she murmured.

Not a body, clearly. But this was bad too, and she understood the assignment, how a cop wouldn't make it past this stage. A white dress shirt, almost gleaming in the night, was crumpled inside the bag. It was splattered with dark stains. She could see the tips of leather shoes under it, scuffed and covered in reddish-brown drips.

Those assholes, Cyra thought, quickly zipping the bag back up.

Even though she couldn't see anyone around, she had no doubt she was being watched. It was too dark to see a hidden camera or a person lurking in the shadows outside the parking lot, but Cyra knew her next moves would determine her worth and entry into the group. Someone in law enforcement wouldn't be able to dispose of the evidence in the bag—her ability to thoroughly disappear these belongings should cement her status as a criminal. One of them.

Cyra willed feelings of revulsion and fear to rise, but she was so focused, so close, she couldn't manage it. Just like with Doris, she knew what she was about to do was wrong, but she needed to follow it through. For Mira. Nothing else mattered. She owed her sister.

Swallowing hard, pressing her tongue against the roof of her mouth and willing the feelings of calm detachment to settle over her, Cyra pulled out a garbage bag, slipped the duffle inside it, and tied it tight, stuffing the whole thing into her backpack.

She didn't dare go back to her apartment. Not carrying what she was carrying, and not without knowing if she was being followed. Instead, Cyra used cash to book a room at one of the cheaper motels near LaGuardia, one that looked run-down, giving a fake name and pretending she missed her flight.

Cyra barely slept. She never really did anymore, but she certainly couldn't while the bloodstained belongings of a dead person rested on the floor near the bathroom.

Cyra stopped sleeping after Mira's death. Bea tried to convince her to try medication or a sleep routine, but Cyra resisted.

Why bother, when nothing felt real anyway? Most nights she wrapped herself in a blanket on the couch and watched nature documentaries as she drifted in and out of consciousness. Eventually, Bea stopped trying to lure her to the bed and let her spend the night alone on the couch. When Bea left, it had been a relief. Cyra could spiral in peace.

Cyra watched *Family Feud* until the early hours of the morning, eyeing the room's deadbolt every so often, occasionally tiptoeing over to check the peephole. There was never anyone there.

When the sun rose, Cyra checked out, bleary-eyed and exhausted, and took the subway to Sheepshead Bay. Her calmness was starting to wear off by the time she got to the kayak rental place Mira brought her to a year ago.

Cyra's eyes felt jittery, her legs leaden. But she approached the rental desk, paying with cash, clambering into the kayak at the dock, paddling her way out from the channel, through Shell Bank Creek, out toward Rockaway Inlet. The backpack stuffed with the duffle bag remained on her back until she reached an area away from any other boaters, far enough from the shore and bridges that she was certain no one could see what she was doing.

The sky was gray. Gentle waves lapped against the kayak as a cold ocean gust sprayed specks of saltwater on Cyra's skin. Her bones felt iced over, like they had freezer burn. Breezy Point was a flat stretch of land directly in front of her; the blurry outline of Coney Island was visible off to her right.

With a dry mouth, Cyra anchored her paddle between her knees, swung the backpack over her aching shoulders, and removed the garbage bag, opening the top so she could pull out the duffle. Next, Cyra dug out the rocks she collected from a park near the rental shop from the bottom of the backpack and unzipped the mouth of the duffle bag, stuffing them inside.

She bobbed on the surf like a seagull, weighing down the duffle bag, crumpling the garbage bag inside it before rezipping the whole thing and unceremoniously sliding it over the edge of the kayak. Cyra watched the blot of darkness sink quickly beneath the surface, hurrying to a watery grave.

Cyra paddled around the area for another half hour, watching, waiting. But the bag never bobbed back up. Satisfied, Cyra bit her lip, ignoring the tiny voice in the back of her head telling her how wrong this was, and steered the kayak back to the rental shop.

She took the long way home. She stopped at several large stores, took a few different buses and trains, trying to shake a tail she wasn't sure she even had. Finally, almost twenty-four hours after she left it, she returned to her apartment in Jamaica.

Back on the dark web, the pixelated skull glowed at her. This time, the answer was even faster, and it made the hair on her arms stand on end:

Well done. I think we're ready to meet in person.

CHAPTER

3

Cyra stood in the middle of her cold apartment, staring at Mira's photo next to her bed, her bare feet like two chunks of ice, listening to the noise of the city coming in through her open window.

She was meeting the gatekeeper of the group today. The final test. A test she took the last week to prepare for.

She didn't tell Eli and Izzie.

In fact, she told them the opposite, to keep them out of her way and their minds at ease.

"Never heard anything back," she told them when they asked what happened. "I guess you were right. It's probably not even real."

But it was. After dumping the duffle bag, Cyra had bought an authentic blonde wig that she learned how to put on by watching drag queen tutorials and shoes with hidden lifts to make her seem taller than her normal five feet five inches. Cyra wasn't a big social media user anyway, but she deleted all her accounts and scrubbed any evidence of her existence from the nursing home website, which was easy since she was in charge of maintaining the page anyway.

There was nothing she could do about Mira's Instagram account or her public photography. She worried a little about her sister's most famous photo, the one of Cyra, but she doubted a group of serial killers were doing deep dives into specific subsections of the photography scene in their spare time. Besides, the change in her appearance should help. The version of Cyra in Mira's portrait looked very different from how she looked now. Taking a photo of someone at their lowest point didn't really accurately capture them.

Mira's self-portrait, on the other hand, was beautiful. Cyra was glad she could look at it without crumbling. Her sister's death had freed her from any attachment. She felt like Buddha, except in a mentally ill way. And yes, it had meant losing her girlfriend Bea, who she genuinely cared about, but it was better this way; not feeling anything.

The numbness started when their mother left.

Cyra had stood on the stairs in the hallway of their childhood home. Mira, only five years old, was crying at her feet, watching their mother collect her things, pretending like she was going out to meet a friend.

"Will you be back soon?" Mira asked plaintively

"Of course," Grace replied, unable to look at her daughters.

"You're too little," Cyra remembered saying as Grace moved her bags toward the door. "You don't hear them fighting at night. I do. They scream at each other. Mommy found a man she likes better than Daddy, and Daddy found out."

"That's enough," hissed Grace. She paused at the threshold of the door, turning back once, looking at her girls huddled on the staircase. "I love you, Cyra and Mira," she said. "OK? I *do* love you."

As she watched their mother walk out the door, the click of the lock muffled by Mira's sniffles, Cyra dug her nails into her palms and felt her anger, grief, and betrayal bleed away. It was replaced by blissful nothingness, a slick layer of ice. The cold coated Cyra's heart so that she went numb, allowing her to stand there on the stairs, calm and steady for Mira.

"I'm surprised you picked a public place," Cyra said as she sat down at the picnic bench, facing the enormous man wearing a Mets cap and huge black sunglasses that covered half his face. "I would have thought you'd want more privacy."

Cyra had looked at herself in the mirror before she left her apartment in Queens and was satisfied with the results. The shoulder-length blonde wig looked legit, and it had been strange to see herself without her usual calico glasses—the contacts she rarely used made her face look narrower, more naked, even with all the makeup she never usually wore. The lift shoes Cyra bought online gave her a few extra inches, and she had even changed up her style—donning a black pencil skirt, ivory blouse, and dark peacoat. Bea's unwanted clothes that she had meant to donate but never did. It was such a departure from Cyra's usual plain t-shirts and joggers. Her style had never been very chic, but after Mira's death she stopped trying at all. Being clean and dressed properly felt like slipping into someone else's skin.

"I thought this would work better for our purposes," the man said. His voice was deep and smooth, his skin was the color of wet soil, and his arms rippled with muscles. "And I thought you'd be more comfortable here. Being a woman and all."

"Here" was a patch of grass off the East Meadow of Central Park, at a weathered picnic table that stood far enough apart from its fellows that the two people sitting there wouldn't be overheard. The air smelled of dead leaves and boiling hot dogs; there was a cart downwind of them, its owner's face obscured in a balaclava, tongs in hand.

Cyra had been hiding near the meeting spot, which was sent to her via longitude and latitude coordinates again, for two hours. Her MMA muscles had made it easy to scramble into a tree fifty yards away, unnoticed. She had chosen to perch in the low branches, careful not to get her skirt dirty, and watched the picnic table. Her counterpart clearly had the same idea, because she had noticed the big man buy a hot dog and then sit at a different table with today's paper for an hour before they were meant to meet up. At 3:00 PM on the dot, he had thrown out his half-eaten dog and newspaper, and sauntered over to the table.

"To be honest, I'd prefer more privacy," Cyra said. She was staring at the man as if she could memorize his features behind the cap and glasses.

Are you the one? Did you kill her?

"Really?" The man cocked his head. "Why's that?"

"Look, I don't want to waste time if this isn't real," Cyra said. "And if this is some kind of entrapment situation . . ."

"You can understand we have similar concerns. Hence the . . . task we asked you to carry out."

We. So, he isn't the only one.

"Were you watching me?"

"There are rules to this," the man said, bluntly ignoring Cyra's question. "I will send them to you through the encrypted chat after this, if you want. You should be aware that I ask questions during intake, but no one else can know any specifics. No names, no access to each other's lives except during meetings, no identifying specific . . . marks. There are more rules, too. We have to be careful. Our meetings are in-person and that means there's an extra layer of caution we need to take."

"I'd hope so."

In-person! I was wrong, they do meet face-to-face. She couldn't tell if she should be excited by the opportunities that would present or be terrified.

Cyra thought for a moment about how stupid she was for doing this. How exposed she was making herself. After the news about Mira broke, Cyra had thought about getting a gun, learning to use it. She watched YouTube tutorials, did some preliminary research. But then she thought about all the sleepless nights alone in her apartment, a gun within reach. The nights got too dark sometimes. Why tempt it?

Instead, a few weeks after Mira's death, Cyra had purchased the switchblade, one that could flip up with a quick push, sharp and serrated, and took to carrying it around in her pocket. She started watching video tutorials online. That and years of experience in kickboxing and MMA training made Cyra feel more prepared than the average person in terms of self-defense. But upon looking at this man, his size, his muscles, she admitted that she might be way out of her league.

"We'll need more from you," the man said.

"I sent you the photo," Cyra stated. "I disposed of the duffle bag. What else do you need from me to know that I'm who I say I am?"

He tilted his head. "Your photo checked out. I know someone who's very good with computers. What you sent wasn't doctored or edited in any way. But some additional proof would be good. We need to know you belong."

Cyra's hands curled into fists. She expected this, and she came prepared. "I'll show you mine if you show me yours. But, of course, I'll need privacy to do that."

The man sat up straighter and steepled his fingers together.

She'd done her research. Not being able to sleep gave her plenty of time to read up on female serial killers. There was a character in her mind, a person she could become. Someone cold and empty who would play a certain role for these people.

"There's a place nearby," the man said. "It's quieter. More private. If you're not too . . . uncomfortable going to a second location."

She couldn't see his eyes, but she imagined a glint behind those sunglasses. Everyone knew that once a killer took you to a second location, your chances of surviving plummeted. But this wasn't a normal situation. This was a series of tests. That, at least, she understood.

"I'll be fine," she said, keeping her voice steady. It was surprisingly easy to do. Or perhaps not surprising, given she had yet to feel a twinge of fear. Fear was gone, bricked off and inaccessible.

Through her research, Cyra learned that evolutionary psychologists theorized that male serial killers act as "hunters," while female serial killers are "gatherers," choosing victims based on the resources they can get from them. But that didn't track with some of the women she read about. Women like Erzsébet Báthory, Darya Nikolayevna Saltykova, and Nannie Doss all seemed to have killed because, well, they *liked* it. The woman Cyra was pretending to be was a hunter too. Not killing for money or survival, but for a thrill.

"You sure you're ready for this?" the man asked, drawing Cyra back to her body.

"Lead the way," she said, getting up and smoothing down her skirt, swinging the chunky black purse she carried over her shoulder. She would show this man what was inside it, and hope that would be the final piece to her entry in the group.

The big man slowly got to his feet, clearly watching her, hawk-like, under the sunglasses. Cyra followed him in silence as they walked down the path toward the park exit on Fifth Avenue. Her skin was prickling, and her insides were vibrating, but it was from a sense of urgency rather than fright. Turning right, away from Mount Sinai, they walked for a few blocks until the man gestured for her to follow him into a side door next to a small deli. He pulled out a rusty key and unlocked the door, heading inside first.

Cyra paused for only a fraction of a second before following him.

Inside, the sounds of the street vanished when the door snapped shut behind them. It was dark for a moment, and Cyra wondered if this was when she'd be killed. Instead, there was a fumbling noise, a grunted curse, and then a weak yellow light flickered above them as the big man let go of the little chain he had pulled to turn it on.

They were standing in what looked to be an unused stock room. It was attached to the deli, that much was certain. Though there were no other doors or windows in the room, Cyra could hear the register *binging* on the other side of the wall, and there were meager piles of paper supplies like toilet tissue and other household cleaning items scattered around the tiny space. In the center of the room was a table that looked like it would be limping if it could walk. She'd never heard of delis having odd add-on closets with street access, but maybe the whole store was a front for their group.

"So?" the big man asked.

"You first."

He shook his head. "Not how this works. You're the stranger. You found us. I need to know you are who you say you are."

"I thought this was an anonymous club. No real names."

"You know what I mean. Do you have anything for me, or are we going to have a problem?"

Cyra dug her nails into the palm of her hand, pressing the tip of her tongue against the roof of her mouth as if she could drive it through her soft palate. Her vision swayed, but she focused on the man in front of her, trying to keep her breath steady. A strange, persistent thought hovered above the approaching anxiety: *It would be so embarrassing to break down in front of this guy.*

She was worried about making a fool of herself in front of a killer. Something told Cyra that wasn't the right priority.

She brought her attention back to her body, to the pressure in her mouth and the pain in her palms. Slowly, she gathered up the numbness waiting below the surface and pulled it up and through, letting it settle over her skin.

She let out an exhale.

I can do this.

"Very well. You already saw the photo of my work, but I have something else," she said, slipping her purse off her shoulder and resting it on the table. She was calm now, steady.

The big man moved toward the other side of the table, and when he saw she was pulling something from the bag, he reached up and removed his sunglasses. His eyes were like little dark marbles, far too small for his face, and giving nothing away. Slowly, Cyra pulled out a plastic freezer bag. It usually lived inside a shoebox in the back of her closet behind a bunch of junk, tucked away in plain sight. Bea had never even noticed it.

Cyra heard the man breathing as she dropped the freezer bag on the table. He stood perfectly still for a moment, then he looked up, eyes boring into her face as if searching for deception.

"It's a hat," he said plainly.

A baseball hat, light blue, stained with brown spots and patches of dirt, was visible within the clear plastic of the bag. It looked worn and beat up, the dried blood soaked into the back of the cap.

Cyra imagined how she would explain this to Bea, Izzie, or Eli. She imagined, countless times, how she would explain this to Mira. But she never found the strength to say it, to tell her sister about the role Cyra played in Mira's first boyfriend's death.

"It was an accident," Cyra pictured herself saying, pleading with Mira to understand. "The day after I confronted PJ for choking you, I was driving home from studying. It was dusk, it was misting, and I was on the back road taking the shortcut home. I saw PJ, on his bike, and I thought about him hurting you. I didn't mean to . . . I just wanted to scare him. I came up behind him fast, and he freaked out, swerved, fell. I didn't even get that close to him. But it was my fault he wiped out. He wasn't wearing a helmet. Just his baseball cap. When I got out of the car to check, he was already gone."

While Cyra wasn't exactly sorry PJ was dead, she still didn't know how to accept the fact that it was her actions that led to his death, so she buried the incident, trying not to think about it too much, which was hard to do in the beginning. Mira was devastated by the accident. The whole town was. But no one guessed Cyra's involvement. The roads were slick and PJ wasn't wearing a helmet. It was clear to everyone that he lost control of the bike and hit his head. Cyra consoled Mira for months, all the while pretending it wasn't her fault.

Cyra's panic attacks started shortly after.

She wanted to tell Mira, eventually. Cyra thought that was why she took PJ's hat that evening. Why she kept it all these years. When she finally came clean to her sister, she wanted proof she was there so Mira would believe her and not think Cyra was losing it. Or perhaps she wanted a reminder of what she did. The horrible choice she made that evening that resulted in a teenager's death. But of course, Cyra never told Mira, and now it was too late. Now her role in PJ's tragic death was a weight she'd carry forever.

But she could still use it to help Mira. She just had to . . . spin it.

"I don't do this anymore," Cyra said, nodding to the hat. "Blood is messy. But he was my first, and I was inexperienced and pissed off, so it happened that way."

"Friend of yours?" the man asked wryly.

"Boyfriend," Cyra said, telling a version of the truth. "He was abusive. Pushed me around, choked me out. One day I got sick of it. Bashed his head in with a rock during a hike upstate."

"What did you do with the body?"

Cyra thought fast, decided it was best to stick to the truth. Or at least, close to the truth. "I left it there. We were in the middle of nowhere. I shifted his body off the trail and let the animals do the work for me."

"You kept his hat."

Cyra's throat worked. She had to get this part right. She did her research. She knew what a cold-blooded killer would say. "Yeah, well, I wanted a piece of him. Call it a trophy. That's what we do, right? Collect trophies?" She pretended to suppress a scoff, as if it was all beneath her.

Then Cyra paused, waiting, her pulse thrumming in impatience as the man considered her words.

"Well," he said after a moment. "I suppose that's good enough for me."

That was it. Cyra passed the test. She was in.

WHIPWORM

On his second day in prison, Ernie Martinez was approached by a man with "WHTE POWR" tattooed on his knuckles who was wielding a sharpened toothbrush.

He's gonna shank me, Ernie thought, knowing he didn't have enough time to properly defend himself from this man who had a head as round and pale as a cue ball. Besides, he was still carrying his lunch tray, and for some reason, he didn't want to drop it. It would be loud and disruptive. If he was going to die, he'd rather die quietly without making a mess.

But before the man could strike, a large shadow loomed over them both. A hand that seemed to be the size of a dinner plate lashed out and twisted the white man's arm, causing him to drop the shiv. A second hand held the big man's full lunch tray above their heads so it wouldn't spill, just like Ernie would do with his drink when he was winding through a crowded bar.

"Move along," Ernie's rescuer growled, and even though the white guy muttered a few barbed comments, he seemed to be castrated without his weapon and scurried away when the big man dropped his arm.

"Thanks," Ernie said, unsure of what prison etiquette dictated he do next. He didn't belong here. Not that he was innocent; he wasn't. But he didn't have the right constitution for jail. Or the right body type. He had always been slight and wiry—fast, the fastest boy on his high school's soccer team, but not particularly intimidating.

"You're new, they're gonna try to fuck with you," the big man said. He was Black and burly, and there was something comforting about his presence that Ernie couldn't put a finger on. "We bunk together. Remember?"

Ernie felt his neck get hot with embarrassment as he realized he did indeed recognize his roommate. He supposed he hadn't paid much attention to anything or anyone since arriving two days ago. He'd been walking around in a strange fog, still stuck on what happened four months prior, what landed him here to begin with.

"Right, sorry."

"Come on, sit with me," Ernie's roommate said, casually leaning over and swiping the shiv from the floor, pocketing it as he glanced around for the guards. None were looking over in their direction, which made Ernie wonder if they had known what WHTE POWR was going to do. "Name's Jackson, but you can call me Python. Everyone does."

Python led Ernie over toward a battered table in the sterile cafeteria, far away from the group of bald men near the buffet line who were now staring daggers at them. Python and Ernie sat across from each other, placing their trays on the sticky table.

"What are you in for?" Ernie asked Python, wondering if that was a rude question. His mother always taught him to be polite and conscientious, and it was hard to dispel those habits even while sitting in jail. Besides, his mother, bless her soul, had died six months ago and wasn't around to disapprove of him anymore.

"Manslaughter." Python said it matter-of-factly. He was hunched over his tray, both forearms down on the table, defensively blocking the food and leaning over so he could scarf down his meal as quickly as possible.

Ernie waited for Python to ask him why he was upstate, but when he didn't, decided he should offer it up himself. "I'm in for assault. I tried to kill someone. I guess. That's what they tell me anyway. I honestly don't know what I was trying to do."

This wasn't strictly true.

Ernie had known what he was doing to the man from the bar, who was named Matt or Max, or something like that, the same way you know what you're doing when you pull up a porn site to masturbate. It was that sense of shame, of doing something wrong, but ignoring it and pretending that if you don't look it directly in the eye, it doesn't count. And Ernie had plenty of experience pretending he wasn't watching the type of porn he watched.

His mother wouldn't have approved. Neither would his father, but the man had walked out on Ernie and his mother when Ernie was eleven, leaving behind only his toolbox and the stench of cigarettes that his mother tried to Febreze away. The whole house smelled of sickly-sweet florals and menthol every day until her death. Then it just smelled of menthol.

When Ernie saw Matt or Max at the bar under the strobing light, his collarbone highlighted in his black V-neck, Ernie knew what he would do. It would be just like the others. The slip of the powder into the drink. The helpful offer to get the man a cab when he started stumbling. Then getting the drugged guy into Ernie's own car instead and driving him someplace nice and quiet where he could press his father's old wrench against the man's throat and photograph him after it was over. Ernie kept those photos, taken with a film camera that he developed in his basement, as memories. He had a thin stack of them tucked into the Bible on his nightstand.

But something had gone wrong with Matt or Max. Ernie blamed himself; he was still grieving his mother's death. That had to be it. He hadn't measured out the right dosage. Because when Ernie tried to help Matt or Max into his car, the other man resisted, suddenly lucid and angry. Matt or Max had yelled at Ernie, tried to go back into the bar.

Ernie, admittedly, lost his cool. He pulled his father's wrench out of his pocket right there on the street, and it took two people to pull him off Matt or Max.

"I didn't have such a great lawyer," Ernie said to Python. "Can't afford much when you own a family deli. But he got them to drop it down to assault instead of attempted murder. I'm sad they took away my wrench though. It was my father's. It had sentimental value."

He was lucky the prosecutors hadn't found anything else, hadn't realized Matt or Max had been drugged. Everyone just assumed it was a drunken bar brawl that got out of hand. The DA hadn't known that the man they caught had killed four people before. In a way, Ernie was lucky. Assault was nothing compared to what he'd done.

Ernie thought about how he would continue his work if he didn't have his father's wrench when he got out in ten years. Stopping wasn't an option, of course. His stint in jail had already taught him that only a few days in—he just needed to be more careful. He owed it to his parents. Ernie knew his father had left them because he sensed that there was a disease inside his son. Ernie couldn't find his father or bring his mother back from the dead, but he could continue his life's work: removing men who dared to explore their deviancy instead of burying it down deep until it rotted and decayed into nothingness.

"Stay alert in here," Python grunted, still hovering over his tray, ignoring Ernie's comment about his charges as if he hadn't heard it. "Don't run your mouth, don't look at anyone. Stick by me and stay quiet."

"You'll help me? Why?"

Python looked up. "Don't really know. Call it penance. I'll have your back."

Warmth melted the center of Ernie's chest. Someone was going to look out for him. Someone was going to take care of him for once. He'd done so much for his mother, especially at the end when the cancer made it hard for her to wash or dress herself. But she had nagged and admonished him until the very end. Even up until the point when she drank the spiked lemonade Ernie made for her containing quadruple the dosage he used on the men at the bars.

Ernie took care of people his whole life. His mother, the customers at the deli, always complaining or looking for items he didn't carry, the women he had brief and unsuccessful relationships with.

Now, for once, someone was offering to take care of him.

Ernie smiled at Python, wondering how many doses it would take to immobilize such a large man.

Python sat on the edge of his bottom bunk, patting the cot and gesturing for Ernie to join him.

"You look me up when you get out, you hear?" Python said, handing his cellmate a business card with a halfway house name and address on it. "It won't be long now. You said they're reviewing your case?"

"Early release for good behavior," Ernie confirmed, taking the card and holding it reverently to his chest.

"You'll be fine," Python insisted. "Keep your nose clean. You'll be out soon."

Ernie would miss his friend. He'd miss the heavy way Python breathed at night in the bunk below him, the way he ate like it was a battle, the way he stared baldly at the guards when they looked at him. Ernie never had a friendship, a real one like this, before. And he didn't want it to end once he was released.

Python accepted him, even had proved his trust by keeping Ernie's secret. He now knew about the men, the bars. Ernie told him a year into his stay. And Python had remained by Ernie's side.

That feeling... being accepted. Being free to express who you really were without judgement... It was something Ernie wanted to share. He remembered what Python said five years earlier: *"Call it penance."*

An idea, a daring, mad idea, had been percolating in Ernie's brain for a while. A way to make more friendships, create more connections, even after he got out and continued his mission.

"I'll see you on the other side," Ernie promised. "But first, I want to run something by you. An idea I had. A way to create community for people like us. Like me."

"What's that?"

Ernie smiled. "Let's call it a support group."

CHAPTER

4

"When did you switch to killing with air at hospitals? That's a big difference from bludgeoning a boyfriend, wouldn't you say?" The big man was leaning against the wall now, looking slightly more relaxed than he did earlier.

"It took me a minute to find my calling," Cyra replied, swallowing away her dry mouth as she returned the plastic bag containing PJ's stained hat to her purse. "Truthfully, my issue wasn't with men; it was with my mother. It was easy to find women who reminded me of her where I work. Older ones, of course, so it wouldn't be a surprise when they died of 'old age.'"

"I see."

"What about you? What's your deal?" Cyra asked, careful not to sound too eager. Her investigation was officially on; the more she knew, the better.

"You can call me Python," the big man said. "I'm the moderator of our group. Well, I run it, but I technically don't belong to it."

"Wait, you're not a . . ."

Python shook his head. "I've taken two lives. But it wasn't for pleasure. It wasn't for . . . fun, like how . . . your kind does. I was hired to 'handle' two people and got caught because the idiot who contracted me bragged at a bar. My cellmate in Sing Sing was one of you. We got along well, and we both were released around the same time." He noticed Cyra's raised eyebrow and said, "I got a reduced sentence for testifying against the idiot who hired me, who was pleading not guilty. Went in when I was twenty, got out in twenty. And Whipworm, he was in for assault, only served five years on account of good behavior. They didn't know about his . . . other stuff."

"I'll bet," Cyra muttered.

"We have rules," Python continued. He mentioned them earlier too, a list he was going to send her. "No real names, no locations, no interactions with members outside the group. No giving each other alibis or leads on . . . victims. Nothing that can tie us back to each other. If one gets caught, they're the only one going down. The more anonymous you can be, the better. I'm pretty sure some of the guys fib about their methods and interests in order to keep themselves safer." He frowned. "You can't trust each other. You may have the same . . . hobby, but that's it. Remember that. The support group is for *support*, to give you a place to be yourself for once. Ask for help with certain . . . activities. It's not supposed to be a place to brag."

"I bet people use it like that though. A place to brag."

"I make sure everyone follows the rules." Python's voice was stern; a schoolteacher warning about the time-out chair. "It's not supposed to be a fun time."

This guy was obsessed with the rules. Cyra swallowed and pushed her shoulders back. "You know, not all of 'our kind' does what we do purely for kicks. Some of us can't control it. Some of us *have* to do what we do."

Python nodded as if he had heard this before.

She was playing this well. Possibly too well? Would he get suspicious if she was too perfect of a fit? But no, she had the advantage, the one she kept forgetting about: she was a woman.

That was weird enough, different enough, that the men should be intrigued.

Cyra said, "I can't believe this is real. I'd heard rumors online and thought it was worth a try, but I assumed it was a prank."

"It's real," Python said, a grimace unfurling on his face as if he'd rather it not be. "It was Whipworm's idea. He said it was a lonely existence. That it would be nice to have a space to talk to like-minded people who really ... got it." He glanced at her. "But not once in the two years we've been meeting have we heard of a woman like you in the area."

"No," Cyra replied, forcing a smile. "You wouldn't, would you? We're rarer than the others. And dare I say harder to catch." She paused. "Why do you meet in person? Isn't that riskier?"

"For sure. But leaving evidence online or having to speak only in code in chatrooms the Feds could potentially hack would be worse. Besides," Python shifted his weight and cleared his throat, "This is how support groups work. There's something about connecting face-to-face that makes it more meaningful."

"Just seems odd," Cyra pushed. "Serial killers aren't known to be chummy."

"You'd be surprised. Even psychopaths want human interaction."

"Or want to check out the competition," Cyra pointed out.

"Whatever you say. You're here, after all."

"How do I know this is real? How do I know you all are who you say you are?"

Python assessed her. "You don't. Trust is a two-way street. I vet all potential new members and even though what you've done so far looks convincing, I have no way of knowing for sure if you're who you say you are. Just like you don't know if we're the real deal yet. It's a leap of faith."

A leap of faith.

The words rang as a memory of Mira unfolded in Cyra's mind; her sister pleading with her five years ago: "Take a chance! A leap of faith. It's New York City, Cyra!"

"What are you gonna do in New York City, Mira?" Cyra had asked her sister. "You just started SUNY. You need to stay in school."

"No," Mira argued. "I hate school, it's stupid. I want to be a photographer, I told you. Nothing ever happens here. Nothing I want to photograph. You said you supported my art. Why get me the camera if you didn't?"

Cyra sighed. Mira wasn't wrong. The camera was insanely expensive, but the look on her sister's face Christmas morning when she opened it made it all worth it.

"Please, Cyra? Move to the city with me. It's too hard to stay here after what happened to PJ. I know it's been years, but I still see him everywhere. I need to start fresh. Will you come with me? I don't want to go alone."

Cyra slumped at Mira's words. It was her fault PJ was gone. He was a bad person and a shitty, dangerous boyfriend, but Cyra couldn't ignore the fact that Mira was devastated by his death. Cyra's actions that evening had inadvertently caused her sister suffering, and she wanted to make up for it. She agreed to move to the city with Mira, help support her dream of being a photographer.

They moved into a cramped two-bedroom in Gowanus and that was where Mira took the portrait of Cyra mid panic attack. The photo featured Cyra reaching out to her sister behind the lens for help, realizing as the shutter clicked that Mira didn't see her as a person at that moment, but as a subject. It took a while to gain traction, but the photo blew up a year and a half ago, winning an award and appearing in a few art blogs. It got Mira a show with famed art critic Arthur McCowen.

After, Cyra moved out to Queens while Mira found a place in Dumbo.

Cyra slammed a box down over the past as if she was trapping a cockroach, shoving it to the back of her mind where it had come from.

She shook herself. Mira was gone, and Cyra failed to save her. She didn't do the one job an older sister is supposed to do, and now there was nothing left to lose. So maybe taking another leap of faith wasn't the worst thing in the world.

Cyra cleared her throat and met Python's eye. "OK. Leap of faith. What happens next?"

The meetings took place in the basement of a shabby former recreation center in Queens. At least, for now. Apparently, according to the rules Python sent her after their encounter, the location changed every time a killer left or was kicked out of the group in order to preserve secrecy.

Having the meetings in Queens worked well for Cyra because at least she didn't have to travel an hour into the city, but it also concerned her because it was only a few miles from her apartment and the thought of one of the maniacs following her home and finishing her off before she could get justice for Mira made her uncomfortable.

The rec center was on a block with a deli, a smattering of residential houses, and a karate studio that looked like it had been used rigorously for a month twenty years ago and then never again. According to Python's instructions, the current meetings started promptly at noon every Tuesday.

Serial killers, strolling through Queens, passing hundreds of people, to casually chat about their crimes. It was unfathomable. Which was perhaps how Cyra managed to remain calm about the fact that she was walking right into the belly of the beast. That, and the fact that she didn't care what happened to her anymore.

Still, Cyra had purposefully planned to show up a few minutes late, not wanting to chance being alone with any of the men until she absolutely had to be. In her bag was a change of clothes and her glasses so she could duck into a coffee shop after the meeting to switch outfits. She planned to double back on the subway, taking multiple wrong stops and changing trains often to ensure she wasn't followed.

Cyra had been instructed to slip in through the gated entrance of the rec center, open the unlocked lobby door, and head down to the basement-level meeting room.

Despite being an unused building, the lobby was still papered with flyers, and the stairs leading down to the lower level had cheerful posters of stock families playing sports. Only a fine layer of dust over the surfaces revealed the building's disuse. Downstairs, the hallway stretched ahead to reveal several meeting rooms and a pair of bathrooms near the staircase. Following instructions, Cyra approached a door with a little black plaque affixed to it. The plaque proclaimed it was the "Lower-Level Reading Room."

She paused at the door. The person she was about to become had to be separate from herself. A killer, a monster. She already looked different; now her insides had to match.

The night before, Cyra practiced facial expressions in front of her makeup mirror while sitting on her couch. She put on a series of horror films, each one more gruesome and violent than the last. She practiced keeping her face still during jump scares, her eyes blank during torture scenes, and her expression bland and neutral when the bad guy slaughtered innocent characters. It was eerie seeing her own face become so emotionless. And how quickly she picked it up.

Cyra took a few deep breaths, as if she was trying to head off a panic attack. She imagined a blast of cold air from the freezer back home rolling over her face.

Confident, this woman is confident, she told herself, pulling her shoulders back, lifting her chin up. Where Cyra hunched, her new persona straightened. Instead of anxiously examining everything around her, Cyra's gaze became still, focused. *Confident and cold.*

She exhaled and entered the room.

The space was finished; a row of slim, rectangular windows pressed up near the ceiling and a collection of school desks were pushed against one wall. Three empty bookshelves stood like sentinels under the windows, and a worn, hideous gray and purple rug carpeted the floor and made the whole room smell like Elmer's glue and dust. A table at the front of the room held a carafe of coffee and, inexplicably, a full plate of deviled eggs, which wasn't helping the smell. The basement was drafty, chilled like a cave, with similar acoustics.

There were eight chairs in a wide semicircle in the middle of the room, and seven of them were occupied. Seven sets of eyes widened as she cracked open the door, seven heads swiveled toward her like prairie dogs.

The stale air felt still—the moment of silence before a thunderclap.

Cyra stepped forward into the space, and for a moment, fear surged inside her heart. She was so startled, she almost stepped back but caught herself at the last second. Her body was shaking and thrumming like a plucked violin string; it wasn't dissimilar to the feeling she would get before panic attacks, but she was thrown off by its sudden reappearance. Cyra hadn't felt fear since the night she got the call about Mira, hearing the apology in the police officer's voice right away and knowing what it meant, hoping it wasn't true.

The rhythmic pounding in her chest, the insistent beating, crushed the fear back until it was shuttered out of existence. What was left was a humming thrill, circulating deep inside her bones.

She walked toward the men in the room.

Python was easily recognizable in the middle of the semicircle, his chair directly facing the door, and he stood up when she entered, a wan smile on his face. "Welcome."

The other six men were openly staring at her, and their expressions varied; Cyra got the distinct sense that some were imagining her naked, while others were imagining her torn to shreds.

"Hey," Cyra said, her body vibrating with adrenaline. This was real. She was here. It was time to perform. Time to make it real. "I'm here for the meeting."

CHAPTER 5

THE MOST UNNERVING thing was how normal most of them looked.

Python was huge, of course, but he technically didn't count as part of their group; there was also a very twitchy, bug-eyed man who seemed unable to sit still in his chair and kept rising for half a second and then sinking back down. But the rest of the group looked like people Cyra wouldn't glance twice at.

Except for one:

He had broad shoulders and obvious gym muscles, sandy brown hair, and piercing blue eyes. A straight nose and bow lips completed his traditional good looks—Cyra was reminded of the football players in high school who were always sniffing around Mira. He was sharply dressed in a crisp button-down and sand-colored chino pants, and he met Cyra's eye with interest, smiling politely.

Something tugged in her chest, and Cyra shivered.

The guy was ridiculously attractive, and Cyra mistrusted him immediately. She'd only dated a few men in her life, enough to know that she usually preferred women, but even when she did sleep with men, she never went near the ones that looked like this.

"This is horseshit." It erupted from the mouth of a tall white guy, all hard angles and sharp limbs sticking out from his chair like a praying mantis folded into itself. He had massive caramel-colored eyes that gave him the incredibly eerie sense of being trustworthy. "She shouldn't be here."

"Hey, this is an equal opportunity group," quipped a wiry-looking man with light brown skin. There was the hint of an accent in his voice. "All are welcome here." He turned to Cyra and gestured toward the free chair, the one next to him. His eyes were kind, and it horrified her. "Please. Feel free."

Cyra was grateful the chair was on the edge of the semicircle. She wouldn't be surrounded on all sides, but still, she didn't want to sit down, which was why she absolutely *had* to.

You can't show them fear. Not now. Not ever. Pretend it's a grief support group.

Bea had suggested Cyra try one after Mira's death. She nagged and nagged until finally Cyra went just to shut her up. It had been awful but not intimidating. Just a haggard cluster of broken people repeating their pain over and over again. Cyra hated it. She didn't understand how it was helpful or healing. She'd refused to talk and never went back.

"That doesn't count as trying," Bea had said. "You didn't even give it a chance. Why can't you have an open mind?"

"Crying in a circle isn't going to help me get over Mira," Cyra had replied.

"It's not about 'getting over' it. It's about moving through it. Letting yourself feel something so you can acknowledge it and try to heal."

"I don't need that," Cyra said. "I need to find out who did this to her."

And now she was here, in this room, with these extremely dangerous men, one of whom could be responsible for her sister's death. After all, how many serial killers could there really be in

New York City? Statistically speaking, it made sense that Mira's murderer was in the group.

Any remaining twinges of fear slipped away, and Cyra straightened her shoulders and lowered herself down next to the man with the kind eyes.

"I'm Whipworm," he said, his voice gentle and welcoming. "I hope you don't mind, but I chose a moniker for you. I was thinking we could call you Mistletoe, if that's OK with you?"

Cyra hesitated, not sure what her play should be here. She felt the rest of the group watching her.

"Cuckoo," a sullen-looking young man sitting on the other side of Whipworm said suddenly, gesturing to his chest without meeting her eye. He had blonde hair and appeared to be the youngest in the group. Cyra pegged him as early twenties, her stomach twisting as she thought about how many people he might have murdered to already be a serial killer at that age.

"I'm Lamprey," the Ken Doll guy said, and it clicked.

"Parasites," Cyra said, remembering the password for the group's darknet account. "Isn't that a little on the nose?"

The man named Lamprey laughed in delight. It was a cold, bitter sound, like icicles snapping. He became less attractive the more she looked at him. "Society wants to call us that. We're just taking it back. Our little inside joke."

"I didn't know mistletoe was a parasite," Cyra said, unsettled by how effortlessly steady her voice was. Her breathing was even, almost meditative. Exhaling with one long, smooth breath, Cyra realized she was unconsciously using the breathing techniques she learned a few years back to help with her panic attacks. "Mistletoe. How Christmasy."

"They steal water and nutrients from trees. You ever seen it in real life? It clumps on to branches and takes what it needs," Lamprey said. "Pretty, too."

Whipworm looked a bit put out, like the other man had stolen his thunder. He slumped a little lower in his chair.

Mistletoe. Cyra knew what this was. The others received monikers that brought to mind images of aggression or darkness. Yet for her, they chose something most often associated with a holiday. Kissing. A dainty and pretty plant. They were trying to infantilize her, defang her, minimize her status. It was their way of putting her in her place—a woman before a killer.

Well, that was fine. Cyra happened to know that the plant was poisonous. When she was in middle school, a neighbor's dog once ate a bunch of mistletoe and was sick all over their yard. If you consumed too much of it, you could die.

If they wanted her to be Mistletoe, she would embrace it. She would bring out the poison they wanted to trivialize.

"Sure. Mistletoe. I suppose it's no different than the nicknames my counterparts have received," Cyra replied.

Whipworm sat up again. "Oh?"

"You know," Cyra explained. "The media loves to give women trite little nicknames that make us sound either like a joke or sex-crazed femme fatales."

Shouldn't have mentioned sex, Cyra thought ruefully, noticing the twitch that rippled through the group at the word.

Whipworm smiled indulgently. "Come on, the media gives men nicknames too. No need to immediately make this a feminist issue."

"'BTK' and 'Son of Sam' have quite a different vibe than 'Grannyball Lecter,'" Cyra couldn't help pointing out.

Lamprey laughed again. There was no humor in it. "Not a fan of Tamara Samsonova, are we?"

"I think she's fine. It's her nickname I have an issue with."

Was this real? Was she really bantering with a room full of murderers like it was normal?

"Who's Tamara . . . Sampson?" the young guy, Cuckoo, asked.

"Samsonova. She was this sixty-eight-year-old Russian lady who got arrested a few years back," Cyra answered, feeling Lamprey watching her. "She was a serial murderer accused of cannibalism. But because she was older and a woman, her crimes became a joke. They called her Grannyball Lecter."

"You're not wrong," Lamprey said silkily, staring at Cyra. "Humor to diminish and deflect."

"Why are we getting a history lesson? Cut the crap. Who are you really?" This came from the pale, pointy man who was now leaning forward with a hostile expression.

Whipworm bent over toward her, and Cyra got a whiff of oaky cologne. "That's Sand Fly. He's a dick, don't mind him."

"No, I'm serious," Sand Fly snapped, nodding at Cyra with his long chin. "Who are you?"

"Excuse me?" Cyra replied, sitting up straighter, but leaving her hands loose in her lap. She inhaled for four counts, paused at the top of her breath, and then released it. "Isn't this anonymous?"

"Sand Fly has money on you being a reporter, but I think you're an undercover agent," said the jittery man Cyra had noticed when she entered. He was now scratching at the inside of his arm, the dark hair flat against his head so greasy it looked wet.

"That's Pea Crab," Whipworm offered in Cyra's ear, making the hair on the back of her neck rise. She wanted to scoot her chair farther away from him, but of course she couldn't do that.

"I told you, I vetted her," Python interjected. He glanced at Lamprey as he said this even though the other man wasn't currently objecting to her presence.

Sand Fly bared his slightly crooked teeth at Python. "You probably just wanted to get your dick wet."

"Watch your mouth," Lamprey said smoothly, his expression calm, but his eyes steely. He looked at Cyra and then pinned down Sand Fly with his gaze. "There's a lady present."

Sand Fly's lip curled, but Cyra noticed that he backed down. She tensed her calves and released them. Lamprey was someone the others respected. Which meant he was dangerous.

"I'm not a reporter or a cop," Cyra announced, dragging the room's attention toward her. "I'd have thought you'd guessed that assuming you went through the same initiation process I did."

"That wasn't initiation," Sand Fly hissed, his words laced with an unspoken threat.

"Sure felt like it. I proved myself several times over. Do I need to kill someone in front of you to get your approval?" Cyra snapped. "Want me to drag one of my angels here and show you how I do them? I like to work privately, I'm sure many of you can relate, but if my *gender* is preventing you from believing me, I can do it."

The room fell silent as Cyra waited for one of them to call her bluff; force her to actually murder someone in front of them. But no one moved, not even Python, who was staying silent and watching the room.

Finally, the last man, a silent, bearded fifty-year-old, the oldest person there, eyes hidden under a brimmed cap, uncrossed his arms and grunted his first words of the meeting: "Let her be. We all trust Python to make these decisions. And if she's somehow not who she says she is . . ." He shrugged, tipped his head back so that he could meet Cyra's eyes. Unbidden, a chill stole over her insides as she took in his weathered skin, the small scar above his left eyebrow, the absolute emptiness yawning in his eyes. "Well, we'll get there if we get there."

It only took that one glance into his eyes to see it. There was something very wrong with this man.

"Are we ever going to start this meeting, or do you still not trust me, Sand Fly?" Python rumbled.

It was clear that Sand Fly did indeed still have an issue, but outnumbered, he shook his head and shoved his hands deep in his denim pockets.

Python looked satisfied though and cleared his throat. "Obviously, we have a new member, so for her benefit, when we do check-in, state your group name and anything else she should be aware of. Remember the rules: no real names, no identifying information for yourself or victims, and keep your share under five minutes." He glanced at Cyra as if to make sure she heard them too. He didn't need to worry; there was no way Cyra would give up any information that might lead the serial killers to dig deeper into her life.

"Sand Fly, since you're so chatty tonight, you can start."

The praying-mantis man rolled his shoulders back and grinned heinously at Cyra. "I'm Sand Fly."

"Hi, Sand Fly," the rest of the group said, making Cyra flinch at the sound of all their voices woven into one twisted chant. It might have been funny, a bizarre mimicry of an AA meeting, if it wasn't so disturbing. She brought her attention back to her breath, dropping her shoulders, letting her chest open in a display of confidence.

"Mistletoe should be aware that I like women like her," Sand Fly continued, leering at Cyra from across the circle, taking in her immaculate outfit and blonde disguise. "But only when I'm slipping a knife into them."

"*Sand Fly.*" Python's tone was warning.

Lamprey clucked his tongue and leaned forward so that his rippled arms were resting across his knees. "Manners," he whispered, a slick sound that somehow cut through the whole room, soft like snakeskin.

Something flashed over Sand Fly's face as he tried to ignore Lamprey, staring at Cyra instead.

They were all testing her, and she knew it. The comments, the glances; even Whipworm and Lamprey's unnerving attempts at welcoming her were meant to throw her off, see what she was made of. Figure out if she was who she said she was.

But she was ready for this. There was a part of Cyra that she always suppressed. The cold, unfeeling part she had to hold back from the world. It had emerged before—when she compartmentalized what happened with PJ, hiding the truth from everyone; when she watched her mother leave her and her sister behind; when she learned about Mira's sexual relationship with Arthur, the "benefactor" who gave Mira her first art show.

Cyra always buried this part of herself, ashamed of it. But now she needed it because Mira was more important than Cyra's humanity. It wasn't worth suppressing the numbness that plagued her anymore. She had to let it out in order to help Mira. She had to fully embrace the character she was playing. The cold, dark Mistletoe, a woman who was unafraid and powerful.

"I wonder what you sound like when you're screaming," Sand Fly said, his voice leathery and hard.

Without warning, he got to his feet.

"Hey," Python cautioned at the same time Lamprey leaned back in his chair, eyes narrowed, assessing.

Cyra's throat clenched and the instinct to flee almost overwhelmed her. Spots of darkness flurried in front of her vision as her pulse skyrocketed. An itch started creeping up her chest, tightening it, making her shoulders cave inward. She was losing it, losing the persona she needed to survive here.

Inhale. Exhale. Inhale. Exhale.

Cyra dug her nails into her palm, using the pain to center herself. She forced her shoulders back, jutting out her jaw, wearing the blank expression she practiced in the mirror last night. In this room, she was not Cyra. She was Mistletoe. And Mistletoe was not afraid.

Cyra exhaled the fear away, deep down into her belly, letting a swell of numbness replace it. Her body tingled, and then stilled. Her emotions melted away.

I am Mistletoe. I am not scared of this man.

The mask fell over her face, and Cyra released the darkness waiting inside.

"It's funny," Cyra said conversationally, suppressing a little yawn as if she heard men talk like this every day. "It's always the men who brag about their conquests that are the least endowed. Or talented. Have you found that to be true, Sand Fly?"

A rash of red sprung up around Sand Fly's pale neck and the corner of his right eye twitched.

Nail on the head.

Lamprey laughed again, looking back at Cyra with an appraising eye. She ignored him.

"Not me," Sand Fly growled, but he couldn't erase the blush on his neck or the furrow in his brow that told the truth. Lower, he muttered, "You stupid fucking bitch."

"Sit down," barked Python.

"Don't tell me what to do." But Sand Fly obliged, blinking furiously and glaring at Cyra.

"Let's move on," Python said, making eye contact with Sand Fly and stretching his tree-trunk arms forward, flexing slightly as he laced his fingers together and worked out a kink in his neck. Sand Fly seemed to get the message and slowly closed his mouth, gaze sliding away from Cyra, fire in his eyes. "Pea Crab?"

The rest of the group slowly went around the semicircle, introducing themselves, though none as aggressively as Sand Fly had. They offered very little about themselves or their lives, as Python requested. Some of the men, like Pea Crab and Cuckoo, seemed content to ignore Cyra outright, avoiding her gaze, pretending she wasn't there. On the other hand, Sand Fly and Lamprey couldn't stop watching her, as if waiting for cracks to appear on her face, revealing her truths. Whipworm seemed completely comfortable to have her next to him, as if she had always been there, but there was a patronizing tone in his voice whenever he spoke to her that revealed a lack of respect.

The only one she couldn't read was the bearded older man in the baseball hat. He neither avoided or stared, and when it was his turn, he simply stated his nickname.

"Mockingbird," he grunted. "I'm a retired trucker. Nothing important to share."

"That's interesting because last time I distinctly remember asking for advice on dealing with injuries from prey, and you mentioned you had some experience with that," Cuckoo said, crossing his arms, his voice bordering on petulant.

"Not sharing today," Mockingbird said.

"But—"

"Don't be an idiot, and you'll be fine," Sand Fly spat, glancing at Cuckoo with disinterest. "I've never once been hurt by these girls. Be prepared, and it won't be an issue."

Mockingbird's eyes narrowed. "Some things you can't prepare for."

"Prepare for every eventuality, that's my motto," Whipworm added.

"Didn't you get caught because you messed up your attempt, Whip?" Lamprey interjected, voice lazy and amused.

"Fuck off, Lamprey."

Cyra's eyes ping-ponged from speaker to speaker, trying to take mental notes, committing everything she heard to memory. At the same time, she made sure her limbs appeared relaxed, her lip curled in a half-interested smirk.

"I want to hear from Mockingbird," Cuckoo whined. "He said he—"

"I'm done talking today, you understand?" Mockingbird was leaning forward in his chair now, affixing Cuckoo with a dead-eyed look that shut the younger man up instantly.

"Alright, let's move on," Python said. "This is your safe space to share what's on your mind, what you might need from the community. Anyone else?"

Sand Fly opened his mouth, but he was cut off by Pea Crab, the shaky man who couldn't sit still. It was hard to figure out his age because he had the look of someone who was put through a washing machine several times on the heavy cycle. "Hi, it's me, Pea Crab."

"Hi, Pea Crab," the group said as one creature.

Pea Crab nodded as if he was a bobblehead, rushing forward before the remnants of his name could fade. "I gotta know, man, how are you getting rid of these bodies without them being found all the time? I—I can't find a good spot. They keep . . . keep finding my people. Like . . . it's a good thing they don't give a shit, but I gotta find a better solution."

"Why don't they give a shit?" Cyra asked. This was what she needed—more information on who these men killed.

Whipworm turned to her again, explaining as if she was a child. "Cops don't really care about dead drug dealers and hookers." Then in a lower voice that didn't carry across the circle, he said, "Pea doesn't really discriminate. He kills to get a fix, or to have a place to squat for a few weeks."

Of course, Cyra thought, looking at Pea Crab with new eyes. *He's using.*

That explained his odd behavior and ragged appearance. It also meant he might not fit the definition of a serial killer. She wondered what he was doing here.

"You're too all over the place," Sand Fly said. "We've told you before; you're going to get caught eventually if you can't stop being so impulsive. If you just drop a body in an alley, it's going to be found. And I doubt you're cleaning up."

"I don't got the time to make it look all pretty and shit like you assholes," Pea Crab snarled, fingernails sinking into the skin around his wrist.

"You're going to draw attention we don't need," Cuckoo said, swiping his blonde hair away from his eyes and frowning.

"I have things to do," Pea Crab replied, but Cyra noticed how his eyes darted to the side and his upper lip twitched. He was withholding something.

"More like meth to smoke," Lamprey said, rolling his eyes. "Cuckoo's right. You're messy."

"And getting messier," Cuckoo pointed out. "You've been devolving over these past few months."

A buzz of energy was traveling up and down Cyra's spine. Now that she had released her fear and anxiety, a thrill was left over, as if she was constantly dropping from the highest point of a rollercoaster.

Cyra noticed Lamprey glancing over at Cuckoo, eyes narrowing. She got the sense that Lamprey liked to play nice with the group, but truly considered himself the Alpha. She wondered if he was there for connection or something else—some form of dominance.

"Water, Pea," Sand Fly interjected. "That's my advice. Wrap 'em, weight 'em, and dump 'em. Remember though that bodies get all bloated in the water, so you'll need more weights than you'd imagine to keep them down there."

Cyra thought about the duffle bag she had weighed down with rocks and sunk in the water off Breezy Point. She expected regret, shame, but as Mistletoe, the memory zipped across her skin with pride instead. She fooled them; she used their own tactics to infiltrate their group.

"Hard to do that in a city without someone seeing you," Pea Crab muttered. "Especially these days with all the cell phones and security cameras and shit."

"That's why moving outside the city is where it's at," Sand Fly said, smirking. "No one peeping at the piers in—"

"Hey," Python cut him off. "No locations. How many times do I have to tell you?"

Sand Fly waved him off. "Yeah, yeah, whatever." Then his attention returned to Cyra. "What about you? What does our newest member think?"

Cyra paused, waiting to see if anyone else would interject, but there was silence. It seemed they were all interested to hear from her on this. It confirmed her suspicions—this wasn't a welcome party; it was another test.

CHAPTER

6

Cyra leaned back in her uncomfortable chair, thoughts whirling.

How could she leverage this to learn something that would help her find the man she was looking for?

"If you're asking about hiding bodies, it really depends on how you're killing them," she finally replied, glancing at Python to see if she would be scolded for breaking a rule. But Python said nothing, just stared off into space while they talked like he was barely there anymore.

"I—It depends," Pea Crab stammered, looking almost confused, like he couldn't remember. His voice floated down to a decibel a little above a whisper.

Cyra tried not to look too eager as she sat forward to hear him better.

It wasn't likely Mira would have crossed paths with this man; she was never into hard drugs, so Cyra didn't think Pea Crab was a likely candidate for Mira's murder. But the more she could learn, the better.

"With a hammer," Cuckoo supplied. "No finesse. He just hits them over the head with his claw hammer."

"Yeah," Pea Crab replied, looking relieved and glancing away. "Yeah, usually with my hammer."

Cyra was beginning to understand how to read Pea Crab. Every time he lied or told a half-truth, he got twitchier and avoided eye contact.

And he's so far gone he can barely remember his kills, but he's clearly talked about them with the group before.

She tried not to think about how many people Pea Crab had murdered—people who could have gotten clean or off the streets. Mistletoe wouldn't care about that, so neither could Cyra.

Something else struck her:

Mira was killed by blunt force trauma.

The attack, according to the police, had been fast and brutal. Mira had been hit on the head, fallen, and then everything else was frenzied overkill. Yet the papers reported that Mira had been found in the park on her back, her face clean of blood. Meaning her killer had turned her over afterwards, something Cyra wasn't sure Pea Crab would have the presence of mind to do.

Besides, the cops seemed to think Mira was attacked with something like a rock, not a hammer.

She pushed the thoughts of her sister's body away.

"Well?" Sand Fly prompted, bringing her back to the room. "Any suggestions for Pea's bodies, Mistletoe?"

She shifted in her seat slightly, straightening her spine, tossing a lock from the blonde wig over one shoulder as if she didn't have a care in the world. "I always do it in plain sight," Cyra said, purposefully lowering her voice as if she was sharing something personal and intimate with a date in a crowded bar. "My angels stay right in their beds. Everyone thinks it's old age or a stroke. Because of where they are, how I do it. *I'm* not messy."

"I'm not hearing a suggestion," Sand Fly said, lips tugging toward the ceiling.

Cyra shot him an irritated glance before turning back to Pea Crab. "He doesn't need one. Whipworm is right. Cops don't care about dead addicts. And from what you're saying, it seems like he's been lucky so far. Maybe that luck will hold out."

It wasn't what they were looking for—they wanted her to expose herself, give a stupid idea or a soft-hearted plea, but she wouldn't give them the satisfaction.

"This isn't productive," Whipworm interjected. "It's not about luck. Pea's been pulling shit like that for a while now and hasn't gotten caught. Helps that he's white, obviously."

"I'm sorry," Cuckoo said, his voice tight like a guitar string. "Are you really trying to make this into a race thing?"

Whipworm frowned. "Of course it's a race thing. You don't think it's interesting how out of this whole group, the only two who've done time are the brown people? Python and I got off easy, too. We actually were released." He jerked his head to his left, at Cyra. "Miss America over here snuffs people in plain sight, and no one blinks twice. Cuckoo runs around with his dick out. Pea just leaves his bodies lying about like they're dirty drawers. And all of you are skipping around scot-free even though you got more bodies than Python and me combined."

Cyra sat still and quiet. It felt extremely strange to be agreeing with someone she knew was fundamentally a bad person, but Whipworm wasn't wrong. She had no doubt that the white members of the group were probably getting away with things Whipworm and Python never would be able to.

"Whipworm . . ." Python murmured. "Stay cool."

"Maybe we haven't got caught because we're smarter about it, huh? Ever think of that?" Lamprey said, leaning back in his chair, eyes sliding over to Cyra.

Whipworm scoffed and looked pointedly at Pea Crab, who was scratching his inner arm frantically like a dog and looking confused at the direction the conversation had taken. "Yeah, man, he's a total genius." He turned to Pea Crab. "You know you shouldn't even be here, right? You barely count as one of us. You just got grandfathered in early. Python would never let you in if you applied today."

Cyra tried not to look too interested, but the conversation was giving her useful information—Pea Crab's disposal methods didn't fit what happened to Mira, and Cuckoo apparently had a sexual component to his kills. That was one of the only things about her sister's death she was grateful for—it had been a fast death, and there was no evidence of sexual assault. Detective Bellows had at least been able to share that with her after they finally released Mira's body.

"The first hit probably knocked her out. The second one was fatal. We don't think she suffered," he told her.

She hadn't been too sure of that. Getting your head bashed in with a rock couldn't feel good, even if you immediately fell unconscious and missed the rest of your death afterwards.

It was still too early to rule anyone out, but as of now, Pea Crab and Cuckoo moved farther down the suspect list. And even though Sand Fly made mention of stabbing not bashing, he was at the top. His hatred for women was obvious, and he could always be lying about his methods of killing.

"Let's wrap up for the day," Python said, after the room remained quiet for a minute. "Feel free to mingle for a bit, grab some refreshments, and then leave separately. Ten minutes apart. I'll be watching," he added, fixating on Sand Fly in particular. "Same time, same place, next week. Remember to check in the night before."

Python turned to Cyra. "The only times we talk to each other are in these meetings. You are to check the forum inbox before each meeting to confirm time and location. Sometimes people leave in between sessions and we need to rotate spots."

"Where else do we meet?" she asked.

"That's a need-to-know basis," Python said firmly. "But we never hit the same place twice."

The men were moving now, standing up from the butt-numbing folding chairs and ambling over to the table with coffee and deviled eggs. Their joints were cracking as they murmured in low voices, occasionally glancing over their shoulders to look at Cyra.

She knew she had to mingle with them, but she approached Python first, who hadn't moved from his seat facing the door, hands clasped in his lap.

"Python."

"Yeah?"

"No," Cyra said. "Python. A snake. Snakes aren't parasites."

The big man chuckled. "I ain't one of you, remember? No way I'm taking on one of those sick little nicknames. No offense. Nah, I was called Python in prison on account of my arms." He looked up at her and winked. "Can crush a man just like a snake."

She couldn't necessarily trust Python, but she'd been alone with him before, and he hadn't hurt her. Cyra made a split-second decision. "Can I leave last?"

She wanted to give the others a chance to leave ahead of her, so she would be able to spot anyone attempting to follow her. And she wanted to set a precedent; if she allowed the men to leave first now, she might be able to follow one of them in the future.

Python's eyes slid over to the table where the rest of the group was gathered and cleared his throat. "Yeah, sure. Listen, I sent you the list of rules. You know we're not allowed to snitch on or hurt anyone else in the group. We're supposed to have each other's backs. But you're . . . different than what they're used to. I think it's for the best that you be careful."

She looked down at him, so calm. "Why don't I disgust you? Why don't we all disgust you, if you're not one of us?"

Python looked surprised. "Who said y'all don't disgust me?"

"Then why are you here?"

His mouth twisted into a half-smile, half-grimace. "My own selfish reasons." But Cyra noticed his eyes flicked toward Whipworm for a brief instant before returning to her. "This group could provide me with a bulletproof alibi. Not that I'm planning to hurt anyone again, but I'm a Black man with a prison record. Anything goes wrong in my neighborhood, I'm the one they're gonna call on. I have an understanding with some of the more . . . upstanding citizens in the group. I get snagged for some bullshit, they give me an alibi."

"I thought no alibis? No outside communication?" she asked, remembering Python's rules.

"I'm different. I agreed to do this, act as a moderator for you folks, specifically because I might need help in the future. You asked why I'm here. That's why," Python said, his voice a low rumble like distant thunder.

But she couldn't forget about how his eyes betrayed him moments earlier, how they had found Whipworm's back like he wasn't even aware of it. Python had to know as well as she did that when push came to shove, none of the men in the group would actually put their neck on the line to give him an alibi. It was just an excuse.

If serial killers could have genuine friends or people who actually cared about them despite their monstrosities, it seemed like Whipworm had one in Python.

"Thanks, Python," Cyra said suddenly. "For giving me a chance."

The big man's smile looked painted on, like a porcelain doll's. "Don't thank me yet."

As she headed over to the refreshment table and the other men, Cyra's limbs felt heavy and thick, weighted from performing Mistletoe's personality, holding herself the right way, thinking of the right things to say. She was losing momentum, like she sometimes did when she was with Izzie and Eli, pretending to be the version of herself that was likable and palatable to her sister's friends. This character she was playing was taxing, but in a strange way. It felt almost . . . too easy. Like it was a trap. It was far too natural to slip into this cold headspace. Cyra had to be careful not to lose herself in the darkness she was embracing. Maybe it was for the best that she limited her time pretending to be Mistletoe. She should wrap this up soon.

"How do you avoid attention with these meetings?" Cyra asked as she sidled up to the table and forced herself to pour a cup of lukewarm coffee under the stares of the men, promising herself she'd only pretend to drink it. "Don't people notice you coming into a nonfunctioning rec center?"

"Hell no, this is Queens, people don't give a shit," Whipworm replied.

"I own the building," Python explained, appearing behind her and reaching for a tea bag that disappeared into his enormous hand. "But like I said, we also rotate meeting spots. You can imagine we have people who don't come back. People who are passing through or realize this isn't for them. When someone leaves, we move locations. You're the first new person we've got since Lamprey and Cuckoo. We moved locations about six months ago and haven't had to rotate since."

Cyra's stomach dropped. If people came and went, what if that meant she missed Mira's killer? What if Mira's killer wasn't in the group at all?

Calm down, she told herself. *Mira died almost two months ago. They said they haven't had anyone leave in six months. There's still a good chance he's here. And if he isn't, maybe someone in the group remembers something about him.*

"Have you had many people come and go?" she asked, feigning nonchalance.

Python shrugged. "Only a couple out-of-towners. People who don't live here. The ones who stay tend to stay for a while."

"But there could be more of us out there, in the city," Cyra pointed out.

"Maybe. Or maybe we're it," Lamprey spoke up, watching her with interest. "We're a dying breed after all. Harder these days to do what we do, what with social media and technology and advancements in DNA gathering. It's easier to mess up now."

"Pea Crab lends credibility to that," Sand Fly muttered, loud enough for everyone to hear.

"Maybe you should go to an NA meeting, Pea," Whipworm said, his lip curling as he stared at the trembling man who was sniffing at the eggs and unconsciously bobbing his head up and down.

"Fuck off," Pea Crab grumbled, turning away from the eggs and chugging his coffee instead.

"By the way, the back door by the dumpsters is always unlocked, even when I'm not here," Python said to Cyra, gesturing up and toward the back of the building.

"Why?" Cyra asked.

"When it's really cold, I tell the homeless guys who live near me that they can get into the building that way. Gets them out of the elements for a bit. They know to only stay until the next morning though." He must have seen the surprise on her face. "I'm not heartless. And they're off limits, by the way. I find out anyone here hurts them, and they're going to have to deal with me."

She wasn't sure what to say to this, how to balance the knowledge of a contract killer who also helped the unhoused in her mind. Cyra stared down at the sad plate of deviled eggs on the table instead, her brows raising.

"Yeah, it was Whipworm's turn to provide the snacks today," Sand Fly said, disappointment clear on his face. "Like anyone is going to eat food he made."

"Oh, for God's sake, I didn't drug them!" Whipworm protested, throwing his hands up and then crossing them over his chest. He lowered his voice and muttered so softly Cyra wasn't sure she heard him right, "None of you are my type anyway."

"Store-bought and still in packaging next time," Python reminded him, but his voice was different when talking to this man; quieter, almost . . . gentle. Cyra remembered that Whipworm and Python were in jail together. That probably explained their bond. "You know the rules."

"Fine, God forbid I try to give us something nice and homemade to eat."

"This isn't a tea party," Cuckoo snapped.

"That doesn't mean we need to lose all sense of respectability and decorum," Whipworm argued.

"Gentlemen, don't scare away our new member with all your squabbling," Lamprey said, watching Cyra's face as she reminded herself to not react, to keep her expression slack like she did in the mirror last night.

"I have to get going anyway," Sand Fly said, ignoring the eggs, which were starting to collect an orange rind over the swirled yolk topping them. "See you guys next week."

He moved around the table, pushing past Pea Crab and pausing at Cyra's shoulder. She tried not to look at him, acknowledge him, but he was so tall she felt him leaning over her. His breath softly fell upon her scalp and for a second, he said nothing, just let his exhalation coat her forehead with a layer of grime no shower could erase. The man smelled like one of those plug-in air fresheners, lemony and too floral to be natural.

Still refusing to look at him, Cyra sensed him lower his head toward her and heard him whisper, "I can't wait to get to know you better."

She suddenly wanted to be home, in bed, under the covers.

This was a nest of monsters; one she'd willingly climbed into.

What's wrong with me?

"Sand Fly." Whipworm's voice came out sharper and slicker than before as he noticed the other man hovering around Cyra's shoulder. "I have an appointment, can you fucking leave so I can get going on time?"

"Relax, Whip, I'm going."

Cyra tried to ignore the flash of relief she felt as the air moved behind her, and Sand Fly traipsed around her and toward the door, sparing one last glance over his shoulder in her direction.

Whipworm looked down at the table, his voice mellowing out again. "Waste of food. I guess I'll take them home."

Cyra felt an absurd stab of pity for the eggs no one had touched, and then blinked it away. She couldn't muster up any pity for her dead sister, her drunk father, or herself, but a platter of deviled eggs that a serial killer made somehow elicited an emotion from her.

She needed to get out of there.

One by one, the other men left, even Mockingbird, silently glancing at Cyra with appraising interest again as he exited. Finally, Cyra was alone with Python, who was folding the chairs and stacking them on their sides in the corner of the room and wiping up the coffee rings on the table they'd used. It struck Cyra as oddly considerate.

"Sand Fly wants to kill me," she said without preamble, watching him.

Python didn't look up, but he nodded. "Probably. He wants to kill every woman. He's got a type, of course, but you being here threatens him. I think his bark is a lot worse than his bite. But stay alert."

"What is his type?" she asked.

But Python shook his head. "I don't know specifically, and if I did, I wouldn't tell you." Then he looked at her, thoughtful. "Look, he's implied he likes rich girls. Stay away from him, don't be alone with him, and you'll be fine. I'm sure you can take care of yourself."

Cyra knew he was thinking of the bloody hat she had shown him. But he didn't know the truth, didn't know the whole story. How she tricked him in order to slip into their group like the parasites they were all imitating.

It didn't matter. Cyra would be the real thing—she would infiltrate them, drain their resources, and leave them an empty husk.

CHAPTER

7

CYRA WAS ON high alert on the way home.

She had ducked into a coffee shop to change out of her disguise, gotten off at the wrong subway stop, doubled back, and switched lines. It took her an hour to go thirty blocks, and the whole way back she couldn't stop thinking about what she should do.

Should I just kill them all?

It was a harrowing thought, and she wasn't sure she had it in her. None of the men in the support group were innocent, obviously, but she was beginning to wonder about the moral ramifications of her attending these meetings while the men hunted and potentially killed more people. If she could stop them, shouldn't she?

But there was no way Python wasn't carrying—a former hitman surrounded by serial killers? He definitely had a weapon; one he was probably far more skilled with than Cyra could hope to be. Cyra's solid self-defense skills made her feel more confident in attending the meetings, but all the MMA training in the world wasn't going to stop a bullet.

As she climbed the steps of the last stop on the F train, rising up into the chilly fall air, leaves whipping around her feet as she passed her laundromat and the Indian food place she once took Mira to, Cyra realized it didn't matter.

The truth was that Cyra couldn't—wouldn't—kill anyone until she knew the truth. Maybe it was sick or selfish, but she had to know who took her sister from her and why, before making any other moves. She owed it to Mira.

As she walked the final blocks toward her apartment, Cyra ran through her suspects.

She didn't know how every member of the group operated yet, and Python warned her that some of them would mislead the others to protect their anonymity. Besides Sand Fly, her gut was telling her that Lamprey and Mockingbird were the two she'd least like to come face-to-face with in a dark alley, but that didn't necessarily mean they were the ones she was looking for.

She was fairly sure she could cross off Pea Crab—Mira's body was intentionally posed, she wasn't his usual kind of target, and he seemed too disorganized to be behind her death.

Cyra chewed it over, approaching her building, stopping short when she recognized the figure standing on her stoop.

Bea was outside the building, looking antsy and fingering the pepper spray keychain she always carried around.

"Hey, Bea."

"Sorry for not texting," her ex-girlfriend said, looking at the pavement. "I was afraid you'd tell me to fuck off, and I really do need to get my last box. My favorite sweater is in there."

"I wouldn't have done that. Tell you to fuck off, I mean," Cyra said, blowing into her fingers to warm them as the air chilled with the slightly darkening sky. Clouds boiled overhead, the sky heaving for a moment like it was considering vomiting on them. "How'd you know I'd be around and not at work?"

"Come on, Cyra, I know you've been barely going in lately. I figured it was a fifty-fifty chance you took the day off. You have to be careful, they're gonna fire you."

"No, they won't. They don't give a shit what I do." Cyra felt her brow twitch involuntarily. Bea always did this. She had a habit of mothering Cyra.

"Well, I had to give it a shot. I saw you deleted all your social media."

"Yep. Time for a change."

"Is that what you're doing? Changing?"

"What else would it be?"

Bea shook her head, glancing down. "Nothing."

"Alright, well, come on up, the box is in the hall closet." Cyra's breathing slowed as she tried not to stare at Bea's familiar face; the ridges of her nose, the half-moon shape of her brows. She remembered tracing those brows with the tips of her fingers, cupping Bea's cheeks in her hands as she kissed her soft lips.

Cyra waited to feel pangs of regret and loss, but none came. Instead, her chest tightened and her jaw tensed. Why couldn't she be normal? Why did she push Bea away instead of opening up to her? Irritation—at herself, at the situation, even at Bea— rose within Cyra. To distract herself, she removed her glasses, pretending to wipe a smudge from the surface. The world was slightly blurry without her lenses, and Cyra was reminded of Mistletoe's contacts tucked away at the bottom of her bag along with the rest of her disguise.

The thought of her serial killer persona stiffened her spine, made her replace her glasses on her face, stifling her annoyance.

Cyra said, "Sorry to keep you waiting. Have you been standing out here for a while?"

Bea shook her head, her beautiful black hair floating around her chin as she spoke. "Not long. I don't miss this neighborhood, though. It's so hard to get to and needs some . . . updating."

"No thanks, I can't afford gentrification. How's your new place?" Cyra asked, unlocking the building door and leading her ex inside.

"Good," Bea replied, clearly trying for nonchalance. "It's not far from that warehouse."

"Where the party was?"

"Yup. Deep in Brooklyn and still way too expensive."

Cyra had only been at that warehouse party where she met Bea because of Mira.

"Come on, it'll be fun," Mira had said eight months ago, her voice muffled like she was holding the phone against her cheek with her shoulder as she often did when she was multitasking at home. "I never see you anymore since you moved to Queens."

"Yeah, well, it's a long commute." Cyra didn't point out that she had moved to Queens because her little sister asked her to clear out of their shared apartment so she could get a new one-bedroom in Dumbo. Mira had claimed she needed more "creative space" after she had been discovered and showcased by prominent art critic Arthur McCowen. She promised it wasn't personal, that Arthur insisted she let her "inner eye work harder" so she had interesting new art to promote at his next show.

"Cyra, come on," Mira had said. "It's not like you're doing anything else. And I miss you."

Cyra had surrendered. "What time?"

That night, Cyra met Bea on the outskirts of the dance circle at the blacklight party Mira had dragged her to in order to take long exposure shots of all the twenty-somethings rolling on molly.

"Having fun?" Bea had shouted in Cyra's ear over the pounding bass. She looked older, closer to Cyra's age, not a college kid like the rest of the party-goers.

Cyra was three vodkas in and had lost Mira a while ago. "Not even a little."

Bea had laughed, and they moved to the street to smoke a cigarette together. Talking to Bea felt easy and natural despite her arresting beauty; she had strong features, light brown skin, and a halo of silken black hair. Cyra had been surprised at how much warmth she felt emanating from this woman's words, how interested she seemed in her.

They exchanged numbers at the end of the night and started dating two weeks later.

After that, Mira teased that she was the reason the two were together, happily taking credit for their relationship even though she had been off in a corner making out with Arthur McCowen, her camera slung around her neck, forgotten.

Bea and Cyra hadn't even made it a year, but it was still the longest relationship Cyra had ever had. She knew she should be feeling sadder about them ending, but she couldn't draw up the energy to care.

She led Bea into the apartment, the one they used to share, and directed her toward the cardboard box of her things that had been shoved under the coat rack for over a month.

"Listen, I wanted to say again that I'm sorry," Bea said, her voice a little wobbly as she reached down and hefted up the box so it could sit against her hip like a baby. "I know my timing sucked. And I'm sorry for leaving you to deal with the fallout of . . . what happened . . . alone. That wasn't cool."

"No, I get it," Cyra said, pulling at a cuticle. "Mira's death was too much. I don't blame you for pulling the ripcord."

"Jesus, Cy, is that what you really think?" Bea exclaimed. "I didn't leave because your sister died. I left because I couldn't watch you emotionally castrate yourself anymore."

"Castrate?"

Bea frowned. "You know what I mean. You cut yourself off from everything, especially any feeling. Especially me."

"I lost my sister."

"And it was terrible, but let's be real, Cy, you had issues with this before Mira's death."

"What do you mean?"

Bea sighed and lifted the box a bit more to snuggle it more securely on her hip. "I'm sorry, Cy. But I was going to end things with you before we found out about Mira. It was just horrible timing. You're . . . you're really detached. From yourself, from me. You're so serious all the time. Even . . . you know . . . in bed. I wanted more fun in my life, and you're so quiet and stoic."

She noticed the expression on Cyra's face and redirected. "Which is a great thing! It's why you're so good at your job, and why the landlord backed down when he tried to inflate the rent, and why Mira knew she could always rely on you to solve her problems. You're going to make someone really happy one day because you're so grounded and . . . steady."

Boring; she's calling you boring, Cyra thought. *Boring stick-in-the-mud.*

If Bea only knew the truth.

Cyra felt a twinge in her heart. She hadn't thought she would marry Bea or anything, but she loved her, in her own way, and to hear that Bea would have dumped her regardless stung. "Well, I'm sorry, too, then. I didn't know I wasn't . . . enough for you."

Bea shook her head as if she was trying to get rid of a wasp. "Don't do that. Don't make it sound like I got tired of you. I didn't. I just got tired of being the only one in this relationship who was trying."

The silence stretched between them, and the remains of their bond fractured. Cyra exhaled, unable to look Bea in the face. Her ex was right. Cyra had been trying to force a moment, force an emotion, but there was no point. There was nothing left to salvage, and it was a disservice to Bea to pretend she was feeling something she wasn't.

"I'm sorry," Cyra whispered. "I'm not trying to guilt trip you. I'm . . . I don't know what else to say."

"Take care of yourself, OK?" Bea said, spinning on her heel abruptly and slipping from the apartment, hiding her face. It hadn't mattered, though; Cyra saw the wet shine in her eyes before she left.

She had to get Sand Fly's leering eyes away from her body; she had to pulverize Bea's words from her mind.

Cyra's wrapped fists slammed into the punching bag in the corner of her apartment over and over; uppercuts, crosses, and jabs flurried down, her thick legs shooting up for sidekicks and round kicks until she was dripping and panting.

Though she started with kickboxing, after Cyra moved to the city, she had joined a mixed-martial-arts gym, learning judo for clinching and jiujitsu for ground fighting. Fighting was what brought Cyra back to herself, back to her body. It was how she erased her mind, how she made it go quiet. It didn't hurt that it made her feel marginally safer around the murderers she was keeping company with either. Her panic attacks got better when she was training, and so did her anger. It was easier to deal with the intensity of the world when she knew she could go to her bag or the mat and work it all out.

She slammed a fist into the bag, quickly darting back, keeping her chin tucked and her other fist protecting her face. Striking was Cyra's specialty, though she had been working on improving her grappling, her weakest area, lately. That and her knife skills.

She lifted the switchblade from her end table and eyed the bag, her right foot sliding forward. They didn't teach knife fighting at her gym; this she learned from the internet. She lashed out at the bag with her right hand, knife held horizontally out in front of her, slicing sideways. Cyra imagined the blade cutting through Sand Fly's triceps like they were fresh butter. Swiftly, she stepped forward with her opposite foot, pulling the knife back, dropping low, stabbing the blade into the bottom half of the bag. She pictured blood spurting from Sand Fly's thigh as she eliminated his mobility. For good measure, she yanked the blade out and sunk it into the center of the bag, as if she could drive it into Sand Fly's heart.

She showered twice after, scrubbing the support group meeting—and Sand Fly's breath—from her skin. She holed up in her apartment for the rest of the afternoon, letting the sunlight drain away, watching horror movies.

Night fell, and Cyra pulled out one of the sad single-meal dinners she bought in bulk every few weeks so she didn't have to think about feeding herself. She peeled back the film and paused, feeling something stagnant and thick pressing around her. She hadn't noticed it before; this heavy presence of absence. No Bea, no Mira. No friends she could text—Cyra was a friendship borrower, forming tenuous relationships with Bea's and Mira's friends instead of her own. Without either of them, she was adrift. Cyra could text Eli or Izzie, but she didn't want to. She didn't want to lie about what she was doing.

And maybe she didn't deserve companionship. Maybe this loneliness was what she deserved. After all, she had done terrible things, some in the past week; she destroyed evidence of a murder, exploited a dead woman she genuinely liked, joined a group of murderers . . . Cyra might have done those things because her back was against the wall, but still. She was better off by herself.

Cyra put the microwave dinner back in the freezer and pulled out a carton of eggs instead. She would make herself a real meal. Even if it was breakfast. She smeared butter in the pan and waited for it to heat, watching little yellow bubbles sizzle and burst.

She thought of Mistletoe, a woman who was a funhouse mirror-image of herself in a different world. A serial murderer who picked elderly women to prey on because she had unresolved trauma with her own mother.

Cyra tapped an egg against the side of the pan and felt it crack beneath her fingers, the gooey yolk slipping out from the crevasse she had created and plopping on to the pan. The whites bloomed solid in seconds. The yolk wobbled daintily, a yellow eye staring up at her.

Mistletoe would be shrewd and self-assured. She would be unafraid; she would be selfish. Things Cyra had never let herself be. She'd walk through the world covered in armor—she killed not for money or lust but for a sense of control.

The other egg was broken and slipped into the pan next to its twin. Edges curling up and browning, the yolks set. Sprinkles of salt and pepper. A slit down the middle of the whites where the two eggs had joined, separating them.

Cyra turned the heat off and moved the pan off the stove, her two eggs googling up at her.

Mistletoe was a necessity moving forward. She was the opposite of Cyra in so many ways. And too similar in others.

Cyra stared at the eggs for a moment. Then she popped open the garbage can with her foot and tilted the pan so that the eggs slid over the lip and into the trash.

She dropped the pan in the sink with a clang, ignoring the protesting hiss of water from the bottom, and swung her coat on. She needed to get out of the apartment for a moment, needed to breathe.

She wanted a beer.

There was a deli on the corner of her block, and she slipped out into the night and powered toward it, the cold licking her face.

The door jangled as she entered, and she remembered hearing a similar sound when she was squished in the storage room with Python the other day, showing him her "evidence," trying to prove to him she was a serial killer.

The beer aisle was even colder than it was outside, and Cyra stood in front of the shelf of forties for several long minutes, imagining the bubbles dancing on her tongue, the warmth in her gut as the alcohol heated up her blood. She would get two. She could drink them both within an hour and be set for the rest of the night. Everything would go away.

Her fingers lingered on the smooth metal of the fridge door, sliding down to the glass and tracing the shapes of the bottles through the door. She hadn't had a craving this strong in months.

Abruptly, she turned and hurried into the candy aisle, swiping her hand through the chocolate section, raining sweets down into her waiting arms. She grabbed a huge jug of iced tea on her way to the checkout and dropped the sugary feast on the counter.

The deli owner and Cyra knew each other in the way deli store owners always know their customers—by habits and faces, not by names or lives.

"One of those nights?" he asked dryly as he began to ring up her items, his brown skin looking washed out under the fluorescent lights above him.

"Gotta feed the beast," Cyra replied.

The man gave her a half-smile. She knew he would have been watching her on the CCTV next to his cash register, saw her lingering near the beer, staring at it longingly. He had seen her in the store drunk before, weaving, and still sold her a six pack. He had been there when she bought several forties and then returned three hours later for another one. He must have noticed when she suddenly stopped buying his alcohol six months ago. But he never said anything.

She was grateful for that.

"Have a good night," he said, and there was an inflection in his voice like he actually meant it.

Something warm released inside Cyra. Here was someone who didn't know about Mira, didn't know a damn thing about Cyra besides the fact she had swapped beer for junk food, and who seemed to care anyway.

She carried the warmth with her until she stepped outside and ran right into a familiar, attractive man.

Lamprey.

CHAPTER

8

SHE WAS PREPARED to meet the serial killers earlier.
But now, on her home turf, mental state wobbly and dented by the trip to the deli, Cyra floundered. The hair on the back of her neck stood, everything suddenly got a lot brighter despite it being night, and her skin awoke with goosebumps.

Lamprey was staring at her with surprise, but Cyra saw the mask of it—how perfect it was, how an acting coach would clap and say, "That's a great imitation of a surprised man!"

He had followed her. Somehow. Despite leaving the meeting a good twenty minutes before her, despite her attempts to cover her tracks.

A pulse of heat shot through her chest. She wasn't wearing her disguise; her blonde wig was tucked away under the bathroom sink; her lift shoes were discarded near the hall closet. Maybe he wouldn't recognize her with her dark hair and glasses? But that was stupid, she saw the truth on his face—he had sought her out. And now he stood in front of her, fifty feet away from her apartment.

She was fucked.

"Mistletoe!" Lamprey exclaimed, moving slightly to the side, his hands finding their way to her shoulders and pulling her with him so that they stood next to the deli's front window, parallel to the open cellar door jutting into the sidewalk's space like a silver bird wing.

Can I shove him into the cellar? Cyra thought, noting it was open for a delivery. *Not a deep fall, but maybe he'll break his neck.*

"What are you doing here?" Cyra managed to spit out. "Why did you follow me?"

"How do you know I don't live in the area, too?"

"Too." Jesus, he knows I live here.

The danger felt like a weighted blanket that was far too heavy, becoming more and more oppressive as the minutes ticked by.

"Cut the shit," Cyra said, thinking that her saving grace was the fact that they were in public, standing on the street corner under the bright lights of the deli. Cars whizzed past, a small group of men were smoking cigarettes and weed across the street, and plenty of people were still walking around—it was only 8:30 in the evening. He couldn't murder her right there, could he? "You're breaking the rules. You're stalking me. Why?"

Lamprey grinned, dropping the pretense of surprise, his frightening smile making Cyra take an unconscious step back, releasing herself from his grip. "Busted. I wanted to make sure you got home OK. Sand Fly's got it out for you."

"Liar."

His grin widened. "It was pretty stupid to leave the meeting last. It made it very easy to hide in a laundromat and follow you from a distance."

Sweat beaded on Cyra's forehead as her heart plummeted.

Oh, hell. How could I be so stupid?

She assumed leaving last would protect her, knowing the killers had already left, giving her time to watch her back and check for shadows, but she didn't spot Lamprey at all. She slipped up, and he took advantage of it.

"You trailed me home," she stated.

"Maybe I was a little suspicious. Maybe I thought you were a cop."

"Do I look like a cop?" Cyra's mind was spinning. She had no idea what game Lamprey was playing, but she had to stay in control of herself. Why hadn't she brought her switchblade? She envisioned slicing the knife across his forearm, ending at his wrist, watching his blood gush out. Her hands were hot and sweaty, and she could almost feel the comforting weight of her forgotten blade in her palm.

"Maybe one of those sexy older ones on TV, you know, the ones who are always tired and never get laid." Lamprey edged closer, his blue eyes wide and his voice simpering.

A woman with a pile of dark hair artfully arranged on top of her head passed by them, glancing once at Lamprey appreciatively, her eyes skimming over his symmetrical face, his built chest that was visible even through his peacoat.

Cyra wanted to shout at her, tell her to never trust men like him, to run the opposite direction if she ever met him or anyone like him at a bar.

He was too attractive. Too confident. A shiny piece of fruit that was rotten inside.

"Cute," Cyra replied, moving around him. "I have to head out now. See you next time, I guess."

"See you, Cyra Griffin."

Cyra's heart sputtered to a stop, and she slowly turned back around, fighting to breathe normally. "Excuse me?"

"*Cyra*," Lamprey said, drawing out her name like it was a snake slithering from his mouth.

"You are mistaken," Cyra tried to say firmly, but the end of her sentence wobbled like a tightrope walker. There was that forgotten emotion again—fear. She pressed against it, trying to shove it away. Fear confused her. Why should she ever be frightened again when the one thing she was the most afraid of already happened?

"I don't think so. I'm a software engineer, but in my spare time I'm a hacker," Lamprey said, his voice casual, effortlessly calm. "I upgraded our . . . recruiting methods when I joined the group. Made it way more secure, put up defenses that would keep the Feds out. Python was pretty good at spotting obvious attempts to infiltrate before me, so the cops never got very far. He uses a software that analyzes the photos we make prospects send. He can always tell if something is faked, but I enhanced the program so that we can also tell if a photo is sourced from court evidence. If a cop tries to use altered images to get their foot in the door, I see right through them. Python lets me know when someone contacts us, and if they're a novice like you, I can access the backend and trace their IP address." He smirked. "The dark web isn't *completely* untraceable."

"So you know I'm not a cop."

"Yeah," He admitted, smiling again. "I saw that picture you sent. It was real. Plus, we block any addresses that are associated with the government or specific government-related sites."

"Did you hack my computer?" Cyra asked, mouth dry.

Lamprey ignored her question. "I thought you looked familiar today. Took me a little bit to figure it out, but finally I did."

A sick feeling was growing in Cyra's belly. "I don't know what you're talking about."

"You see, I move in some very, ah, elite circles. I love art."

Cyra's stomach dropped.

"I remembered this great portrait from, oh, a little while back. Of this girl having a panic attack. Her face was so striking." Lamprey smiled. "It took a minute with the different hair and no glasses, but I finally recognized you."

Mira had a cat when they were children. Bernard.

One time Cyra woke up to a scrabbling noise in the early hours of the morning. She realized it was coming from the bathroom right across the hall from the room she shared with her sister, who could sleep through a nuclear war. Cyra tiptoed out across the carpeted floor and on to the cold tiles of the bathroom, her heart in her throat. She swept aside the shower curtain to reveal an extremely satisfied Bernard, crouched like a gargoyle, looking down on his catch: a small mouse charging around the tub in terror, leaving little bloody footprints, unable to scale the slippery walls and escape. Cyra had screamed and woken her father, then ran back to bed and hid her face in her pillow, not wanting to see what her father would do with the injured mouse.

Pinned by Lamprey's appraising eyes, Cyra finally understood what that mouse must have felt like.

"Once I remembered where I'd seen you, it was easy to figure out your real name from there," Lamprey continued as Cyra worked to keep her face under control. "That photo was a real goldmine. Don't worry, I didn't tell Python anything. Just that we should be safe with you."

She was screwed. That meant he knew all about Mira's death and the pending investigation. Did he have access to her emails as well? Was that how hacking worked? Was he able to actually get into her computer using her IP address?

"Great, so you know I'm not trying to turn you into the police," Cyra said, trying to keep her voice as matter-of-fact as possible.

"Ah, yes, but you are looking for something, aren't you? Or rather, some*one*." Lamprey leaned forward and Cyra caught a whiff of his scent; mint and cologne, with something musky detectable underneath, like the smell of a horse. "Which one of us are you betting on? Personally, I think it's Mockingbird, but you never know. Your sister would have appealed to several people in our little group."

The part that scraped against Cyra the hardest was that the world would fall in love with Lamprey if he was ever caught. Good-looking, educated, charming. She was aware of the fetishization of serial killers, of the internet's obsession with them (but only the white ones), of the studios who would clamor to make a movie of his life. But they wouldn't understand. They wouldn't realize that up close and personal, there was nothing appealing about this man.

Cyra's hand shot out and latched on Lamprey's arm. Her fingers met cold metal; his thin gold watch immediately began heating up under the warmth of her palm. Lamprey started, shock flickering across his face before he masked it with another slow smile as she began to tighten her fingers, digging into his cold skin. "You'd save me a lot of trouble if you confessed to my sister's murder now."

Lamprey laughed. "I like you, *Mistletoe.* And if it was me, I think I would actually tell you. I want to see what you'd do."

"Shut up."

"Don't be so nasty, Cyra."

"Congratulations, you found out my real name, but I got into this group for a reason," Cyra hissed. She had to convince him she was dangerous. "I wouldn't get in without evidence, would I? I'm still a killer."

Lines formed between Lamprey's brows and his jaw tightened, but his smile stayed fixed. "I know how the application process works. I know you must have shown something convincing. But I don't believe you hurt anyone, *Cyra.* You're not like us." He suddenly lunged closer until the two of them were only inches apart. "Not yet, anyway."

"No real names," she demanded, scrambling to maintain some semblance of power here. Everything was spinning, moving too fast. "You have no idea what I've done." She thought of the story she told Python about PJ. Maybe that would work on Lamprey too? Or was it too late?

She gritted her teeth. Should she try to eliminate him now? What were the chances he was the one who killed Mira?

"Ooh," Lamprey trilled, watching her face. His other hand came out of nowhere and clamped down on top of hers, still clutching his arm and watch. It was like they were playing that game Mira and Cyra used to play as kids where they would stack their hands on top of one another's in alternating order, pulling out the hand at the bottom of the pile and slapping it on top so the cycle continued. "You're thinking of killing me, aren't you? Oh, I really do like you, Mistletoe. Listen, your secret is safe with me."

To anyone else on the street they probably looked like lovers playing a flirty game; arms twisted up between each other.

Cyra's muscles tensed and her thighs ached; she wanted to lunge at him and take him down with a double leg move. Her heart was pounding so hard she was worried she'd trigger a panic attack. She fought the urge to pull her hand out from under his, to return her body back to herself. Appearing weak right now was not an option, not to this man. "Why on earth would I believe you?"

"Because I want something from you," Lamprey said. Noticing the expression on her face, he amended. "I know you're not a cop. But I think someone in the group is a rat. Maybe an undercover, maybe just a snitch. I don't know yet. But I can't trust anyone else to help me ferret him out. Except you. I know who you are, so you're going to help me."

"What do you mean? How do you not know anyone else in the group? I thought you said you helped with the application process."

Lamprey grimaced. "Believe it or not, I was the last person to join before you. I just started offering my vetting services to Python. Everyone else was already established in the group, and I can't work from nothing. Obviously, I don't know their real names, and I don't have access to their original messages or photos. It's not like any of them are going to let me borrow their devices either. Not to mention, I'm sure most of them were clever enough to use a library computer far from their real home. And not be photographed by a rising star in the art world. Unlike you."

Cyra knew he was trying to get a reaction from her, so she kept her snarl inside her bones. "Then what makes you think someone in the group is a mole?"

He shook his head. "Just a feeling."

She glowered at him.

He knit his brows together and added, "And sometimes I see things online in the stupid true crime forums warning against people that sound an awful lot like the men in our group. With physical descriptions and everything. I have no proof yet. But you'll help me get some."

Cyra shook her head violently. "I'm not helping you with that. I have my priority."

Lamprey leaned in closer, his long lashes inches from her face. "You will help. Because if not, I'll expose you to the rest of the group."

A boulder fell in Cyra's stomach. She still didn't know if Lamprey killed Mira or not, but judging by his behavior he could very well be the person she was looking for. However, if he revealed who she really was to the group before she could confirm anything, it would all be for nothing.

As if reading her thoughts, Lamprey smiled again and said, "I didn't kill your sister. But if you need more incentive, I'll help you figure that out too. Because if someone in this group did kill her, I need to know who."

She swallowed. "Why?"

He paused, the smile slipping for a fraction of a second. "I read about the murder in the paper. And it was sloppy. We have an understanding here; be smart with the bodies. That's why Pea Crab is on thin ice, leaving people in trap houses and alleys.

He's not really one of us, you know. The rest of us are competent. Sand Fly sinks his in the river, Mockingbird is a trucker, he leaves them in woods on the road . . ."

"And you?" Cyra asked, feeling sweat from her hand slick against the gold watch under her palm.

Lamprey's grin returned. "Now that would be telling. The point is, we don't just leave our darlings out in the open, and we don't hunt exclusively in the city."

This was news to Cyra, and she finally pulled away from Lamprey's grasp, chilled by his use of the word "darlings," shaking her arm out and leaning forward. "What do you mean?"

"I think Python made an exception for your . . . story," Lamprey paused and quirked up a brow. "Because you're a woman, you know. Interesting and new. An unofficial rule of the group is that we limit our kills in the five boroughs."

"But why? There are millions of people here. Isn't it easier to disappear someone in a city this size?"

"Of course. And we do, but only sometimes. This is how I know you're not really one of us, by the way," Lamprey added, glancing down at the reddening marks on his arm from where Cyra had grabbed him. He adjusted his golden wristwatch so that it faced upwards again and looked back up at her, his smile gone, his face cold. "We don't shit where we eat. It's harder to get caught if you spread out your successes, not leave glaring signals back to your doorstep. A pretty blonde girl viciously attacked in a popular public park is a real stupid move. I'm sure the cops are all over that, even if they aren't telling you everything they know."

You could have waited for the cops to do their job, the little voice in the back of Cyra's head piped up. *You didn't have to be in this position, being threatened by a serial killer, if you just had more patience.*

Except Cyra didn't want the same thing the cops wanted. She wanted vengeance, not a cushy jail cell for the person who ripped away Mira's life.

"OK, so you think my sister's killer is in this group?" Cyra asked, dropping all pretense now that it seemed like Lamprey wasn't interested in immediately killing her.

"There's a chance." Lamprey admitted. His face darkened a touch. "Pea Crab is a mess. He's a junkie, and he's getting worse. He said he used to take the trains outside the city and find a homeless person every year, but I think that was a lie. He just kills whoever gets in the way of his next fix and leaves them there to be found later. He's not a real . . . parasite." Lamprey glanced once behind him as he said "parasite," as if checking for eavesdroppers.

"You're saying he could be devolving," Cyra said, using a word she had come upon during her research. "Losing control of his urges as he spirals."

"Look who ran an internet search on serial killers," Lamprey snapped. Then he looked thoughtful. "You're not the first to point that out." Before Cyra could ask what he meant, he continued, "Yes, he's devolving."

"But my sister wasn't into drugs or anything like that."

Lamprey's smile was back. "Are you sure?"

Cyra's fingers twitched, and she had to hold herself back from scoring her fingernails across Lamprey's face. "I know my sister."

"You *knew* your sister," Lamprey corrected, smirking.

He was playing with her, she realized, releasing the fists she had formed and taking a deep breath. Lamprey was trying to get her riled up. To make her reveal something? To off-balance her? Simply because he enjoyed it? Cyra wasn't sure, but what she did know was that she couldn't let him infiltrate her mind.

"If I help you find out who's the rat in your group, you'll help me figure out who killed my sister?" Cyra asked.

"I swear it."

"That doesn't comfort me much," Cyra said acidly. "You'll also agree to not kill me? I have things to do. People to avenge.

This only works if it's like a *Silence of the Lambs*-type relationship where you would find it rude to murder me after we've worked together."

"But of course," Lamprey replied, his smile deepening until he looked almost unhinged. Then, suddenly, it dropped off his face. "You have my word. I won't hurt you. I'll help you find who killed your sister. As long as you help me, too."

"You know, you're making it pretty obvious that you're the one who killed her," Cyra said, trying to keep her voice steady and detached, finally calm enough to infuse more of Mistletoe's persona back into her body.

Lamprey shook his head. "You'll see, in the end. I didn't know your sister, just her art. And only just. She wasn't that good." He leaned forward again, the smile back. "But now I know you, and I'd be honored to help you."

Cyra didn't see how she had a choice. He was blackmailing her. If she refused, he'd expose her to the group or kill her, or both. Either way she ended up dead, and Mira's murder went unpunished. She couldn't trust him as far as she could shove him, but she had to play nice. For now, at least.

"Fine," she spat. "Now leave. I want to watch you walk away."

"You know I already know where you live," Lamprey said, nodding over her shoulder. "I followed you, remember?"

"Still."

"Wow, not even going to invite me inside for a cup of tea?"

"Tell me your real name."

Lamprey actually took a step back, his face etched in surprise. "What?"

"You know mine. It's only fair I know yours, too," Cyra demanded. Feeling the upper hand within reach, she stepped forward, edging the man a bit closer to the open cellar door. "How else am I supposed to trust you? And don't lie. You're not the only one who knows how to use a computer. I'll check online to make sure you're being honest."

"What makes you think I have an online presence?" Lamprey asked, not noticing how close he had gotten to the black hole in the ground in front of the deli.

"You looking like that? You couldn't resist. Especially if your whole shtick is luring people in by being 'normal' and 'friendly.'"

"Think you've got me pegged, huh?" Lamprey's face had shuttered, smile gone, expression wiped blank, ugliness creeping out. "Fine. Jason Weston."

Cyra demanded he spell it correctly for her, putting the name in the Notes app on her phone, and then stared the serial killer down. "We should only call each other by our group names when we interact. For safety's sake. The real names are insurance. Examples of trust." The last word slipped from her mouth like it had a bad taste. As if she'd ever be able to trust him. Or him, her.

Lamprey looked at her for a moment. "You're not one of us. But I think you could be."

The hair on Cyra's arms stood up inside her jacket and the soles of her feet grew hot. She didn't think; she raised both her hands and pushed Lamprey, sending him teetering into the open cellar. The man gave a yelp of surprise as he fell backward.

Cyra stood at the maw of the cellar for a moment, not daring to look, her heart beating in her throat.

Why did I do that? He's really going to kill me now. If he's not . . .

"Bitch!"

Not dead then.

Cyra leaned over the open doors and found Lamprey sprawled on the dirty floor, lower half still draped on the steps, torso and head smudged with dust from the deli's basement.

"I am not one of you," Cyra hissed from above him, looking down. "But I will do whatever it takes to find my sister's killer. Understand?"

She bent over backward to prove herself to the support group, to pretend she was one of them, but now that Lamprey had met her true self, she couldn't stand being compared to these men. They were sick, hurting people for pleasure and excitement. Everything Cyra did, every mistake or questionable act she ever did was for Mira. To protect her.

They were not the same.

Lamprey was slowly getting to his feet, disgustedly wiping off his fancy peacoat and patting his legs as if to make sure he hadn't broken anything. He had only fallen five feet, and Cyra was relieved she hadn't done any actual damage. The last thing she needed was to be arrested for assault. Or murder.

Lamprey stood still at the bottom of the steps for a second, looking up at Cyra. She imagined what she must look like from his angle—backlit by the streetlights, her wispy dark hair blowing against her cheeks, her muscled body hidden by a thick black sweater, eyes burning.

Lamprey's anger seemed to flare as his fists bunched and his brow twisted, but he took a deep breath and it leaked out of him. He gazed up at her instead, eyes narrowed in appraisal. He wasn't taunting her anymore, wasn't playing a game. He saw a glimpse of her that had elicited something that looked almost like . . . respect.

"Interesting," he said softly, eyes not leaving Cyra's. "Very interesting."

Cyra wanted to slam the cellar door on top of him, leaving him down there in the dirt and the darkness where he belonged, but instead she gave him one last cold look, and then turned away, walking home with her bag of candy.

Cyra worked the next morning, which was just as well.

It meant she couldn't stay up all night googling Jason Weston. Cyra was a little surprised he told her his real name, but he must have been confident that there was nothing of substance she could find online. And sure enough, his name was just common enough that he easily disappeared into a sea of other men. She did spend two hours looking through his Twitter profile, the only social media account she managed to find him on, her skin crawling at how *regular* he presented online. He hadn't been active in months, but back when he did engage, it was only retweets from comedians, some tweets about new software he was using, and, randomly, a history of "liking" John Deere posts.

Since it had been so easy to find his account, which used his full first and last name in his handle, Cyra had no doubt that this was the social media page Lamprey used to make himself seem like a real person and not a monster, but it was still eerie to see what he presented and what she knew to be his true self. They were at odds with each other. If Cyra hadn't met Lamprey at the meeting, would she have been fooled into thinking he was normal too?

Cyra shook herself, shuddering. She was going to be late to work if she didn't hurry. The nursing home was only a few subway stops away, part of the reason she had moved to Queens in the first place, but she frequently rolled in fifteen, twenty minutes late since Mira's death.

The staff at Cardinal Hill Nursing Home had been more than understanding when she cut her hours after Mira's death, but the truth was that doing marketing for a nursing home wasn't a gig that needed forty hours a week anyway. Cyra knew she was lucky, even before Mira's death, to work somewhere that pretty much let her do what she wanted.

Cyra floated through her tasks, scheduling social media posts, photographing the residents playing mah-jong in the common room, updating budgets on digital ads, uncomfortably aware of the fact that Lamprey must also know where she worked, until her phone buzzed.

How are you doing?

Eli, texting her in the group chat they had with Izzie, which meant that Izzie asked him to check in with her and this was his way of proving he did.

We want to see you this weekend, Izzie replied, not waiting for Cyra to respond. *Come over. Wine and cheese night.*

Cyra leaned against the wall of the hall she had been walking down on the way to her cramped office. Wine and cheese night was something the four of them would do—really, it was something Izzie, Eli, and Mira would do and occasionally invite Cyra to. Cyra would come maybe half the time, but was avoiding them since she got sober.

She went to one right before Mira's death, but she didn't like to think about it.

Cyra's fingers hovered over the phone screen, trying to decide on a good excuse.

A third text popped up in the group chat as if Izzie had known what Cyra was thinking:

It's either this or we come out there and help you clean out your apartment! I know it's a mess.

She wasn't wrong, but the presumption scraped against Cyra. They weren't friends. Eli and Izzie were *Mira's* friends. And yes, the two had been making a huge effort since her sister's death, but Cyra was concerned that this wasn't due to them wanting to check on her—she suspected they were trying to replace the hole Mira left in their group.

And if they thought Cyra was a replacement for Mira, they were sorely mistaken.

But still, Cyra would have to go to Wine and Cheese. There was no way she wanted them at her place, looking at the dirty clothes on the floor, the pathology and criminal studies books scattered on every surface, the parts of her serial killer disguise she was too lazy to put away.

She'd go for an hour and hope they wouldn't ask her too many questions.

As she tapped away a response, chest clenching, Cyra imagined how she would have to behave at this dinner. She would have to fake smiles, feign interest in conversations she had no energy for. She would have to project emotions she didn't have. She was already exhausted.

She pushed her shoulders back, lifted her chest, imitating the body language she used as Mistletoe in her first meeting. A wave of chilled calmness spread across her skin.

It'll be fine, she thought, sending a series of cheerful emojis in the group chat. *You are good at pretending.*

SAND FLY

Edward didn't learn to hate girls until Briana Bower.
Before Briana, he liked them. Well, maybe not "liked," but at least didn't despise them. Girls were like the hair that clogged the drain of his family's shower: kind of gross and an inconvenience, but nothing to get worked up about if the water still ran properly.

Before Briana, Edward thought his trepidation around girls was simply due to their unfamiliarity. They were a house full of boys, after all. He didn't have much experience with females. Edward's mother had died when Billy and Joseph were eight, and Edward was only four.

All the memories Edward had of his mother were unpleasant. Flashes of her crying, cringing away from his father, looking at Edward as if waiting to see something in him that never appeared.

Sometimes Edward would ask Billy and Joseph to tell him stories about their mother, but they both called him a crybaby and pretended like they didn't care that she was gone. They were older, twins, bonded closer than anyone else, and they didn't let Edward forget it.

"Why do you care?" Joseph would tease. "She didn't love you. She didn't love any of us!"

"That's why she did what she did," Billy added.

And asking his father was a bad idea.

Edward mostly avoided the girls at school, especially when he started high school and shot up like a stinkweed, arms and legs dangling in the hallways like Gumby.

When Briana Bower approached him during gym class sophomore year, three days after his sixteenth birthday, Edward had the sudden urge to squeeze his elongated body under the wooden bleachers to get away from her.

She was so beautiful. Almost too beautiful. Glossy hair like in the magazines, lips as plump as ripe peaches. When she got up close to him, Edward could see that her eyebrows weren't symmetrical—it somehow made her look even prettier. The most popular girl in his grade was coming up to him and smiling.

"I like your shoes," Briana said, glancing down at the Reebok pump sneakers Edward's father had gotten all the boys for Christmas that year. "Super neat."

"Uh, thanks." Edward was hyperaware of the little bubbles of acne pulsing on his forehead, the stench of his underarms, not quite hairy enough yet, from dribbling the basketball around cones Coach Hatter set up in the gym.

Edward froze, not knowing what to say next. An image popped into his mind, wicked and dripping with desire—Briana on her knees, looking up at him with her bruised fruit lips, emulating the things Edward had seen in the dirty magazine he stole from Billy's bedroom a year ago.

"So, hey, the Sadie Hawkins dance is Friday," Briana said, snapping her bubblegum and twirling one of her long pigtails. She grinned at him.

"OK."

Briana laughed. "Do you wanna come with me?"

When Edward was ten, Billy ordered him to walk the family dog, a Shepard-mix Joseph had named Demon. Edward was half the size of the dog at that point, all skin and bones, and he complained that their father wouldn't like it. But the other Darby brothers were too busy playing Street Fighter on the Super NES. So, Edward leashed up Demon and the second they got down the driveway, sensing the weakness in his handler, the dog had shot away down the street. He must have smelled freedom. Perhaps tasted it, too, because the dog never returned. Edward got in big trouble—his father loved that dog and had given him extra lashes that night even though Edward tried to protest that it wasn't his fault.

Briana's words made Edward feel like maybe he understood Demon's mad dash a little better. The dog saw something he wanted, and he went for it.

"That would be cool," Edward replied, wincing as his voice cracked at the end of the sentence, the worst place for it because it lingered in the mind.

"Rad! I'll see you then!" Briana flounced off back toward her group of girlfriends, who were watching them but pretending not to.

Edward had dreams about Briana every night that week, ruining his sheets and turning them inside out each time, too ashamed to let his brothers see him do the same laundry multiple times in a row. He wondered if he should get her a corsage. She liked pink, he knew that. All her Lisa Frank folders and notebooks were in garish pink shades. Maybe he could get her carnations.

He mentioned it to his father. He needed money if he was going to get her a corsage.

"A date? Good for you. She hot?" his father asked, looking up from his ballgame and Bud with raised eyebrows.

Edward nodded, his sunken, bony chest puffing out a little. "And the most popular girl in the grade."

"Atta boy." His father dug a ten-dollar bill from his wallet and handed it over.

On Friday night, Edward met Briana at her house and walked her six blocks to the school, wishing he could have rented a limo or something. She looked stunning in a white minidress. Edward wondered if he could lick the hot pink lip gloss off her mouth later. His penis bulged against his briefs under his dress slacks, the black pair he'd worn for his mother's funeral. He thought of the closed casket, his mother lying inside with a hole in her head. He thought of the priest making some shifty comments about her immortal sin and how they had to pray extra hard for her soul since she chose to die in such a disgraceful way.

Edward's erection pushed harder against his underwear and he cleared his throat as if hoping it would push it back down.

"Thanks for taking me." Briana chirped as they entered the school, joining the throng of other hormonal teenagers making eyes at each other.

"I'd take you anywhere," Edward replied.

Nice, he thought. *You're on point tonight.*

It only took him forty-five minutes to lose track of Briana. He offered to get them both punch from the snack table and when he returned to where he left her, at the bundle of white and silver balloons near the gym's entrance, she was gone. He hunted for her, but it was like she had disappeared into the folds of the universe. Maybe she had gone back to whatever pink and purple splattered world the Lisa Frank animals came from.

Edward's stomach started cramping like it did every time he heard his father raise his voice. His palms got slick just like they did when he felt the nip of the belt buckle against his bare back. He spent the rest of the dance looking for Briana and pretending he wasn't. The chaperons had to kick him out after everyone else had left because he kept telling himself she'd be back any second now.

Edward walked home alone, the night pressing in on him, crowding his breathing and bleeding the warmth from his body. He thought about the last time he saw his mother. He didn't remember much. Just that she had been frantic and crying. A toy truck had been clenched in his little fist, and Edward had sat in the middle of the floor and watched as his father chased his mother into the bedroom.

The next thing Edward remembered was a sharp cracking sound, like an oven pan being dropped against a concrete floor.

Seconds later his father had stormed from the bedroom, barely glancing at his youngest son as he tucked something black and L-shaped into the waistband of his pants.

Edward had put the truck down. He was done playing anyway. The truck's wheels were sticking; it was unable to move forward.

CHAPTER

9

CYRA WALKED THE few avenues from the subway to Eli and Izzie's apartment on Sixth and Garfield on Saturday evening.

She let the unseasonably warm breeze brush her loose hair as she approached the not-quite-a-Brownstone-but-hoping-to-be-mistaken-for-one where they rented a basement apartment.

Dead leaves curled and crunched under Cyra's big black boots as she spied a family out for a stroll up ahead on the block, laughing at something the youngest daughter had said—the little girl looked about six and wore a pink puffy jacket that was far too warm for the day's weather. Cyra paused in front of Eli and Izzie's, watching the family get farther and farther away up the block. The mother's arm was wrapped around her partner, the two of them leaning toward each other, watching their two daughters skip ahead, chanting some kind of rhyme Cyra couldn't make out. The family was a unit, clearly complete and content. Jealousy, a swollen and tender fruit, burst in her gut, leaking out inside her. She was glad those little girls wouldn't grow up the way she and Mira had but still . . . she wished their unfettered joy was a little quieter. A little less public.

Cyra shook her head and turned toward Izzie and Eli's building.

A year after Cyra and Mira moved to New York City, Mira met Izzie. Mira, no art prospects yet but waitressing on weekends, had gone to the Brooklyn Museum one Wednesday morning to "get inspiration" while Cyra was working at her marketing job at the nursing home. Mira met Izzie there, guiding a field trip of kindergarteners, and ended up trotting around the exhibits with the group.

"She was so easy to talk to," Mira had told Cyra that night. "She's a little older than me, but she got this amazing teaching job and moved here from the Midwest. So we're both newbies. We're going to go to happy hour tomorrow. You should come!"

But Cyra had declined; she knew how effervescent her sister was around new people. It was better to let Mira do her thing without her trying to include Cyra in the conversations like a clunky third wheel.

Mira and Izzie became fast friends, and Cyra had worked hard to be happy for Mira instead of feeling like she was being replaced. Izzie was on Mira's wavelength, unlike Cyra, who mostly wanted to hang out at home or go to quiet coffee shops.

A few months into their friendship, Mira and Izzie dragged Cyra out to a Park Slope dive bar called American Cheez, and there they met Eli, who was Izzie's age, a few years younger than Cyra.

Eli initially approached Mira, shyly introducing himself to her and their group. Cyra had watched, proud of her sister, as Mira clocked Izzie's interest; the way she laughed at Eli's jokes and leaned in closer to him when he was talking. When Eli asked if he could buy Mira a drink, she encouraged Eli to buy shots for their whole table instead, and smiled when Izzie and Eli started bonding over being transplants from the Midwest.

And that was it. After that night, it was the three of them, best friends, even when Eli and Izzie started dating and got serious.

Cyra always felt a little out of place around them, and not because she was older, much closer to thirty than they were. The three of them had similar energies, seemed to fold together in their own little group seamlessly.

Now, without Mira, the group had fractured, and Cyra wasn't sure what Izzie wanted from her. She'd never be able to be Mira.

"Cyra?" Eli was standing at the wrought-iron door tucked under the stone steps leading to the first floor entrance. He was in his socks, leaning his head out, brows furrowed, wearing a thick flannel and dark jeans. "You OK?"

"Of course." Cyra hurried inside the little gated entryway that held the building's trashcans and a teeny plot of hard-packed soil with a few half-dead bushes.

"Come on in," Eli welcomed her, stepping back so that she could slip through their gated front door, which she had always admired with its swirling black patterns, and past the second storm door. "Great weather we had today, right? Nothing like a random seventy-degree day at the beginning of November. Did you get outside and do anything nice? Did you do anything fun for Halloween? We handed out candy to the trick or treaters. It gets wild here!" Eli's voice seemed louder than usual as he led her into the tiny hallway where they kept their coats and shoes. "Can I take your coat?" He reached out for Cyra's denim jacket, and then lowered his voice considerably. "Don't tell Izzie about the serial killer support group."

Cyra raised an eyebrow. "I'm pretty sure she already knows, remember?"

Eli flapped his hand toward the floor, indicating she lower her voice. "No, not that. Don't tell her that you joined."

Cyra paused in the middle of handing him her jacket, and then slowly stepped forward to get closer to him. "What are you talking about?"

"Cyra, I know you," Eli whispered. In a much-louder-than-normal voice he said, "Where'd you get this jacket? I totally need one like it." Perhaps realizing how stupid he sounded, Eli made a face, then turned back to Cyra. "I knew when I told you that you'd never be able to leave it alone. And I noticed . . . I noticed you deleted all your social media profiles. I told Izzie it was probably you taking a social detox so you didn't have to see Mira popping up on everyone's feeds, but I realized what that really meant."

"I don't know what you're talking about," Cyra said carefully as Eli hung her jacket up and looked at her with wide eyes.

"We don't have to go into it now, in fact, I'd rather we don't," Eli said quickly. "But please. Be careful. And don't tell Izzie. She wouldn't understand. She'd get so upset. She's already pissed at me for putting my job in danger to tell you something that could get you killed."

"You don't have to worry," Cyra replied, stepping away from him, her eyes sliding past his face. "There's nothing to tell, so I won't say anything. Come on, do you really think I'd be able to infiltrate a group like that? Izzie was right all along."

"You're good, I'll give you that," Eli muttered. "It's like talking to a store mannequin. No expression." In his louder voice he said, "Come on, Izzie's in here, she got a great brie from The Good Wife."

Their apartment was cozy and well lit; the living room was tucked up against the front windows, which looked out on to the sidewalk, and Izzie stood in the open-plan kitchen, hair pulled back into a ponytail. She was bent over a large platter, arranging cheese with painstaking concentration. Several bottles of red were laid out on the coffee table along with a bowl of candy corn, the only remaining treats from the recent holiday. Cyra clenched her back teeth, wondering how she was going to hide the fact that she wasn't drinking without Mira there to take up all the attention.

Cyra knew she shouldn't hide her sobriety, but it didn't feel like the right time to tell people. It hadn't felt like the right time six months ago either when she made the decision and told only

Bea. Getting sober was both easier and harder than Cyra expected—she didn't go to meetings; she didn't do rehab. She wasn't sure what to call herself—she didn't think she was an alcoholic, but she also knew she didn't drink normally. She tried one AA meeting and immediately knew it wasn't for her. Instead, she wrapped up her fists and threw punches at the bag in her apartment every time she felt like drinking.

The first few months were tough, but her body seemed relieved to get away from the alcohol. And until the close call at the deli the night she ran into Lamprey, Cyra hadn't craved a drink since the summer. Even with Mira's death.

Cyra supposed she wasn't telling Eli and Izzie because they'd ask questions. They'd want to define her, dissect her reasons for quitting, and expect a bunch of dramatic emotions. They would want her to make it a Big Deal with long talks about her feelings, and truthfully, Cyra didn't have the bandwidth for that. It was easier to continue hiding her sobriety. For now.

"Hey, Izzie, thanks for inviting me."

"Oh gosh, Cyra, it's so good to see you!" Izzie said, looking up from her cheese and offering a smile that was far too wide.

"You too." For a beat, it was silent, and Cyra knew they were all remembering the last time they gathered here, when Eli told them about the support group. "I brought artisanal jam," Cyra said, breaking the silence and handing them a little paper bag. Izzie and Eli liked crap like that; they enjoyed trying to emulate the "cool parent" vibes of Park Slope. Cyra had stopped at the most hipster-looking shop she could find on the walk from the train and bought several twelve-dollar jars of jam, glad she was no longer worrying about what was in her rapidly-depleting bank account since Mira's death.

"Ooh, thank you!" Izzie squealed, fluidly moving around the counter and snatching the bag from Cyra. "These will pair excellently with the Manchego."

"Uh-huh. Sure will."

"Here, I'll pour you a glass, have a seat, relax!" Eli said, ushering Cyra toward the velvet blue couch pushed up against the curtained windows.

Cyra sat, running a thumb against the soft material of the velvet couch, forcing a smile as Eli handed her a brimming glass of wine, gingerly placing it back on the coffee table when he turned to help set up the rest of the cheese while Izzie opened up Cyra's jam.

It was obvious, Cyra thought; Mira's absence. It hung over them like the thick smoke of a bonfire that had just been doused in water. She could almost smell her sister's beachy perfume next to her on the couch, see glints of her golden hair in the Edison bulb lighting.

"So glad we got to do this together," Izzie called out from the kitchen. "I think it's good to keep these traditions. And I didn't want the last Wine and Cheese night to be the one we ended on anyway. That was . . . rough."

Cyra could see Izzie's grimace from her spot on the couch. Eli visibly winced and nudged his girlfriend's elbow, shooting her a meaningful look.

"Let's not dwell on the past," Eli said, trying to redirect.

"Oh, of course," Izzie agreed, infusing a false brightness in her words. "Don't worry, Cyra. Mira would have forgiven you. Eventually."

"Izzie," Eli hissed.

"I'm trying to help," she whispered hotly.

Cyra dropped her head into her hands, fingers digging into her temples as if she could reach inside her brain and smear away the thoughts surfacing. Nausea rose in Cyra's stomach along with the memory of the last time they had been together at a Wine and Cheese night like this one. She spent the last two months dutifully pushing that night away, forcing it to the back of her mind as if she could erase it entirely. She had nearly forgotten; it was so easy to deny the truth.

It was too hard to admit that Mira, the person she loved the most, the person she did everything for, hated Cyra at the end of her life.

The last Wine and Cheese night was a month before Mira's death. Cyra had been late, as usual, since her commute from Queens was the longest. Her sister, Izzie, and Eli were already into a bottle, laughing at some new, stupid meme Mira had shown them, cheese forgotten on the coffee table in favor of wine-stained lips.

Cyra had poured herself half a glass, pretending to sip from it on occasion and letting the others do the bulk of the drinking while she picked at the cheese. It had been fine, normal, although a little boring to be sober for, until Mira had gotten a notification on her phone and the smile dropped from her face like a stone in a well.

"Fuck!" she had screeched, leaping to her feet, not even noticing that she spilled half a glass of wine all over the coffee table.

"What, what?!" Izzie yelled, jumping up too, going over to Mira's shoulder and peering at the phone screen. "Oh. Oh no."

"What's going on?" Eli had asked. A look of real fear had been plastered to his face that made Cyra wonder what he knew.

"There's an article about Mira in Brush Culture," Izzie said, her voice hushed. She looked up at her boyfriend. "You know, that art and culture blog that got really huge last year after interviewing Wells Chandler. It's run by that art critic, James Oppenheimer."

"Isn't that a good thing?" Eli had asked.

Cyra had known it wasn't. The cheese she wolfed down felt like it was spoiling inside of her, and a terrible aftertaste forced its way up her throat. Her fingers buzzed.

"No, it's not a good thing!" Mira shrieked, scrolling now, her eyes almost a blur as she sped-read the article. "It's not about my art at all! It's about Arthur!" She burst into tears, throwing the phone at Izzie. "You do it, I can't!"

Dutifully, Izzie caught the phone and went through it slowly, reading what Cyra already knew was there. "It says that Arthur McCowen put on Mira's first show only because she was . . ."

"Say it!" Mira screeched.

". . . Sleeping with him." Izzie cleared her throat, embarrassed.

Mira wailed and collapsed on to the floor, pressing her fists against her eyes. Cyra wanted so badly to go to her, to wrap her in her arms, but she couldn't. Not after what she had done. Instead, Eli leapt to his feet and skirted around his girlfriend so he could kneel down next to Mira, placing a soothing hand on her back and murmuring quiet consolations to her that she ignored through her tears.

Izzie shot Mira a concerned look, but continued. "It's really gross journalism. It's basically a hit piece on Mira, saying that there are so many hard-working artists in the industry and she's getting opportunities others aren't by . . . using her . . . sexuality."

"No." It was the first thing Cyra had said since the news broke, but it slipped from her mouth in anger. That wasn't right. It wasn't what they had talked about.

"I know," Izzie replied, misunderstanding. "Oh, fuck." She blanched and looked up from the phone at Cyra, her eyes searching.

Shit.

"What now?" Mira cried. "What?"

"Nothing," Izzie stammered, still unable to look away from Cyra's face, which was growing hot and flushed.

"Give it to me," Mira snapped, throwing off Eli's arm and leaping at her friend faster than any of them could have predicted she move. Mira yanked the phone from Izzie's hand and started reading out loud. "*'Even Griffin's own sister, Cyra Griffin, subject of Griffin's breakout piece,* Portrait of a Panic Attack, *acknowledges that her younger sibling has been afforded leverage in the industry that others have not.'*"

"Cyra," Eli had breathed.

"Oh, there's a quote from my *sister*, too!" Mira said, her voice dropping three registers, now sounding guttural and inhuman. "*'Mira is incredibly talented, but she shouldn't need to sleep with someone to get to where she's meant to be.'*"

"No!" Cyra yelled, scrambling to her feet. "No, he cut off the rest of what I said! I swear, it wasn't supposed to be a smear piece, Mira. Never. I would never do that to you."

"Oh, really? Then what is this?" Mira shouted, shaking her phone at her sister, her eyes dry and glassy now.

"It's out of context! I went on to say that Arthur was clearly taking advantage of you! He was using you! It was supposed to be a #MeToo thing, not some kind of bullshit slut-shaming gossip rag piece," Cyra protested, hands sweating. "I swear, Mira, I was trying to protect you. I never thought he would write it like this."

It had been scary enough knowing how mad Mira would have been seeing her boyfriend in the news labeled as someone who abused their power, but to have the tables turned and point the finger at *Mira* was worse. Cyra's skin bristled. She couldn't believe James had bastardized her interview like that. She had given him all the information she had found—how Arthur seemed to have a new "muse" every few years, how she was always some young, impressionable artist, new to the city, how he'd jumpstart her career and then she'd fade away after he got bored and found a new girl. Cyra had been able to tell right away that he was using her sister, but Mira was so excited to have her first show, so excited to have an older, knowledgeable man in the art world interested in her, she wouldn't hear it.

It was just like PJ—Mira being taken advantage of; Mira being abused without being able to accept it. But Cyra couldn't handle Arthur the way she handled PJ. So, Cyra had reached out to Brush Culture to try to expose him. But in the process, she exposed her sister instead.

"Oh, fantastic, now Arthur is texting me," Mira deadpanned, her face growing tighter and tighter as she read the texts that flashed across her screen. She looked up at Cyra, stark betrayal written across her face. "He's dumping me. Both as a girlfriend and a client. Says he can't trust me anymore. So, congratulations, Cyra. You got your wish. You did it again—you chased away another man who loved me."

"Mira, no," Cyra cried out, trying to move around the coffee table to get to her. "I'm not trying to hurt you! I'm trying to protect you—why can't you see that?"

"Because every time you try, I end up getting hurt!" Mira yelled.

"You are picking terrible men! They use you! Arthur was going to leave you regardless, I was trying to take him down before he hurt you further," Cyra shouted, her voice matching her sister's. They had never spoken to each other like this. Even after PJ's death, Mira had wanted her sister's comfort. Now, she looked like she would tear out Cyra's hair if she could.

I can never tell her the truth about PJ now, Cyra remembered thinking at the time, before shaking that thought away.

"You've hurt me more than any of them ever could!" Mira screamed wildly. "I hate you, Cyra! I wish you were dead!"

Then she had turned and fled into the night, her hiccupping sobs echoing behind her.

"I'll go after her," Eli had said, unable to look at Cyra. "Make sure she's OK."

He ducked out, and Cyra stood stock-still, watching Izzie shakily mop up the spilled wine on the coffee table.

"You should probably go home." Izzie whispered.

"Izzie, I didn't . . . I swear . . . it wasn't supposed to be like that."

"I believe you. But she won't. And I need her to stay here tonight so I can keep an eye on her. So, please, Cyra, leave."

Cyra had left. It was the last time she saw her sister alive.

CHAPTER 10

Cyra stared at the faded stain on the coffee table, the remnant of that night, and had to stop herself from touching it. It felt like a part of her sister. Her lips had touched that wine, and now it was etched into this wooden coffee table forever. The coffee table had more of her sister than Cyra did.

After the damning article in Brush Culture, Mira lost all the shows she had booked, the buzz around her photography dried up, and her Instagram had filled up with nasty messages. Cyra couldn't take it—she knew she should stop, not get involved again, but she couldn't sit back and do nothing while Mira got all the heat.

Cyra created a number of social media accounts. She started posting everywhere, trying to redirect the blame toward Arthur. People began to notice, engaging with her posts, which she kept anonymous or as catfish accounts, and started to turn their attention to Arthur as well.

But it wasn't enough. Cyra used one of her fake accounts to message Arthur directly. She'd be up at two in the morning, eyes burning, hunched in the bathroom to avoid Bea's questions if she woke up and caught her, studiously blackmailing Arthur McCowen.

I have evidence, she would write. *I will show the world what you've done.*

Your life is over.

See this Twitter post? I have people on my side now. They're paying attention. We're coming for you.

He never answered, but Cyra pushed and pushed as public opinion slowly shifted against him.

Two weeks after the article dropped, Arthur took a dive from the top floor of a parking garage.

Cyra had a panic attack the day after.

She tried to reach out to Mira to see how she was taking Arthur's suicide, but her sister had blocked her on everything.

The ironic thing was that after Arthur's death, women started to trickle forward on social media, sharing their stories of him and how he pressured them into a sexual relationship in return for putting on their shows.

Eventually, the truth Cyra had been trying to shed light on came out, but it had destroyed her sister in the process.

Cyra had hoped that Mira could forgive her, hoped that she would at least talk to her. But she wouldn't.

"She needs time," Izzie told Cyra when she tried to talk to her sister through her. "I know she won't feel this way forever, you just have to give her space. I think she knows deep down that you were trying to help her. But she's not ready to talk to you yet."

So, Mira had stayed with Izzie and Eli until the morning she got up to go for a sunrise run in Prospect Park and was killed by someone who ambushed her by the boathouse.

And that was it. No more chance of reconciliation. No more protecting her sister. No more making up for her past mistakes. All Cyra could do was find the person who killed Mira, who took away the chance for them to be sisters again.

Now, Cyra was closer to the truth, now she had suspects. She could finally do what needed to be done to right the wrongs she cast on her sister.

"You OK?" Eli asked, jolting Cyra back to the present moment. He was hovering above her, and she took her hands away from her head to gaze up at him. "Sorry about that. We shouldn't have brought it up."

"It's fine," Cyra replied, dropping her hands and leaning back, imagining her expression smoothing out and flattening the way it did when she was watching horror movies and practicing her Mistletoe face. "Forget it."

Cyra faked her way through the night with Eli and Izzie, grateful, at least, that they didn't bring up Mira or mention anything else about the last Wine and Cheese event. At one point Izzie noticed that Cyra hadn't drained her glass, and Cyra pleaded a headache, getting the bright idea to use it as an excuse to leave early, unable to keep from staring at the faint stain of her sister on the coffee table.

"I'll walk you to the train," Eli said, helping his girlfriend clear up the glasses.

"No, Eli, it's fine, it's not a far walk."

But Eli shook his head. "The whole neighborhood is on high alert. People, especially people like Mira, don't get killed in Prospect Park. And since it's been over a month without any arrests, people are staying nervous."

Cyra thought of the family she saw on the sidewalk earlier, happy and laughing. They hadn't seemed nervous. But maybe that was because they were together, and when you're surrounded by love it's hard to imagine a scenario when you might not be.

"Let him walk you," Izzie begged. "I'm sure it's fine, but it never hurts to be safe."

Cyra didn't mention that her literal years of MMA training were probably enough to keep her safe during a five-minute walk.

Then, to Cyra's horror, Eli's eyes filled with tears. "I couldn't do anything for Mira. Let me do this. At least I can keep you safe."

Cyra didn't think Eli, with his noodle arms and bird body, would be much help against any of the men in the support group, but for the first time she thought about what kind of guilt Eli and Izzie might be harboring considering Mira was staying with them when she died. The two of them had latched on to Cyra after the news broke, and she assumed it was because they knew she would be chewed up by how Mira and Cyra had left things. But maybe it was because they felt just as helpless as she did. Unable to do anything to save the girl they had all loved.

"She was my best friend," Izzie said, her eyes wet now too.

Cyra glanced at the bottles on the coffee table and realized that Eli and Izzie had been undaunted by her lack of drinking; they must have had a bottle and a half of wine between the two of them.

Seems like the part of the evening where we don't talk about Mira is over, Cyra thought, glad it was at least happening on her way out the door.

"Why aren't you sadder?" Izzie burst out, watching Cyra's face.

"Izzie!" Eli scolded. He turned to Cyra. "She doesn't mean that, she's just emotional. She had too much wine."

"Shut up," Izzie replied, and the disgust in her voice shocked Cyra. She never heard Izzie sound so venomous. "Of course I'm emotional. The question is, why isn't *she*?"

Cyra felt her body and brain slow down and still, like it had when she went to the meeting. She was gathering herself together, so she wouldn't say or do anything she'd regret.

"I think I should leave." Cyra couldn't possibly make these two understand. They didn't know how it felt—the complicated mix of anger and numbness.

"Please, let me walk you," Eli said, lurching forward, a meaningful look in his eye.

Cyra sighed. He probably wanted to talk her out of returning to the support group. Well, she'd just deny it again. But she clearly wasn't getting out of there without him. "Fine. Izzie, thank you for inviting me over. I hope you get some rest tonight."

"Fuck you, Cyra," Izzie said, tears overflowing now. "Fuck you for betraying her. For making that article come into existence. For stranding your sister here. This is all your fault. It wouldn't have happened if it wasn't for you."

"Hey," Eli started, but Cyra waved him off.

"I know," she said instead, looking steadily at Izzie from across the room. "I'm sorry."

Then she turned, grabbed her jacket from the hallway, and strode to the front door without waiting for Eli, who she could hear scrambling behind her.

"Drink some water," she heard Eli tell his girlfriend as he charged out into the night after her.

"You should stay with her," Cyra said as he caught up to her on the sidewalk. "She needs you. She's upset."

Eli winced, a conflicted look passing over his face. "She needs to cool off. When she's like that . . . she gets more and more wound up if you try to talk sense into her. She'll be calmer when I come back, and then I can talk to her. I'm sorry she said those things."

Cyra shook her head. "I don't blame her for feeling that way. She's not wrong. If I hadn't done what I did, Mira would probably still be alive."

"Is that why you're putting yourself in such danger?" Eli asked as they reached the end of the block and crossed the avenue, heading toward the Union Street subway stop. "You can pretend all you want, Cyra, but I know you're trying to get involved with that group. I just don't know how deep you are." When Cyra didn't answer, hands shoved into her jean jacket, Eli continued. "It's not your fault, Cyra. What happened to Mira was not your doing. And I know you think she hated you, but I promise you, she didn't. It's just . . . sometimes when you love someone that much, it's also easy to hate them. But hate like that, hate between sisters, it doesn't have real teeth. She would have forgiven you. I swear."

But Eli couldn't know that. He was friendly with Mira, of course, but it wasn't like *Izzie* was telling Cyra this. If she had, Cyra might have believed her. Izzie and Mira were best friends. Eli was the best friend's boyfriend. He had no idea what was going on in Mira's head. And he didn't know about PJ, about what Cyra did to Arthur after the article was published. Maybe Cyra didn't deserve her sister's forgiveness.

"You really don't need to walk me the whole way."

"Look, Cyra, Izzie's delivery was terrible, but she's kind of right," Eli said, almost jogging to keep up with Cyra despite her short stature. "You seem very closed off. I mean, you were never an open book, but I'm worried you're not letting yourself feel anything anymore."

Cyra stopped short, Eli almost running into her. She spun to face him, the brownstones illuminated in the streetlights, the families of Park Slope all tucked up in their cozy homes, leaving the sidewalks empty except for a sprinkling of fallen leaves and discarded trash fluttering down the street in the breeze.

"I don't need a psychology lecture from you," Cyra said firmly. "I'm handling the death of my sister the way I need to handle it. Period."

Eli looked cowed. "Yes, but . . ."

"What did you think would happen," Cyra hissed suddenly, moving closer to him. "When you gave me that info you stole from work? Did you really expect I wouldn't do anything with it? Did you think I'd go, 'Oh, OK, cool, Mira was the victim of a serial killer,' and move on with my life?"

"Cyra, I—"

"What was it?"

". . . What?"

"The thing that made the cops think she was part of a pattern?" Cyra asked. "Bellows wouldn't tell me."

"I don't know." But the way Eli wouldn't meet her eyes, the way he shifted his feet so that they were pointed away from her, told Cyra that he was lying. He knew—that was why he brought it to her to begin with. He wanted her to dig deeper and find the truth.

"Eli. She's my little sister. You wanted to help; that's why you told me about the support group. Don't half-ass this."

"I could lose my job." His voice was small.

"You already could," Cyra pointed out. "You aren't screwing yourself over any more than you already did. Might as well make it count."

Eli looked around the street as if he was expecting a squadron of police officers to pop up at any second and clap handcuffs on his bony wrists. Then he sighed and leaned forward, whispering, "I didn't put it together until a few weeks after she died. Remember I said a year ago I brought home a file about the support group? Well, there were other files too. With a bit of information about the signatures of people they suspect are operating in the greater New York area. One of them was a man who would always cross his victims' ankles over each other. When your sister was found . . ." Eli swallowed hard, as if all the wine he consumed was threatening to come back up. "Her ankles were crossed. And since the autopsy showed she was hit from behind and . . . passed away on her front, someone intentionally turned her over after she died and crossed her ankles. Posing her. That's it, though, that's all the information I have."

"And no one else knows about that detail besides the cops?"

"That's right. They are intentionally withholding it from the public."

"Any other similarities between my sister's case and these other victims?"

"No," Eli said, looking a little green now at Cyra's detached tone. "They were all killed differently. The ankles being crossed was the only thing that connected them."

"I need to see those records," Cyra said. "I need to see if there is anything about the other victims that can help me determine which serial killer might be responsible. How far back do the killings go, for example? Or what kind of victimology patterns do they fit?" She thought about what Lamprey said the other day about not always hunting in the boroughs. "Were they all killed in the city or other areas?"

"Jesus, stop, stop," Eli exclaimed, taking a step away from her. "I don't know. I don't remember. I tried to erase all that shit from my brain as soon as I read it. I didn't know when I took that file that it would get into . . . any of that stuff. I was just curious about the dark web aspect; I didn't want to stick around to read about murdered women."

No, he wouldn't, would he? It was more convenient to forget about the victims so that they didn't seem as real.

"I need to know," Cyra demanded.

"No, you don't, you don't need those images in your head."

"Eli," Cyra said, her voice low. "What do you think they talk about in those meetings? Let's say that I hypothetically went to one and met them in person . . ." Eli's face changed from green to white and his jaw dropped a bit. He had guessed she made contact. He probably hadn't thought she'd actually try to *attend* a meeting. "Do you think they'd talk about sunshine and daisies?"

"Cyra, no."

"I need to know," she repeated.

Eli bit his lip. "I can't access any more of those digital files. They track that, seeing who checks out what. I was only able to do it last year because our system was down for maintenance for a week, and I got curious, wanted to look into some of the high-clearance files. But they've been going through some of the older physical files because of the connection now to Mira's case."

"So, then you can check and tell me." Eli visibly trembled, and Cyra reached out and grabbed his hand. "You said you didn't do anything for Mira. This is your chance to do something for her. Help me figure out who did this to her. Please."

Eli's face worked, but finally he nodded. "You're right. OK. I can't get you the actual file, but I may be able to snoop around and at least point you in the right direction."

"Thank you." Cyra meant it, and she inflected as much feeling as she could into her voice.

"But Cyra, are you sure?" When she looked at him quizzically, Eli continued, "I mean, are you sure this is the route you want to take? Instead of, you know, letting the police do it? Even if you pull it off, it's so dangerous. You could be killed, too. Or . . . get in trouble . . ."

Ah, he knows what you're planning, the voice in the back of her head said.

"I won't do anything stupid," Cyra assured him. She slowed her breathing, curled her fingers so her nails nicked her palms, tapping into some of Mistletoe's personality the same way she did at the meeting. The heat drained from her body, replaced by a blanket of ice. When she spoke, her voice was different, low, intimate. Lying, effortlessly. "I promise. I want to find out who did it first, and then I'll turn him over to the cops. I don't know if I'd have the stomach to do anything else anyway. I'm not like whoever killed her."

Eli nodded, although a shadow crossed his face that made Cyra think he was perhaps choosing to believe her because that was easier for both him and his job. "Good. Just be careful. And when you think you're getting close, go back to Bellows and tell him what you think. He'll check it out. But don't . . . you know . . ."

"I'd never throw you under the bus, Eli," Cyra said, being honest this time. "You've already helped so much, and I won't forget that."

He gave her a watery smile. "Come on, let's get you to the train."

But as they walked the rest of the way in companionable silence, Cyra couldn't help thinking that Eli was intentionally burying his head in the sand—he had to know what Cyra's intentions were and had decided to not care, which was why he put his career in jeopardy in the first place.

Maybe Mira's death gave everyone she knew a different texture of guilt they had to carry around with them. Mira's father held a bottle, her friends compromised their values, and her sister shredded her humanity in the name of justice.

CHAPTER 11

Cyra stood in front of her bathroom mirror Sunday evening, checking her Mistletoe disguise again, her ropey muscled limbs—her second secret weapon besides the switchblade—hidden under long sleeves and dress slacks. Despite her shorter stature, Cyra had always been strong. "Low center of gravity," her father used to say. "Can't knock you down. Not like your sister; she'll blow away in a good breeze." Her extensive fighting training had made her body even more compact and coiled.

Peering at her reflection, Cyra wished she could wear her eyeglasses—every time she wore her contacts she saw her mother looking back at her. But appearance aside, she was pleased with the progress she'd made so far.

Lamprey had thrown a wrench in her plans, but maybe it was a good thing. She couldn't trust him, of course, but if he could help her figure out who killed Mira, especially if *he* killed Mira, it would be worth it to keep him close.

As Cyra stared at herself in the mirror, she noticed a quiet humming in her chest, gradually growing louder along with a bouncy sensation in her stomach. It took a moment for her to place the feeling—excitement.

Cyra's reflection flinched, her eye twitching.

You can't feel proper grief or find moments of happiness, but you can get excited at the prospect of chatting with psychopaths? What's wrong with you?

"Breathe. Get yourself under control," Cyra commanded her reflection and inhaled, holding her breath at the top before exhaling, fogging up a circular patch of the mirror. She watched her features still and her expression slacken. She leaned forward, impressed with how controlled and emotionless her face looked. "Interesting."

She wondered if this was how she looked when she practiced Mistletoe's confidence on Eli yesterday.

It's not excitement, Cyra told herself. *It has to be nerves. I have to go back into the lion's den in two days. It's performance jitters.*

The humming continued all night and into the next day. When she checked in with Python via the dark web chatbox Monday night, she received a simple: *Same time, same place.*

When Tuesday finally rolled around again, Cyra was ready to return to the rec basement for her second meeting. It would be the first time she'd be seeing Lamprey since pushing him down the cellar steps, and she hadn't forgotten their deal. Did Cyra believe him—was there another person in the group who wasn't who they said they were?

She wasn't sure, and she honestly wasn't sure she cared either.

Cyra checked herself in a compact mirror before entering the rec center. Her blonde wig was sitting naturally. It was strange to feel taller in her lifted shoes. It was a sensation she wasn't used to; she never really wore heels. Staring at her reflection, Cyra marveled at how unlike Mira she still looked, even when she shared her blonde hair and removed her glasses. Their coloring was too different, face shapes opposite each other. Even blonde, no one would guess at first glance that Cyra and Mira had been sisters.

Cyra had tried hard to not be jealous of her younger sister. Even when they were teenagers, and Cyra realized how much more beautiful Mira was than her. Even when it became clear that their father preferred Mira. Instead, Cyra was proud to keep Mira safe since their useless mother hadn't been around to do so. But that meant there was no one around to take care of Cyra when she had panic attacks.

They started after the awful incident with PJ. A sharp pain in the center of her chest like a burr the size of a mango was stuck in her lungs. The scrape of her breath as she tried to get air but couldn't, her throat closing up. The pinpricks up and down her arms, the sweat that beaded on her face, the waves of nausea. And worst of all, the way her heart rocketed against her chest like it was trying to break free of her body.

The first few times it happened Cyra went to urgent care, convinced she was dying. Eventually, one of the nurses told Cyra she was experiencing panic attacks and suggested therapy. But Holden Griffin, the sole breadwinner of the family, couldn't afford it on his lousy insurance. At least, that's what he told Cyra. Of course, he managed to find money later on for Mira's first photography class and her prom dress.

Cyra learned to manage her panic on her own instead. She began to feel the differences in her body when the attacks were coming on, like how the air changes before a storm. When anxiety would smash into her with thunder and lightning, Cyra would go somewhere quiet, clench her fingers, and repeat to herself over and over again, sometimes for hours, "It's going to be OK, get through the next ten minutes, and it'll be over." It was her private ritual, the only way she knew to combat the world-shattering intensity of the attacks.

When Mira's photo of Cyra having a panic attack blew up and got Mira featured in Arthur McCowen's showcase, Cyra's private ritual became very public.

Cyra snapped the compact mirror shut, shutting down the memory at the same time.

She returned to her steady breathing, pushing her anger, betrayal, and discontent down deeper with every exhale. It all slipped away like shampoo down a drain. This time, it was far easier to coax out the hollowness hiding in her body. It was like stepping into a cave; everything was cold, dark, and empty. She flexed her fists but didn't even need to dig her nails into her palms this time. Her body was eager to release any pain, any memories that tethered her to the version of herself she had to be for others. The tattered remains of Cyra Griffin were walled off, and her absence was filled by the persona of Mistletoe—the crueler, starker persona she needed to embrace to fit in with these men.

She felt for her knife in the pocket of her slacks, feeling its comfortable weight, and then she slipped back into the basement room, this time ten minutes early, eager to watch the others enter.

Python was already there, and she was surprised to find his presence almost . . . comforting. Maybe it was because she knew he was a killer, but not a serial one, knowing that out of all of them, he was the least likely to be involved in Mira's death. The vague contempt he seemed to hold for the men in the group didn't hurt either.

Python apparently hadn't wanted to deal with another deviled egg situation because there was a box of sealed grocery store doughnuts stacked on the table besides the coffee this time.

"Why doesn't anyone worry about the coffee being poisoned?" Cyra asked, pouring herself some from the carafe and nodding at the group's moderator, who was currently arranging chairs.

"I always bring the coffee. I guess I'm trustworthy. We usually rotate who brings the snacks. Figured I'd do it today to avoid any issues again."

"I love doughnuts."

"Don't open them yet," Python warned, not bothering to look at her while he continued setting up. "The boys will want to see they're sealed before eating them."

"They always this paranoid?"

Python finally glanced up at her, shaking out one of the folding chairs with one hand and smacking it on the floor with a muffled *clang*. "You must be new."

"Well, duh."

"No, I mean, to killing." Python nudged one of the chairs farther away from its fellows so they were more evenly-spaced. "A lot of these guys have been at this for a long time. You don't stay unnoticed without some paranoia."

They aren't unnoticed. Cyra thought of the file Eli had promised to help her with. *They're just unfound. For now.*

"I'm not new," Cyra said. "I thought you would have picked up on that."

Python shrugged. "I guess everyone has different styles. But as a woman, you should be even more paranoid."

She watched him carefully as he finished organizing the chairs, glanced up at the clock above her head, and eyed the door. "You think one of them is gonna try to kill me, don't you?"

Python didn't reply, cut his eyes away from her. Cyra strode to the chair on the edge of the semicircle she had adopted last time and made to sit down, then changed her mind. "Why let me join, then?" she asked, moving instead to a chair in the middle, the one that faced the table and gave a good view of the door. The one Sand Fly had occupied last time.

"It's not my business," Python muttered. Louder, he said, "You wanted to join, this group is for people like you who wanna talk about their . . . predilections, so I let you join."

"Someone kills me, they'd be breaking the rules of the group."

Python nodded. "They'd be dealt with."

But not stopped.

She noted that Python wasn't offering protection of any kind. Just retribution.

Cyra stared at him again, watching the flickers of emotion that danced across his face. Python was so much easier to read than Lamprey. Even as herself, she was good at observing the unsaid in people's expressions. It was how she knew her mother was leaving them and how she knew Mira was being used by Arthur. As she studied Python, she thought of something. "That's why you're the moderator. You're the hired gun, aren't you? If anyone in the group hurts someone else in the group, you'll kill them."

Python grunted. "It's implied. Everyone knows. It keeps order here. They need that, need to know there are consequences to their actions if they join our circle. Whipworm hired me as protection for the first year, but now I mostly do it for my own benefit. Keep an eye on Whip, make sure he doesn't get sent back to the big house."

"You two are close."

"I saved his life in prison. We've had each other's backs since then." Python's voice changed when talking about Whipworm, getting quieter, more mellifluous.

"You said he hired you for the first year," Cyra noted, splaying her legs out in front of the chair and folding her hands across her lap, imitating Sand Fly's posture from last week. "How long has this group been going then? You said two years, right?"

Python's eyes flickered down Cyra's body, but it didn't seem like he was checking her out. He was examining her pose, brow furrowing as he realized what she was doing. "Been about two and a half years now, yeah."

"Started with just the two of you?"

"Yeah, and then Mockingbird joined up. Guess Whipworm had run into him before he went away and looked him up after. Mockingbird had this crazy story about breaking his leg and needing a support system. The others trickled in after that."

"Wait, is that what Cuckoo was referring to last week when he was needling Mockingbird about an injury from a victim?" Cyra asked, sitting up a little.

"Yup. He doesn't like to talk about it much though. I think he's embarrassed."

Mockingbird was the one person in the group Cyra couldn't get a read on, and he seemed like the most likely person to be a lone wolf. She was honestly shocked he was in the group at all. He barely talked. Although, maybe that was due to her presence. Maybe he was chattier without her around. He was fairly reticent to discuss his injury last week, glaring at Cuckoo as if he wanted to rip his lips off.

"So weird. I thought most of us liked to be alone. To find there's a group of us who want to meet was . . . interesting."

"And yet you joined," Python pointed out.

"Yeah. I know why I did. I just wonder about the others."

"It's the same for a lot of them. They joined because they were curious. Or because they wanted to check out the competition. Or because they were sick of always wearing a mask and wanted someone to see their true selves. Or . . . because they needed an audience."

Ah. There it was, the thing she had overlooked. From her research, she knew that some serial killers thrived on attention. They needed to feel like there were eyes on them. They were the ones who antagonized law enforcement or created their own nicknames. The support group was a way to get an audience without the danger of being caught.

"You sure you wanna be doing that?" Python asked, pointedly nodding at the seat Cyra had stolen from Sand Fly and the posture she had adopted to mimic his.

"Sure do," Cyra said, stretching her legs further, lips curling. "Some of them need to stop seeing me as a woman and start seeing me as one of them." She looked at Python. "Then they'll stop thinking of me as something they can kill."

The sound of a door smacking open echoed from outside the room—perhaps from upstairs. Someone was here; the serial killers were starting to arrive.

Python grunted again, his sound of acquisition, and a minute later Sand Fly walked through the door, his eyes landing right on Cyra.

It was worth it to see the look on his face.

That spot was *his*, and she had taken it away from him.

He remained stock still for a moment, watching her. She wondered if he'd say something or try to move her.

Instead, Sand Fly poured himself a cup of coffee, eyed the doughnuts appraisingly, nodded at Python, and then slid down in the seat next to Cyra, moving his chair slightly so that he pressed up closer to her. She didn't move a muscle, just turned her head toward him and said, "Great weather we've been having this week, huh?"

Before he could answer, Lamprey strolled into the room, his eyes narrowing for a second as he focused on Cyra and Sand Fly, then smiled in approval. Mockingbird was right behind him, and a few minutes later Cuckoo showed up. Whipworm swept in a minute before their start time holding another platter covered in plastic wrap that he placed on the table.

"Oh, not again," Sand Fly complained.

"I made flautas," Whipworm said, hurt. "I thought this would be better. They were fried, cooked, so they're safe."

"I don't think that's how it works," Cuckoo said, rolling his eyes.

"It's my mother's recipe."

"Sorry, Whip," Python said in his gravelly voice. "No one's gonna eat them. Come on, man, you gotta stop trying. Just stick with the regular food."

"God, you assholes are the worst!" Whipworm said, genuine hurt on his face. He tried to slam the platter of flautas into the tiny trash near the door, but the platter was too large, and it bounced off the rim of the can and landed on the carpet. "Great!" Whipworm bent over and started to clean up the mess.

"Follow the damn rules," Lamprey scolded, sounding bored, watching the other man scrape flecks of loose rice off the floor from a flauta that seemed to have exploded on impact.

"Where's Pea Crab?" Cyra asked, silencing the room.

"Yeah, where is he?" Cuckoo said, twisting around to gaze at the door as if Pea Crab would burst in now that they were thinking of him.

"Are we surprised he's late?" This came from Mockingbird, and Cyra worked to not jump at hearing his unfamiliar voice come from her right. He so rarely spoke that she had forgotten what he sounded like: gruff, but with a strange pitch, like he was intentionally making his voice sound lower.

"Pea messaged me last night," Python announced. "He can't make it today."

"Don't the rules dictate that we need to move locations then?" Cyra asked. "What if he's with a cop right now spilling his guts?" She didn't have to fake her concern; Cyra needed the meetings to continue for as long as possible. It wouldn't do to have the group shut down or members arrested before she found out the truth.

Python shook his head, and Lamprey smirked. Whipworm caught Cyra's eye from the doorway and mouthed, "Needed a fix."

"It's OK, Pea Crab is . . . different," Python allowed. "He'll be back next week. In the meantime, we should start."

A tiny shiver of fear slipped through Cyra's Mistletoe defenses, but the coldness inside her snapped it away. It sounded like Pea Crab did this kind of thing on occasion. If the killers weren't worried about him betraying them, neither should she.

Whipworm stacked his rejected flautas on top of the tiny trash and stomped over to the circle, eyes hooded and dark. He did a double-take seeing Cyra in Sand Fly's usual spot, and then settled down next to Lamprey, who had taken her old chair.

She felt ready. She knew how things would go this time; she could do this.

Cyra's second meeting started.

PEA CRAB

I T WAS JUST that everyone and everything was so loud all the time and nothing ever got quiet and that's why he had to have them, had to put anything and everything in his system, had to go, go, go and get his fix because he needed it and no one else could understand that, not even the group. And Ray loved the group, he loved, loved, loved it because he didn't have to worry about pretending like he did for the rest of his life.

The voices started when he was little and he didn't remember exactly when but he remembered that they were so loud, loud, loud and he just wanted them to be quiet for a little bit, you know? It wouldn't have been too bad if it had just been one voice even if the voice was yelling at him because he was used to yelling (Momma always yelled before she had her drinks) but it wasn't one voice it was many, many, many voices and some of them yelled but some of them whispered and that was worse. The whisper voices cut through the other noises and told him to do bad things to his body and when he tried to stop himself (Momma would say *What did you do to your arm you stupid boy*) the voices got worse.

But then one day in high school, Ray was with his buddy Phillip and Phillip was an eel, Phillip was slippery and lived in a dark hole, and he took Ray to his dark hole and showed him the drugs he stole from his older brother and showed him the syringe and stuck it into his own arm and then his eyes got all dreamy, and he sighed like he had been holding the world's breath instead of his own. And when Ray took the needle and copied Phillip and felt the warm rush through his veins he gasped because they were gone! The voices melted away, and they were finally quiet and Ray could think, think, think for the first time. But he didn't want to think. Ray wanted to drift away on this amazing feeling forever, and he loved Phillip for giving it to him.

The next day when the drugs had worn off, and Ray's voices were back and telling him to hurt himself and hurt himself and hurt himself, he wanted to scream because now he knew what life was like without them and he wanted that always.

Shut up, Ray cried, *shut up shut up*. But they didn't. So Ray returned to Phillip's dark hole and asked for the needle again but this time Phillip was selfish, and he said Ray had enough yesterday. *It's mine*, Phillip said and Ray began to panic because he wasn't going to share and if Phillip didn't share, Ray was going to die, and he didn't want to die. Even though the voices wanted him to die. He didn't want to leave Momma because even though she was a drunk they loved each other because that's what family is.

Please. Share, Ray begged.

Phillip still refused and Ray was so angry because he had finally found a solution to his problem and finally found something that would stop him from hurting himself and here was Phillip being greedy and that wasn't right. So Ray picked up a rusty orange hammer from the table (Table? Didn't Phillip live in a hole? Why did it now look like a house?) and he smashed the hammer against Phillip's head and the other boy dropped like a brick into a pond. Plop, plop, plop. Ray tore the house (hole?) apart until he found the needle and a collection of little baggies with a tacky substance inside that looked like the brown sugar Momma sometimes spooned into her mouth when she didn't feel like cooking.

When the voices had quieted down again, Ray felt really bad for what he did to Phillip. It was too late now though. Phillip didn't have real parents—foster parents looked after him but they were not very good parents, not like Momma, and they weren't home so Ray dragged Phillip outside into the wooded area behind the house and then, because the voices were quiet and it was a nice day, he dragged him even further and further away.

Eventually he set Phillip down when he realized his arms were aching, and he left him under a big tree deep in the woods and then walked back with the needle and the little bags in his pocket and felt so amazing, amazing, amazing that he knew Phillip would forgive him. Because Phillip had introduced him to the drugs and the truth was that it was never the voices that made him hurt people. It was the drugs. The drugs were the ones that made him smack heads with hammers and rifle through pockets for cash. Maybe he could have got by with the voices eventually and learned to live with them, but the drugs were more important. He killed for the drugs, drugs, drugs, not the voices.

Now Ray crouched in the apartment he was squatting in remembering this and remembering Phillip as he shifted his fingers around in a new baggie (not the same one because that was long gone and now Ray was much older and wiser). The apartment was dingy and dark and lit up by like a hundred squat fat candles he found tossed in the trash behind a church and their flickering light cast funny shadows on the walls, but Ray didn't care because soon he would be high again and everything would be perfect. Ray was almost always high; he had a baseline that he had to keep otherwise the voices might come back and that couldn't happen because he thought that if he heard them saying to kill himself now he probably would do it, and he didn't want to die so it was better he stayed high.

Ray took his socks off and sat on the creaky wooden floor and splayed his toes apart so he could slide the needle into the space between his toes and depress the plunger and ahh, yes bliss, bliss, bliss. Ray slumped against the moth-eaten couch and for a second he felt bad because he could see the blood splatter on the back of the couch and that was from Scooter's head (from when Ray smashed the hammer into it). Where was Scooter anyway? Ray wasn't sure because he knew he moved him and left him somewhere after the group told him last week to be more careful with his bodies but he couldn't remember where he left him. Ray was glad to have the group because they got it (they understood)—he didn't like killing these people but he had to because they didn't share and they wouldn't give him what he needed to keep himself alive. Ray thought that if people weren't so selfish the world would be a better place.

The door creaked and swung open and he blinked because oh, he knew this person, this was his friend (friend?) from the support group. He was supposed to meet them tomorrow. (It was tomorrow right? Or maybe it was today. Yesterday? Soon.) *Hello*, Ray said, *Hello, hello what are you doing here, why are you here and how did you find me? Isn't this against the rules?*

His friend walked closer and closer and there was something sharp and metallic in his friend's hand, it winked at him in the candlelight, it was smiling at Ray.

Don't scream, his friend said.

Oh, oh, oh, Ray said as the words fell out of his mouth like slugs and the world tipped over sideways as something hot ran across his throat (he couldn't feel it, could he?) and something wet spilled down his neck.

Now it is now.

Think of it this way, his friend says as Ray tries to breathe. Why can't he breathe, why is everything going dim and where are his drugs and why does he feel a breeze on the inside of his throat? *You'll be happier now. This is no way to live. Goodbye.*

Ray does not let go of his needle, even when he stops breathing.

CHAPTER

12

"It's been a while," Whipworm admitted, running a hand through his hair. "I know you guys understand. The period in between starts off fine, normal. But the longer I go without it, the more antsy I become."

"Sounds like you're due for a night out," Sand Fly said, smirking.

They started the meeting on the topic of cooling off periods, the time they waited between kills. Cyra hadn't contributed yet; like Mockingbird, she was leaning back in her chair, listening and watching. She made sure to keep her body language relaxed and confident, but internally she was on high-alert, mentally sorting everything the men said, categorizing them from most likely to least likely to be involved with Mira's death. Pinpointing if anyone killed two months ago would be a huge clue.

"I have to do it twice a year, or I go out of my mind," Sand Fly offered, scratching the side of his angular nose. His nails were disturbingly long.

"Once a year for me," Cuckoo added. "I don't get the urge as often, but it always comes the same time every year, and it's always so strong."

"What about you, Mock?" Whipworm asked, trying to engage the older man.

It seemed like Mockingbird wasn't going to answer, lips tight and face drawn, but finally he said, "About every two years. Depending. Less now that I'm retired."

"Same," Lamprey chimed in, his eyes darting toward Cyra before settling on Whipworm. "Well, it used to be like that. When I was younger. I don't have much of a real timeline anymore. I do it when the urge strikes. Which could be anytime. But it's been more frequent in the past few years. Mistletoe, what about you?"

Lamprey was putting her on the spot on purpose, and Cyra was hyperaware of the mood shift as the men feigned casual interest, turning their eyes toward her. It wasn't the right time to step into the spotlight; she needed them to continue sharing. She needed to determine which one of them might have killed last.

"Here I was thinking you boys were the real deal, but those are some long cooling off periods," she said instead, crossing her legs and smiling at them blandly.

Sand Fly's eyes narrowed, and Cuckoo squinted at her. She caught Lamprey's catlike smile from the corner of her eye, and she sensed he knew what she was doing.

Cyra couldn't straight up ask the group if anyone killed a girl two months ago. But she noticed that if one person shared an answer or experience, the others tended to jump in, almost as if they were one-upping each other.

She turned to Whipworm to address him directly. "When's the last time you made a kill?"

"Well, that's the thing," Whipworm said, jutting out his lower lip, simpering. "It's a little nerve-wracking, to be entirely honest. It'll be my first time since getting released from prison."

"Seriously?" Lamprey asked, raising his brows. "You've talked in the past about dudes you were stalking."

"Stalking isn't the same as killing," Whipworm replied. "I like to keep my skills sharp. Check out the scene and see what's what.

I want to be sure this time. I got caught because I made a mistake. That can't happen again. I want to really plan it this time."

"Ah, you're finding someone ahead of time, aren't you?" Sand Fly interjected knowingly, nodding his head in approval.

"Yeah," Whipworm said, a little sheepishly. "I used to pick someone randomly while out. But I want to grow. Get better. That's why I've been practicing following potential targets."

"Stalking is an art form," Cuckoo said with an eagerness that reminded Cyra of a younger kid trying to keep up with older children on a playground.

Shit, Cyra realized. *We've moved on to a different topic.*

Whipworm's admission derailed the kill timeline conversation. She couldn't turn it back now without looking suspicious. But it wasn't all bad. If Whipworm was telling the truth, he hadn't killed in quite some time and might not be the person she was looking for. This was a marathon, not a sprint. She wasn't going to be able to collect all the information she needed in just two sessions, and maybe this stalking discussion could help her too. Mira's attack seemed random, impulsive. The more she knew about how these men operated, the more of a sense she would get of Mira's killer.

"Following people? That's my shit," Sand Fly said, scratching his nose again. Cyra perked up, watching him. Touching his nose could be a tell, a way to mask a lie. "I can definitely give you advice there. Bet Lamprey has helpful tips too. I know he likes to follow his 'darlings.'"

And now Sand Fly was deflecting. Interesting.

Lamprey's cheek twitched, and he glanced at Cyra, a wink of mirth in his eyes before answering. "Oh, yeah. Following people isn't that hard. Most people are stupid."

Dick, she thought, but the anger was watery and tapped down by the overwhelming control Mistletoe's persona had over her countenance. She was also aware of the very real implication that Lamprey targeted her as his next 'darling' since he followed her home, but he promised earlier that wasn't the case. He insisted he wanted them to help each other. Was he lying? He was harder to read than Sand Fly.

Cyra became aware of how bizarre this situation was—her sitting here listening to these awful, disturbing conversations without any connection to the reality of it. In that moment, she felt a rush of gratitude for Mistletoe. Her coldness, her lack of empathy, made it easier to muster the courage to attend these meetings and hear what she was hearing without breaking down.

"You're on the right track," Sand Fly said to Whipworm. "The most important thing about following someone is learning their patterns. Does your target take the same route home from work every day? Do they go to the gym? When? People are creatures of habit. Find their habits, and that'll make following them—and grabbing them—much easier."

"Keep your distance," Lamprey added. "Use mirrors, watch from a car, don't be obvious. Changing your appearance helps, especially if they know you or have seen you around before. Remember, if you can see them, they can see you. So if you can't get good gear or access a hiding place to watch from, figure out how you can become invisible in plain sight."

"Hm," Whipworm said. "Thanks, man. That's actually pretty helpful." He chewed his bottom lip thoughtfully, then abruptly turned to Python. "Should we move on? Someone else can share now."

Python nodded. "Sure."

Whipworm got to his feet and ambled over to the snack table, grabbing a doughnut and sticking it in his mouth. "I need a snack break. Anyone else want one?" he asked, words muffled around the pastry clamped between his lips.

Cyra wasn't hungry, but she wanted to appear unconcerned and calm. What better way to prove her comfort in the group than by eating in front of them? "I'll take one."

Whipworm, in a gesture of consideration, brought the whole box over to her so she could select a doughnut herself. He offered the box around, but no one else showed interest, so he returned the doughnuts to the table and sat back down, mumbling under his breath, "My flautas would have been better."

Everyone ignored him.

Cyra bit into the doughnut. It was stale. Flakes of icing melted on her tongue. The dough had the consistency of silly putty and tasted vaguely of rancid oranges. She gnashed her teeth against the chewy pastry, deeply regretting her decision to eat it but having gone too far to spit it out.

Python cleared his throat. "Sand Fly? Would you like to go next?"

Sand Fly shrugged, but his eyes lit up and he shifted forward in his seat, swiping his tongue across his upper lip. He looked like an enlarged stick insect. "Sure. So—"

"Introduce yourself," Python reminded him. His biceps, the size of small children, seemed to flex unconsciously as he spoke.

"Every time, Python, really?"

"We follow the rules."

Sand Fly rolled his eyes but acquiesced. "Fine. Hi, y'all, obviously you know me as Sand Fly."

"Hi, Sand Fly," the group intoned.

"I actually have news today," Sand Fly said, running his pale fingers through his dark hair, reminiscent of maggots twisting in freshly turned earth. "There was this new girl I was interested in—I think I mentioned her a couple weeks ago? Face that could light up a basement at midnight, megawatt smile. Well, things progressed. I was taking it slow, you know, getting to figure her out and see what she was into, that kind of thing. But, finally, last night, I was ready. And it was . . . magical. Really, really magical." The man sighed in contentment as if reliving the experience. He crossed his legs and grinned. "I can't stop thinking about her. Janice. God, that beauty."

"Hey," Python interrupted. "You know the rules. No names."

"Right, sorry, Python." But Sand Fly's grin spread wider. He wanted the others to know. To wonder about her. To picture her.

Cyra's stomach started churning when she realized she didn't want to think about this woman named Janice. Janice wasn't real to Cyra, not when she was Mistletoe. In this room, Janice was only a story.

"She can't be as sweet as that girl I told you guys about," Cuckoo said, challenging Sand Fly. "The one from last spring. Remember her? You certainly seemed jealous when I talked about how she begged."

"Please, they all do that," Sand Fly spat. "She wasn't special."

"She was *exquisite*."

"Oh, yeah, you're all so tough with your frail, little bird girls," Whipworm interjected, his hands flapping in his lap. "Want a challenge? Want a real thrill? Try overpowering a two-hundred-and-fifty-pound athlete with your bare hands."

Lamprey barked out a laugh. "Overpower? You drug them at bars, Whipworm, and then lure them to your car. Those dudes are barely conscious when you kill them. That's not the flex you think it is."

"Ah, shut up, Lamprey."

Sand Fly let out a high-pitched giggle from his perch near the middle of the semicircle. The sticky table where the gritty coffee and lackluster pastries sat was visible behind him, making the whole scene seem somehow normal. A twisted parody of an AA meeting.

Python's brows furrowed. "That's enough of that, I think. Remember, you're all on the same team. Let's keep it moving. Who's next?" His massive head swiveled around, eyes landing on Cyra, trying to choke down the piece of doughnut that had gotten lodged in her throat during Sand Fly's little monologue. "Mistletoe, how about you?"

Immediately, the other men in the room perked up as if they had smelled something mouthwatering.

She couldn't distract them this time. She had to share.

You've prepared for this.

Cyra swallowed hard, forcing the hunk of doughnut down toward her stomach, and cleared her throat. She didn't smile. Not for this. It would have looked wrong, strange, for a woman to have the same kind of lurid joy the men had when describing their conquests. She had a part to play. Hands hidden in her lap, she slowly dug her nails into the flesh of her palm and concentrated.

"It's been slow for me," she said, focusing on the floor, feeling their eyes lock on her, hanging on to her every word like she was spoon-feeding them good doughnuts instead of these shitty stale ones. Only Python looked at her calmly and without rapaciousness. "I have to be careful. There's only so much I can do without my employer getting suspicious. But I've picked out my next one. She's ancient. She looks like a pruney finger, like when you're in the bath too long? Like that, but it's her whole body." Cuckoo twitched across the circle. The movement sent a ripple of tics throughout the group; lifting shoulders, tongues darting out from lips, brows furrowing, fingers flexing. Cyra continued as if she hadn't noticed. "She reminds me of my mother. Next week I'll do it."

"How?" It came from Sand Fly, his lip curling.

"Careful," Python warned. "No specifics. Nothing that could identify you or your mark."

"I'd bet any amount it's poison," Whipworm said. "Women always use poison."

"Cowardly, if you ask me," Sand Fly spat.

"Woman's weapon," Whipworm agreed.

"You think so?" Cyra asked, leaning forward so they could all get a good look at her face, the doughnut rolling around her stomach like calcified sugar. "You have to be smart for poison. You have to be up close and personal. You have to watch them slump over in their beds. See the life go from their eyes. You have to have the stomach to watch a body do all the fascinating little things a body does after it stops being useful. Poison isn't the weapon of a woman. It's the weapon of the heartless."

The room was silent. They were all leaning toward her like trees deep in the forest who arch desperately toward the sun, trunks twisting in an effort to feel the light.

She waited until she could practically hear them frothing at the mouth. "A little shot of air. Less evidence than poison."

The room burst into burbling chatter.

"Hey, that's enough. Settle down." Python didn't have to bellow, though he could have. His firm, soft tone was disquieting enough that the room fell silent.

Cyra glanced around surreptitiously. She thought Sand Fly's hand was drifting toward his crotch, but she didn't want to look closer to check. Cuckoo was making a strange throat-clearing sound, and she could feel Lamprey's gaze burning a hole in her chest. Whipworm was smiling. Mockingbird was staring at her, brows furrowed. Only Python seemed to have a hold of himself, but that was to be expected.

"Anything else you want to share with the group?" Sand Fly asked, his pale skin flushed around the neck.

Her eyes snapped toward him. "No."

Sand Fly looked like he was about to respond, his face tightening, but Python cut in. "Let's thank Mistletoe for sharing."

"Thank you, Mistletoe," the group chorused, but their voices were louder now, sparked, eager. They sounded less like a group of schoolchildren and more like a chanting mob who could smell blood. She was the fresh chum in the water.

"Well, we're out of time for tonight," Python continued, perhaps sensing the shift in energy in the group. "Thank you to all our sharers tonight. Pea Crab said he'll be with us next time. If he's not . . . Well, I'll let you know our new location next week.

Don't forget to check-in as usual the night before. Be smart out there, and stagger your leaving times."

There was a flurry of movement as the meeting concluded and the safe space of their little bubble burst.

Cyra moved fast and purposefully. She felt Lamprey's eyes following her as she strode over to the coatrack and removed her peacoat and black wool hat.

"I hope we get to hear the details next week," a voice came at her ear.

It took extreme control to not jump at the wet words. Instead, she turned around, a placid expression on her face, her voice cool. "We'll see."

Sand Fly stared at her, smirking, until Lamprey appeared, nudging him with his elbow. "Not bothering our lovely Mistletoe, are you?"

Sand Fly narrowed his eyes and took a step back. He was sharp and angular, taller than everyone else in the group, but Lamprey had a reputation. And muscles.

"Of course not," Sand Fly said, lips somehow chapped and wet at the same time. He ran his tongue over his teeth, which looked like a broken fence, and glanced back at her. "See you next week."

"You will," she replied, pretending to be unconcerned as he made for the coatrack.

Lamprey looked at her a moment longer, smiled, and then turned away.

It wasn't until she had gotten outside the room, leaving first this time and ducking into the women's restroom near the stairs, that Cyra finally lost control.

Checking the lock on the bathroom door, body shaking uncontrollably, Cyra stared at her expressionless face in the mirror, waiting for her real self to break free, waiting for tears to fall, for her composure to crack.

When it didn't, despite her trembling limbs, the queasiness that manifested during the end of the meeting rose swiftly and she squatted over the toilet, vomiting up the stale doughnut.

What the hell is wrong with me? Why am I not having a bigger reaction? Why am I not more disturbed?

Cyra wanted to be disgusted with the serial killers, but it was herself she was the most revolted by. She hurriedly reached inside, rooting around her heart as if she could forcefully yank out a more appropriate emotion—fear, rage, sorrow. But the mask of Mistletoe was tight, and it didn't allow for anything to sneak through.

Go back to yourself, she thought frantically, aware of how comfortable the persona was starting to feel. She didn't want to take Mistletoe off. She didn't want to feel the shame and horror from sitting through these meetings.

But she had to. She needed to get back to her real life.

Cyra closed her eyes and thought of Mira's face, her laugh, her infectious energy. The edges of Mistletoe slipped, Cyra's breath started to come fast and hitched, and she released the coldness of her counterpart.

The bathroom floor was hard against Cyra's knees. She forgot about germs and how disgusting an abandoned rec center's toilet might be and rested her sweaty forehead against the cool rim, choking back tears. If she started crying now, she would never stop. She had to keep it together. She had to focus.

Maybe Sand Fly was boasting. Trying to establish himself as an Alpha. Or trying to scare her, the female newbie. But maybe he was telling the truth. Maybe he did murder some poor woman named Janice last night.

Could she find the woman? Alert the authorities? But the impossibility of it loomed ahead of her. She didn't even know Sand Fly's real name, let alone where he hunted. Maybe Lamprey could help? But he said he didn't know the names of the other members either.

A few months into their relationship, Bea and Cyra had curled up on the futon to watch a decadently shot, ominously narrated Netflix special on Midwest serial killers. They both hated it, but for different reasons.

"Remember that show, *Are You Afraid of the Dark?* It was like that. Like, 'Oo, we're trying to scare you because this is such scary shit!'" Cyra said after it was over.

But Bea frowned at the screen, paused on the credits, her arms wrapped tightly around her chest. "It skipped over the victims entirely. It was like *they* were the footnotes and these sickos were the main characters. It should be the other way around. What is everyone's obsession with men who are fundamentally evil? Why do we need all these lurid movies and documentaries and books about them? And why do the people who suffer the most because of them always get forgotten?"

Cyra felt guilty for not picking up on the same themes Bea had, but she felt worse now because she did it again, except on a much larger, much more terrible scale.

She forgot or, more likely, willfully pushed aside the existence of the people these men killed. Or planned to kill. She knew, obviously, that they were murderers, active ones at that. But she hadn't allowed herself to really acknowledge what they might be out there doing. Her entire focus had been on the killers themselves—and which one of them could have hurt Mira. She was focused on only one victim. The one that mattered to her. She was no better than the armchair detectives doxing innocent people or the subtly gleeful white women who clutched their pearls in horror but secretly thought they were too clever to fall for a serial killer's tricks.

Cyra was part of the problem. She even helped hide a victim's belongings.

But she couldn't fix it. Not yet, not now. Perhaps it made her a bad person, but her priority had to remain unchanged.

Mira. She was doing it for Mira. Not Janice. Not the man whose clothes she sank.

But she decided something. Whether or not Sand Fly killed her sister, he had to be dealt with. After she found Mira's killer, she would do something about the rest of the group.

Cyra clambered to her feet and wiped her brow, taking a few sheets of toilet paper and spitting into them, flushing the wad and washing her hands before exiting the bathroom. She'd been in there for almost thirty minutes, so she was sure she was the last one downstairs, but she peeked into the basement room anyway to make sure.

It was empty—table clear of doughnuts and coffee; chairs stacked in the corner.

Cyra was about to turn and leave when she spotted something strange lying on the floor. It was a four-by-six inch piece of white paper underneath the table that she was almost positive hadn't been there earlier.

She glanced around again to make sure she was alone, and then scurried forward and scooped up the piece of paper. It had a heavy weight—glossy photo paper—but the edges were a bit torn and there was a crease in the middle where it had been folded. At first, Cyra thought it was blank. But then she flipped it over and her breath caught in her throat.

It was a photo of Pea Crab.

Or, more specifically, of Pea Crab's body.

Cyra brought the photo closer to her face, her mouth dry.

The body was recognizably Pea Crab; he was lying on his back, one arm flung out to the side, legs twisted up underneath him as if he had fallen and tried to catch himself at the last second. His eyes were open, and an expression of bewilderment was on his face. It wouldn't be unbelievable to assume that Pea Crab, clearly hurting for a fix after their last meeting, had overdosed. Except that a wide, red smile was slashed across his throat. It was a clean line, straight and steady. There was no blood in the photo besides the congealed clumps on his neck, and the body looked like it was lying on the concrete floor of a warehouse or maybe a basement.

She lowered the hand holding the photo and took a deep breath. This was real. She was holding evidence of a murder in her hands. And clearly, one of the serial killers had done it. But why? Because Pea Crab was a liability? And more important, how had they found him? Python and Lamprey had both emphasized how important anonymity was to the group, and how careful the others were to keep themselves separate outside this room.

Although, if Cyra was going to pick one of the men as the easiest, least prepared target, it would be Pea Crab. She doubted he covered his tracks well when leaving the rec center. It was possible one of the others followed him.

What do I do here? Cyra thought. *I could stick it in a mailbox; hope someone turns it over to the cops.*

There didn't seem like much to go on from the photo, and what if they found her fingerprints on it? She'd been printed back when she started her job at the nursing home and couldn't risk the cops asking her how her hands got on a picture of a dead man. And she couldn't have them interfering with the group, not yet, not before she got a real lead for Mira.

Besides, Pea Crab was a serial killer. He murdered people as casually as getting milk from the store.

She had no sympathy for him. She couldn't spare it.

"Whatcha got there?"

Cyra nearly jumped out of her skin, whirling around to see Lamprey leaning in the doorway, watching her. She didn't hear him come in at all; he was so quiet. Today he was wearing a light blue button-down under his tan hunting jacket, and his hair had a movie-star tousled look that turned her stomach.

"What are you doing here?"

"You hurried out so quickly," Lamprey said, face stony. "I saw you slip into the bathroom, so I left and doubled back," he added, watching her face. "I thought we should reconnect after our last meeting."

Was he going to hurt her for the cellar stairs stunt?

He could be the one who killed Pea Crab. It could be even more dangerous to let him know she found the photo. (Intentionally dropped, or accidentally?) But it was a risk she had to take—she had to distract him. She waved the photo at him as if to beckon him closer.

At the same time, Cyra slipped the hand not holding the photo into the pocket of her black slacks, pulling out her switchblade and hiding it within the sleeve of her cardigan. Lamprey pushed off from the doorframe and walked closer. When he was within a few feet of her, Cyra stretched her arm out and brandished the photo at him. "Pea Crab is dead. And someone in the group did it."

Lamprey's face went smooth and blank as he took the photo from her. "I see." His fingertip traced the outline of the dead man's body, and he brought the image closer to his face, scouring it. Cyra wasn't sure he was doing it for the same reasons she had.

"Well?"

"Well, what?"

"Did you do it?"

Lamprey looked up, bringing the photo away from his face. "Pea Crab was a liability. He could have blown up the whole group. Brought us all down. It was only a matter of time before he got caught. Stick him in a precinct without a fix for two days and he'd crack like a rotten egg, tell them everything in the hopes they'd let him score. Although, hey, maybe they wouldn't have believed him, given the state he was in."

Cyra clenched her jaw and tightened her grip on the switchblade, feeling for the lever that would pop the blade out. "So you killed him."

Lamprey watched her for a moment, eyes deep pools with no bottoms. "No," he finally said, and Cyra couldn't tell if he was lying or not. "I didn't. But I understand why someone did. And I even agree with it. It was a defensive move."

"Who do you think did it?"

Lamprey's brow creased, ever so slightly. "Slit throat. Both Sand Fly and Cuckoo have said they use knives." Cyra perked up at this, making a mental note. "But no one in our group specifically slits throats. Although, if you were smart, you wouldn't kill Pea with your signature move anyway. Too obvious."

"Mockingbird?" Cyra offered. "He's quiet. Dangerous."

Lamprey nodded thoughtfully, looking back down at the photo. "It's possible. He's the one I know the least about. Very careful, very seasoned. He's been doing this longer than Cuckoo has been alive."

"But does he care enough about the group to try to protect it like that?" Cyra asked.

Lamprey glanced up at her again, eyebrows lifted. "You're right, I'm not sure he would. To protect himself? Certainly. But if something happened to compromise the group, I have no doubt Mockingbird would be far away before the cops could even sniff out his last name. He's a trucker, you know. It's the one thing he's shared often. Guy like him? I bet he's got hideyholes all over the country."

"OK, so then, what do we do?" Cyra pointed at the photo. "Someone offed one of the members. We have to tell . . . someone. Everyone?" She floundered, realizing she was banking on Lamprey's help with this and hating it. What the hell were the rules or obligations when a serial killer got murdered? And why was she asking another one for his moral advice on the matter?

"Where did you find this?"

Cyra told him how she spotted it and her suspicions that it had been dropped or intentionally left behind after the meeting.

Lamprey was quiet while she spoke, once again tracing the body in the photo with a finger. "We do nothing for now."

"What?"

"I'll keep this, just in case," Lamprey said, folding the photo in half along the crease and slipping it into his pocket. "You don't show all your cards until you know who you're playing against."

"So, we just do . . . nothing . . ."

"For now." Lamprey smiled.

"It's against the rules," Cyra pointed out. "Whoever did it will be killed by Python."

Lamprey scoffed, his face breaking into derision. "Python. Yeah, OK, we'll see."

"What?"

"The man isn't as hard as he pretends to be," Lamprey said. "I don't know what he told you, but the real reason he went to jail? He pled guilty. He felt *bad*. For contract kills. For murder he was lucky enough to be *paid* for. He doesn't have that cold-blooded instinct in him—he's all bark, no bite. Not like you." Lamprey grinned, nodding at Cyra. "Hiding a knife in your sleeve so you can stab me if I get too close."

Cyra sighed and shook her hand free from the cardigan sleeve, revealing the switchblade clamped in her fist. "I know how to use it. And I always carry it. So when you start thinking about chopping me up or whatever sick shit you do, remember that I'm prepared, unlike your other victims."

Lamprey didn't take the bait and correct her on his killing or disposal methods. "I already told you; I'm not going to kill you. We're friends now, kitten." He dragged the word "friends" out so that it sounded far more menacing than it should.

"Don't call me that," Cyra snapped before she could stop herself. She internally flinched. She'd just ensured he would call her "kitten" every chance he got now. Trying to distract him, she asked, "Did Python tell you that? About his case?"

"Of course not, that would shatter this hardbody thug persona he's created," Lamprey said, ignoring Cyra's frown at his casually racist characterization. "I found his prison records when I joined. I wanted to know who this dude running our group was. I can't get anything from our nicknames, but prison nicknames and a general release date? That I can trace."

"Then . . . you know his real name."

"Correct."

"What is it?"

"What do I get if I tell you?" Lamprey was smiling again.

"You get to walk away with all your organs still inside your body," Cyra said, keeping her voice as calm as possible. She was getting the sense that Lamprey responded to control and dominance. He thought he was in charge of their relationship, but Cyra made herself seem like a threat the other night when she pushed him down the stairs, and she had to keep that up. She hoped he'd be less likely to attack her if she put up a strong front. "What's his name?"

"He didn't kill your sister, if that's what you're thinking," Lamprey said, his smile fading a little as it became clear Cyra wasn't going to banter with him. "He's not like us."

"Wait . . . that means you must know Whipworm's real name, too. They were cellmates."

Lamprey's smile flashed back on his face in an instant. "Oh, yeah, I forgot to mention that the other night."

Cyra actually took a step closer to him, the knife still tight in her sweaty hand. "How am I supposed to trust you if you keep lying?"

"Relax, kitten, it's not Whipworm." Lamprey said. "He didn't kill your sister nor is he the snitch."

"How the hell do you know?"

"Have you not picked up on this yet?" Lamprey asked. "I thought you were clever. Whipworm only kills men. He's never said it outright, but I don't think he's much interested in women. If you get my drift."

She remembered now. Whipworm had said something along those lines at the meeting today, but she had been so fixated on not reacting that it hadn't really sunk in.

"Your sister wasn't his type in any sense of the word. And he seems to prefer to strangle his selections."

The realization hit her. "You stalked him too. Found him outside the group."

Lamprey nodded once, and then stepped closer, closing the distance between them so that they were only a few feet apart. "Both him and Python. It wasn't hard. Two birds, one stone. They don't follow the group's biggest rule." He leaned in. "*No outside contact.* Unless Whipworm's hunting, of course. Dilly-dallying around, looking for his next victim. He likes to do that alone." He raised one eyebrow at her, smirking.

Cyra shook her head. "I don't give a shit what Python and Whipworm get into on the side unless it has to do with my sister."

Lamprey looked displeased with her disinterest, but shrugged. "I can't confidently say they one hundred percent weren't involved, but it's really unlikely."

Which Cyra had to take with a grain of salt because it was coming from his mouth. Still, though, she was inclined to agree with him. What reason would either Python or Whipworm have for going to Prospect Park and randomly murdering a girl out for a jog?

You're acting like these guys think rationally, the voice in the back of her head whispered. *They don't. They're* serial killers. *You can't predict what they'll do.*

"How do you know neither of them are the snitch?"

"They started this group," Lamprey said. "Why would they try to destroy it? I can't see them doing that. Plus, I have their prison records. They're both the real deal; I know they killed people."

"Give me their names," Cyra demanded.

"I will," Lamprey promised. "Once you help me determine who the rat is."

"That's not our deal." Cyra's hands were getting hotter, and she suddenly wanted out of that basement, out of the building, out of the whole city.

"You've got a head start," Lamprey said. "I've already told you it's not Python or Whipworm. And Pea's dead. Not that I thought it would be him anyway. Kid could barely keep his head on straight, and I don't think he had the time to go scrolling through true crime sites to warn people about us. That leaves three options."

"I don't give a shit!" Cyra hissed, her composure slipping. "I want to figure out who killed Mira."

"Then you'll help me."

"No."

Lamprey moved so fast Cyra barely had time to blink before one hand was wrapped around the wrist holding the switchblade, the other grabbing her free hand and twisting it behind her. Cyra gasped as Lamprey bent the wrist on the hand holding the blade back, and she automatically released the knife, sending it thumping to the carpet.

Cyra stilled, assessing the situation. Lamprey's hold was slightly painful but weak. He was barely restraining her left hand, the one that hadn't been clutching the knife. She was fairly certain she could break his grip and escape, but she knew, almost instinctively, that was not the right move here. Lamprey might have researched her, but there was no way he knew about her MMA training. She hadn't visited her gym since joining the group, practicing at home instead, and even when her social media accounts were active, she rarely posted and never about fighting. MMA was her secret weapon. She wasn't ready to reveal it yet.

She sensed Lamprey waiting, ready to take his cue from her next action.

Cyra was squashed against Lamprey's chest, her heartbeat banging into his own as she was suddenly struck with a spike of agitation that she absolutely under no circumstance could show to this man.

One of the books she read about serial killers told her that there were generally four different types: visionary, mission-oriented, hedonistic, and power/control-oriented. If she read Lamprey correctly, he was the power/control type. He liked exerting control over helpless people. And if Cyra gave him nothing to be in control over—no fear, no concern, no fight to get away—maybe she could get out of this.

Although she longed to activate her MMA skills—breaking his grip, striking hard and fast, then taking him down—she held back. Cyra forced her expression to slacken, let her wrists grow limp in Lamprey's big hands, and looked up at him with steady eyes. "Let go of me, Jason. Don't be stupid."

At his real name, Lamprey started. Cyra could feel his breath against her cheeks, smell the coffee and spearmint gum on his lips. His eyes searched her face, looking for terror, looking for a fight. He wanted her to want to live.

Seeing nothing he hoped for in her expression, Lamprey dropped her hands as suddenly as he had grabbed them. "I was only playing. Don't worry, kitten. I'd never hurt you. We're a team. I'll see you soon, OK? We have work to do."

Lamprey winked at her, his temperament subdued now, and turned, leaving the room.

Cyra waited until she heard the clank of the door upstairs, until he'd been gone five minutes, before finally bending down to grab the switchblade, her hand shaking so bad it took her three tries to pick it up. She felt springy, as if she just jumped out of a plane. It wasn't until she had the knife back in her hand that Cyra realized her nervous, shaken response wasn't from fear. She frowned, unsettled by her reaction.

The encounter with Lamprey hadn't frightened her—it thrilled her.

CHAPTER

13

Back at her apartment, Cyra made a list with two columns.

"Snitch" was on the top of the left; "Killer" was on the top of the right. She carefully wrote down each man's nickname in both columns, then crossed out Python's and Whipworm's names from the left. She left Pea Crab off both lists. He was dead now, and no longer her problem. Sand Fly was an obvious candidate for the Killer column, although she struggled to decide whether or not to trust what he shared in the meetings. He told them that he killed only twice a year, and if he recently murdered Janice, that would mean his timeline didn't add up with Mira's death. Of course, he could be lying.

She looked at Lamprey's name, written in jagged pencil strokes.

This was a dangerous game. As tough as she was with all her fighting training, Cyra wasn't sure she would be a match for a fully-fledged murderer. Lamprey was toying with her earlier, and she was certain she hadn't seen the extent of his real strength. If push came to shove, would her self-defense experience be enough to beat someone like him?

She had to play nice with Lamprey and try to keep her distance at the same time. Which could be difficult given he knew where she lived, but she was hoping that being on the third floor of a locked building might deter him.

Cyra looked down at the "Snitch" column. Finding the mole in the group could be an asset. It could potentially help her narrow down the people on the other side of the list.

Her pencil hovered over Python's and Whipworm's names, remembering what Lamprey said about them being unlikely to have killed Mira. She slashed a line through their names but resolved to keep an eye on them.

Cyra pushed back from her little kitchen table and turned, taking in the studio apartment. It was a wreck. She couldn't remember the last time she'd cleaned, and she wondered if it had looked this bad when Bea stopped by last week. Her ex probably thought she was losing it from grief, but Cyra had been too busy to consider doing laundry or cleaning up the old takeout containers on the counter. But now, shaken from the encounter with Lamprey and needing to reset her brain, Cyra changed into a stretched-out tank top, tossed her hair back into a bun, and attacked the dirty apartment.

Clothes went in the hamper, garbage was collected and dropped down the chute in the hallway, the Mistletoe disguise was packed away properly, the bathroom was scrubbed, the kitchen cleaned, the unused bed sheets replaced and made.

When Cyra collapsed onto her futon three hours later it was dark, and she was breathing heavily, the tank top stained with halos of her sweat. She felt good. Better than she had in a while. She looked around the studio, her eyes falling on the framed self-portrait of Mira by her bed.

Getting to her feet again, Cyra marched over to the minuscule hall closet and pushed aside her thick winter coat so she could pull out the twelve-by-fifteen-inch framed photo Mira gave her for their birthday last year. The frame jostled against a shoebox on its way out. Cyra winced and pushed the shoebox further back; it contained PJ's bloodstained hat, and Cyra didn't like to look at it very often. Once a year, she would take it out and think about the terrible thing she did, wondering if that year would be the year she would tell Mira. Every year, she convinced herself otherwise, shoving it back in its hiding spot so she could pretend it didn't exist.

Cyra carried the frame over to the table and placed it upright, so that her own face was staring back at her.

Mira had snapped *Portrait of a Panic Attack* in their first year of living in New York City, but it hadn't caught anyone's attention until a little over a year ago when Mira submitted it to a small photography publication. It went viral for a few days, sparking the interest of Arthur McCowen.

Cyra reached down and traced the lines of her own face with a fingertip, instantly stopping when the memory of Lamprey doing the same with the photo of Pea Crab's body slipped into her mind.

Those first months of living in the city were tough for Cyra. Mira had flourished, her joy at the freedom and energy she felt being away from home palpable as she explored their new city. But Cyra was paralyzed by the change.

The panic attack happened in their first apartment. It was a Saturday night, a bottle of wine next to Cyra's bed and *Real Housewives of Potomac* playing on the TV in her tiny bedroom. Cyra thought Mira was out, and the attack hit her so quickly she only had time to put down her wine glass, turn off the TV, and sit in the darkness of the room, hands wrapped around her knees as she rode the waves. She repeated her mantra, "Just get through the next ten minutes and you'll be OK," over and over as her throat constricted and her eyes streamed and her stomach twisted.

The bedroom door bursting open almost gave Cyra an actual heart attack. Mira spilled into the room, the brightness of the hallway behind her bleeding into the darkness that was keeping Cyra grounded.

The memories came to her in pictures, snapshots just like Mira's photos, as if the whole scene was something Cyra saw splayed out in a darkroom and wasn't something she had actually lived through.

Mira's bleary eyes and wine-stained lips. The slinky black dress she had worn to meet her new friends in Park Slope. The camera slung around her neck that she had taken with her that night. Mira raising the camera. Pointing it at her sister. Cyra's hand coming up in defense.

"Mira, no."

And the whirring snap and blinding flash as she took a photo.

Cyra looked down at the black and white photograph of herself on the table. This was the photo that had created Mira's signature style—black and white high contrast portraits in dim lighting. In the photo, Cyra was kneeling in the very center of her bed, eyes hysterical and wide, wet with tears. Cyra's mouth was ajar, mascara smeared and blotchy. One hand was digging into her knee, the other was midmovement, a gesture toward the camera. The rest of the bedroom was a stark black; the ridges and plains of her face and bare arms standing out. She looked like an island in a sea of darkness.

But it was Cyra's expression that had really made the portrait go viral. It was the expression of a woman who was drowning and knew it.

So relatable, one comment said when Cyra found the photo on a Reddit mental health thread with thousands of upvotes.

The photographer perfectly captured the hopelessness you feel when having a panic attack, someone else wrote. *Everyone should see this, it's so important!*

The comment had eight thousand upvotes.

Only a few people seemed to think of Cyra as more than a subject.

Idk how I feel about this, one person had responded. *This girl doesn't look like she wanted her photo taken. Feels exploitative.*

But Mira was so proud of the photo. "I'm really sorry. I was drunk when I took it. And I helped you right after, remember? Got you to calm down a bit. It's just . . . I think it's the best thing I've ever done."

Cyra agreed to let her use it. She honestly didn't think it would go anywhere. And for a while, it didn't. Cyra had almost forgotten about the photo when Mira submitted it to the photography magazine. She certainly didn't think it would be published, go viral, and land Mira in a sticky situation with another man who was taking advantage of her.

Cyra swallowed, looking down at the photo she hated. When Mira had given it to her as a present, Cyra had pretended to be pleased and then stuffed it in her closet, only bringing it out if Mira came to visit.

Part of her wanted to hang it up in the apartment now. A way to honor her sister.

Cyra shook her head. She picked up the photo and walked it back to the closet, leaning it against the back wall so that she didn't have to look at her own distraught expression anymore. She closed the closet door with a snap and leaned against it for a moment, breathing deeply.

"I have to get out of here," she muttered, pressing her hands against her cheeks, which felt hot and clammy despite the fact that Cyra barely kept the heat on in her apartment.

After a quick shower and change of clothes, Cyra found herself at the grocery store a few blocks away. She'd been putting off getting paper towels for three weeks now, and she wanted to restock her frozen meals, which were running low.

She stood in the freezer aisle, a shabby red plastic basket slung over her forearm. Opening the door, icy air fogged up her glasses as she reached in and grabbed a microwavable burrito. Pausing for a moment, letting the cold permeate her skin, Cyra took a deep inhale and released it. There was a slight tingling in her extremities, followed by a numbness that kept her alert and focused instead of sleepy and heavy. The sensation was similar to how she felt when pretending to be Mistletoe. And similar to how it felt when she was trying to stop a panic attack.

Cyra tossed the burrito in her basket and let the freezer door close.

When the clouds faded from the lenses of her glasses, Cyra noticed a man standing a few feet away, watching her. He was in his midforties with a craggy face and a reddish-blond beard. A shopping cart full of burgers, mac and cheese, and not a single vegetable rested in front of him. Caught staring at her, he grinned.

"Nice ass," he said, gripping his shopping cart and navigating it around her before she could answer.

Automatically, Cyra turned so her back was to the freezer door, corded muscles in her arms tense as the man passed her by without a second glance, apparently satisfied with the interaction.

The freezer door was closed, but ice lingered inside Cyra's chest. Her heart hammered, and she took several long, deep breaths to steady herself before slowly ambling down the aisle, trailing after the bearded man.

It was late afternoon, and the grocery store was fairly crowded, making it easier for Cyra to put people between her and the man while still keeping him within her sights. She watched as he put a six pack of Miller High Life into his cart and then wound his way to the checkout, leering at the young girl at the register as she scanned his items.

Somewhere along the way, Cyra had put down her basket. She slipped into the "10 Items or Less Line" and bought a pack of gum, timing it so that she was leaving the store just after the bearded man, who was weighed down with three large grocery bags. As she headed to the exit, she caught a glimpse of her reflection in the tinted windows of the store and did a double-take. She didn't recognize her mannerisms at first; her shoulders were pulled back, her chin was tilted up, and she looked taller, even without her lifts. It took her a second to place it, to realize what she was doing: becoming Mistletoe. It was almost unconscious, and though Cyra thought she should perhaps be concerned about that, all she could feel was relief as she let herself sink into the skin of her support group persona.

As she followed the bearded man, she remembered Lamprey's and Sand Fly's tips. She didn't trail the man too closely; she crossed the street to put some distance between them, weaving through people and watching him through gaps in the passing cars.

The bearded man turned off the avenue and Cyra followed him to a dingy walkup, pretending to scroll through her phone while actually using her camera to zoom in, watching as the man punched in a door code and entered his apartment's lobby, disappearing from view.

Now I know where you live, she thought.

She imagined this man as Mira's killer. She imagined staking his place out, learning his habits, his comings and goings, figuring out his apartment number and memorizing the door code. When she was ready and knew they wouldn't be disturbed, she would slip inside and knock on his door. Cyra imagined stabbing the man, over and over. Getting justice for her sister by bringing him to his knees in a pool of his own blood.

Her pulse sped up at the thought, and Cyra blinked, expecting disgust or guilt at the violent spiral her mind had taken. But there was nothing.

Cyra whirled away from the building, tightening her grip on her phone, slumping her shoulders and wrapping her hands around her torso as she speed-walked away from the man's block.

She pushed against the emptiness inside her, startled by how unyielding it felt.

Go away, she thought.

Cyra pictured Mira's mischievous grin and bubbly laugh, forcing Mistletoe's personality to finally dissolve.

Cyra longed to embrace that calm, calculating, unemotional instinct. But of course, she couldn't. That was absurd; Mistletoe wasn't real, and more importantly, Mistletoe was a murderer. But pretending to be her felt so *natural*.

With a queasy jolt, Cyra realized she hadn't experienced a panic attack since creating Mistletoe.

Cyra practically ran the rest of the way home, hoping to leave the unsettled feeling in her gut on the pavement behind her.

CHAPTER 14

Cyra worked Wednesday and Thursday, and on Friday evening, when she was practicing her striking in her apartment, Eli called her.

"I got it," he said, his whispery voice making her think he was squished in his bathroom so Izzie couldn't eavesdrop.

"The file?" Cyra ripped off her boxing gloves and dropped them next to the punching bag, trying to wipe sweat from her forehead with the back of her equally sweaty arm.

"Not the whole thing," Eli murmured. "But I took photos of the key pages. I can email them to you."

Cyra thought of Lamprey, his hacking abilities. She had no idea how hacking worked, if he was able to access her emails. She couldn't risk it.

"No," she said quickly. "Let's meet up. Can you print me copies?"

"I guess, but that seems more dangerous. I don't really want physical versions of this floating around."

"Trust me, Eli, this is safer. And I won't keep them. I'll read them and shred them. I promise."

Eli still hadn't seemed comfortable, but Cyra pushed until he agreed to meet her at Brooklyn Bridge Park in a few hours.

It was annoying how everyone who lived in Brooklyn seemed to forget there were other boroughs in the city; Eli and Izzie never wanted to leave. Even Mira, when she was alive, would drag her feet in making the trek to Cyra's apartment in Queens. But today, Cyra didn't care that she had to be on the train for another hour to meet up with Eli. If she could get access to information Lamprey didn't have, she'd have a much-needed advantage.

Cyra met Eli at the edge of the park, past the wide swathes of yellowed bushes, where he was standing on the edge of the pier, leaning against the safety railing and staring across the water that looked as hard and cold as granite.

"It's freezing down here," Cyra complained as she approached him, unable to ignore the spectacular view despite the relentless wind and promise of ice in the air. The Brooklyn Bridge sprawled out on their right, tethering itself to the shore and stretching to lower Manhattan. In front of them was the city's skyline, familiar all over the world but still not something Cyra had ever gotten used to. It made her feel so small when they first moved here, so powerless. "Can we go to a coffee shop?"

Eli turned to meet her, shaking his head. He was dressed in a matching knit hat and scarf and a camel corduroy sherpa jacket that couldn't be providing much warmth. Cyra supposed fashion was more important than comfort for hipsters. "No way, this is too sensitive. Can't risk someone seeing or overhearing."

"Let's make this fast then," Cyra said, stepping next to him, feeling her hands start to go numb already. She forgot her gloves in her haste to meet him and the sensation of her fingers freezing reminded her of what happened the other day at the grocery store. She shoved the memory into the back of her mind, ignoring it and its implications.

Eli reached inside his corduroy coat and pulled out a thin manila folder. Cyra didn't dare open it here; she pictured the wind immediately snatching at the pages with greedy fingers and tossing them into the gray water—or worse, into the face of some unassuming person who'd turn them in. Instead, Cyra tucked the file into her WNYC tote bag and pressed it close to her body.

"Thank you," she said over the wind. "Seriously. I appreciate it."

"Cyra?"

"Yeah?"

"This is wrong." Eli's eyes seemed to be tearing in the wind. "This isn't how this should be handled."

"Not this again," Cyra sighed, wondering if it would be exceedingly rude to take off now that she had the information.

Eli looked at her, the two of them alone on the edge of the park, surrounded by water and dying plants. "You know, my grandma used to say that if you danced with the Devil long enough, he'd end up thinking he could have more. She always said the only way to save yourself was to say no to the dance in the first place."

Cyra scoffed. "Sounds a little slut-shamey."

"Yeah, well, different era. But the message holds true. If you keep hanging around these men, what will it do to you? To your soul?"

Cyra couldn't respond. She didn't want to think about it, she didn't want to acknowledge that the same question was on her mind lately. She looked out at One World Trade Center instead, its bluish silver peak jutting proudly into the gray sky. What did Eli know about her soul anyway? How did he know it wasn't destroyed already? Maybe it started disintegrating the day their mother left, and then flaked off a bit more every time Cyra couldn't catch her breath or had to protect Mira or look the other way when her father provided her little sister with something they couldn't afford. Maybe the last of Cyra's soul slipped away and into the sewers when she got the call that her sibling was found dead under suspicious circumstances in Prospect Park.

"Oh, fuck."

Cyra looked back at Eli. He was staring at something over her shoulder with bugged out eyes, biting his lower lip. She spun to see Izzie marching over the dead grass, hopping down to the pavement of the pier.

"I knew it," she shouted when she was close enough, the wind snatching her words and making them muffled. "Are you serious, Eli?"

"You followed me?" Eli demanded, moving around Cyra and meeting his girlfriend before she could reach the safety railing. "What the hell, Iz?"

"Of course I did," Izzie exclaimed. "All your 'walks' these past months. You've been so secretive and withdrawn lately. So, what is this, huh?"

Eli looked torn, glancing at Cyra's tote, then back at his girlfriend's tight face. For her part, Cyra was a bit taken aback. It seemed like everyone was doing some light stalking this week.

But Cyra couldn't let Eli admit the truth. Izzie would lose her mind if she knew Eli stole again from work, and the fewer people who knew about what Cyra was doing with the support group, the better.

"Izzie, I'm sorry, it's my fault," Cyra said before Eli could reply. "I needed advice. On how to fix things with you."

Eli and Izzie both froze, turning their attention to Cyra. Eli looked alarmed; Izzie looked intrigued enough that she forgot to snarl in anger when she replied. "What?"

"We haven't spoken since Wine and Cheese," Cyra said, which was a truth she was only now realizing. She rarely reached out to Izzie first; it was always the younger girl initiating the conversations. "I know you were upset. I know *I* made you upset. I wanted to ask Eli how I could make it right. He knows you the best, loves you the most, so I thought he could help."

At her words, Izzie's face softened. "No, Cyra, I shouldn't have yelled at you that night. I was embarrassed, that's why I haven't reached out." She turned to Eli. "You still should have told me. You lied. Said you were going to the library. That's not OK."

"I'm sorry. It wasn't like that," Eli said, reaching out and holding her shoulders, trying to play along. He was surprisingly good at keeping eye contact with Izzie as he lied to her face. "I didn't want to upset you even more. I know you've been so . . . emotional lately."

"My best friend died!"

"I know, but there have been days you can't leave the bed, and then other days you just sit on the couch and glower at me." Eli looked abashed. "Sorry. I know it's hard for you. But I didn't want to like, trigger you or anything if you were still upset about Wine and Cheese night."

"I told him not to tell you," Cyra offered. "It's my fault."

Izzie sighed heavily, gently removing Eli's hands from her shoulders. "I didn't want Wine and Cheese to end like that. It's just been really hard, you know? It's not fair to blame you for Mira's death. I don't know why I did that."

Cyra did. She'd seen it before. After their mother left, after it became clear she wasn't coming back, Mira had turned on Cyra for a few months. She'd have temper tantrums frequently, unable to understand what happened and why. Mira's tantrums would mostly happen when their father was working late, and Cyra, only ten herself, was left to babysit her little sister—learning to feed her microwaveable mac and cheese and pieces of toast for dinner.

"You made Mommy go away!" Mira would scream, her little fists balled up, face red from crying. "It's all your fault!"

Cyra hadn't known what to say to that. Especially because she had been wondering if that was true herself. What exactly had she done (or maybe, not done) that had driven their mother away? Mira was too little, so it had to be something Cyra was responsible for. Otherwise, why would a mother ever leave her family?

When she got older, Cyra realized that Mira, in her grief, had needed someone to blame. It hadn't hurt any less when it was happening, but Cyra understood. Maybe that was what Izzie needed the other night; someone to take her pain out on.

"It's going to be OK," Cyra told Izzie, using the same soothing voice she used to use on Mira when she was upset about a boy or paying their rent. "I know you were a good friend to my sister. I'm sure she knows that too, wherever she is."

Cyra didn't believe Mira was sitting on a cloud in the sky benignly looking down at them, but that was clearly what Izzie needed to hear, because she offered Cyra a conciliatory smile.

Eli was glancing between the two of them, looking uncertain and lost, but if he continued to keep his mouth shut about the support group, Cyra could do what needed to be done. Catching Mira's killer was the best way Cyra could give Izzie closure.

Izzie said, "I'm sorry for saying you're the reason Mira died. It was uncalled for. I'm glad you're still in our lives."

Something moved under Cyra's chest, a small bloom of tenderness. "Me too."

"I can't believe this is real," Eli murmured. "I can't believe she's really gone."

Izzie looked at him, voice clogged with emotion. "Why did it have to be this way? She should still be here."

The three of them stood shivering on the empty pier for a minute. Cyra felt the gap of Mira like a missing tooth.

As she looked back out across the water, she wondered how many of the serial killer support group's victims were weighed down beneath the waves.

Waiting until she got home to flip open the manila file folder Eli had given her took Cyra every ounce of willpower in her body. On the train ride back, she clutched the tote bag to her chest and stared straight ahead, chewing the inside of her mouth to keep herself from ripping the file open right there in the subway car.

Back inside her apartment, Cyra flung her coat and shoes in the middle of the clean floor and yanked the folder from the bag, dropped to the futon, and tore it open feverishly. The first page she skimmed so quickly that she didn't retain any of the information, and she had to start over.

Calm down, she told herself. *Take a breath and do this properly.*

Cyra recentered herself and exhaled loudly through her mouth.

The pages Eli gave her were print outs from his cellphone; clear images of physical sheets of paper describing the details of a case from 1999. Lines immediately jumped out at Cyra:

Victim showed signs of manual strangulation . . .

Victim was found on her back with her left ankle crossed over the right . . .

No sign of sexual assault . . .

Medical examiner puts the TOD at early in the morning on April 14, 1999 . . .

Settling in, a wash of stillness coming over her, Cyra sifted through the other papers, skimming them first, and then reading more slowly. Eli was right—he hadn't been able to get her everything, but there were two specific cases and a one-sheet that seemed to be a summary of the patterns and analysis of the suspected serial killer in the folder.

The first case was from 1999. A twenty-two-year-old white woman named Hanna Javitz had been found strangled in a dump on Staten Island. Her ankles had been crossed, but besides that, there was nothing that stood out about the murder. She was a cashier at a 7/11 and had been busted for marijuana charges a year before her death. Definitely not what you'd consider a low-risk victim, and Cyra wondered if Hanna was one of the murderer's first kills.

The second case was from 2007—a thirty-year old from Hudson had been found in the brush near the river upstate. There were almost no similarities to the 1999 case—Miriam Barnes was married with two kids, was a real estate agent, and was Black. She had been shot in the head and left right off a well-trafficked trail near the river. But her ankles were crossed, left over the right.

Cyra squinted at the pages. From her own research, which was validated by some of information on the one-sheet, she knew how unusual it was for serials to switch up victimology, especially in regards to race. Even changing the method of murder was odd.

There was no hesitation present in any of the documented cases that we are aware of, indicating that these victims are likely the work of a more experienced killer, the one-sheet read.

The one-sheet appeared to be prepared by none other than Detective Bellows, the man who was in charge of Mira's case. Cyra suspected that was the reason he was assigned to, or asked to be assigned to, her sister's murder. He'd obviously been watching this killer for a while, gathering reports from the Feds and creating his own internal one-sheet to hand out to his team so they could keep their eyes peeled.

Unknown suspect is likely a white male in his mid- to late-forties with a blue-collar job that allows or assigns frequent travel, Bellows wrote. *Suspect is disorganized in his methodology and victimology, but despite that, crime scenes have lacked any kind of physical evidence, leading us to believe he has above-average intelligence.*

In his report, Bellows mentioned two other cases—Eli must not have been able to pull those. Apparently two other bodies popped up with a similar signature; a forty-year-old woman in 2010 and an eighteen-year-old in 2015, but Cyra didn't know the specifics. It was 2019 now, which meant if Mira was killed by this man, his cooling-off period was becoming shorter. He went from six years between kills, to five, to four. Cyra wished there was more information about who he could be, why he was doing this, in any of the pages, but the cops seemed to have as little information as she did.

What she did know was that this killer had clearly been operating for at least twenty years, which already helped. Cyra scrambled to her feet, placing a hand to her head as all the blood rushed there, and stumbled toward the table where she had left the pad with the list of names.

Returning to the couch, she looked at the names in the "Killer" column and slowly crossed off Cuckoo's. The guy was so young he wouldn't have even been born when the first killing happened. It couldn't be him. She had crossed out Python's and Whipworm's names last week, and she felt more justified in that decision now. They were in prison for at least the 2015 murder, and she was inclined to agree with Bellows's assertion that the suspect was an older white man. With Pea Crab dead (and also too young to have been involved), there were three names left on the list: Sand Fly, Mockingbird, and Lamprey.

Her eyes caught on one of the final lines of the one-sheet.

At the bottom of the report, Bellows had typed:

Suspect appears to fall into the category of a hedonistic serial killer and should be approached with extreme caution as he has had access to firearms and other weapons in the past.

Cyra tapped a finger against her paper.

The one who would fit best given his age was Mockingbird. But the information here was at odds with what Lamprey let slip about the man—Mockingbird, a trucker, killed people on the road and left them in wooded areas.

"But it's coming from Lamprey," Cyra reminded herself out loud. "You can't trust him."

Besides, she thought, *the report said that the suspect probably traveled a lot for work, and that* did *fit Mockingbird.*

She turned her attention to Sand Fly. He looked to be in his late thirties or early forties, but he seemed to be pretty set on young women ("Rich," Python had said), whom he'd stab. Mira was young, but she wasn't stabbed. Plus, some of these other victims varied from what Cyra guessed Sand Fly's usual "type" was.

That left Lamprey. The problem was that he was youngest of the three, not that much older than she was. She pegged him at thirty-two, thirty-three. Which would make him a teenager during the 1999 kill. Not impossible, but unlikely. And she had already seen him in action; picked him out as being a power/control killer.

"But you know the least about his methods," Cyra said to herself, furrowing her brow and pinching the bridge of her nose.

Lamprey was tight-lipped about how and who he killed, and it wasn't like that information was on his Twitter page. He also inserted himself into her investigation, the way some killers do with the cops on the TV shows Mira used to be obsessed with.

The person she was looking for could be Lamprey.

Or her earlier concern could be valid: the man she was seeking might not be in the support group at all. Maybe Mira's killer joined the group a while back and left before he could share about her murder, or perhaps he never joined to begin with.

No, she had to move forward operating under the same conditions—she *had* to figure out if one of these three men killed Mira. If she exhausted all possible options, and it looked like none of them were the man she was looking for, she'd reevaluate.

Statistically-speaking, the murderer is probably in the group, Cyra thought in an effort to cheer herself up. *And you've already narrowed it down so much.*

Cyra closed the file and leaned back on the futon, letting a long breath escape her chest. She tried to look at the positives; she knew more now than she did yesterday, and she had some actual evidence to help direct her instead of being forced to trust Lamprey's words.

But her goal still felt so far out of grasp.

Cyra finally let herself think the thing she'd been avoiding for months: *Who am I without Mira? Who am I without someone to protect?*

Mira was Cyra's shadow and sun both. She trailed after Cyra, even sharing her birthday, yet still managed to outshine her. Cyra, always torn between a stinging pride and a deep need to keep Mira safe, let her sister become her whole world, even when Mira pushed her away or created space between them. Even when Mira showed everyone the bleakest moment of Cyra's life. Cyra built her life around her sister because it was easier to micromanage Mira's life than to confront the emptiness of Cyra's own. Cyra's fragile, surface-level friendships, her often fraught and short-lived relationships, the effort it took to portray the emotions people so often seemed to want from her—she didn't like thinking of her own problems. She preferred fixing Mira's. Even now, in death, Cyra was trying to solve an issue for her sister.

If she was being truly honest, Cyra sometimes thought of Mira as her greatest project. A shining example of her competence as a sister and a person. She might admit that without her, Cyra felt useless, a horse without a cart.

But Cyra hadn't been honest for a while, and she saw no reason to start again now.

CUCKOO

CHARLIE FELT AWFUL after killing the prostitute, he really did. So awful, in fact, that he had thrown up and spent the rest of the evening sweating and crouching over the toilet like he had a virus. He knew that this proved he was a good person who had to do a terrible thing.

All of this was bigger than him. It was more important than ethics or the law or some hooker dressed in drag. One day he would be able to forgive himself for the things he did. The thought comforted him.

The thought that comforted him more, though, was seeing his name in the papers one day. There would be stories written about him. Articles. Blog posts and Reddit threads. Maybe he would even get his own docuseries or Netflix special. Wouldn't that be something? Why did other men get that fame? They didn't even deserve it. With their sick ways and messy tactics. It wasn't fair. Charlie deserved the future he envisioned for himself.

Everyone would know his name. He would finally be something.

His parents knew. They had always told him, even when he was a little boy, that he was destined for greatness. In fact, everyone did. His uncles all commented on how strapping he was. His parent's friends openly wished their own kids would be as obedient. Only one person ever doubted him.

Ms. Carroll. Charlie's third grade teacher.

She had frizzy red hair and bushy eyebrows, and she always wore blue. She had all different shades of blue in her wardrobe; navy, midnight, periwinkle, baby, aqua, ultramarine, sapphire, teal, and other hues Charlie didn't know the names of. She gave them hard pop quizzes and doted upon the children less deserving of her attention; the ones who had the cheap sneakers or were too stupid to read the chapter books Charlie tore through. Ms. Carroll would talk gently in her low voice to Davy Miles, who everyone knew was slow and not worth the time, and try to get him to understand the math problems the rest of them had already finished. She would pull Lizzie Pippen to the side after class and offer to give her extra tutoring even though Lizzie had a deadbeat daddy according to Charlie's mom.

Charlie tried so hard to get Ms. Carroll to see that he was exceptional, much more interesting and talented than the rejects she babied. He never got a question wrong on a quiz, never turned in homework late. The other kids all looked at Charlie in awe, especially when he showed them his new RAZR phone. But still, Ms. Carroll didn't give Charlie the praise he knew he deserved.

One day after they were dismissed for gym class, Charlie hung back and tapped on Ms. Carroll's hip to get her attention.

"Yes, Charlie?" Her voice was flat and calm. Charlie didn't like that. He was used to adults looking at him with sparkling eyes and indulgent expressions, like he was the best caramel chocolate in a box full of coconut and strawberry filling.

"You gotta spend more time on the people that matter," Charlie informed her, repeating almost word-for-word what his father had told him at the beginning of the school year when he told Charlie he had to stop being friends with Constantine because his parents didn't speak English.

Ms. Carroll's bushy brows scrunched together like a hairy caterpillar. "Excuse me? Can you explain what you mean by that, Charlie?"

"Davy is dumb, and Lizzie is trash," Charlie explained, his chest swelling with importance. It was sad that no one had told Ms. Carroll this. She was making a fool of herself, and it wasn't fair; she was pretty and smart, she should know better. "Everyone knows it. My mom says Lizzie has 'daddy issues.' I don't have daddy issues. My daddy is the best police officer in the state. In the whole world, probably. So, you should really spend more time with me at school, OK?"

Ms. Carroll took a seat at her little desk and placed her hands in her lap. She was staring at Charlie. She licked her lips and cleared her throat. "I'm sorry you feel I've been neglecting you, Charlie."

"What's that mean?"

"Neglecting? It means not paying enough attention."

"Oh, yes. You've been very neglecting."

"But that doesn't mean it's OK to call names," Ms. Carroll said, and she reached out to straighten some papers she had left on her desk. "It's not nice to say those things about your classmates."

"Ms. Carroll," Charlie said, smiling at her like he did with his much younger cousins. "You sound silly."

"I'm sorry you feel that way, but you have to follow my rules."

Charlie laughed. "My daddy says I only have to follow his rules." Then he cocked his head, looking at her. "Ms. Carroll, you're not my daddy. Your voice kinda sounds like his, though."

Something strange happened to Ms. Carroll's face. It was like someone had twisted a paper bag from the inside, their hand clenching the bag so it crumpled into itself. "I know who your daddy is, and I know who you are. Your daddy has been on the local news saying that people like me are an 'abomination' who don't deserve to live authentically. Your daddy . . ." Ms. Carroll hissed, and her voice was now ragged. ". . . Your daddy didn't like that my boyfriend lingered too long at a stoplight. He especially didn't like the brown color of his skin. And he really didn't like when we filed a suit against him when he broke my boyfriend's arm dragging him from his car. And you," her voice rose an octave, her eyes wide and hollow like a doll's. "I hear the comments you make to the other children. I won't allow it anymore. I should have stopped it months ago. You're not special. You're not above the rules."

All her words fell out like throw up, quickly, as if she couldn't stop them. Ms. Carroll was panting, her chest heaving under her sea-colored blouse. Blotches had appeared on her neck and cheeks. She was looking at Charlie in a way he didn't understand. He also didn't understand half of what she said—all he did know was that she was definitely insulting him.

"You can't say that!" he shrieked, and ran from the room.

That night, sniffling because he thought it would make him more sympathetic, Charlie told his parents what Ms. Carroll had said. Charlie's father was especially pissed off.

For a few more days, Ms. Carroll floated through the classroom, swathed in blue like the Virgin Mary and ignored the kids whom she should have praised.

But by the end of the week, she was gone.

"Don't you worry, son," Charlie's father told him when he asked what happened to Ms. Carroll. "I took care of the situation. Couldn't have a deviant, and one who was bullying my son at that, teaching young children."

The other kids in Charlie's class shared rumors that Ms. Carroll was moved to the crappy public school because she had a mental breakdown. They said that was why she had yelled at

Charlie. Even Lizzie came up to Charlie and said he was brave for not crying when the teacher flipped out on him. A new teacher, an old lady named Mrs. Yancy, took over. She looked at Charlie's scores and cherubic smile and gave him what he'd been looking for.

But every so often, Charlie thought about Ms. Carroll and the mean things she had said. He'd think about what she was doing at the high school, and which kids she was ignoring there. And every time he saw a cloudless sky or a plastic container filled with blueberries, he would grit his teeth and remember.

By the end of the year, Charlie hated the color blue.

CHAPTER

15

Cyra was surprised at how ready she felt for another meeting already, but part of her was worried it came from an eagerness to spend more time as Mistletoe, away from the intensity and exhaustion of real life.

Donning her disguise, Cyra hopped on the train to the rec center. At Parsons Boulevard, a man swaggered on to the subway, raving and cursing, eyes sliding along the passengers as if searching for someone. Though it was a frequent occurrence, Cyra never really got used to it, and she averted her gaze.

"You bitch!" the man screamed, everyone around him studiously ignoring his breakdown the way only New Yorkers could. "You bitch, I see you!"

Cyra glanced up and found the man's wild eyes locked on her.

She waited for fear but found only cold. Her breath automatically steadied, and her fists curled in. A blanket of calm fell over her as she welcomed the stillness of Mistletoe. It was the fastest and easiest transformation yet. Cyra jutted her chin up, meeting the screaming man's eye, and his fervor seemed to break. It was as if he saw something reflected in her gaze that cut through the thunder inside his head—something he wanted no part of.

He mumbled something incoherent and stumbled away, not speaking again until he approached the very end of the car, far away from Cyra.

For the first time, a small whisper of pleasure curled in Cyra's chest. Mistletoe might be a parasite like the other killers, but she was also powerful. That was something Cyra could respect.

She wore Mistletoe's mask through the train ride, trying to ignore how comfortable the persona was starting to feel. How much easier it was to be this other woman instead of herself.

When she reached the rec center, she was prepared.

"Where's Pea Crab?" Whipworm said at the start of their meeting, eyeing the empty chair that stood out among their semicircle like a missing egg in a full carton.

No one said anything, even though Cyra couldn't help glancing at Lamprey. He raised his shoulders toward his ears, his face smooth and calm. "Maybe he's on a bender."

There were absolutely no tells Cyra could pick out on his face or body, and she felt a zing of fear. Lamprey was good. Too good.

Python frowned. "He never messaged last night. We'll have to move locations. Those are the rules. But . . . I know a few spots he might hang out at. I can ask around after this. Try to see if anyone found an OD."

"Wait, what's that?" Lamprey said suddenly, pointing at something white on the floor underneath Pea Crab's chair.

Cyra's jaw twitched. What was he doing?

The men twisted in their seats or ducked their heads, following the point of Lamprey's finger. Mockingbird, the closest to Pea Crab's empty chair, slowly reached down and picked up the slip of paper.

Cyra watched his face very carefully, but his eyes remained dead and cool as he scanned what Mistletoe knew was on the photo. Wordlessly, Mockingbird rose to his feet and stumped over to Python, handing him the photo.

Cyra felt like she was watching a six-way tennis match. She didn't know who to focus on, which face to examine for micro-expressions she barely knew how to read.

Eyes on the prize, reminded a voice from deep inside her. *Does it really matter who killed Pea Crab?*

"Fuck," Python said, taking the photo of Pea Crab's body in his meaty fingers.

Whipworm leaned over his shoulder and automatically grabbed the other man's upper arm, his knuckles turning white against Python's dark skin.

"What the hell is going on?" Cuckoo complained, jumping to his feet and rushing over.

Sand Fly followed, but Mockingbird ambled over to the coffee carafe and poured himself a new cup, steam spiraling up like storm clouds. Lamprey shot Cyra one glance, swift, challenging, and then crowded around the others, feigning interest.

"Everyone back up," Python growled, clambering to his feet, the photo clenched in his hand, his other arm swinging forward and scattering the serial killers like marbles. "We have a situation; I need to think."

"Nothing to think about," Mockingbird said, his voice carrying over the chatter from the others. "Group's been compromised. Unless he broke a rule, and you did it?"

"I didn't kill him," Python said, his voice low.

The room dissolved into chaos. Voices lifted above each other, the group an orchestra of suspicion.

"Someone killed Pea Crab!"

"Someone in this group?"

"Obviously."

"You don't know that."

"Really? How'd that photo get here then?"

Cyra was the only one who stayed seated. She thought of Lamprey's insistence that there was a rat in the group. Was it the same person who killed Pea Crab? And why had

Lamprey decided to play this card now, so soon after saying he wouldn't?

"Everyone needs to calm down," Python roared over the din. "We need to figure this out."

"No one's gonna cop to it," Whipworm said, rubbing his hands across his face. "What are we supposed to do?"

"Mockingbird's gone." Cyra's high voice, so different from the others, rang out like a windchime.

The others froze, then looked around wildly.

She was right.

The older man had slipped out of the room without anyone noticing while they were arguing.

"Well, it was him, then," Sand Fly determined with a huff.

"You seem pretty keen on laying the blame on someone else," Lamprey said silkily.

"You know that's not what I'm doing," Sand Fly hissed.

"If Mockingbird doesn't have to stay, neither do I," Cuckoo said, jamming his hands into his jeans pockets and hunching his shoulders like a scolded child. He made his way toward the door as the swell of voices rose again, Python trying desperately to keep some semblance of order.

"Cuckoo, come back," Whipworm called out.

"Was he your type, Whip?" Sand Fly accused. "Is that why you killed him?"

"What? That's not my work and you know it!"

Cyra wondered how many of the men were armed right now. How easily could this turn into a bloodbath?

Suddenly, she felt Lamprey's breath near her ear. "I'm going to distract Python. Follow Cuckoo. I'll meet you at the deli at eleven tonight."

She understood—they had missed the chance to follow Mockingbird, but if she trailed Cuckoo now, she could potentially get more information about him. This must have been Lamprey's plan—a way to ferret out the rat.

For a fraction of a second, Cyra paused, unmoving.

She already determined Cuckoo was far too young to be Mira's killer. Tracking him would be useless to her. Lamprey just wanted help in finding the snitch in the group.

He seemed to sense her thoughts, because before he moved away to Python's side, Lamprey leaned forward again and whispered, "Do this for me, and I'll give you the names I have. There are more than you know."

That little shit! I knew he was lying about not knowing anything else, she thought.

And even though Lamprey was high on her list, there were two other men she had to consider too. If he knew their real names, she needed them.

As Lamprey moved toward Python, blocking his view of the door, she got to her feet and scurried out of the room and up the stairs, running on to the sidewalk where she swiveled around wildly in the brisk air.

There.

She caught a glimpse of Cuckoo's blonde head at the end of the block, and she strode purposefully after him, not wanting to draw attention by running. Glancing behind her once to make sure none of the other men had followed her, Cyra ripped the blonde wig off her head, wincing as the shoddy glue job pulled at the little hairs on her scalp. A woman passing her in the other direction gave her a weird look, but Cyra didn't care. She shoved the wig into the shoulder bag she brought and yanked out a dark blue beanie, jamming it over her head. There was nothing she could do about her outfit—she didn't have time to change her slick black slacks and J Crew jacket, but hopefully the change in hair would be enough to keep Cuckoo from realizing she was following him.

She hoped he wouldn't get into a car. Then she'd be screwed.

But Cuckoo turned down College Point Boulevard and headed in the direction of the cemetery that lay, sprawling and brown, a few blocks away.

It was the middle of the day, but the streets of Flushing, Queens were still busy. Cyra let a few people get between her and Cuckoo as she slumped her shoulders, trying to make herself seem smaller. She wished she could take off her lifted shoes and be short again.

They passed an Ethiopian restaurant, a string of liquor stores, and then Cuckoo turned down a more residential block with a series of squat, brown brick apartment buildings crammed up next to a cluster of two-family homes. This block was less populated, and Cyra slowed down to let Cuckoo get farther out ahead of her, remembering Lamprey's advice on stalking—and the way she trailed the bearded man she followed from the grocery store.

When the buildings on the right fell away, replaced by a cemetery, Cuckoo glanced over his shoulder.

Cyra's breath hitched, but the younger man's eyes glazed right over her, searching behind her. She sighed as he turned back. He was looking for one of the members of the group, and far enough behind him, without her blonde hair, his brain hadn't registered her as Mistletoe.

It's funny the things our minds can look past when we don't know exactly what we are looking for, Cyra thought.

When a gap appeared in the cemetery gate up ahead, a small opening that led to a footpath for visitors, she was surprised when Cuckoo turned onto it.

This would be tricky. If he looked behind him again once he was in the cemetery, he would realize she was following him, blonde or not. But she'd come this far. She couldn't turn back now.

When she reached the gap in the wrought-iron fence, Cyra ducked into the cemetery and immediately slipped behind a large black obelisk that shone in the tentative sunlight. When she peeped out from the other side, she could make out Cuckoo cutting across the crunchy dead grass, weaving in between gravestones, heading toward the other side of the cemetery.

Maybe he was visiting a victim.

Carefully, mouth dry, Cyra began to follow him again. She felt like Elmer Fudd tracking Bugs Bunny, hopping behind monuments and larger gravestones, pressing herself against the cold side of a mausoleum when she saw Cuckoo's head start to shift as if he was going to turn around again. He seemed to know where he was going, but to her it looked like he was picking his way through the wide space as if at random.

The cemetery was empty besides the two of them and the thousands of dead people. Queens was covered in cemeteries. Mira used to say it was the Dead Borough, and the only way most people would agree to visit it was in a coffin. Clouds were bundling together above, threatening to blot out the weak sunlight, and Cyra hadn't dressed properly for a cemetery trek; her hands were freezing and her legs underneath her slacks felt like two lead pipes.

Finally, Cuckoo reached the other side of the cemetery. She watched from behind a huge grave marked "Robinson" as Cuckoo fastened his hands around the black bars of the fence and scrambled up and over the top, landing on the sidewalk on the other side like a cat. He straightened and looked around again, causing her to duck down behind the dead Robinson. When she dared to look out again, Cuckoo had turned away.

Could she make the climb over the fence in her neat Mistletoe outfit?

But Cuckoo was crossing the street, walking away from the cemetery, and if she didn't move now, she would lose him.

Scurrying over to the fence, Cyra wrapped her bare hands around the bars, feeling the rough scrape of iron underneath her palms, waiting until Cuckoo was blocked by some trees before pulling down, pressing her lifted shoes against the base of the fence, and yanking herself upwards. Her fighting muscles activated, biceps flexing beneath her jacket as she heaved herself upwards. There were spikes half a foot long at the top of the fence, and she grabbed one of them to steady herself, then awkwardly pulled herself over, the tight seams of her slacks restricting her legs; her stupid shoulder bag catching one of the spikes.

"Should have thrown it over first," she spat.

She pulled the bag free, which dislodged her, and she tumbled to the sidewalk four feet below. Her palms burned from where they had grazed against the pavement, but she wasn't injured—the only bruises were on her ego.

"Fuck women's clothing," she muttered. "God forbid we be able to scale fences easily."

Brushing herself off, she hurried up the block in the direction Cuckoo had disappeared in, noticing that the houses on this side of the cemetery were spaced a little farther apart, boasting tiny brown yards and Christmas decorations already in windows and draped over porches.

When she got to the end of the block, she turned, and there he was.

Cuckoo was walking up to a ranch-style home with a light green awning over the door and several lawn signs about slowing down when you drive jammed into the cold earth. A white "Back the Badge" sign accompanied them, which she thought was an odd choice for a killer.

As Cuckoo pulled keys out of his pocket, Cyra stepped behind a large oak with naked branches and a little sign underneath it that said "Curb your dog."

She was close enough to hear the key scrape in the lock, then a different sound, a jaunty jingling that she immediately recognized.

"Of course. He's got great timing," Cyra heard Cuckoo grumble. Then he cleared his throat and must have answered the call because his voice changed. "Bellows. Hey—no, I know, I just had to stop at home to get something . . . Yes, sorry, sir, yes—"

Cuckoo's voice was abruptly cut off as he stepped inside the house and the door snapped shut.

Cyra pressed her forehead against the tree, feeling the bark dig into her skin.

There were other men named Bellows. There could be a different explanation for why Cuckoo called him "sir." After all, what were the chances that the detective assigned to Mira's case in Brooklyn knew this man who attended serial killer support group meetings in Queens?

But then she looked at the "Back the Badge" yard sign again. Cyra's suspicion could be one hundred percent absolutely correct:

Cuckoo was a cop.

CHAPTER

16

SHE SHOULD LEAVE, Cyra knew that.

But she couldn't. There were too many things that didn't add up. Was Cuckoo really a police officer? Was he undercover? Bellows clearly knew about the whispers of the support group since it was Eli who had passed that information along to Cyra. But the phone call Cyra overheard sounded strange, and from what Cyra knew about undercover cops, there were much more rigid rules around how they could contact their team in order to protect their cover. Would Bellows really ring Cuckoo up on his personal cell?

She needed to know more.

Cuckoo was too young to be the man who killed the women in the files Eli gave her, but as far as she was concerned, he was back on the list. Copycat killers existed, and if Cuckoo was a cop, he would have access to the same records Cyra saw.

Cyra watched the house for a few minutes, ignoring her shivering body, waiting to see if Cuckoo would come back out. When it stayed quiet, she peered around, finding the street empty, and darted forward. Moving quickly and silently, she pressed up against the side of the house and slipped around toward the back. The windows at the front were heavily curtained, but maybe she could see something from the flat, concrete backyard.

She started to move toward the picture window when she became aware of several things all at once: someone was behind her, their breath suddenly against her neck, and something hard was pressing against the base of her spine.

"Don't fucking move."

There was a click behind her back, and Cyra realized the hard object was a gun. Feeling a flush of frustration, Cyra tried to steady her breath and remain calm.

I can handle this, she tried to assure herself.

"Don't shoot, Cuckoo," Cyra said. "That would be a mistake."

"Get inside," Cuckoo growled, his voice against her ear, pushing her forward. "Or I'll do it here, neighbors be damned."

They shifted forward together, an awkward tandem shuffle toward the screen door above the tiny back porch that looked as if it had been built by Cuckoo himself, new wood and wobbly railings.

"Inside," Cuckoo hissed again, reaching out to open the screen door with one hand and shoving Cyra into the house.

"Jesus, you don't have to manhandle me," Cyra muttered as she stumbled into what looked to be the kitchen, quickly casting her eyes around for some kind of weapon. The knife block was on the counter, but on the other side of the room. She doubted she could get there fast enough to grab one. Her switchblade was at the bottom of her shoulder bag since this pair of Mistletoe slacks didn't have pockets.

Fuck Women's Clothing, Part 2, Cyra thought bitterly as Cuckoo swept inside, letting the door slam shut behind him. He lifted his Glock 19, pointing it at her chest.

If she wasn't sure he was a cop before, Cyra was certain now. The recognizable service pistol, the way he held it, perfectly uniform and steady, feet apart, thumbs forward on the gun all spoke to him being on the force.

Dirty cop? Or undercover?

"Drop the bag, and then let me see your hands," Cuckoo said, the slightest hint of shakiness in his voice.

As Cyra obeyed, she watched his face. Up this close, Cuckoo looked even younger than he did in the basement. He must have been right out of the police academy.

"You're a cop." Cyra stated the obvious.

"Does anyone else know?" Cuckoo demanded.

Cyra shrugged, embracing Mistletoe's predator-like stillness to keep herself calm. "I don't think so, but Lamprey is definitely suspicious of you. He sent me to follow you today. For a cop, you were really easy to trail. Maybe you should work on that."

"Shut up," Cuckoo said, his voice harsh, finger moving over to the trigger.

Something strange was going on here. Cuckoo wasn't acting like any police officer she'd ever met, and she was getting concerned that he might try to kill her right there in his house. She had to take a risk, throw him off. If he was dirty, she was dead. If he wasn't, it might save her life.

"I'm not one of them," she said. "I snuck into the group under false pretenses."

Cuckoo let out a strangled laugh. "Yeah, sure."

"I'm serious. My name is Cyra Griffin."

Cuckoo's finger lifted from the trigger. "You're . . . telling me your name? Why is it familiar?" He said the last part as if talking to himself. Then he squared his shoulders. "No, I don't believe you. I know you had to show proof to get in that group, and I've heard you talk in there. You're dead inside."

"Well, that's rude." Cyra wrinkled her nose, but secretly she was relieved. Her acting must have been convincing. "Look, I can prove it. Prove that I'm not a serial killer."

"How?" The gun was steady on her.

She swallowed. "My name is familiar because Mira Griffin is . . . was my sister. I heard you on the phone with Detective

Bellows. He's in charge of Mira's case. If you really work for the Seventy-Eighth, you'll know I'm telling the truth. And you'll know why I'm looking in this group for the person responsible for her death."

"My God," he breathed, and the gun hitched down a fraction of an inch. "I thought you looked vaguely familiar. I thought maybe I'd seen you in a mugshot or something. That happens sometimes . . . But now that you mention it, you look like her."

She couldn't help it. A bloom of warmth cut through the chill in her chest. "You . . . you think we look alike?"

"Sure, exact same eyes and nose," Cuckoo said. "I stared at her photo enough in the weeks after it happened. Didn't place it until now, though."

"So you believe me?"

The gun hovered back up again as Cuckoo stared at her, naked confusion flickering across his face. "How did you get into the group?"

"I work at a nursing home," Cyra explained. "I showed Python a photo of a dead client and pretended I killed her." She didn't dare mention the story she told Python about PJ. Cuckoo might get the wrong idea. "They had me dispose of a victim's belongings."

Cuckoo winced. "They made me get rid of someone's *head*."

Cyra wondered what she would've done if that had been her test—would it have stopped her? She nodded at him in commiseration. "I'm not like them. I'm just trying to figure out which one of them killed my sister, man."

Cuckoo let out a heavy exhale and finally lowered the gun. "Ms. Griffin, no offense, but you're a wildcard. What you're doing is extremely dangerous."

"And what are *you* doing?" Cyra asked, glancing around at her surroundings fully for the first time now that there wasn't a gun in her face.

"I can't say."

She could only see the kitchen they were standing in and part of the living room through the arched entryway, but everything from appliances to furniture looked outdated and fussy, like it was the home of a much older woman.

Cuckoo noticed her looking and seemed to read her mind. "My mom left me this place when she died. Cancer. I think I'm the only twenty-two-year-old on the force with his own house. It's a bitch to get to Brooklyn every day I'm on shift."

"What about your father?"

Cuckoo's eyelid twitched. "He was killed in the line of duty. Two years ago."

Legacy cop. Probably not dirty. But also doesn't seem to be undercover either. What's going on here?

"Sorry to hear that. What's your name?" Cyra asked. There was something shifting in her abdomen, a spiral of unease lengthening and curling up, floating toward her brain. Something still wasn't right.

Cuckoo hesitated for a moment, then said, "Charlie Guardia."

The tendril of unease touched her brain, and she couldn't stop herself. "Seriously, what are you doing in the group? You're not undercover, are you?"

Cuckoo—Charlie, looked at her askance. "Sure I am."

"How did *you* get in the group then? Besides the . . . head thing," Cyra asked, remembering what Lamprey said about how he was the last to join before her. He must have joined up right after Charlie, so he wouldn't have been able to trace Charlie's messages. Yet Charlie was clearly one of the members Lamprey was suspicious of otherwise he wouldn't have had Cyra follow him. "You have to show proof to get in."

Charlie's face turned blotchy and she noticed his hands clench toward his sides. "I—I tricked them."

Lying, he's lying.

Charlie being a poor liar made his behavior in the meetings all the more suspicious. He seemed engaged and enthusiastic during the group sessions, which made Cyra believe this contrite cop was his public persona, a performance. Cuckoo was far too invested and excited by the killing conversations to not be one of them at heart.

"I guess you heard about the support group from work?" Cyra asked.

"Yeah, how'd you get that information anyway? You show up a few months after your sister's death by dumb luck? Bellows wouldn't have told you any of that . . ."

"He didn't," Cyra said cagily. If Charlie wasn't going to be upfront with her, she would show him the same courtesy. She quickly changed the topic. "Let me guess: You're doing this on your own. The force didn't sanction this."

From the bleak expression on Charlie's face, she nailed it.

"I couldn't believe no one was doing anything!" Charlie said. "Like, we knew how to get into the site, we knew how to contact the group, but no one was trying because every previous attempt failed before the meetup stage. I get there are legality issues for us, but come on."

"So, you decided to go rogue and try yourself."

Just like I did.

"Yeah, and it worked!" Charlie's youth was obvious now. His round cheeks were rosy and lit up with his excitement, his gun forgotten at his side. "I've been under since the summer began, gathering intel and taking notes. If I can go to my bosses and get these men arrested, I'll have done something really good for the world! People will be so happy!"

Ah, I see, Cyra thought.

He wanted the accolades. It was a desperate, obvious desire written all over his face. This man-child had delusions of bringing the whole force down upon the support group, being championed by his peers and the public, and getting all the credit for catching some of the most dangerous killers in the country.

He was a child, searching for praise, too stupid to realize he was doing it all wrong.

"I get it," Cyra said. She decided to try a different tactic and softened her voice, leaning forward a little toward him. "You're doing this without them knowing, so you have to make sure you bring them each head on a silver platter so they forgive you for breaking the rules."

"Ask for forgiveness, not permission, right?"

"That's right." Cyra nodded, stepping closer to him now that he seemed less likely to shoot her. "And are you close? Do you know their names?"

Charlie's eyes darkened. "Not yet. But I'm gathering info. I'm making progress." His lips twitched as he lied.

Cyra knew—he wasn't any closer to finding their names than she was. And then she realized she was missing the obvious. "You've been going online, right? Warning people, trying to save them and protect them against these monsters?"

Charlie's face lightened again, and he enthusiastically nodded. "Yeah, just doing my part, you know. True crime and serial killers are very popular these days. I'm trying to warn people. It's my job to keep them safe."

That was it. Charlie was the rat Lamprey was looking for.

How the fuck did this little idiot scam his way into the group?

Cyra was baffled. Python clearly wasn't stupid; how did he not realize what Charlie was? There was only one way . . .

"Charlie," Cyra said, her voice very gentle and low now. She stepped even closer to him and tried to smile in a reassuring way. "I know how it feels. I know how hard this must have been for you."

"It's been awful," Charlie agreed, brow wrinkling. "To hear them talk about people like that every week . . . To have to pretend I was the same!"

"And it must have been extra hard because you had to do something really bad to infiltrate them, right?" Charlie looked away, but Cyra, close enough to touch him now, reached out and slowly picked up the hand without the gun and held it. "It's OK. I understand. What you're doing is . . . brave. You're going to help find my sister's killer. I don't care what you did. And I can see you're a good person, and it's weighing heavy on you. It's OK, Charlie . . . You can tell me."

Her words seemed to strike a chord with him. He met her eye and sniffed, giving her a watery smile.

At least one of them was a good liar.

"I feel so bad about it," Charlie said, squeezing her hand. "But I knew they'd want proof. So I . . . I went to an area I'd heard about through the grapevine at work. I picked up a . . ."

"Sex worker?" Cyra offered, urging him on, surprised he was telling her this. He really was an idiot. She was also surprised he had lasted for so many months in the group without being caught. Then again, he was clearly unstable, so it wasn't like he had to pretend that much.

"Yeah," Charlie said, lip trembling. "I felt bad, so bad. But it had to be done; I knew I could make a real difference if I got into the group."

"What happened?"

"Well, I had to pick someone who wouldn't be missed, so I took one of those cross-dressers, you know the ones."

Charlie's voice seemed to be coming from far away; Cyra's ears felt clogged and hot at his words. Within her, rage, fresh, molten, bubbled out, spilling over any remnants of Mistletoe she was still carrying inside her. Cyra froze and forced herself to not drop Charlie's hand.

"I gave Python directions to the body," Charlie choked out. "God, it was terrible, I pray for that prostitute every morning. But it worked. I got in."

Cyra clenched her jaw so hard it hurt, then released it, trying to breathe. "Did anyone come looking for her? The sex worker?"

Charlie quirked a brow at her word choice but shook his head. "No, that was the point, to pick someone who wouldn't be missed. I wrapped it up good after Python took a look and took it to a dump. I kept an eye out, but they never found the body. Our dumps are a decent place to hide things you don't want found."

Now Cyra really did drop his hand. Charlie had killed someone. And not just someone. Someone he clearly thought of as disposable, someone he thought wouldn't be missed because of who she was.

Bea might be Cyra's ex, but she still cared about her, and Bea was a trans woman. The asshole standing in front of her would call a woman he killed *"it?"* As if being trans or being a sex worker made someone less than. If he had killed Bea, would he assume she wouldn't be missed too? How dare he. Cyra couldn't forgive what Charlie had done.

In some ways, he was worse than Lamprey. Charlie thought he was a good person. He was justifying what he'd done—killing someone. But he was too stupid and twisted to realize that he'd never get the fame he was looking for. The police would lock him up for more reasons than one, or he'd slip up at a meeting and get himself killed. Cyra was shocked he lasted as long as he did, given how little common sense he appeared to have.

The man who held a gun on her had disappeared entirely. All Cyra could see now was an eager and ignorant little boy who was in way over his head.

Maybe she should pity him. But then she remembered how he talked about the woman he killed and that instinct vanished.

"Now what?" she asked. "Now that we both know the truth about each other?"

Charlie sucked his cheeks in. "It's too dangerous for you to be in that group. I totally understand why you felt you had to join. You want to find your sister's killer, right? Well, let me handle it. I'm already in there, I know these guys, I have their trust. And when my research is complete, and I turn it over to the captain, your sister will get justice."

Cyra almost laughed. Almost.

He was deluded. Maybe this was why Python let him in. There was clearly something not right about Charlie. If he channeled that toward the group, they might very well believe he was one of them.

"And you'll . . . let me go?" It was the only thing she was worried about. Would Charlie try to shut her up now that she knew the truth? She had to play it right. "You wouldn't hurt me, right? You're just doing your job."

"I would never hurt someone on purpose," he said, puffing his chest. "I had to do a bad thing, but I'm not a bad guy."

"That's right."

"But . . . you'll stop coming to group? You won't tell?"

Even his words were stunted like a child's. Asking her if she'd tell on him like they were in the schoolyard. He told her his father and mother both died recently—and he was living in their home, alone. She wondered if those losses shook something loose in his psyche. Perhaps he had regressed mentally.

"I won't say a word, I promise," Cyra assured him. "But be careful, OK?" She knew it was what he'd want to hear.

Charlie nodded solemnly. "Of course. And I'm sorry, you know, for the gun thing. I really thought that was going to end badly for a minute there."

"Would you have killed me?"

"I think I would have had to." Charlie shook his head sadly. "But I'm glad I didn't."

Cyra bared her teeth in a smile. "Me too."

The streets were dark when she met Lamprey in front of the deli.

The cellar doors were closed. The sidewalk was empty, only a few smokers lingered in front of the Chinese food place on the corner; it was too cold for anyone else.

"Well?" Lamprey asked as she walked up. "Find anything? Today was a clusterfuck, I could use a win."

Cyra wanted to hear about what happened after she left the group. If they had decided what to do about Pea Crab, if Python decided to rotate meeting locations. But that could be saved for another day.

She wrestled, momentarily, with her decision on her way home from Cuckoo's earlier. He wasn't a serial killer, but he wasn't normal either. He was broken, clearly, but she had to draw the line somewhere, and she couldn't forget about Bea talking about the forgotten victims from the Netflix special.

Cyra knew about Charlie Guardia's victim. And she wouldn't forget her.

Perhaps doing this made her just as bad as Cuckoo. But Cyra didn't care. There was a rage in her that she hadn't felt in a long time, and she didn't know what else to do with it. She wanted someone to pay for all the victims, all the women, who were disappeared simply because they were deemed less worthy.

"It's Cuckoo," she said, watching as Lamprey's face changed at her words. "His real name is Charlie Guardia. He's a rogue cop. Here's his address."

CHAPTER

17

Cyra called out of work the next day and met Lamprey in Forest Park at three in the afternoon.

A thermos of hot tea was clasped in her hands to warm her as she waited for him on a park bench outside the cluster of trees that led to winding trails and abandoned train tracks in the woods behind her.

"I have to admit, I'm surprised," Lamprey said as he sat down next to her, dressed in his peacoat and a thick blue scarf that brought out his eyes and complimented his sandy hair. He looked so normal, so human.

He made her feel sick.

"You shouldn't be. Charlie is an idiot. I don't know how he didn't accidentally reveal himself to you guys before now." Cyra didn't look at Lamprey as he sat down, bringing her thermos up to her lips and enjoying the puff of heat from the drinking slot warming her nose.

"Not that," Lamprey corrected her. Then he shook his head. "Although you're right. He was an idiot. I had already pinpointed him as the likely leak. He kept using all these textbook terms to describe us. 'Organized, devolving,' all this shit that he'd casually pepper into conversation. He was a bad liar, but I thought maybe he was trying to cover his anonymity. Should have just trusted my instincts. Knew he was off. Didn't think he was a cop, though. That was a fun twist."

Cyra noticed the past tense. "It's . . . taken care of?"

"See, this is what surprises me," Lamprey said instead of answering her question, leaning toward her on the bench, his body facing hers as she resolutely looked away. "I think I misjudged you."

He reached out and took her limp gloved hand in one of his bare ones. Cyra could see the rounds of his knuckles pressing up against the whiteness of his skin like they were trying to break free toward the surface. She didn't pull her hand away, but still didn't face him. The tree line next to her was a thicket of dead branches and old trash. Cyra focused on a plastic bag that was wrapped around the forked arms of a leafless bush.

Lamprey squeezed her hand. "I was wrong. You *are* one of us, kitten. You are, I can sense it. All you need are three bodies to be like me."

The plastic bag wasn't disintegrating—it would be another thousand years before that happened—but the sides of it were shredded as if by claws, and Cyra didn't understand how it had gotten so hopelessly twisted around the park shrubbery. It was like someone had intentionally woven it in between the branches. Why would anyone do that? There was a garbage can ten feet away.

"Kitten?"

"I'm not like you," she finally whispered.

She felt his smile. "They won't find him, if that's what you're concerned about."

The tears in the bag were fluttering frantically in the wind.

Cyra thought again about how someone on the outside would look at the two of them and think they were dating—would assume from their body language that they were having a lover's spat, and Lamprey was trying to cheer her up. The thought churned her stomach.

"I'm tired, Lamprey," she said. "Did you kill my sister?"

He scooted closer to her. "No. I told you."

"And you're a liar who's already misled me multiple times."

"Not about this. I killed a cop for you."

Cyra sucked cold air in through her teeth and lowered the thermos. "You did that for yourself."

She couldn't think about Cuckoo. She didn't want the details. That would make it real—make what she did *real*—and she couldn't handle that. Not now.

Lamprey's hand was tightening, no longer a gentle squeeze but a fierce vice. "I know he did something that pissed you off. You didn't tell me everything, but I know you wouldn't have given me a map right to his doorstep if he hadn't offended you. You told me because you wanted me to get rid of him. And that's fine. But be honest with yourself here, kitten. If I'm the bad guy, so are you."

Cyra tried to yank away her hand, but Lamprey didn't let go, and she quickly stopped, not wanting to excite him by struggling. Instead, she looked away from the plastic bag and faced him for the first time. "You're right. I'm not a good person. But you're the one that needs to earn my trust. The names. Of everyone else in the group. And anything else you know about them. Now."

Lamprey stared at her for a minute, eyes locked on hers, until he finally released her hand and sat back. "Whip is Ernie Martinez. Python is Jackson Carmichael."

"Mockingbird and Sand Fly," Cyra demanded.

"I don't know their names."

"You said you did. You said you knew something more."

"They're not as interesting as me, kitten," Lamprey said, a flicker of a smile playing on his face.

"Jason." His real name was like a thick poison on her lips, but it worked; he blinked and the smile disappeared.

"I don't know his name and I'm not sure how this would help, but I'm pretty sure Sand Fly is impotent," Lamprey said, his voice expressionless now. "He's obsessed with young women and stabbing them, and it doesn't take a shitty cop like Cuckoo to tell you those two things are related."

"What else?"

Lamprey sighed, like she was nagging him to take out the trash. "Based on things he's said before in meetings, my hunch is that he lives north of the city, on the water. A town like Rye or Mamaroneck. He rarely hunts in the actual boroughs."

"Any idea how long he's been at it?"

"A while, I think." Lamprey stroked his chin thoughtfully, staring off over Cyra's head as if quickly getting bored of the conversation. "He likes the well-off girls. The ones from good families with fancy handbags and crap. He finds a new girl to obsess over; follows her, watches her, sometimes engages with her, and then, well, you know. You heard him the other day at the meeting."

Lamprey shot her a grin, watching to see if it would disarm her. When she didn't react, simply asked, "And Mockingbird?" his smile twitched and faded.

"You know about as much as I do. You've seen him in meetings. He's a retired trucker. Rarely shares. But he's been doing this forever. And he's the best at getting rid of bodies because he knows all these back roads in deep forests and places where you can dig a hole and never have to worry about it." He glanced back at her. "But once he slipped up. He wore a cap with a red truck on the front. I thought it was a generic trucker hat, but when he was leaving, there was a last name stitched in red on the back above the closure: 'Walker.' He must have forgotten it was there, otherwise he would have never worn it. Still, haven't made much progress with that. You know how many truckers with the last name Walker there are, kitten?"

"And you?" Cyra's voice was low as she shifted on the bench, placing her thermos down on the slats between them and looking directly at Lamprey's pale face. She saw his lips curling up, and she shook her head. "I kept my end of our deal. I found your rat."

"You got lucky, you stumbled into it," Lamprey murmured, watching her mouth. "I gave him to you on a silver platter. I did all the hard work."

"Tell me."

"Why do you want to know all the dirty details?" Lamprey asked, reaching out toward her again, this time pushing a lock of her dark hair away from her eyes.

"Did you kill my sister?" she asked once more.

"No, kitten, and I won't repeat myself again." An edge had entered Lamprey's voice and Cyra wondered if that meant he was annoyed or defensive because she was getting closer.

"Well, I know you killed Pea Crab."

Lamprey looked delighted. "Oh, I love that trick!" He pulled his hand back and clapped once, looking at her with sparkling eyes. Cyra was sure this move had worked on people, especially straight women, many times before, but all she could see was his mask, pulled back over his true self. "Say an accusation as a statement instead of a question in the hopes I'll say, 'But how did you know?' No, sorry, kitten. Didn't kill him either. Although Mockingbird ran out of that meeting real fast, didn't he?"

"You think he did it?"

Lamprey shrugged. "Wouldn't be surprised. After Cuckoo and you left, Python said he wouldn't cancel the next meeting, but he was 'investigating' Pea's death. Like he's a PI or something. What a joke."

"There's still going to be a meeting next week?" Cyra was surprised. The group seemed like it had splintered completely. Cuckoo and Pea Crab were gone, Mockingbird could be halfway to Canada by now, and the rest of them were clearly on high alert. "If they realize Cuckoo is dead too, they're going to think someone is picking them off."

Lamprey gave her a curious look, but only said, "They won't know about Cuckoo. I don't take photos like whoever it was who killed Pea. They'll assume he got spooked and decided to stop coming. I'm sure Mockingbird won't show up either. We'll have to change meeting locations." He cleared his throat. "You're right, though, kitten. You helped me. And I promised if you did, I'd help you."

Cyra sat up straighter, feeling the comforting weight of the switchblade in her front pocket. "What are you saying?"

Lamprey slung one arm on the back of the bench, looking casual and handsome and empty of a conscience. "If you want, I can hack into your sister's devices."

Cyra's body separated, briefly, from her mind. She was flung up into the sky like a bottle rocket, peaking, and then tumbling back down to slam into her own skin again.

The police were able to access Mira's phone records, but they hadn't been able to get into her actual cell phone. No one, including Cyra, knew Mira's passcode. The cops were working to get override access from the cell phone company, but that could take a while. Since nothing unusual had shown up on Mira's phone records, the cops weren't pushing it all too hard, probably focusing on the serial killer angle instead. But Mira's phone was recovered with her body, so the police were keeping it in evidence. Her laptop, on the other hand, also locked, was left at her apartment in Dumbo and was therefore apparently deemed unimportant to the investigation, since Mira was staying in Park Slope with Eli and Izzie at the time of her death. Bellows consented to release the laptop to Cyra's possession after their cursory inspection of it went nowhere.

Cyra chewed her bottom lip, considering Lamprey's offer. Serial killers were hard to catch because their kills were so random. The chance of one of her three suspects making contact with Mira was incredibly low, especially if it was Lamprey. Why would he offer to do this if there was incriminating evidence of him to be found? On the other hand, Mira was on and off the dating apps—maybe Mira met someone there and moved their correspondence to text or email.

"Mira's phone is still in evidence at the police station," Cyra explained. "But I have her laptop. They couldn't get into it."

"If you can't get me physical access, I can't help with the phone," Lamprey said, and Cyra's heart sank. "But you get me the computer, and I can break into it, no problem."

"I–I'll have to think about it." She didn't know how she felt about Lamprey having access to her sister's inner world. It felt wrong to have someone like him going through Mira's virtual belongings. After all, Mira's laptop and phone were linked via the Cloud, so most of Mira's texts would be on the laptop too.

But she couldn't be sentimental if she was going to find out the truth.

"At the next meeting," Lamprey offered. "If you agree, bring the laptop and wear something red so I know to double back after and get it from you." He grinned, teeth like tombstones.

"Do you think Python will have the meeting in a different place? What if it's not as accessible as the rec center?"

"Don't worry," Lamprey said. "We haven't switched meeting spots since I joined, but Python apparently picks places that are quiet and insulated. It shouldn't be an issue."

"Fine, I'll think about it," Cyra said again. "I've got to go."

She left Lamprey alone on the bench, no longer concerned about him trailing her. He was right, in a way.

She was a bad guy now, too.

MOCKINGBIRD

Vic Walker always wondered what he would do if someone came into the rest stop bathroom while he was drowning a victim.

He liked to imagine himself moving swiftly, pinning the intruder to the wall by their neck and then finishing both unlucky people off at the same time. But logically he thought it would be a bit messier than that. It took a surprising amount of strength to drown someone in a toilet bowl, and that was Vic's nonnegotiable. He could have all the fun he wanted with his victims, but they could not die unless he had his hand on the nape of their neck, pressing their faces into the cracked porcelain, letting the water lap against his hand as they thrashed.

Regardless, he had been at this for almost a decade and not a single person had ever interrupted him. Maybe it was because he killed late at night, at the most remote, grimiest rest stops. Maybe it was because something was looking out for him. Vic wasn't religious, but he had to admit that he was luckier than most people. Maybe there was a reason for that.

The hitchhiker he had picked up earlier looked to be around twenty and was female. Vic didn't really care about gender either way. He'd pick someone based on their eyes, not what was between their legs. Vic liked expressive, large eyes. Ones that would widen and become bloodshot and terrified when they realized what was happening. That was the part he liked the most about his victims.

Victims.

He liked calling them that because it played on his own name. Victor and His Victims. Sounded like a punk rock band.

Vic took a certain amount of pride in knowing what he was and why he did what he did. He had read all the serial killer books; he had sifted through all the internet threads when they started to become a thing, and he'd learned how to use a laptop. He liked that he didn't fit into any patterns. He liked that he changed up who he picked and how often he killed. He liked that he hadn't been abused or experienced any childhood trauma. Vic had grown up in Kunkle, Indiana with a loving family and no worries in the world, and he had started pulling the legs off insects when he was three.

He was meant to be this way, simple as that.

"Please," the hitchhiker begged from the sleeper cab behind him. She must have worked the gag free. How annoying. Vic didn't feel like stopping to fix it, though. Besides, he was only four hours from one of his favorite rest stops. "Please just let me go."

Vic turned up the radio. Patsy Cline was on. He sang along, his voice rumbling in harmony with the engine.

The road stretched out ahead of him, headlights from the truck he was driving cross-country cutting through the darkness and bleeding away the night.

Soft sobbing came from behind him, and Vic tried to ignore his irritation. He had this one for a day or two now and he was already getting tired of her. She had huge blue eyes, which was what made him stop for her to begin with. But he wasn't getting the reaction he wanted. The hitchhiker's eyes would dim like a dying flare. It was like she would go somewhere else, which took all the fun out of it.

Oh, well. Not everyone could be a winner.

The hitchhiker finally fell asleep, or else entered some blissfully quiet catatonic state, and Vic drifted off into the music for the next four hours until he finally reached the rest stop. There were certain places that held special significance for Vic. He wasn't sure why—he just liked the feel of them. He often picked dump sites near wooded areas because they were easy, and once his victims were dead, they didn't matter, but the rest stops were important. The last time he'd been to this one was in 2002 and it had gone spectacularly well. Even though this girl was a dud, he felt certain that her final performance would be worth it.

Vic hopped into the sleeper cab and grabbed the girl, who was limp and unconscious. Her wrists and ankles were bound, but he liked to cut the ties at this point. It was like drowning a kitten if they were still trussed up, boring and slightly pathetic.

"Wake up." Vic used his pocketknife to slice through the rope and shook the girl's shoulders roughly, but she didn't move. This happened sometimes. They'd pass out from fear, exhaustion, pain. She'd wake up once he got her into the warmth and light and tossed some water on her face. Vic grunted in displeasure and lifted the hitchhiker into a fireman's carry, exiting the truck, his heavy boots clomping across the empty parking lot.

The rest stop was small and half the safety lights were broken. It was close to 3:00 AM, normal trucker hours, but Vic's fourteen-wheeler was the only one there. The air tasted like snow and asphalt. He could smell the bathrooms from halfway across the lot. He wondered about the last time they were cleaned and chose the women's—probably less disgusting and even less of a chance of them getting interrupted. Not many female truckers or travelers who would brave a spot like this at this time of night.

He dumped the girl on the filthy floor, hoping the fall would jar her awake, but her eyes remained closed.

Scoffing, Vic turned and selected the stall he'd used, kicking in the door so that it ricocheted off the stall's wall and bounced back, the whole line of toilets rattling with the sound. If that didn't wake her, he didn't know what would.

"Rise and shine," Vic announced, turning back around just in time to see the bathroom door gently drift shut with a soft clunk.

The floor was empty. The girl was gone.

"Fuck!"

Vic sprinted from the bathroom and burst back outside. The hitchhiker was racing across the lot, screaming at the top of her lungs even though there was no one around for miles.

This didn't happen.

Not to Vic.

He didn't lose control; he didn't lose victims. Not ever. How had that bitch played dead so well? He raced after her—she would never make it. She'd been without real food for days. She was living off sips of Gatorade and the beef jerky Vic didn't want. Her legs were spindly, and her body was not how it used to be. There would be no daring escape for her. And while Vic liked a little fight, this was too much. He would make the drowning slow, a final lesson to her to never cross him.

But the hitchhiker ran anyway, moving like a shot deer that doesn't know it's already dead. Would she try to get back into the truck and drive off? Vic had left the keys in the cab, but surely, he could catch up with her before she got there.

But the girl didn't head for the truck. She swerved off the lot and tore toward the safety railing that separated the rest stop from a chewed-up drop-off.

"Nothing over there for you, little girl," Vic yelled as he sped up, getting closer and closer to her now. He was starting to enjoy himself. She glanced over her shoulder, saw how close he was to her, and finally, *finally*, her big blue eyes widened in the panic he was looking for. Maybe he would incorporate this little game in future kills. It made him feel like a powerful lion, out on a hunt.

The hitchhiker reached the thick metal safety railing and flung herself over it, stumbling toward the edge of the drop-off, the inkiness of the bottom of the ravine below swallowing any light from the parking lot.

"Don't you do it!" Vic shouted, suddenly realizing she might jump. The drop wasn't very high, only about twenty feet, so she might not die if she leaped off it, but he would be pissed if she broke her neck before he could get to her.

Vic hopped the rail with ease and reached for her, only a few feet away, already feeling her hair in his hand as he pushed her head under water. She was steps from the drop-off edge, but she had turned to watch him jump over the safety guard, now motionless.

As he grabbed for her, at the very last second, she twisted.

Her lithe frame ducked and swerved, Vic's hand passing by her harmlessly as he growled in frustration. "You little—"

She pivoted, much, much faster than she had been moving minutes earlier, and while Vic was unbalanced, she swung around behind him, put both hands on his back, and shoved.

Momentum and gravity worked together; there was nothing Vic could do to stop it. He toppled forward off the drop-off edge, managing to turn his body so that at least he wasn't falling head-first, plummeting down to the dark ground below.

Something in his leg snapped on impact and a bright blistering pain shot through his entire body as Vic screamed in rage. He couldn't see much down in the ravine; he was on his back now, one leg burning, the other twisted up under it. There were halos of artificial light backlighting the top of the drop-off, the edge from which he'd fallen, and Vic watched the shape of the hitchhiker stare down in the blackness for a moment before moving away.

He wasn't dead, and his back wasn't broken. But his leg sure was, and it took Vic three hours to find a way out of the ravine in the pitch black, using the rest stop lights as a guide. By the time he limped and dragged himself back to the parking lot, he was exhausted. His truck was still there, which was good. But the girl was gone. No sign of her.

Gritting his teeth, letting his anger fuel him back into the driver's seat, Vic wondered if she had headed back down the road toward the highway. Or if she had disappeared into the woods, panicked and terrified, to die of exposure. It wasn't like she had a coat. But what she did have was three hours head start, and she clearly hadn't been as weak or oblivious as she had made him think she was. She somehow noticed the drop-off from the truck even while feigning unconsciousness and had wriggled from his grasp right when she had him where she wanted him near the edge.

Vic had to admit she was gone. He wasn't going to find her, and his priority now was to get to a different town, far from here, fix his leg, and hope that she would freeze to death. He wasn't much worried about her being able to identify him, but he needed to get as far from here as possible.

As he drove, the pain sending flashes of white across his vision, Vic thought about what his father had told him when he didn't make the softball team in middle school.

"It's OK, Victor," his father said, taking him for ice cream when he saw how upset his son was. "It's OK to fail. You know why? Because it's always a lesson. There's always something good you can take away from a failure. And then it stops being a failure at all, you see? Because now you know how to do it right the next time."

Vic took great comfort in killing his father and burying him in the woods before he left home at age eighteen, but his words were even more comforting now.

The hitchhiker might have gotten away from him, but he would never let anything like this ever happen again.

Vic would do it right next time.

CHAPTER

18

Cyra was lying on her back on her apartment floor, staring up at the ceiling, replaying her conversation with Lamprey.

She was struggling with the understanding that if she survived this self-imposed mission, she'd never be the same person.

She'd always known that, in a way. Bea probably noticed it too—the transformation Cyra had been edging toward, shedding everything about her old life as she committed to this one thing, her humanity be damned. Looking back, Cyra was happy Bea got out when she did. Cyra probably wouldn't have had the strength to end things herself, and there was no way sweet and playful Bea would have been able to understand how deep Cyra had gotten. How easily she opened the door to her own darkness, a pulsing throbbing thing that was spreading its roots inside her—admitting that it was comforting to embrace Mistletoe because she echoed the natural emptiness that yawned inside Cyra too. After spending her whole life forcing emotions for other people, it was a relief to unlock the parts of herself she denied for so long, to accept the ease of navigating as someone charming and cold, shaped by steel and broken rocks.

"I don't want to police anyone's grief," Bea had told Cyra a month after Mira's death. "But if you need to cry, babe, you should. Don't hide from it."

"I'll try harder to be sad," Cyra tried to tease her. But her words fell flat and wilted away.

"No, that's not what I'm saying at all," Bea had said quickly. "I just don't want you to numb yourself from this pain."

And in a rare moment of honesty, Cyra had decided to open up a little. "Sometimes I feel like I am carrying around this little chestnut of pain. And I've been carrying it for a long time, basically since I was a kid and my mom left. And every time something bad happens, I stuff it inside this chestnut and bury it in the soil. People talk about how if you bury feelings, they'll explode later, but that doesn't happen with me. My buried things die and become nothing. I feel nothing because if it hurts, I get rid of it."

Bea stared at her a moment, and then enveloped her in a hug. The two of them had sat on the tiny futon in the studio, tucked into each other's arms for a long time.

But even that burst of sincerity wasn't enough to keep Bea.

It was for the best. The person she was becoming now, the amount of time she was letting Mistletoe out, bleeding over into her real life like poorly painted watercolor strokes, was not someone Bea would have liked. She would have called it what it was—a way to self-destruct without drinking or suicide; a way for Cyra to punish herself for what happened to Mira.

The decision she'd made—betraying Charlie to Lamprey—was not one that could be undone. Cyra had one goal for infiltrating the support group. Charlie wasn't it. There was a line drawn, thick and clear, in the sand. Cyra had looked at it, then looked at Charlie Guardia, and decided to step right over it.

Cyra knew she should feel some version of guilt or regret over her actions since joining the group. But she didn't. There was a strange shift happening, as if she was the one pretending and Mistletoe was the real person.

I don't feel guilty because I did all of it for a reason. To help Mira. I don't have the time and space to mourn all their individual victims like Bea would, but if I can destroy a few of these men on my way to Mira's killer, that's the best way I can honor the people they killed.

Cyra needed to believe that.

Mira once told Cyra that after seven years, you become an entirely new collection of cells. Mira had thought the idea so beautiful—that your entire cellular body could become new, constantly replicating and reproducing so that you were essentially a new human every seven years. But when Cyra had looked it up, curious, she didn't have the heart to tell her sister it was a myth. In reality, some cells, like those in the skin, could be replaced in only a matter of months, while others, such as certain neurons in the brain, stayed the same your whole life.

People can try to change, they can hope to evolve and become better, but there are some parts of them that will always remain the same.

Cyra rolled off her back, stars flooding her eyes at the sudden movement, and crawled over to the bed. She groped underneath the bed skirt and pulled out a plastic container. Just like the shoebox in her hall closet, this bin wasn't labeled; she would always know what was in there. Cyra popped the top off and reached inside, pulling out Mira's sleek silver laptop.

She didn't want to give it to Lamprey. She didn't trust him. But she also needed to know, needed to see what was on it if there was any chance it could help her. Skin crawling at the thought of Lamprey's hands where Mira's used to be, Cyra pulled the laptop close and whispered, "I'm sorry, Mira."

Eli and Izzie tried to see her again that weekend, but she brushed them off, saying she had to work. Cyra had initially toyed with the idea of asking Eli if he knew Charlie but decided against it.

Just because they worked in the same building didn't mean they'd ever seen each other, and when people inevitably noticed Charlie was missing, she didn't want anything to be traced back to her. Or Eli.

The night before the next meeting, Cyra logged into the dark web address and pulled up the chatbox. It had become second nature at this point, and her pulse was steady as she messaged Python.

Confirming attendance for tomorrow, she typed. *If we're still on? I left early last time. Seemed like it was getting hairy in there.*

The message blinked on the white screen for a few minutes before the reply finally came: *We're still on. 1 PM. We have things to discuss. Here are the new coordinates.*

They were changing locations after all. Cyra wondered if that meant Python figured out who offed Pea Crab and wasn't telling that person the new meeting spot.

Looking up the location, Cyra groaned to see it was deep in the Bronx. It would take her forever to get there, but her irritation was dampened a little when she clicked the street view and saw the building's exterior. A church.

She started to laugh. How perfect. A group of the biggest sinners to ever sin meeting in a church to discuss murder. Python must have a twisted sense of humor.

The next day, Cyra dressed in her Mistletoe outfit in her apartment, remembering Lamprey's instructions to wear something red if she agreed to him hacking Mira's laptop. She carefully pulled on thick stockings, a dark skirt, and a starchy white blouse. Cyra adjusted her blonde wig and placed a crimson headband on top of it, watching her reflection carefully in the bathroom mirror. She thought about how much effort it used to take to become Mistletoe. Now, deepening her breathing, squeezing her fists, Cyra closed her eyes, picturing Mira's prone body in the park, and when she opened her eyes and met her gaze in the mirror, she was looking at Mistletoe.

Cyra dropped the switchblade in the pocket of the skirt, which she bought for a Mistletoe outfit specifically because it had pockets, stuck Mira's laptop in her bag, and slipped out the door.

She was betraying Mira again, but hopefully this time it would be worth it.

CHAPTER

19

The church, as it turned out, was in disuse, like the rec center. It took up half a block in Kingsbridge Heights, a residential area. The streets were calm and quiet when Cyra arrived. The church looked different from the street view image, which must have been from a few years back.

Scaffolding and a construction fence circled part of the church, but Cyra found an opening easily enough and slipped in, noting that, despite being under construction, there was no one around. There were porta-potties and some two-by-fours stacked against the eastern side of the building, but the site was empty despite it being the middle of a weekday.

The huge front doors were unlocked, and Cyra stepped cautiously into the vestibule, spotting Python right away. He was standing on the marbled floor in front of two double doors with glass windows that led to the pews and pulpit, visible through the panes behind him.

"We're going down that way," he explained, pointing to a door off to the side of the vestibule. "Church basement."

"You sure like basements, don't you?"

"They used to use it for AA meetings and family gatherings," Python replied, looking tired and tense. "It works for our purposes."

"How do you find these places?" Cyra asked, glancing behind him and examining the lines of pews and the dark altar. Sunlight poured in through the stained-glass windows, leaving puddles of color on the white floor. With no one around, smelling of dust and old wax, the church felt eerie and haunted.

"I know people. I hear things. This place fell on hard times. Needed renovations, but then the construction company went under halfway through. They haven't been able to continue yet. It's unused, for now. It'll work in the short term." He added, "I was waiting for everyone up here so no one got lost. We better head down. You're the last one."

She followed him to the left of the vestibule, the two of them clomping down creaky stairs that spit them out onto a landing leading to a wide, empty space. It was much larger than the rec center basement, but there were no egress windows here, just watery yellow lighting from overheads. There was no snack table either. A line of stacked folding chairs rested against one wall, untouched. The carpet was worn and blue, and leaning against the walls of the room were the Stations of the Cross. They were all out of order; the one closest to them depicted Jesus dying on the cross, but the one a few feet away from it portrayed Jesus meeting Mary. The church must have moved the gilded portraits down here during the start of the renovations, which was why they weren't hung. It gave the room an odd, disjointed look.

The whole space smelled strongly of sawdust, and cobwebs gathered in the corners.

The others were waiting for them, standing aimlessly near the center of the room. Cyra was shocked to see Mockingbird.

There were only five of them left now.

"Cuckoo's not coming, I guess," Whipworm said, peering behind Cyra.

"No," Python replied. "That's one of the reasons we moved. I didn't receive a check-in from him last night. He's out."

"I almost didn't come back myself," Lamprey said, glancing at Cyra's red headband, the ghost of a smile on his lips. "Do we know what the hell is going on, or is it pretty clear to anyone else now that Cuckoo was the one who offed Pea?"

"We don't know that," Python said. He looked drawn, deflated somehow, despite his size. Like someone had punctured a Macy's Thanksgiving parade balloon and it was slowly collapsing in on itself. "I'll be honest, I don't think this here group continues after today."

"We're splintering," Whipworm agreed, and Python gave him a grateful, tender look that he immediately replaced with a scowl when he noticed Cyra watching.

Lamprey was staring again at Cyra, giving her a knowing look. She remembered what he said weeks ago about Python having all bark and no bite. He wasn't qualified to be moderating this group—he was an ex-con trying to wrangle a bunch of serial killers. He couldn't find Pea Crab's killer any more than she could.

But Cyra couldn't have the group disband. Not before she got what she came for.

"I don't know about anyone else, but I need this group. I need these meetings," she said, as five other heads turned toward her. Sand Fly was unnervingly quiet, dark eyes boring into her chest. "Out there, I have to be someone else. Someone soft and sweet and stupid. I have to dumb myself, my true self, down because society can't handle who I am at my best. I know I'm new, but these meetings have been a breath of fresh air. I don't have to pretend. I can be myself and know I won't be judged for it. I'd like to continue."

"Well said," Lamprey murmured loud enough for everyone to hear, a hint of sarcasm in his voice as he looked at Cyra.

Sand Fly's eyes flicked between Lamprey and Cyra, a shadow crossing his expression before he cleared his throat. "We were fine before you joined. Maybe it's you. Maybe you killed Pea Crab."

"Oh, come on," Cyra said sweetly. "We both know you don't believe I'm capable of that. I'm a girl, right? I don't make messes."

Sand Fly's face darkened further, but Python interrupted their standoff. "It's real nice of you to share your feelings, Mistletoe, but it doesn't change the fact that this shit is falling apart."

"Then fix it." This came from Mockingbird, standing the farthest away from the group and the closest to the stairwell.

The room turned toward him, immediately magnetized by the rarity of his voice.

"How?" demanded Whipworm, stepping forward and angling himself so that he was standing in front of Python, almost protectively.

"This is why you're here, isn't it? You're supposed to be the neutral party who will kill anyone who breaks the rules," Mockingbird said, addressing Python.

"I am," Python replied, swiping Whipworm away and crossing the room to come face-to-face with Mockingbird. "I've been looking into it. But if you want to confess to killing Pea, that would make my life a lot easier. I could handle your ass right here, right now."

For the first time in the month she'd known him, Cyra saw Mockingbird smile. She thought Lamprey's grins were unnerving; they had nothing on Mockingbird. He was missing one of his upper canines and his teeth were stained a gradient yellow, probably from smoking. She had caught whiffs of cigarettes the few times she had passed near him. But it wasn't just that his mouth was unappealing—his smile was one that made you remember that teeth are bones jutting from our heads, there to rip and chew.

"I wouldn't still be here if I killed him," Mockingbird said. "Now get the fuck out of my face."

"Hey, let's all calm down," Whipworm said, scurrying forward and pulling Python away from Mockingbird. "Let's have our meeting today and—"

"I don't think so," Python said, his jaw clenched as he stared at Mockingbird with naked aggression. "Better to give us all some time to go home and think."

"OK, how about this?" Whipworm offered frantically, and Cyra focused on him as he pushed away Python and stood between him and Mockingbird. "Let's do something different. Let's agree to meet here on Saturday night. Six o'clock. And we could make a deal. Pea Crab's killer doesn't come. He," Whipworm glanced at Cyra, "Or she, would agree to never come back to the group. Disappear. We wouldn't be able to find you. This is a free pass. You did it, you can leave. We won't kill you. You don't want to be here anymore, you can leave, too. OK?" His voice was pitched slightly higher than usual, and Cyra was able to read his tone, see the truth in his hopeful eyes.

"A hall pass," Python said in his low voice, looking at Whipworm thoughtfully. "Maybe . . ."

Cyra wondered if it was as obvious to everyone else what she had finally realized.

"And if we all show up?" Lamprey asked.

Whipworm sucked in his cheeks. "Then we have an answer. Cuckoo was the one who did it."

She hid a disbelieving smirk with her hand. Cuckoo was dead, but his absence from the group didn't absolve anyone else even if they didn't know that. Whipworm was essentially suggesting a scapegoat.

She felt the rest of the group absorb Whipworm's words, betting that most of them were coming to the same understanding she had. Lamprey in particular caught her eye and gave her a wink.

Sand Fly scoffed. "I think—"

"Yeah," Python interrupted, fixing Sand Fly with a threatening look. The other man reluctantly closed his mouth, anger simmering on his face. "Yeah, I think that would be acceptable. That's the new plan."

That cemented it: Whipworm had killed Pea Crab, and Python knew it. She suspected Whipworm did it to protect the group, wanting to eliminate the person who was most likely to get caught and spill the beans, but he didn't think it through. He took that photo for whatever reason, and now he was putting Python in an awkward position. Cyra wondered if Whipworm told Python he'd killed the other man or if Python just knew.

"Fine," Mockingbird grunted.

"Works for me," Lamprey said.

Sand Fly and Cyra nodded their assent, but an ephemeral plan was starting to coalesce in her mind. A way to take care of a problem. It meant she needed to get what she wanted before Saturday. A tight timeline but potentially doable.

"No point in continuing today, then," Python said. "Go on. Ten-minute increments. I'm still watching."

CHAPTER

20

Cyra left first, darting into one of the porta-potties outside the church, which was thankfully not as horrible as it could have been, waiting for half an hour, giving the others time to clear out and Lamprey time to double back.

She glanced at herself in the little square mirror affixed to the plastic wall of the portable bathroom. Her cheeks were sunken and there were half shadows under her eyes. Cyra couldn't remember the last time she ate a full, hot meal. She'd been stuffing peanut butter and jelly sandwiches into her mouth for the past week. Her body was something she had to fill up like gas in a car. Food wasn't for pleasure or taste anymore; it was to keep her from passing out on the street.

She turned away from her sallow face and pushed outside, reentering the empty church basement. Cyra pulled one of the folding chairs away from the stack leaning against the wall and opened it, placing it in the center of the room. She took off her coat and arranged it on the back of the chair. Dipping a hand into her bag, she withdrew Mira's laptop and placed it gently on the seat.

A sound from behind made her turn.

"I brought—" she started to say, but cut herself off when she saw who was standing near the stairwell.

She expected Lamprey's broad figure, but instead Sand Fly's angular, sharp body stepped forward, approaching her slowly.

Something cold and slimy poured down Cyra's spine, pooling in the base of her stomach as the taller man crept toward her, making steady movements like he was trying to approach a skittish cat.

"I knew it," Sand Fly whispered.

"What are you doing here?" Cyra asked, desperately trying to bring back Mistletoe's bravado and composure. But for the first time, Cyra couldn't get a good grasp on her, couldn't slip the mask on over her own face.

It wasn't a game anymore. This was real.

"I came back to see if I was right. And I was. Something is going on with you," Sand Fly hissed. "You and Lamprey, right? That's bullshit, Mistletoe. Of all the men in this group, you pick him? Such a cliché. I hate assholes like him. Think they're so great, God's gift to women. But no fraternizing within the group, it's not allowed!" Sand Fly let out a little yelp of laughter that cut through Cyra's bones. "This will be fun. I'm going to like taking something away from him."

"Fuck," Cyra spat. She didn't have time to get the switchblade out from her skirt pocket; Sand Fly launched himself toward her, head down, clearly intending to body slam her into the ground.

But Cyra trained for this. She hopped into her fighting stance, bending her knees, bracing for impact. When he hit her, forehead bashing into her sternum, Cyra executed a sprawl, shooting her legs out behind her, allowing her weight to collapse forward on to Sand Fly's head. With an opponent of average height, this move would have allowed her to get the advantage, maybe even takedown and headlock him. But Sand Fly was much taller than Cyra, and when he felt the sudden heaviness of her chest on top of him, he was able to wiggle free, sending her stumbling to one knee as he overcorrected.

Everything looked both high-definition and blurry at the same time, like she was in a super-stylized video game.

Cyra rolled away once she hit the ground and yanked her switchblade from her pocket, flipping open the knife with one swift, practiced movement, holding it in a tight sideways grip before lunging forward and slashing at Sand Fly's face.

Sand Fly twisted away, avoiding her reach, and paused at the zenith of his movement to assess her as she stepped away, back in her fighting stance. Then he smiled. "Got some training, huh? That's cute, but that won't cut it here."

He dove forward, one hand headed straight for her right arm to restrain and disarm her.

It happened so fast. Cyra's left fist shot out, knocking aside Sand Fly's, and then her blade moved almost on its own, jabbing up rapidly as if she was doing an uppercut punch, sliding into the soft jelly of the man's right eye.

Sand Fly screamed, and Cyra shushed him, automatically, as if he was disturbing the peace in a library.

Cyra wrenched her hand back, Sand Fly's eye squelching as she pulled the blade from it.

"You fucking bitch!" he screeched as she scooted away from him, trying to get her bearings.

Sand Fly was writhing on the ground between her and the door. The knife hung loosely in her hand. She didn't want to get a closer look at the smears of Sand Fly that were painting the blade. Cyra should finish him off now, before it was too late.

But she couldn't. Not yet. Not without knowing. "Did you murder a girl in Prospect Park in September?"

Sand Fly slapped one of his hands over his bleeding eye, groaning as he struggled to sit up. "I'm going to take it real slow with you," he panted, rising to his feet. His one good eye was weeping and bulging with rage.

"Did you murder a girl in Prospect Park in September?" Cyra repeated. Even she could hear how hysterical she sounded, her pitch high and frantic.

Red oozing from the fingers clamped against his right eye, Sand Fly lifted the edge of his black bomber jacket and revealed a sheath against his flat, pale stomach, swiftly removing an ugly serrated knife with his free hand.

Cyra hesitated. He could be the man she was looking for. And he was wounded. But on the other hand, she'd brought a thumbtack to a knife fight with a man whose joy in life was stabbing young women. And Cyra couldn't avenge Mira if she was dead.

She flung herself toward the right, hoping to use Sand Fly's now-blind spot to get around him to the staircase. The room was large enough that if she was fast, she could avoid him completely.

Sand Fly roared and twisted, anticipating her move. She skirted him, staying on his injured side, and threw herself toward the stairs. Cyra felt him behind her, breathing heavily, getting closer, and he was taller, longer, faster than her and her short legs . . .

"Bitch!" he screamed again, and something hot sliced down her back.

The exit was close, so close, but there was a wetness trickling down Cyra's spine.

Then footsteps clattered down the stairs and Cyra shrieked, veering toward the right, nearly crashing into the wall as she narrowly avoided the new figure running into the room: Lamprey.

He moved fast. So fast. He was like liquid mercury, slipping to the side and pivoting, letting Sand Fly skid by him and stumble to a stop on the stairs' landing.

Lamprey took in the scene: Cyra pressed against the wall, switchblade dripping, eyes huge; Sand Fly at the stairs, injured eye leaking, vicious hunting knife streaked with a brushstroke of red.

Is that mine? Cyra thought, looking at the blood on Sand Fly's blade as her back started to sting and prickle.

A terrible thought came as Lamprey's gaze ricocheted between the two of them and their two knives. There were two serial killers. One Cyra. If they decided to team up, she would have no chance in hell of escaping. She would die here in this church basement, probably painfully and slowly. Her hand trembled.

"Jason," she said, as his gaze skimmed her face. She was worried all her composure was gone, that he would see her fear and love it.

He didn't respond; time paused, the three of them in a strange lopsided triangle with Sand Fly blocking the exit and bleeding through his fingers.

Then the spell broke.

"She's mine!" Sand Fly snarled, locking his one good eye on Lamprey.

"I don't think so," Lamprey replied, and there was no mirth on his face now, no hint of a smirk in his voice. His face was bare, and his eyes were blue pits of nothing. His pretty façade was gone. All that was left was the ugly emptiness of his true self.

This was the real Jason Weston. The psychopath. The serial killer.

Sand Fly charged him.

Cyra and Mira once watched a nature documentary about walruses. Cyra remembered the fight between two males the camera crew had captured; there was no finesse in that brutal battle between the two walruses vying for a spot as the beach's alpha male. It was pure violence—a smashing of bodies together, a clash of tusks and ignorance of flayed skin. Mira had cried when the larger walrus gored his competitor, slouching away to his harem, leaving the other male's body raw and pockmarked in the sand. Cyra had tried to explain to her that it was nature; they didn't think about right or wrong, it was about survival.

Watching Lamprey dispatch Sand Fly felt like watching that documentary again, except this time Cyra could hear the thwacks of skin, feel the heat from the warring bodies, see in gritty detail the fight between two males who thought they owned other people.

It was over fast.

Sand Fly's hunting knife was suddenly in Lamprey's hand, then tossed to the side as Lamprey's fingers fastened around the angular man's throat as he writhed and bucked underneath him.

"Wait!" Cyra cried out, as Sand Fly's movements slowed, his hands reaching toward Lamprey's face as if moving through syrup. "Wait, fuck. Did you kill her?" Cyra raced over to the two men, forgetting her stinging back, forgetting the danger. She dropped down to her knees beside Lamprey and shook Sand Fly's shoulder, getting his blood on her hands. "Mira Griffin. The blonde girl in Prospect Park. Did you kill her?!"

But it was too late.

Sand Fly's hands flopped down to frame his ruined face, his right eye a bloody hole, his left staring up at the ceiling, unseeing.

"Why did you do that!" Cyra shrieked, pummeling Lamprey's muscled arms as he unlocked his fingers from around Sand Fly's bruised neck. "It could have been him! I needed to know!"

Lamprey turned, quick as a viper, seizing her wrists and shooting to his feet, dragging her upwards with him. "Thanks for sticking him in the eye. Made it a lot faster. Though, really, he wouldn't have been a match for me on his best day. He's like a stick insect. What was he thinking? I've got eighty pounds on him. The idiot."

"It could have been him!" Cyra's switchblade was somehow on the floor now. Her back was itchy, something wet was sticking against the inside of her lovely blouse. Her arms hung loosely in Lamprey's fierce grip, and nothing felt real.

He would kill her now, and she'd never know who took Mira away from her.

"He got you? Hey. *Hey. Cyra*, pay attention, you can't check out right now."

"What?" Cyra looked up at Lamprey's square face as if she had forgotten he was there.

"His knife. It was bloody. He got you?"

"My . . . back, I think."

"You calm yet?" Lamprey asked, shaking her arms.

Cyra gave a listless nod, and he dropped her wrists, putting a hand on her shoulder and spinning her around to see her back. She barely flinched when he lifted her collar and peered down inside the back of her shirt to survey the damage.

"You'll be fine," Lamprey declared, dropping the collar and stepping away from her. "It's just a bad scratch. Clean it when you get home and cover it in gauze. You got lucky. Don't even need stitches."

Cyra didn't care. How could he care? *Why* did he care?

His words sunk in.

"You're not murdering me."

Lamprey raised an eyebrow. "Would you like me to?"

Having him protect her was almost worse than him trying to attack her. It made no sense, so it could only signal something dangerous. Something he wanted from her. Cyra looked down at Sand Fly's crumpled body. "He didn't answer me. I don't know if he killed Mira."

Lamprey shrugged. "Sorry, but it had to be done. Process of elimination, right? If Mockingbird turns out not to be who you're looking for, it was probably Sand Fly. Case solved."

"Or you," Cyra said absently.

"Still a suspect even after I saved your life? Some thanks I get," Lamprey said, his usual sardonic tone creeping back into his voice.

Cyra couldn't think about that. Couldn't accept that she might not be standing here breathing if Lamprey hadn't showed up. "Why did you do that?"

"I owed you," Lamprey replied immediately. "I like to square up my debts. You helped me, you stuck to your word. I'll stick to mine. Now, I came back for that laptop. Are we still doing this, or what?"

Cyra had completely forgotten about the laptop, but now she looked over at the chair that had miraculously remained upright despite the struggle. Mira's laptop was still sitting indignantly in the middle of it, framed by Cyra's coat on the back of the chair, waiting for them to stop fucking around and get to business.

Lamprey followed her eyes and walked over, eyeing it. "I'll need to take it home to jailbreak it, you understand that, right? I need my software."

Cyra had been afraid of that, worried about what Lamprey might do or see without her there to monitor him. It wasn't like she could go to his home. That was too reckless, even for her. But the concern she felt hours earlier was gone now, as if she couldn't summon up the energy to care.

"You should go," Lamprey said softly. "I have to deal with this. It might take a while."

The idea of leaving Mira's laptop with him felt like leaving Mira alone with him. She would have never allowed that in real life. But she didn't have a choice. And Cyra didn't like how she was feeling—raw, exposed, emotional. She needed to regroup and recalibrate. She wasn't a stranger to violence, but having someone brutally attack her, and then watching them be ruthlessly murdered right in front of her eyes shook her more than she cared to admit.

Cyra nodded. "How long?"

"The laptop? I'm not sure. A few days, maybe. I can get a burner phone, message you when it's done."

"Hurry. Please."

"I'll do my best," Lamprey promised.

"And . . . you . . . you have my phone number." It wasn't a question. Cyra was tired, so tired, of feeling ten steps behind Lamprey. He saved her life, but there had to be a reason. He was playing her, she knew it. There was always something up his sleeve he wasn't showing her. He was dangerous, and she needed to take care of it. She didn't trust him. Not for a second.

Lamprey smiled, pretending to be bashful, but dropped the act when Cyra didn't react. "You want me to do this or not?"

Cyra thought of Mira and what she would think if she could see her now. What she would say if she saw how deep Cyra had gone, how much darkness she had allowed inside herself already. Would Mira care? Or would she think it was what Cyra deserved after what she had done to her?

Cyra managed to nod.

"Good. Then get out. I have work to do."

She swiped her coat from the back of the chair, turned, and plodded from the room, stepping around Sand Fly's body as she left. She stopped in the porta-potty to squirt hand sanitizer on her hands, wipe away the blood with her shirt, and cover all evidence of the fight with her buttoned up coat.

It wasn't until Cyra was halfway home that she remembered her switchblade was still lying on the floor of the church basement next to a dead body.

CHAPTER

21

At home, Cyra washed the cut on her back in the shower, watching pink streams of water circle the drain and thinking about how lucky she'd been. How Lamprey would want something more for saving her life.

She bundled herself up in the thick blue robe she kept hanging on the back of the bathroom door and fell into bed, wondering when the nursing home would fire her. She was going to call out of work again tomorrow. And while they let her do what she wanted and were sympathetic following Mira's death, Cyra knew that type of understanding went only so far.

She was running out of time.

But she couldn't worry about that now. She hugged a pillow to her chest and curled around it, her body aching. The trauma of the day—of the past month, really—was catching up with her.

A fantasy, painted in drippy watercolor, bloomed in her mind—getting dressed, going down to the deli, getting a six pack of beer, drinking them one-by-one under the covers while watching a mindless reality show.

Cyra had never been a big drinker. Not in high school, nor college. She'd have a cocktail or two when a friend or whoever she was casually dating at the time dragged her out, but that was about it. And Cyra had always avoided whiskey. She saw, even before Mira died, how much her father loved it. In the list of things her father loved, Cyra always knew she came after Mira, but it was harder to admit that she followed whiskey too.

When Mira convinced Cyra to move to the city with her, Cyra discovered how much she could forget when she drank alcohol. When Mira would go out to parties, Cyra would get a six-pack and drink alone. She thought of it as self-care. Her alone time where she could further push down her feelings and worries and numb out.

But as time in the city slipped by, Cyra found herself drinking more and more to feel less and less, and her panic attacks got worse. It was almost like clockwork. The day or two after a binge-drinking session, Cyra would have a panic attack.

Six months ago, Cyra went to the liquor store when Bea was visiting her brother for the weekend and bought a bottle of Maker's Mark. She drank half of it while staring at the framed photo of herself midpanic attack.

The next morning, disgusted with herself, Cyra threw out all the bottles in the apartment. She texted Bea and told her she was done with drinking. Cyra wasn't sure why she didn't tell Mira about her sobriety. Why it was only Bea she trusted enough with her decision to quit. She hoped she would have told her sister eventually. Maybe when she hit the one-year mark. Maybe that would have been the thing that brought them back together and helped Mira forgive her.

Now she'd never know. She'd never get to tell Mira any of her secrets.

The fantasy of going to the store and getting a few beers grew stronger, but it also sounded like so much work. Work, and a distraction from what she really needed to do, which was prepare. Cyra's mind was made up: Lamprey needed to be dealt with. If Lamprey did kill Mira, he would never admit it. He was having too much fun stringing her along.

The idea that formed during the meeting was in full bloom now. Cyra would get the information she needed from Lamprey before Saturday, and then betray him to the group that night. Tell them he killed Cuckoo; place the blame for Pea Crab on his shoulders as well. And let the men do what they did best: kill.

Kitten. Meet me at the church in an hour. It's too cold to stand in front of the deli.

The text had come through Friday evening from an unlisted number, but Cyra knew from the horrible pet name that it was from Lamprey. She wondered if he was lying, if he preferred to meet in the Bronx because it was closer to wherever he really lived, maybe outside the boroughs.

Is it done? She had texted back.

Yes. You want to see this.

Fine. But rec center, not church.

It was closer to her apartment, and she didn't want anyone else catching them like Sand Fly did.

Cyra donned her Mistletoe disguise even though she didn't need it for Lamprey. It made her feel more confident. As she buttoned her blouse, she thought about Lamprey's fingers brushing her skin, pulling at her shirt collar as he checked on her wound. Her body tensed, remembering the same hands were responsible for the death of who knows how many people.

Her skin pricked with goosebumps.

Cyra felt the loss of her switchblade intensely. She would pat her pocket absently only to remember it was gone, a lump in her throat at the thought of a weapon with her prints and a dead man's blood on it in Lamprey's possession. Cyra had been having nightmares about Sand Fly lately. Dreams where he pinned her underneath his spindly body like he was a giant spider, both his eyes bloody holes that dripped hot wax on to her face.

I wonder if Lamprey plans to kill me tonight.

Cyra took a kitchen knife from her block, one with a four-inch blade that she carefully put in the pocket of her winter coat, and left, letting her body relax into apathy, hiding away any residual shock from the other day's attack.

The outside of the rec center looked like it was sagging—she had only ever seen the building during the day, and it looked extra derelict in the night. She skirted around the edge of the building, down the alley it shared with an Indian food place, and headed toward the back door near the dumpsters that Python said was always unlocked.

Remembering Python's habit of letting people stay in the center when it was cold, Cyra entered quietly. Seeing no one else, she slipped downstairs and into the basement room.

Cyra tapped the outside of her jacket pocket, feeling for the kitchen knife, before stepping fully into the room. Lamprey was already there, sitting at the flimsy table, Mira's laptop open in front of him, bathing his face in a harsh blue glow in the otherwise dark room.

"How's your back?" Lamprey asked without looking up from the screen as Cyra stopped a few feet away from the table, watching him.

"It's fine. You got it unlocked?" She didn't want him to see how unnerved his feigned concern made her.

"Yep, I was able to get in for you," Lamprey said, looking up from the laptop. "The wig, again, really? It's just me."

"Never can be too careful."

"One day you'll show me the real you," Lamprey insisted, smiling, and Cyra's hand drifted a little closer to her jacket pocket at the implication. He curled his fingers toward her, asking her to approach, as he turned back to the laptop. "I'll show you what I found. Your sister's phone I obviously can't access, but it was connected via the Cloud to her laptop, so most of her texts are backed up here. She left her email up, so I didn't even need to hack her account. Apparently she was emailing from her phone quite a bit in the weeks before her death. Besides that, there's not much on her computer besides hundreds of photography files. And what looks like some old school papers." Lamprey looked over and realized Cyra hadn't moved. "What's up? Don't you want to see?"

This is wrong! Cyra screamed from inside her head. *That's my sister's private world.*

She shook herself, deepening her breaths, curling her nails into her palms, squeezing tight until she felt skin break. She was not Mira's sister right now; she was her avenger. She was Mistletoe. Cyra drew the darkness, the coldness, over her shoulders like a cloak, letting it settle over any protestations. She straightened, calmer.

Cyra cleared her throat, pushing her hesitations back. She marched over to the table. "You couldn't resist snooping? That's my dead sister's private information."

Lamprey grinned. "We both knew I wasn't gonna hack it and walk away. Come on, kitten. Grow up."

"Fuck you, Lamprey. I'm guessing you found something?"

Lamprey, seated, reached out and brushed a hand against her hip. "Oh, yeah, I found something alright."

Cyra swiped his hand away. "Focus. Tell me."

Lamprey grinned, smoothing his hair back where the breeze from her hand ruffled it, but didn't try to touch her again. Instead, he pushed the laptop toward her and got to his feet, towering over Cyra.

"I won't take away the excitement," he said. "I'm sure you'll want to explore yourself. There are some emails that you'll find very interesting."

"Just tell me," Cyra said in frustration, reaching for the laptop. "Who was it? Which of them was she talking to?" Her desperation was slipping out now, so strong that her detached persona was shunted to the side and overpowered.

Pay attention to him, a voice hissed from the back of her mind. *Don't let him distract you!*

As much as she wanted to fixate on the laptop screen with her sister's texts and emails, she couldn't let her guard down around Lamprey. Turning from the screen and facing him, hand close to her pocket, Cyra clenched her jaw. "What was it? What did you find?" she asked again.

Lamprey, like her, was still wearing his coat. It was warmer in the rec center than it was outside, but it was still chilly. The right side of his face was cast in the whiteish glow from the laptop, giving the left side a ghoulish, shadowed look. His smile seemed lopsided and more poisonous than ever.

"You were so sure it was one of us," Lamprey said, his voice low and humming, like the sound her refrigerator made late at night.

Cyra stilled. "It was."

"Was it? You've done your homework. You know that in most cases when a woman is killed it was her partner who did it."

"Mira was single."

But that wasn't strictly true. She was always on the dating apps; she liked meeting new people and would often go on multiple dates a month with different men. If Arthur McCowen was still alive at the time of Mira's death, no doubt the police would have looked at him very closely. But Arthur was pretty much the one person Cyra was able to rule out entirely being that he died weeks before Mira did after Cyra bullied him relentlessly online.

"She was seeing someone," Lamprey said, his tone indicating he knew he was driving a nail into her skin. "Someone she didn't tell you about. I wonder why? Did you do something to her?" His words were liquid belladonna, dripping from his mouth.

"Stop fucking with me!" Cyra snapped, immediately regretting it as Lamprey's face twisted further in the darkness, an eager look in his eye. "I'm leaving."

She shut the laptop and slipped it into her shoulder bag but didn't move, not quite trusting Lamprey to let her walk away. She wanted to be prepared for whatever he would do next.

"I never really asked," Lamprey said when she made no move toward the door. "Why you thought it was one of us. I mean, I saw all the articles on Mira Griffin's death, I knew she was murdered. But why go to serial killers instead of the more obvious suspects?" When she stayed quiet, staring at him like a watchful owl, his eyes widened. "Oh, I see. You got inside information, didn't you?"

Cyra didn't want to tell him, didn't want to reveal her trump card yet, but maybe his reaction would be a clue. "Her ankles were crossed over each other when she was found. It was an already established pattern. The cops told me." The last part was an outright lie, but he didn't need to know that.

Lamprey didn't blink. "I see. Well, that means nothing to me, but we're pretty careful to keep things like that to ourselves in the group. As you correctly assumed, it can be very revealing."

Cyra still had no idea if he was the person she was looking for. It was impossible to tell when he was lying or not. He seemed neither surprised nor defensive hearing about the crossed ankles, but she couldn't trust that what he was presenting was genuine.

Lamprey stretched, reaching his arms up toward the ceiling, rolling out a crick in his neck. Cyra's hand jumped inside of her coat pocket at the sudden movement, and she took a step back to give herself space. But he simply let out a satisfied groan as he unlaced his fingers and swept his arms back down to his side.

"I'm off, I have somewhere to be tonight," Lamprey said, offering her another grin. "Unless you have something better to tempt me with."

"You really found something on there? Or did you plant something?"

In that eerie way of his, Lamprey dropped his smile like a bag of bricks and the empty, nothing expression of his true face replaced it. "Read her emails. And think about where you got that insider information from. Smart girl like you, you'll figure it out."

Then he was gone, striding from the room so quickly that Cyra barely had a chance to make space for him. A whiff of cologne and toothpaste drifted by in his wake and her stomach turned.

Nothing Lamprey said could be trusted. He lied about knowing the names of group members, he constantly evaded her questions about himself, he blackmailed her into working with him to identify the group's rat, and he could have planted evidence on Mira's laptop. The fact that he seemed to be trying to steer her away from the support group was more evidence against him.

But Cyra couldn't help it. She had to see. She had to know. And she couldn't wait to get home.

She closed the door of the room, took out her knife and the laptop and put them both on the table and pulled up Lamprey's abandoned chair.

She sat in the darkness and began to read her sister's emails.

CHAPTER

22

Wanting to show self-control and prove that Lamprey couldn't hook her that easily, Cyra sifted through some of Mira's texts first.

She felt gross, going through Mira's private words, but she couldn't let Lamprey's eyes be the last ones to see Mira's thoughts.

Mira's laptop wasn't with her in Brooklyn at the time of her death, so her most recent texts were from a week prior. Most of the messages were from Eli and Izzie, both separately and in group chats. Eli's messages were memes and videos. Izzie's were long rambling messages about her relationship. Apparently, Izzie had some insecurity issues.

Arthur's name was in Mira's message list as well, a little eggplant emoji next to his contact. Knowing he wasn't responsible for Mira's death and wanting her sister to keep some of her privacy, she ignored that thread. There were some things sisters shouldn't share with each other.

Cyra quickly moved on to the emails.

At first, she wasn't sure what Lamprey was referring to. There were a lot of spam emails that Mira hadn't deleted—her inbox had a horrifyingly high four-digit number bolded in black over the little mail icon. Cyra fixated instead on the emails that had clearly been opened and replied to. There were a lot of photography-related communications, but they had dried up after the article, along with any emails from Arthur.

Then she found them.

Email exchanges going back almost a year between Mira and a Yahoo account with the handle DragonsAreReal. The messages seemed to start one-sided, with DragonsAreReal professing feelings and admiration, and Mira offering vague responses, but not entirely shutting them down. This went on for months, until, over this past summer, Mira started to reciprocate.

I know what you mean, she wrote when DragonsAreReal mentioned how hard it was to deny their feelings toward her. *Sometimes I regret how things played out. I knew you were interested in me, but I wasn't ready. How would things have turned out if it was me and you instead?*

The emails were short and nonidentifying until that point. A deeply uneasy feeling was rising inside Cyra's chest.

Don't we owe it to ourselves to give it a try? DragonsAreReal wrote on July 16th.

But I don't wanna lose your friendship, Mira had responded fifteen minutes later. *And besides, it would break her. We can't do that to her. She's my bff.*

"Oh, Mira, no," Cyra murmured out loud, placing her head in her hands for a moment and squeezing her eyes shut, remembering how Eli met Mira and Izzie in a bar and had expressed interest in Mira initially, not Izzie.

I can't sleep thinking of you on the couch out there, all alone, he had written after the disastrous Wine and Cheese night shortly before Mira's death.

Then come here. I need to feel you.

Both their messages had the "Sent from my phone" tag at the bottom, letting Cyra know they were emailing covertly from their devices while Izzie slept.

Cyra pinched the bridge of her nose, frowning.

Eli and Mira must have used email because leaving texts or DMs on either of their phones where Izzie could easily see would have been stupid, but emails, tucked away in a folder that could be deleted off your phone entirely was safer.

The most recent email exchange, the day before Mira's death, had a different vibe.

I don't understand. We're so good together. You can't throw us away, Eli had written.

But I can't throw Izzie away either, Mira had replied. *I'm sorry, but it has to be this way. I can't do it anymore. She loves you. You have to forget about me.*

And his response, a minute later, in bold, all capital letters: *I CAN'T.*

Eli was clearly in love with Mira, probably had been for a long time, and from the tone of his emails, seemed obsessed. And Mira, always terrible at picking men, fell into the most clichéd love triangle she could find. The best friend and the boyfriend. What had she done? At least it seemed like Mira had come to her senses at the end, realizing she couldn't keep hurting Izzie. Although, her decision to be a good person had come at a price.

Cyra stared at the screen, her eyes starting to ache from the contrast of the dark basement and the bright laptop.

Could Lamprey have planted these emails? He could still be behind this. But no, how could he know the nuances of these relationships well enough to convincingly replicate them online? She was trying to avoid the truth—Cyra followed the wrong trail. Her hands were hot as she thought about how eagerly Eli had told her about the support group when it became clear she wasn't going to stop searching for Mira's murderer. She thought about how he had gotten her the files and how easily he had accessed information about signatures and methods.

"No, this is crazy," Cyra whispered, pushing away from the table and standing up, looking around the dark room, the wind whistling against the egress windows above her.

It would mean Eli killed her sister because he couldn't live without her. It would mean he remembered the ankle-crossing signature he'd read about in a file. It would mean he saw an opportunity to shift the blame, gently placing Mira's left ankle over her right one in Prospect Park, and then hurrying home to console Izzie when the news broke. It would mean he sent Cyra on a wild goose chase to take the spotlight off himself.

"Mira, you should have told me," Cyra said, moving forward again and gently touching the laptop screen.

But why would she? After what Cyra did with PJ, and how she betrayed Mira with Arthur, her sister had no reason to confide in her about Eli.

I'm so sorry. Then, louder in her head, a cold voice: *I will make it right.*

Her heartbeat settled, the muscles in her face relaxed. In this room, in Mistletoe's disguise, it was easy to make a decision.

Cyra looked at the laptop and the empty room. Tomorrow evening, she would return to the church in the Bronx, get there early, and tell Python Lamprey was responsible for the breakdown of the group. With an easy scapegoat, Python would kill Lamprey, getting him out of Cyra's way, clearing the path for her to pay Eli a little visit.

Both Lamprey and Eli would get what they deserved.

CHAPTER

23

SHE KNEW PYTHON would be at the church early.

Cyra only had to beat Lamprey there.

She was starting to feel like she spent more time with the serial killers than at her job. She hadn't worked all week; called out sick again. Cyra knew she would be let go soon, she had heard the warning in her boss's voice, but she couldn't be bothered to care. Not now.

As she trotted up the church steps, the brisk evening breeze tousling strands of her wig, she enjoyed the stillness inside her. Python wasn't in the church entryway this time, and Cyra paused to glance at the pews and lines of votive candles through the vestibule doors, barely visible without sunlight. Cyra wasn't religious, but she appreciated the atmosphere of the church—expectant and empty, like her.

This time, she didn't need to do any breathing exercises or adjust her body language—the transformation to Mistletoe came naturally and immediately. She was already inside Cyra, part of her. What she thought was her real self now felt ephemeral, relieved to make room for the coldness Cyra cultivated for a month under Mistletoe's mask.

Calm, confident, Cyra made her way to the stairs and descended into the church basement.

The last time Cyra was down here, there was blood speckled on the carpet and a dead man sprawled out on the floor. But Lamprey did well. No bleach stains or rusty spots marred the blue carpet. It looked exactly the same as it did before Sand Fly attacked her.

As expected, Python was there early, setting up the chairs in a semicircle in the center of the room, the low ceiling only a few feet from the top of his head.

"You're early," Python said, sparing her a glance.

"I have to tell you something," Cyra said.

"You confessing to Pea Crab?"

She shot him a look. "We both know who did that."

Steps sounded on the staircase behind her, and cursing internally, realizing she'd lost her shot to talk to Python alone, Cyra moved further into the room as Whipworm and Mockingbird entered.

Oh, well. Maybe this works better anyway.

Whipworm and Mockingbird didn't even get a chance to say hello.

"Lamprey killed Pea Crab," she said, unable to help glancing at the spot where Sand Fly's body had been. "And Cuckoo."

"What?" Python straightened, forgetting about adjusting the chairs he'd been setting up in the middle of the room. "How would you know that?"

This was the risky part. But it didn't matter. She no longer cared about the group; the person she was looking for had never been there to begin with. "I've been sleeping with him."

Whipworm turned red, but Mockingbird tilted his head at her with interest.

Python frowned. "That's against the rules. No outside contact, remember?"

"It didn't happen outside, it happened inside, after our meetings," Cyra lied, a shiver of disgust at the mere thought of touching Lamprey coursing up and down her back.

"That's semantics," Python growled.

"Who cares?" Cyra said, spurred on by the thought of Lamprey walking down the stairs at any second. "He broke a bigger rule. Listen to me, Python. I didn't know until the last time, I swear. But he killed Pea Crab. And . . . he killed Cuckoo and Sand Fly, too. You ever notice how vague he is in his shares? It's because he's not into killing women—he's into killing *us*. He wants to be the top dog. He wants to prove himself as the Alpha—even in a group of serial killers, he wants to be the most dangerous one."

"Sand Fly is dead?" Mockingbird said casually, with mild interest, as if he was asking what the specials were at a diner.

Whipworm was shaking his head emphatically, but Python looked concerned. "Why didn't he kill you then?" Python asked, crossing his arms and staring at Cyra.

"I don't know." This, at least, she could answer with complete honesty. Lamprey had plenty of chances to off her already. He'd even saved her life. But that wasn't a comforting thought. It meant he had something worse waiting for her. "Look, I'm telling you the truth. He told me about Pea and Cuckoo, but I saw Sand Fly with my own eyes. Sand Fly came back to the church last week after the meeting. I guess he forgot something. And Lamprey killed him to keep us a secret."

"Lamprey *was* the one who pointed out the photo of Pea that day," Python said thoughtfully, glancing at Whipworm, a little wrinkle appearing between his eyebrows.

"Why are you telling us this?" Whipworm demanded. He was looking anxiously at the stairwell, a sentiment Cyra shared; this needed to be done quickly.

"Because he's going to kill us all," Cyra said, a hint of impatience in her voice. "He's picking us off one by one. He'll get me too, in the end, I have no doubt about that." It was true, she didn't.

"He can try," Mockingbird grunted. The corner of his lip twitched like he was suppressing a smile.

"You need to do something," Cyra petitioned Python. "You wanted to know who killed Pea, right? Well, this is your answer. Lamprey's killed *three* of us."

She watched as Python and Whipworm met eyes briefly, her suspicions from the other day confirmed. Python knew damn well that Lamprey hadn't killed Pea Crab, but he wasn't going to pass up a free scapegoat in order to protect Whipworm.

"Do you have any evidence?" Mockingbird asked, genuinely curious.

"This isn't a court of law," Whipworm said, his face calm but fingers twitching by his sides. He must have come to the same conclusion Python did: Cyra's accusation, true or not, solved their problem. "Three of our members are missing. That's not a coincidence. Python?"

"He'll come in through the front doors," the big man said. "I'll wait for him down here. I'll take care of everything."

A thrill of excitement and relief shot through Cyra. He was going to solve the Lamprey problem for her, just as she hoped.

"What about us?" Mockingbird wanted to know.

"Go upstairs now," Python said. "There's another exit at the back of the church. Go past the altar and the sacristy, and you'll see it. I'll stay here."

"Not alone," Whipworm said. "It's Lamprey. I'll stay with you. Help out."

There was a brief softness in Python's eyes as he looked at Whipworm. He nodded once, then turned to Cyra and Mockingbird. "Go, now."

"Good luck," Mockingbird muttered.

Cyra felt like she should say something, but there was nothing left in her throat. She nodded to Python and Whipworm, and followed Mockingbird upstairs.

The vestibule was empty; it was still ten minutes before their set meeting time. Instead of going out the front, Mockingbird pushed against the inner church doors and the two of them stepped into the silent space.

"This way," Mockingbird grunted, shuffling over to the far left side of the church so they would be hidden under the eaves and by the pews if Lamprey happened to glance through the doors in the vestibule.

The church was dark, the sun already set. The stained glass let in a faint tinted glow from the bruised navy sky, but otherwise, it was difficult to see much. The pews were long lines of parallel shadows, and the altar was a dark mass rising ahead of them. Unheated, the church was freezing and Cyra's nose felt ice-tipped.

"I wonder if Python is armed," Cyra whispered. She'd seen Lamprey in action. She knew how fast and powerful he was. But she was pleased with the odds. Python alone was probably a match for him; Whipworm at his side would put the nail in the coffin.

They passed a holy water font, barren and bone-dry. Their footsteps were soft and pattering on the marble floor. Even in the darkness, Cyra noticed Mockingbird's limp. She recalled that he was the one who was injured by a past victim.

Remember that, she told herself, and almost nodded.

"Is *Lamprey* armed?" Mockingbird asked, reminding her that she was suddenly alone with him for the first time.

Cyra's mouth dried out, but she carried on as if she didn't have a care in the world, her heartbeat steady. "I'm not sure. He might have swiped Sand Fly's hunting knife. I don't think he's the type to carry a gun."

"No, you're right. Not him," Mockingbird replied. "He's old-school, like me. Does things with his hands."

They reached the altar, sidestepping around the unlit votive candles surrounding the portrait of the Virgin Mary. Cyra cast a glance over her shoulder, but she couldn't see any movement from the front of the church. Any sounds from the front doors or basement were muffled by the city leaking in from the windows; car horns, the whistle of the wind, a siren going by in the distance. Cyra didn't know if Lamprey was inside the church yet. He could already be in the basement for all she knew.

The two of them trailed across the altar, passing the pulpit, tabernacle, and pews for altar servers. Eyes adjusting to the lack of light, Cyra could see that the back of the altar featured a huge marble table in front of a Baroque sculpture that almost reached the domed ceiling. The sculpture consisted of pillars and carved angels, and half-hidden behind it was a squat door that must lead to the sacristy and promised exit. Mockingbird paused in front of the door, turning back to look at her.

Cyra missed her switchblade; the kitchen knife felt unwieldy in her pocket, but she still considered using it.

You can't. He's too prepared. And he'd expect it from you, especially after what you told them.

"The group is over," Cyra said instead, waiting to see what Mockingbird was going to do.

"I know. Half of us are dead, and the other half are eating each other alive like wolves."

She cocked her head, squinting at him in the low light, watching for sudden movements. "Why aren't you attacking me?"

Mockingbird let out a wheezy laugh, and then lowered his voice, glancing over her shoulder toward the front of the church. Everything inside was quiet and bathed in heavy shadow. "You don't have the right eyes for me, sweetheart. No offense."

The right eyes? She wanted to gut him. But it wasn't the correct time. Too much hung in the balance. Instead, Cyra slipped the comment about eyes away into the corner of her brain where she kept notes on the serial killers.

"We should leave one at a time. Like usual," Mockingbird suggested. "Do you want to go first?"

She didn't like the idea of this man at her back. Cyra shook her head. "All you."

"Well, it's been fun," Mockingbird said, placing a hand on the doorknob.

"Hey," Cyra whispered as the older man opened the door, his craggy face barely visible from the light dribbling in from the stained glass. "Why'd you join this group to begin with? You don't seem like the social type."

Mockingbird paused with his meaty fingers on the door handle. He seemed to be considering whether or not to answer her. Finally, he licked his top lip and said, "I live a solitary life. Part of the job. And it's what I like. But when I do have to interact with people, I like to hear from people who don't think they're better than me." He gave her a look like maybe he categorized her in that group and continued. "Those guys down there, they may be killers and liars, but they respect me. They understand what I do and why I do it."

It was the most she ever heard Mockingbird talk. His voice was thick, with a slight regional drawl. He might have grown up on Long Island or Queens. Or he could be faking it.

"You're implying I don't," she replied, curious. Had he guessed she wasn't who she said she was?

"You couldn't. You say you're like us, but it's different for women," Mockingbird said, his voice soft now. "You don't have the bodies we do. You don't have the animal drive to hunt." He squinted at her in the darkness. "For women, killing is a game. Petty revenge and broken hearts. Women kill for death. Men kill for life. It gives us air. And that's something you could never understand."

He didn't wait for her to respond. The door clunked open, and Mockingbird vanished into the dark of the sacristy.

Cyra didn't love the idea of waiting around knowing what was going down in the basement, but it was better than getting into a battle with Mockingbird. She had her priorities right now, and she couldn't take any chances before she dispatched her sister's murderer. Cyra stepped away from the door and pressed herself behind the massive sculpture, hiding herself from view from the front of the church, waiting.

In the shadows, several yards away from the sacristy door, Cyra pictured Mira's face, bright and smiling. She waited for Mistletoe's mask to fall away like it did the other times she felt stuck in her alter ego's persona. Nothing happened. Cyra brought up memories of Mira, curled under a blanket, eating ice cream straight from the container, laughing. Fondness twitched in Cyra's chest, but that was it. There was no mask to remove.

Mistletoe started as a way to trick the men, but she slowly became a refuge, a place for Cyra to be the version of herself she hid from for years. Cyra feared Mistletoe in the beginning because she felt *too* real, *too* comfortable. But now her heart was floating and her limbs were light. The version of herself she presented the world was there still, within reach inside her, but she had no desire to wear it anymore.

Mistletoe's darkness filled the broken cavity in her chest. Cyra didn't need dramatic emotions or forced behaviors to be whole when the emptiness could be her anchor instead.

There was a scuffling noise behind her, a muffled thump, as if it was coming from far away. Cyra dared a glance around the edge of her hiding place, peering into the darkening church. She could just make out the vestibule doors, but there were no lights to see any movement.

A softer sound, more human, like a moan or a cry, echoed beyond the pews. Then a final, resounding *clunk* before the church descended back into silence.

Cyra swallowed. She wasn't sure what was going on, but it was time to make her exit. She heard a click from the sacristy door behind her; the snick of a doorknob turning.

She spun around and saw Lamprey, splattered in blood.

CHAPTER

24

Lamprey shut the sacristy door behind him with a soft thud.

He was a few yards away from her spot behind the sculpture, and upon seeing her, Lamprey stepped out from the shadows and into a weak stream of streetlight filtering in from the stained-glass windows high above them. She was able to get a better look at the blood splashed on his face and neck.

A rush flooded Cyra's ears as if she was standing too close to the edge of the platform when the train pulled in. Her throat was scratchy and dry, and her limbs were buzzing. She slowly stepped to the side so her back was no longer pressed against the Baroque sculpture, keeping her gaze trained on Lamprey, whose face was blank.

It was clear her plan hadn't worked. And judging by the blood on Lamprey's face and the confident way he was holding himself, he escaped unscathed while the others did not. Was the blood from Python and Whipworm? Mockingbird?

Cyra ground her molars and inhaled through her nose. She had about ten seconds to say the exact right thing or Lamprey would attack—of that she had no doubt.

The stale open air of the church cooled her back and the weight of the kitchen knife was heavy in her pocket, but she didn't pull it out yet. She couldn't afford any sudden movements. She needed to unnerve him. To behave the opposite of how he expected her to act.

Cyra looked right at Lamprey's stony face and said, "Hey. Are you OK?"

Lamprey blinked, and a hint of expression came back to his face like a blush. "What, this? I'm fine, kitten. Thanks for the concern." He wiped a finger against the blood on his cheek and drew it back, examining the dark smear on his fingertip in the low light.

"Did you meet Mockingbird?" She nodded to his bloody face.

"Nope. Missed him."

"How'd you know I'd be in here, then?" Cyra asked, crossing her arms over her chest as if to keep her heartbeat in a cage. She tilted her head, looking at Lamprey without malice or accusation. It wasn't hard—her body was reacting as if she was afraid; her heart racing, her muscles tensing, but all she felt was anticipation.

"I like to know our meeting spots," he replied, lowering his hand and gazing at her. "I explored the church the other day, getting familiar with its layout. I didn't see you or Mock at the front, so I knew you were probably creeping around inside somewhere. Maybe using the side or back exit. Thanks for waiting for me." And there was his smile, the creepy, saccharine one that conveyed he knew what he was saying wasn't the truth.

But he was talking, which was a good sign. He was still more interested in bantering with her than murdering her. She needed to encourage that. Maybe even . . . use it. Could she manipulate Lamprey's obvious enjoyment of their cat-and-mouse game to her advantage? Clearly, her trap didn't work. But if she could trick him, distract him, *use* him, then she could slip away later, escaping his plans for her.

"You were ready for Python and Whipworm," Cyra guessed.

Lamprey nodded. "To be honest, I was impressed you had the balls to set that up. It's what I would have done too. I'm not mad, kitten. You got what you wanted and tried to clean up your mess after. I'm about to do the same."

"What happened down there?" Cyra added a touch of awe to her voice, raising her brows as if impressed. "You don't look hurt at all."

Lamprey paused, assessing her. "I wasn't."

"I shouldn't be surprised," Cyra said, giving him a knowing nod. "You're good at this."

"I'll take that as a compliment. Flattery is new from you," Lamprey noted, watching her face.

Cyra wasn't sure if he could tell she was faking it or if he genuinely believed she was impressed, but he was avoiding her original question. She repeated, "What happened?"

Lamprey sighed. "Whip tried to sneak up behind me while Python made some big speech about how I broke everyone's trust, and I caught him off guard. Stuck your little switchblade in the side of Whipworm's neck, and then threw it into Python's chest. Took off right after. I had to make sure I'd be able to catch you back here."

"Are they dead?" Cyra asked, realizing the sounds she heard from the front of the church could have been Python carrying Whipworm out, getting him away from the threat of Lamprey.

Lamprey shrugged. "Python definitely isn't. Your blade was little. I'm decent at knife-throwing, but it only caught him under the collarbone. But Whipworm . . ." Lamprey grinned. "If he's not dead already, he will be soon if Python doesn't get him to a hospital. But who knows. Maybe they're in the ER right now. Maybe the doctor will put that switchblade in a plastic evidence bag for the cops. Maybe the cops will dust it for prints and find yours; I made sure to wear gloves, you know."

"You were setting me up," Cyra observed.

"It crossed my mind," Lamprey admitted, looking down at his nails and examining one of his cuticles. "It felt like a waste to not do something with your little knife. But I think, in the end, this was always where we'd end up."

"Of course," Cyra said, her voice infused with power and assuredness. She allowed the tiniest hint of intimacy to creep in her tone so that her next words dripped out slowly like honey. "Or we could continue having fun."

Lamprey froze completely, glancing up from his nails to stare at her. "Oh?"

"You enjoy this," Cyra stated, uncrossing her arms and taking a step forward toward him. This manipulation had to be perfect. It had to be flawless. And to do that, she needed to infuse a bit of truth. "I enjoy it too. I've learned from you, Lamprey. And I like the power Mistletoe gives me. I like that I'm not scared or out of control. I like that I'm not pretending to feel things I don't anymore, and I like that I'm ready to do what needs to be done to get justice for my sister."

Lamprey lowered his hands, mirroring Cyra's body language. He stepped forward too, until they were only a foot apart. The line she was walking was dangerously thin. Lamprey was close to the edge, she could feel predatory energy emanating from his stance, but she could pull him back.

The church was silent around them, the faint scent of incense hanging in the air.

"What are you proposing, kitten?"

"Working together."

Lamprey's lips twitched before he caught himself and smoothed out his expression. "We already found the rat. The group is done. What else would I want from you?"

"Tonight, I'm going to confront the man who killed my sister," Cyra said, a flicker of heat licking her stomach as she pictured Eli. "You could come. Help out. I have an idea."

"Why would I do that?"

For the first time ever, Cyra smiled at Lamprey, and its effect was immediate. His eyes widened, and he jerked slightly toward her, his gaze on her mouth. "Because after, we'll do one of yours," Cyra said.

"Yes." His response was instant and firm.

Cyra's face didn't change, her breath didn't whoosh out of her chest, but the muscles in her legs loosened and her stomach relaxed. All those hours she spent with Lamprey paid off. She read him correctly, she bought herself some time.

Although, she knew Lamprey could be manipulating her as well. Trying to lure her into a state of false security. She couldn't trust him, not for a moment, but she was betting Lamprey was too invested now to kill her.

"What's next?" Lamprey asked, watching Cyra. "You said you had an idea."

This dynamic was unusual for them. In the past, it was Cyra asking Lamprey for things; Lamprey pulling the strings. His deference to her now felt like a test, but the support group taught Cyra how to think on her feet, and once again, she smiled at Lamprey, watching his eyes track her lips.

"I have Eli's email. If I give it to you, can you send him an untraceable message? One that would permanently delete itself after reading?"

Lamprey's mouth curved up, mimicking hers. "You know I can."

Cyra nodded. She hadn't planned for this part. She was going to text Eli after support group and tell him to meet her alone in Prospect Park, but maybe this was better. More punishing for him. "Tell him you know what he did. Be vague. Threatening. Say if he doesn't agree to meet you tonight at 10:00 PM at the Prospect Park Boathouse, you'll go to his bosses. It would be so easy to arrest him right at work."

The more she thought about it, the more perfect this pivot seemed. She would give Lamprey Eli's dummy email, the one he used to message Mira. She knew he would pay attention to anything that came to that address. And Cyra was familiar with the power of blackmail after what she did to Arthur McCowen. Eli would make an excuse to hide the truth from Izzie, keeping her out of the way so Cyra could do what needed to be done. If she texted him as herself, there was no guarantee he wouldn't show up with Izzie in tow like last time.

Lamprey grinned. "Ah, your inside source, I see. OK, but I'll have to go home to do this. I need my equipment. And then?"

"We'll both go to Prospect Park. You meet him there. Distract him. I'll take care of the rest. I don't actually need you at the park, but I'm assuming you'll want to be involved. Want to see it happen."

"Correct," Lamprey said, nearly purring. "I'm curious to see if you can follow through. Or if you'll try to betray me again."

"I promise, I won't," Cyra said, remembering how Lamprey made a similar promise to her weeks ago when he vowed not to hurt her. She wondered if he was lying then the way she was now. "We'll need something to weigh down a body, too."

"I have something I can bring," Lamprey offered. "I've got sandbags. I can bring several. They're heavy. Should be more than enough weight."

"Good."

"And after? After we disappear your little friend's body?"

Cyra bore down on her disgust and disinterest and did something she had never done before—she reached out and gently squeezed Lamprey's shoulder. "Then we do yours."

Lamprey, eyes suddenly vacant and shallow, afforded her a thin-lipped smile before glancing down at her hand. "You seem different, lately. You're talking to me now like . . . Well, like you talked in the meetings. Like Mistletoe."

Cyra shrugged. "OK?"

"Which one is the act, I wonder?" Lamprey said, lifting Cyra's hand from his shoulder and holding it a moment, his palms cold and dry against her knuckles. "The bereft sister looking for justice or the cold-blooded woman in front of me?"

Cyra pulled away her hand gently, eyes boring into Lamprey's face. "Who says I can't be both?" She placed her hands on her hips. "Now, do we have a deal or not?"

The ghost of a smirk crossed Lamprey's face as the shadows in the church lengthened around them. "Yeah. You have yourself a deal, kitten."

Prospect Park was vacant this time of night, the moon out and illuminating the empty paved paths and lonely benches. Cyra passed a man wrapped in a sleeping bag on one of the park benches near the entrance, but she didn't see anyone else besides a few bold dog walkers headed back home for the night. She was confident she and Eli wouldn't be disturbed this late. Everyone in the neighborhood was still on edge since Mira's murder. There wouldn't be many people out, especially in this freezing weather.

Cyra was wearing nondescript, dark clothes and a black knit cap that covered her hair. She stopped back home after her encounter at the church with Lamprey to change and give him time to contact Eli. Cyra's phone buzzed an hour and a half ago with a text from Lamprey's burner phone: *All set. See you soon.*

A black, thick knitted scarf Mira gave Cyra for the birthday they shared was wrapped loosely around Cyra's face, obscuring her nose, mouth, and jaw, hiding her features from view. The kitchen knife was stowed in her coat pocket, but that was a last resort.

Mira died because Eli bashed her head in with a rock. That action should be repaid in kind.

An eagerness was coursing through Cyra's body as she moved quietly through the dark park, avoiding patches of light on the pavement from the streetlamps. She was so close to finishing this. She glanced at the ground from time to time, keeping her eyes peeled, and finally swooped low, clutching a fist-sized rock with a jagged, sharp edge. Cyra pocketed it.

When she reached the boathouse, Cyra stood in a deep cluster of shadows thrown by the trees next to Lullwater Bridge, hidden from view. She peered around, realizing she was the first one there as she cast her gaze over the lake and the building beyond it. During the summer, people would take boats and kayaks out on the little lake; Mira and Cyra went together once. They had taken a selfie in front of the boathouse, and Cyra felt honored when Mira posted it to her Instagram even though it wasn't her usual aesthetic.

My forever best friend, Mira captioned it.

Cyra stared at the boathouse. It was a beautiful Beaux-Arts style building with Tuscan columns and wide floor-to-ceiling windows, lit up beyond the bridge. Lollipop street lamps surrounded the boathouse, making it shine like a beacon in the dark.

She was grateful that her sister might have gotten to look at such a pretty structure before she bled out on the dirt near the lake's edge. Mira was killed and found early in the morning, not too far from where Cyra stood now. It was Eli's dumb luck that none of the other sunrise joggers saw anything.

"I'm here," Cyra whispered hoarsely into the night. "I'm with you. It's almost over."

A twig snapped, and Cyra twisted, spotting Lamprey picking his way across the bridge and pausing at the end, casually leaning against the railing as if he was waiting to meet a date. It was too dark to see his eyes, but Cyra could sense his alertness. He knew she was there; she could see the curve of his smile from her hiding spot.

Oh, how she wished she could kill him. But she had to focus. Eli was the priority, and nothing could distract her from that.

Cyra peered around, making sure they were still alone.

At 10:00 PM on the dot, footsteps fell on the path that crossed Lullwater Bridge, and Eli's familiar form came into view, his head turning nervously as he scanned his surroundings until he clocked Lamprey waiting for him at the end of the bridge.

Eli wore a sleek bomber jacket with a red infinity scarf. He looked like a piece of uncooked spaghetti standing next to Lamprey's muscled shape.

Eli stopped a few feet away, apparently correctly deciding he needed to give himself some space between his body and this strange man, before Lamprey pushed himself off the bridge and moved forward. Eli was forced to take another couple steps back, turning slightly so his back was to Cyra.

Perfect. Lamprey must have done that on purpose.

Cyra began to move, every step calculated and silent, checking the ground below her carefully to make sure she wasn't going to land on a stick or a dead leaf, approaching the bridge like a stalking panther. She pulled her scarf down slightly, revealing the lower half of her face.

"Who are you?" Eli said, his voice croaky and clearly frightened. "How did you get that email address? I only gave it to one person."

Lamprey didn't answer Eli's question. He drawled, "I know some fascinating stuff about you."

"What do you want?" Eli demanded. "What is this?"

"Relax, I just want to chat." Lamprey's voice was cold and hard.

"Blackmail is illegal," Eli said, voice wavering. "How did you get that email address?"

"Mira gave it to me," Lamprey hissed.

"W—what the fuck," Eli stammered. "Mira is . . . M—Mira is dead."

They hadn't planned for this particular exchange, but Cyra suppressed a pleased smile as she continued her approach, getting closer now. It was a nice touch. An unexpected knife twist by Lamprey.

"You did something bad, didn't you?" Lamprey said, a note of taunting in his voice.

"What do you mean?" Eli asked nervously. "Who are you?"

Lamprey smiled. "You were having an affair with Mira Griffin."

Eli started shaking his head automatically. "I swear . . . please . . . It was a mistake—"

"And then you killed her, didn't you?"

"Wait, no, hang on—"

"That was a very naughty thing to do."

Cyra slipped the rock from her pocket, pleased with how beautifully it fit in her hand, the smooth side easy to grip, the sharp edge pointed like the ridge of a cliff.

She was only a few feet away from Eli now. She could see his dark hair, edges golden from the park lights. She could smell his leather-scented cologne; hear his teeth chatter from the cold.

Lamprey's eyes landed on her, looking over Eli's shoulder, an expectant expression on his face. He wasn't smirking or grinning now. He was waiting. Watching.

Eli seemed to realize the other man had lost interest and began to turn around, following Lamprey's gaze.

But Cyra didn't want to see his face. She was envisioning Mira instead, her sister crumpled on the ground a hundred yards away, bleeding out from a hole smashed into her skull. She was thinking about all the conversations she would never have with her sister again, all the apologies she would never get to say. All the memories lost, flushed away by a man who thought Mira was his.

A surge of cold rose up over Cyra's head like water, drenching her heart, leaving a still lake of numbness in its wake. There was nothing left to stop her.

This man killed her sister. She wanted him dead.

Cyra raised the rock and slammed it down on the back of Eli's head.

The noise that escaped Eli's mouth was gargled and half-hearted. He stumbled forward, reaching out to Lamprey as if he expected the man to catch him and hold him up, but Lamprey side-stepped Eli, letting him fall to his knees.

Eli turned, disoriented, looking up at Cyra standing above him, a wet rock in her outstretched hand. His eyes bulged with recognition, and then crinkled in pain and horror as she lunged forward again.

The next strike knocked Eli out entirely. The third, fueled by the strength in Cyra's powerful arms, ended it. Eli collapsed on to his side, face streaked with crimson, eyes blank, mouth puckered as if he had been trying to say something with his last breath. The blood pouring from his wounds steamed slightly in the cold night air.

Cyra was panting. The hand holding the rock was sticky and hot with blood. She walked over to the bridge and dropped the stone into the water below, the splash echoing through the quiet night. Her heart was pounding from the effort, and Cyra didn't notice the stinging in her eyes until she returned to Eli's body. The threat of tears was washed away with one deep breath. There was no sadness or regret. Those things were dead now, like Eli.

"You have the bags?" Lamprey asked, coming over to where Cyra was standing over Eli's body.

She nodded, pulling several extra-large garbage bags from underneath her coat. "The weights?" Cyra asked Lamprey, her voice raw and somber.

"I left them on the other side of the bridge. I'll grab the duffle bag. I brought clean-up solution too."

Glancing around to make sure they were still alone, Cyra took the water bottle mixed with bleach that Lamprey handed her and poured it over the spots on the pavement where Eli's blood had spilled. She returned the empty bottle to the duffle bag, helping Lamprey unpack the sand bags. Cyra dug in Eli's pockets, ignoring his fading warmth, until she found his phone, which she turned off.

"Take his wallet too," Lamprey instructed. "Dump them both separately on your way home. It'll slow down identification."

Cyra obeyed, and the two of them shifted Eli's body, wrapping it in the garbage bags, packing the heavy sandbags inside as well. Producing a roll of duct tape from his own coat pocket, Lamprey helped Cyra wind it around Eli, holding the bags in place.

It took both of their considerable strength to lift Eli and drop him over the bridge into the lake. This time, the splash back from the water reached Cyra's face, freckling her skin, rolling down her cheeks.

The two of them stood in the center of the bridge for a moment, watching the ripples fade away in the glowing light from the boathouse across the water.

"He'll be found, eventually," Lamprey pointed out.

"I know," Cyra replied. "It's not that deep here. But it'll buy us time."

Lamprey moved back from the bridge's railing, turning to face her. "I'm proud of you."

Cyra swallowed nausea. Mistletoe's apathy was strong, but a bubble of revulsion at herself for being someone Lamprey could be proud of gurgled in Cyra's gut.

"Thanks for the help," Cyra said instead, not looking at his face. She didn't want to see how impressed he was with her.

Lamprey's hand brushed against her cheek. "I'll see you soon. I can't wait for mine."

Cyra nodded, but she wasn't going to be waiting around for Lamprey to pick a woman to kill together. Tomorrow, she was leaving the city for good. He would try to follow her once he realized she was gone. But she would be ready. Lamprey could hunt her, but Cyra would be the real predator.

"Yeah," she said. "Give me a few days to rest. Then we'll plan."

Cyra turned, the trees watching silently as a murderer walked away, just as they did for Mira.

LAMPREY

Matilda was the perfect baby, and Jason hated her. Her fat little hands, her giant blue eyes, the way she opened her tulip petal mouth and tried to coo.

Jason's father said it was a phase. He would get over his jealousy, he said, and be the best big brother in the world.

Jason was only four, but he knew that his father was wrong. He would never like the baby. Never.

And he didn't. Matilda got older and started walking, putting her grubby hands on all of Jason's special toys. She started talking and taking away his mother's attention with her stupid baby words. She started school and brought home ugly drawings on colored paper and trailed after Jason, babbling about her life.

One day, when Jason pushed his sister in front of his father, his father took him into the backyard and led him down to the little green bench in front of the pond on their property. Jason loved the pond—it was slimy and covered in algae and sometimes there were frogs in there. He always wanted to catch a frog and squeeze it until it popped, but he could never get one.

The pond was his and his father's special place.

Jason's mother hated it. She said it was dangerous to have a pond with two small children who could wander into it, and

Jason got mad when he heard her say that because he wasn't small, not anymore.

You have to be a good big brother, Jason's father told him that day in front of the pond. Tildy looks up to you.

I don't like her, Jason said.

She's little, but she'll get older soon and then you'll be friends. Until then, remember that you'll always be my little man, Jason's father said, and he fastened his gold wristwatch around Jason's arm. It was far too big, and slipped off immediately, but Jason took to carrying it around with him. His most treasured possession.

When Matilda was five, Jason set her pigtails on fire.

It happened early one morning before being carted off to school, after Jason's father had already left for work. Jason's mother had screamed and put Matilda out. His little sister cried and cried and wouldn't stop. Jason had expected to get in trouble. He knew he'd be yelled at. But instead, his mother just stared at him like he was a scary bug and whisked Matilda away to her bedroom.

She didn't tell Jason's father what happened. She said that Matilda had been standing too close to the stove during breakfast and her hair caught fire. Matilda didn't correct her. She stopped talking.

Three weeks later, Jason cornered Matilda in the laundry room and was trying to convince her to drink the blue liquid their mother kept on top of the washer when his mother caught him.

A day later, Jason's mother kept him home from school and waited for his father to leave for his job at the car lot. Jason liked his father. He liked that he sold people cars and bought himself fancy wristwatches that he then gave to his son. Jason's father loved him. He was proud of him. Even though he was only nine, Jason could tell.

But the man who showed up at their door that day and sat down with Jason in the living room wasn't like his father. He was shrimpy and pale. He didn't have his father's large hands or thick moustache. He was as different from Jason's father as he could be.

He sat Jason down while his mother hovered in the living room entryway until the man, Dr. Young, who said he was something called a psychologist, made her go into the kitchen.

Dr. Young asked Jason all sorts of questions about Matilda and his thoughts and feelings. He asked what Jason liked about Matilda, and Jason said nothing. He asked why Jason had lit her hair on fire, and Jason said it was because he didn't like her. Then Dr. Young wanted to know if Jason was trying to hurt her, and Jason had rolled his eyes because he thought that was obvious.

Yes, he told Dr. Young. I want her to be dead.

Then Dr. Young nodded and told Jason to stay there, he was going to talk to his mother. But Jason wasn't stupid, he wasn't going to "stay there." He got up and printed himself against the wall that stuck out between the kitchen and the living room and listened as Dr. Young said some mean things about him to his mother.

Dr. Young said he couldn't diagnose a child as a sociopath, but that he thought Jason was dangerous to Matilda.

Jason was annoyed. He decided that telling the truth was obviously the wrong move. He would be more careful in the future. He would not tell the truth ever again if it was going to be used to make him seem mean. Matilda was annoying; anyone else would have set her hair on fire too.

Dr. Young made sympathetic noises to Jason's mother, and then there were a series of gross, wet kissy noises that made Jason stick his tongue out. He poked his head around the wall and saw Dr. Young's skinny little body holding his mother's and felt sick.

Jason went to his room and thought about ways to get rid of Matilda.

The next day, when the school bus dropped him off, the house was empty and quiet.

Matilda and his mother were gone.

———

Jason's father convinced Jason's mother to visit for Christmas.

A few months had passed since she had left them, and she hadn't wanted to come. But Jason's father had threatened to stop sending her money to pay the rent for the new apartment she had gotten for her and Matilda. Jason heard his father screaming this over the phone late one night after he had drunk a lot of beer.

Jason's father was drinking more and more since he found out that Jason's mother ran away with Matilda. He would work a lot and drink his beer and give Jason weird looks even though Jason was sure his mother hadn't told his father the truth.

Jason was excited for Christmas. He had asked for a new Power Rangers action figure set, and he thought he was going to get it. And it would be nice to see his mother again. He didn't think he would miss her, but he did. She made the best food. His father didn't know how to cook. Jason was sick of hot dogs and mac and cheese.

Christmas Day was not cold enough for snow, which annoyed Jason. He was further annoyed when he saw Matilda at the front door, her hand clutched tightly in his mother's grasp.

The family, back together again for the first time in months, exchanged presents.

Jason did not get the Power Rangers action figure set.

When Jason's father dragged his mother into the kitchen and started whispering angry things at her so that Matilda and Jason couldn't hear in the living room under the tree, Jason took his sister's hand.

Come on, Tildy, he said to her. Don't worry. I have a present for you.

Matilda seemed to be talking again, but her voice was different and soft. She told him she wanted to stay inside. She said she wanted their mother.

Matilda got their mother all the time. How unfair of her to remind Jason.

Come on, Jason insisted. It will be fun.

He squeezed her pudgy hand and dragged her the long way past the kitchen through the dining room, quietly opening the sliding glass door. Jason could hear his parents' voices raising now. His mother was yelling and sounded scared. Jason closed the sliding door behind him gently. He pulled his little sister down the lawn, their bare feet crunching over the cold dead grass.

We're going to catch frogs, Jason said.

Then he led his little sister into the pond.

CHAPTER

25

Cyra didn't return to her apartment that night. Instead, she walked from Prospect Park to the Brooklyn Bridge, wandering toward FDR Drive. She threw away Eli's wallet and phone in two different trash cans along the way.

Her feet began to ache as the night wore on and got colder. The streets got quieter, and the air smelled of snow. When Cyra reached the Queensboro Bridge, she crossed it, headed back into her borough, walking miles and miles on Queens Boulevard as the sky slowly began to lighten. She passed delivery trucks making their rounds and morning joggers. She thought of nothing, especially not Eli's face.

Her feet were blistered and bleeding by the time she reached her usual subway stop nearly seven hours later, the last one on the F line. The sun was rising now, birds chirping as Cyra approached her block.

A jangling noise came from Cyra's bag, cutting through her reverie. Her breath caught to see Izzie's name on her phone screen—she was requesting a video call. Cyra almost didn't answer, but at the last minute, she figured she owed her sister's best friend this one last courtesy. She was right by the deli

Lamprey followed her to, so she stepped to the side of the street, leaning against a pole with a parking sign attached to the top.

"Hey."

Izzie's face appeared on Cyra's phone screen, stark and wide-eyed. "Cyra, have you heard from Eli? He didn't come home last night. He said he was going to meet a friend for a drink, but he never came back. I've been calling and calling him, but his phone is dead or not on or something. I'm . . . I'm freaking out."

Cyra admired her calm, unmoving face on the little screen next to Izzie's. She didn't flinch. Not a flicker of emotion or deceit crossed her expression. "Sorry, no. I haven't heard from him."

"Where are you so early?" Izzie asked, momentarily distracted by the sky behind Cyra's head.

"Ran out of toilet paper," Cyra said ruefully. Her legs ached from her absurdly long walk.

"I think I'm gonna call the police," Izzie said, her own background moving; she was clearly pacing through their apartment. Her hair was greasy and her eyes bloodshot. It didn't look like she slept either.

"Maybe he stayed with his friend and his phone died," Cyra offered, glancing around. The street was still quiet. Only a few dog walkers and runners were around, but Cyra turned down the volume on her phone anyway.

"No," Izzie snapped. "He wouldn't do that."

"Do you know what bar he went to?"

"He didn't say." Izzie's voice was frayed and haggard.

"I'm sure he'll turn up." Cyra realized her voice was bordering on callous, and she made an effort to soften it. Izzie lost her best friend, and soon she would realize her boyfriend was gone too. Cyra couldn't muster up the ability to feel bad for her, but she could give her one final kindness. A way to ease the pain of Eli's disappearance while at the same time keeping Izzie from calling the cops before Cyra could get out of town. Besides, Izzie deserved to know her boyfriend was a cheater. "Izzie, I should tell you something."

"What?"

"I was able to get into Mira's laptop," Cyra said, speaking slowly and gently. "I saw her messages. Eli and Mira were having an affair. I'm so sorry, but it's possible . . . it's possible he has more women on the side. It's possible he's with one of them."

Izzie stopped pacing, staring at the screen. "Are you fucking serious, Cyra?"

"I'm sorry. I think you should know."

"No, no!" Izzie snapped. "How did you even get into Mira's emails?"

"I guessed her password," Cyra lied, but something about Izzie's words stuck in her head.

She brought the screen closer to her face, examining Izzie. The other girl's brows weren't raised, her face hadn't fallen. Her mouth was open in a perfect little O, she was still ranting at the phone, but her initial reaction had been a second too late, and the facsimile of shock wasn't sitting authentically on her expression now. Her eyes were blank, unperturbed.

After all that time trying to decipher the ambiguous and multilayered expressions of the faces in the support group and reading the tones of their voices to parse out the lies, Cyra could read Izzie as easily as a billboard.

Her words rang in Cyra's head: *"How did you even get into Mira's emails?"*

Cyra hadn't told Izzie Eli and Mira were communicating via *email*. She specifically said "messages."

Izzie had already known Eli was cheating. Cyra should have guessed that Mira and Eli, neither of whom were well-versed in the art of subtlety, would have been noticed by Izzie. That changed things.

Cyra didn't give Eli a chance to defend himself verbally or physically, but she remembered the shock in his eyes, the horror. She heard his protestations toward Lamprey before she appeared behind him. He sounded genuinely surprised at the accusation he killed Mira. At the time, she thought it was shock that he was caught, confident that he'd gotten away with it. But maybe... maybe he really hadn't seen it coming. Because maybe he wasn't the one who killed Mira. Cyra knew how tightly-wound Izzie was. She knew Izzie had anger and insecurity issues.

Sourness curdled at the bottom of her stomach.

Oh God. What if I made a mistake?

"Hello? Earth to Cyra!" came Izzie's shrill voice through the phone. "Why are you telling me this anyway? Are you trying to hurt me?"

"Did you know he was cheating?" Cyra asked, voice wooden.

"Of course not!" Izzie said, but she looked away from the camera and her eye twitched. "Look, I have to go. I need to figure out where my boyfriend is."

Before Cyra could answer, Izzie hung up.

Electricity was running through Cyra's veins; she needed to confront Izzie. She needed to talk to her and see if there was any validity to her suspicions. She had to get back to Park Slope. But first, she needed to attend to her feet; she could feel her popped blisters leaking in her shoes. Cyra limped the last block to her apartment, let herself in, and raced up the stairs, ignoring the burst blisters and sore legs from her all-night walk.

The magnitude of her potential mistake loomed over her head, and numbness spread over her, thick and layered. She had killed Eli so fast, without giving him time to defend himself or explain. Her disconnect from her emotions was why she was able to dispatch him so quickly, but it might have been to her detriment.

Cyra unlocked her apartment door and stepped inside the quiet.

She kicked off her shoes, not daring to peel off her socks and check the wet spots she could feel on her feet. Instead, Cyra pulled on a pair of broken-in sneakers. She shucked off her peacoat, leaving the kitchen knife in the pocket for now. She needed something warmer underneath; she was chilled from her excursion.

Ignoring the light switch, she hurried over to her dresser for a sweater before freezing halfway there.

Someone was sitting on her futon.

"Hell," Cyra breathed, spinning toward her discarded jacket on the floor near the door.

Knife, knife, I need that knife, was tattooing itself across her brain.

But she was closer to the couch than the door, and her reaction was too slow, her sore legs wobbly beneath her. She felt fingers on her neck, yanking her back, throwing her down to the ground.

The air fell out of her stomach with an abrupt flatness as she hit the floor. She lay gasping as Lamprey moved between her and the exit, blocking her path to not just the door and her knife, but also to the kitchen, her only other hope for a weapon.

Lamprey's face looked like a charcoal sketch. Backlit by the weak hall bulb, his expression was blank.

Cyra clutched her stomach as she struggled to sit up, skin vibrating.

"Oh. It's you. What are you doing here?" she croaked. "How'd you get inside?"

Lamprey didn't smile. "This is what I do. I pick locks."

"Why are you here?" Cyra asked again, shifting backward, closer to her bed. The pain was starting to recede from her stomach. "I said we'd connect in a few days to plan your turn."

"You know why, kitten. It's time."

Lamprey watched, unmoving but coiled like a tight spring ready to be unleashed as Cyra used the bed frame to haul herself to her feet, fists clenched. Her training suddenly didn't feel like it would be much use face-to-face with a real killer, especially after no sleep and nearly twenty miles of walking. But maybe she could still salvage this.

"You promised," Cyra reminded him, her voice calm, stating a fact. "You said you wouldn't hurt me."

"I lied."

"We were going to be a team. What about your turn?"

"This *is* my turn," Lamprey said, his voice like velvet now. "You agreed to this."

Cyra always knew this was coming at some point, but she didn't expect it so soon after Eli's death. She really thought Lamprey was intrigued by her proposition to hunt together, but she should have known he already identified his next target: her.

"I can't die yet," Cyra said honestly. "I have to deal with Izzie first."

Lamprey quirked up an eyebrow. "Izzie?"

"Mira's friend. I think . . . I think I might have made a mistake. Izzie already knew about the affair. Her response was off. Maybe I was right, and Eli was the one who killed Mira, but I have to be sure. I have to go talk to Izzie."

"If it makes you feel better, I can pay her a visit someday."

"It doesn't," Cyra snapped. "You know me dealing with this on my own was the whole fucking point of me joining the group. I have to find my sister's killer. I have to confirm I killed the right person. And if I didn't, I have to rectify that. You are not going to take that away from me, Jason."

In the past, when she used his real name, Lamprey had shaken himself like a dog, remembering their agreement, settling down. But now it seemed to spur him on—his eyes leveled at her; he moved forward one step at a time. Maybe his reaction to his name in the past was an act meant to pacify her, soothe her into thinking she had some control.

"You won't believe me, but I am sorry it has to end this way," Lamprey said. "Think of it this way; I'm helping you reunite with your sister."

"Why now?" Cyra asked, desperate to keep him talking, wondering if her neighbors would do anything if she started screaming or if they'd just turn the volume up on their TV. "Why didn't you kill me any of the other times you had me alone?"

Lamprey looked at her like she was an idiot. "Because I liked you, Cyra. And when I like someone, I need our special moment together to be perfect. None of those other times would have been perfect. It wasn't what I envisioned for you." He leaned forward, breathing deeply as if he could sniff her from five feet away, and Cyra clambered over the bed, pressing herself against the opposite wall, putting the mattress between her and him. "God, I think you're the most special woman, Cyra. And I want to keep you that way forever."

"Is that what you say to all the girls?" she spat as Lamprey looked down at the bed blocking him as if it had sprouted up in front of him without warning.

"No." Lamprey's voice took on a dreamy quality as he gazed at her from across the sheets. "My darlings are wonderful and interesting. But none of them have ever captivated me like you have. And that's because you're different. You're like me."

Then he moved.

His body rippled like a snake as he leaped over the bed, clearing it with upsetting ease. Cyra hissed and backed away, the door behind her now and Lamprey near the windows. Seeing a chance, Cyra tried to bolt toward the front door again, but Lamprey was on her so quickly she barely had time to turn around and put her fists up before he snatched at her wrists.

"Don't you see?" Lamprey whispered, yanking her to his chest like he had done after killing Sand Fly, so close he could have leaned forward and pressed his lips against her forehead. "Me, the group, everything you did to get here, right now: We are part of you. We live inside you. You learned from us. I know it. I saw how you killed that man in the park. And I applaud your growth. It's been thrilling to watch. But it's over, Cyra."

It was his use of her real name that told her he was serious. This time, there would be no manipulation, no trickery. He was done with her. Now he wanted to destroy his toy so no one else could play with it.

The last time Lamprey had her by the wrists, Cyra held back, not wanting to reveal her martial arts skills before the right moment. *This* was the right moment.

Twisting her wrists sharply and moving her elbows out, Cyra broke Lamprey's grip and headbutted her forehead toward his perfectly straight nose. At the very last second, he recoiled and she made contact with his cheekbone instead. The reverberation sang through Cyra's skull, and Lamprey cursed in pain. Cyra thrust her knee upwards violently, right into Lamprey's groin. He gasped, face paling.

Swiftly stepping back, Cyra planted her feet, widened her stance, put up her left fist in front of her chin, pivoted on her back foot, and shot a hefty cross into Lamprey's jaw. He toppled backward on the bed, his face reddening where Cyra punched him.

Cyra didn't waste any time. She raced over to the kitchen, which was closer than her crumpled jacket in the hall, and flipped a switch, blasting the apartment with bright, white light. She slipped a seven-inch carving knife free from the butcher block.

Lamprey was groaning and gathering himself, and there was a moment when Cyra saw her escape. She could make it to the front door. She could pound on a neighbor's door, pray they opened up, or she could run down to the street and get a passerby to call 911. But that was what a scared person would do. And Cyra wasn't scared of him. She hated him.

Lamprey looked up, a note of apprehension on his face as he realized she could easily escape. He pushed off the bed, rubbing his jaw, and got back on his feet, pausing. He was waiting for her decision.

Cyra glanced toward the door, and then down at her knife, held in a hammer grip, thumb pointing toward the ceiling, the way the online tutorials taught her.

She locked eyes with him, and she knew he saw the truth reflected there. This was their private war. It had been the entire time. He didn't kill Mira, but he played with Cyra since day one. She was going to end it now.

She wasn't leaving.

CHAPTER

26

Lamprey watched carefully as Cyra crossed back toward the middle of the apartment, still giving him a wide berth, but positioning herself so that she had room—as much as possible in the cramped space—to move so she wouldn't be trapped against a wall.

"Someone's had martial arts training I see," Lamprey said, his voice a little froggy from Cyra's assault, but still pleased. "Clever to keep that hidden. You really *are* special. And I'm not even surprised. It's what I'd expect from you. But this is hardly a fair fight. You also have a knife."

"Do you think I'm stupid?" Cyra asked. They were about fifteen feet apart, and she knew how fast he moved. She needed to stay alert. "Where's Sand Fly's big hunting knife, huh?"

"Bottom of the Hudson. I don't really enjoy knives. I think they're . . . unrefined."

"You expect me to believe you're unarmed?"

"Come here and find out." In a flash, the old Lamprey was back, grinning at her and batting his eyelashes absurdly.

And because he didn't think she would, because he had dropped his predatory guard for a moment to taunt her, Cyra made her move.

She leapt over the squat coffee table covered in dirty dishes and darted forward. She sliced out to the side with her blade as a sharp exhale fell from Lamprey's mouth and he swiveled. A spurt of crimson arced through the air as her knife caught the edge of Lamprey's shoulder, but he dodged her fast enough that the wound was minor. He was moving away from the bed and toward the far right wall, pinning himself in where Cyra was minutes earlier.

For a moment, Cyra felt something that went beyond the surge of adrenaline—a fierce exhale moved through her taut muscles, the rippling body she had trained for years. She wasn't a gazelle, legs pumping, heart fraying, trying to escape; she was a lion, fanged and fighting. In those few seconds, she understood. She understood how intoxicating it was to be the hunter.

But she had also walked all night, and her feet were bleeding in her shoes.

The momentum of her attack sent Cyra skidding to a clumsy halt only steps away from Lamprey, who dropped his exaggerated grin and offered her a small, dangerous smile instead.

"Hello, kitten," he whispered, and lunged.

They collided, Cyra keeping a hold of her knife so tightly her forearm began to cramp. Lamprey's right hand snaked around her throat as Cyra's free one pulled back and slammed a fist against the side of his head.

The two of them tumbled to the ground, Cyra beneath Lamprey. They were rolled up against her dresser now; Cyra could feel crumpled clothes beneath the small of her back, digging into her skin as she writhed under the much larger man.

Cyra tried to get into a guard position, where she could wrap her legs around Lamprey's torso, bringing his head down so she could stab him, but Lamprey was stronger, heavier, and sensed her instincts. He straddled her hips, pinning her to the ground, rendering her legs, already tired and sore from her walk, virtually useless.

"Hush, kitten, it will be over soon," Lamprey said, his voice consoling, but his eyes two chips of ice. One hand pressed against her throat while the other reached for her knife.

But Cyra wasn't going to let him take another blade from her. With black spots forming at the edges of her vision, she evaded his left hand and thrust the knife upwards, deep into Lamprey's side.

A harsh exhale fell from Lamprey's lips, and he glanced down as if confused to see a knife handle protruding from his ribcage. He moved his other hand to Cyra's throat as well, doubling the pressure.

Cyra tried to yank the blade from his torso so she could attack again, or at least speed up his bleeding, but her arms weren't working anymore. Her hand dropped to the floor with a soft thud as blackness fuzzed across her eyes, lines shifting and crisscrossing like an Etch-A-Sketch.

"Good . . . aim . . ." Lamprey panted as lines of blood started to dribble from his wound. He seemed to be struggling to breathe, same as her, yet different. "Now it's a waiting game. Who . . . will . . . give in . . . first?"

Cyra thought that at the moment of her death she would see Mira's face. Or maybe even the whole family; Mira and their parents, standing there, giving her strength, taking care of her. But there was nothing except the face of a man who had murdered countless other people, staring down at her.

Cyra's mother had abandoned her. Her father hadn't favored her. And her sister . . .

The truth was that Mira had used her. She had used Cyra to get to New York City, she had used her to jumpstart her photography career, and she had used her as someone to blame every time things went sideways.

Cyra loved her family. And one by one, they all left her. It made sense they would leave her in death as well.

No. She might have done some shitty things, but you still owe Mira. And you still need to know if you killed the right person.

Cyra's hands were numb, her vision was going, and her legs were shaky. She wasn't sure she had the strength to perform the move she needed to do, but she had one shot. She had to take it—now.

Cyra brought her feet underneath her knees, and then, with her last bit of power, thrust her hips hard toward the ceiling. Lamprey, still on her abdomen, was jarred loose by the sudden movement, body tipping forward toward Cyra's front half, some of his weight slipping from her throat. Taking advantage of his imbalance, Cyra twisted her hips laterally, freed her knees and finished the mount escape by locking her legs around Lamprey's midsection, drawing him toward her and into guard.

She seized the handle of the knife sticking out from Lamprey's side, her lungs gasping for oxygen as she wrenched it free with a wet squelching sound.

The pressure on her throat eased for a second as Lamprey wheezed in pain, and Cyra, bringing Lamprey's neck closer to her head by squeezing her knees, slashed the tip of the knife up toward Lamprey's carotid artery. The skin of his neck split like the soft rind of a peach, and hot blood cascaded over Cyra's face as she whipped the knife back.

Cyra released her guard hold and kicked Lamprey away from her body. He fell against the floor, hands moving to his own throat as if programmed to do so, as if the need to try to stem the life leaving his body was a reflex he couldn't control. Wet gurgling noises were coming from the man's mouth as he slumped over to the side, the upper half of his body propped up by Cyra's dresser.

She wanted to make some profound final statement, tell Lamprey that she bested him after all. It would have felt cinematic and full circle. But life wasn't a movie, and Cyra's esophagus felt like a crushed straw. Instead, she met Lamprey's eyes and watched as they stilled. Only the fact that his chest stopped moving clued her in to his death. His eyes were just as empty as they were in life.

Cyra lay on the floor for a minute, dragging air into her chest with raw inhales that sounded like a car breaking down. Her neck felt beyond bruised, and it hurt to move her head, but she felt alive, energized, lighter. Sitting up, wincing from the pain, she scooted away from Lamprey's body and rested her back against the bedframe. Streaked in blood, the expression frozen on Lamprey's face wasn't fear or rage, it was disappointment.

Cyra sat there long enough that her breathing eventually slowed and returned to normal. The only sound in the apartment was the drip of Lamprey's blood on her floorboards; a sound that was becoming more and more infrequent as the blood congealed and stopped flowing.

Reaching forward and pulling the knife up with her as she got unsteadily to her feet, Cyra wobbled her way over to the bathroom to clean up. Staring at herself in the mirror, smeared with red, eyes bloodshot and neck tattooed with imprints of Lamprey's fingers, she wondered if she should rethink confronting Izzie. Maybe she was overreacting. Izzie knowing about the cheating didn't necessarily mean she had anything to do with Mira's death. Cyra could disappear; convince herself she killed the right person.

But her instinct was telling her otherwise. Izzie lied several times on that video call, and Cyra needed to know why. Cyra needed the truth.

Cyra peeled off her ruined clothes and dropped them to the floor of the bathroom. She allowed herself a brief shower while the body of a man who once saved her life cooled outside the door.

CHAPTER 27

Cyra hailed a yellow cab outside her apartment and took it to Izzie's. She was no longer concerned with staying anonymous or not leaving a trail. She would deal with this loose end, and then leave the city as quickly as possible.

It was a beautiful day, cold and crisp but with a brilliant blue sky. She leaned against the window of the cab and watched the houses, decorated for the holidays, whiz by.

Her breathing was steady, her heart rate was even.

When the cab deposited her in front of Izzie's apartment, Cyra rang the doorbell, adjusting the scarf she was wearing to cover the bruises already forming on her neck.

"Cyra?" Izzie asked incredulously, opening the door. "Wait, do you know where Eli is? I still can't find him; I called all his friends and no one's heard from him. That was fucked up, what you said on the phone, by the way." The younger woman was rambling, and she looked even more disheveled in person than she did on the phone screen.

"Can I come in?" Cyra croaked. "I need to talk to you."

"Your voice sounds weird," Izzie observed, brow furrowing, but she stepped aside, and the two of them entered the belly of the apartment.

"What happened in here?" Cyra asked as she walked inside. It looked like a bomb went off. There were clothes everywhere, papers scattered all around. Both Eli's and Izzie's laptops were open on the kitchen table, face to face. An empty bottle of wine sat next to the computers, a stained glass beside it.

"You got in my head, that's what happened," Izzie hissed. "I started looking for more evidence of cheating. But I can't find anything, and Eli must have changed his computer's password."

Clearly, Izzie was breaking down. Having lost track of her boyfriend seemed to have spun her out of control completely.

"You knew," Cyra stated. "When did you figure it out, Izzie?"

The two of them stood a few feet apart, in the center of the mess. For a moment, Cyra thought Izzie would lie. But then, finally, she sighed, slumping. Izzie's face fell, her chest caved inwards. She gazed down at her feet, hands trembling. "After Wine and Cheese. When she stayed with us." She didn't say, "Just before her death," but Cyra heard it anyway.

"Did you catch them?"

"I saw them!" Izzie cried. "On the couch, *my* couch, with *my* best friend. He left our bed to stick his tongue in her when I was in the other room. I always knew he had a soft spot for her. I knew he liked her when we first met. But I thought . . . I thought I was enough. I guess I was wrong."

"Did you know Mira broke it off with Eli?" Cyra asked, her muscles beginning to tighten. Her hand drifted into the pocket of her coat so she could stroke the edge of the knife handle.

"What?" This time, Izzie's reaction looked real; her pupils dilated, her cheeks flushed, her browed arced toward her hairline.

"You didn't know that part," Cyra observed.

"It doesn't matter," Izzie burst out, her neck corded and tight now. "She would have gone back to him eventually. She wanted everything I had, even my boyfriend. She would have taken him from me! He's all I have! Mira had you and her father, Arthur, and all her Tinder dates' attention. She was going to be a famous photographer; she was loved by everyone. But that wasn't enough, she had to take my man!"

"And that's why you killed her," Cyra said, her words falling like stones.

She expected Izzie to deny it, but the trick that hadn't worked on Lamprey—stating an accusation like it was fact—worked on the younger girl. Izzie's face grew red. She drew herself up to her full height, lip curled, eyes narrowed and hot, and snapped, "I had no choice!"

Cyra slumped slightly before forcing herself to straighten again. She thought of Eli's broken skull, his warm blood. So it was true. She made a mistake.

She remembered Mockingbird's words. He said women kill for revenge or heartbreak. Izzie had killed for both.

"How did you know about the crossed ankles?" Cyra asked, the one missing piece, the one that had sent her on a wild goose chase.

Izzie shrugged, and Cyra noticed her words were slurred. She glanced again at the empty wine bottle on the table behind Izzie. Izzie said, "I started going through Eli's phone when he was showering to make sure he wasn't texting other girls. But then one day I saw he downloaded this weird file, and I read it, and I was disgusted, but what could I do? It's not like I could have brought it up to him and been like, 'Hey babe, I found this while I was snooping, let's chat about it.' It always stuck with me. When it happened . . . I . . . I panicked. I remembered the file; it popped back into my head like it had been waiting for me all that time."

Cyra's hands were starting to tremble slightly, and she made the effort to return to a place of steadiness. She had a second chance here to right a wrong. She couldn't mess it up.

I killed an innocent person, Cyra thought, and clamped down on the sentiment so hard and fast it was shattered immediately, not giving it anytime to root and summon an emotion. *He wasn't that innocent. He was obsessed with Mira. He made her a target for Izzie.*

"I can't believe I missed the Mira thing at first," Izzie said, dragging her hands through her hair, giving her a crazed, frantic look. "The texts he sent her were always completely normal. I didn't know they were emailing each other. I trusted them both." Her voice broke, and she snarled, really snarled, like an animal, as if to make up for it.

"You replicated a serial killer's signature to get away with murdering your best friend," Cyra stated, hand fastened tightly around the knife in her pocket now.

"I *had* to," Izzie repeated, turning her fiery eyes on Cyra. She blinked, as if seeing her for the first time. "I'm really sorry, Cy. I didn't mean to do it. I decided to join her on one of her crack-of-dawn runs so I could talk to her alone, and when we took a break at the boathouse, I couldn't hold it in anymore. I confronted her, she denied it, and it made me so angry . . . It just happened."

Izzie was claiming it wasn't premeditated, but that couldn't be right. Cyra's jaw clenched and she exhaled slowly. "If it hadn't been planned, you would have told Eli where you were going that morning. But you'd already decided to kill her, so you didn't want to implicate yourself. No one ever mentioned you being on the run with my sister, which meant you kept it quiet."

"No, I swear! I didn't plan it," Izzie said, her hands shaking as she stared at Cyra. "I wanted to talk to her alone, girl to girl. I just . . . I lost it! She *laughed* at me when I told her I knew! She said I was imagining things, and then she turned her back on me. Like I didn't matter. Next thing I knew she was laying on the ground, and I had a rock in my hand. It was like I blacked out."

"And then you realized what you did, so you turned her over and posed her body," Cyra said, voice cold. "I bet she was covered in your DNA, but since she was living with you, the police overlooked it."

"Don't blame me," Izzie said, her tone rising. "*You* ruined it. It's always been you. You did that stupid article, and that's what made Mira move in with us, and that's why Eli cheated. It's your fault. Yours."

Cyra saw Eli's face in her mind. She misjudged him. He wasn't a killer. Just another stupid boy who only thought with his dick.

Cyra squeezed her eyes shut. She couldn't bring Eli back. She couldn't revive the life she took, and Eli was partially to blame for all of this anyway. Remorse didn't benefit her, so there was no reason to feel it. But she made Mira a promise, and the least she could do was make Eli's death mean something.

Cyra opened her eyes, pulling out the knife from her coat pocket.

"I won't apologize for this," Cyra said, her voice low. "You did it to yourself."

"What is that? What are you doing?" Izzie spat, lurching back. "Don't fuck with me Cyra. I killed someone. I killed your *sister*. You have no idea . . ."

Izzie's energy was changing. Cyra felt the swell of it, a manic, toothy desperation. Izzie's eyes were darkening, and Cyra knew she was witnessing what her sister had turned away from a few months ago.

But Cyra was not Mira. And Izzie should have remembered that.

Ignoring how every movement jostled her tender neck and sore legs, Cyra mimicked Lamprey, darting forward in one fluid motion, twisting and reaching Izzie's side before she could move away. She could stab her, right now, and end it. But she wanted Izzie to have the time to know what was happening, so instead, Cyra sent a fist into Izzie's torso, knocking the other girl off-balance. Izzie shrieked, but instead of running away or cowering, she spat on the ground and lunged forward. Cyra quick-stepped back, and executed a roundhouse kick, sending Izzie crashing against the kitchen table. The empty bottle toppled over; the wine glass shattered on the floor. The two laptops clattered against each other.

After taking on Sand Fly and Lamprey, overpowering Izzie was like throwing around a kitten. It felt too easy, and that made Cyra hesitate. She didn't have the same buzz in her bones she had when fighting Sand Fly or Lamprey. If the opponent was too weak, the win didn't feel earned.

There was something unearthly in Izzie's expression as she got back to her feet. "It's not my fault," she said, and there was no remorse in her voice.

Cyra's hesitation vanished. Earned? Izzie *earned* this the moment she killed Mira. Cyra could barely push the words through her bruised throat. "She trusted you. She loved you."

"Come on, Cy," Izzie slurred, stepping forward despite the naked knife in Cyra's hand. "I told you; it was an accident. You're better than this."

"No," Cyra replied, a thrill running through her veins. "I'm not."

Cyra moved toward the other woman, quick and sharp, watching the understanding rise in Izzie's eyes as she realized Cyra was serious, dangerous.

Cyra's knife flashed as it cut through the air, finding a home in Izzie's flesh.

After, Cyra stood alone in the middle of the apartment. She expected to feel exhausted, the lack of sleep and intense physical activity finally catching up with her, but just like with Lamprey, Cyra's chest felt lighter, steps springier. Her shoulders were lifted, and her breath was easy. Cyra slid her blood-stained coat from her shoulders, letting it drop at her feet, resolving to take one of Izzie's from the coatrack on her way out.

There were shards all over the floor from the shattered wine glass, and blood spray decorated the walls. One of Izzie's golden earrings, a little hoop of metal, glinted on the floor. It had been ripped from Izzie's head during the struggle. The apartment where Cyra spent so much time with Mira and her friends was a complete wreck. And now all three of them, Mira, Eli, and Izzie, were dead.

Cyra looked down at Izzie's chalky face, the wounds slashed across her chest and neck. As Izzie's blood coagulated on the floor beneath her body, Cyra knelt by the younger woman's feet. She lifted Izzie's left leg, already heavy and inflexible like a wooden stilt, and crossed her left ankle over her right.

Now, Cyra thought, *we are done.*

CHAPTER

28

When Cyra got home, she moved fast. Her body ached and her feet were painful, but leaving a schoolteacher's corpse in her apartment after a loud fight in a nice neighborhood was different than sinking a body in a lake. Cyra needed to get out of town immediately. She threw some clothes and her emergency cash stash into a black duffle bag. She would catch a train upstate, stopping at her father's house. He'd be so drunk he wouldn't even notice her entering the basement and collecting the twenty grand in cash he kept in a tin box down there.

Besides the cash and some clothes, everything else would have to stay. Her phone, laptop, keys, wallet. She would start over with a new purpose in mind.

Cyra knew it would be hard, almost impossible, to find Mockingbird now. He'd be on the road, leaving the city behind as the dust settled. All she had was his last name, Walker, and his job. But she knew what he looked like. She knew he didn't carry a gun because he liked to kill in the old-fashioned way. She knew he had a thing for eyes and sported a limp. And she knew that with the right planning and enough time, she could find him and surprise him.

She wondered briefly if Whipworm died; if she should circle back to New York sometime and kill him too. But there was always time.

There were more people out there like Lamprey and Mockingbird. More people who needed to be eliminated. Because of Mira, Cyra stumbled into a viper's nest, and now that she had seen the infestation, she couldn't go back to pretending these people didn't exist.

Besides, there was still an unknown man out there murdering women and crossing their ankles.

Cyra looked at Mira's laptop, sitting open on her kitchen table. It was a shame she couldn't bring it. The last part of her sister. She knew she didn't have the time, but Cyra couldn't help herself—she sat at the table and took one last look at Mira's emails.

On a whim, Cyra navigated back to Mira's inbox and typed her own name into the search bar. A flurry of old emails popped up from back when they lived together and Cyra would send Mira rent requests. But there was something new, too—a draft, unsent, to Cyra's email address that Mira wrote the day before her death.

The hand tracing the trackpad shook slightly as Cyra opened the unsent email, eyes blurring as she scanned it.

Cy,

> *Every day I wonder why you did what you did and it hurts so bad to know you couldn't come to talk to me about your worries with Arthur. I'm not stupid. I know he was using me, but you didn't even think about how I was using him too. I'm not some child you have to run around and save all the time. And you owe me about a million apologies. But I don't hate you, you're my big sister, I love you so much. I need some time, OK? Separate from you. I know we live in*

different boroughs but even here I can feel you. I need to be on my own for a bit and figure this out. I'll always love you. I mean, you're my sister. I can't not have you in my life. Just let me live it my way. We're not kids anymore. You don't have to take care of me. Take care of yourself now.

XO Mira

Cyra pulled away from the laptop, trying to memorize the words. Then she hovered the mouse above the garbage can icon and hit "Delete forever."

She closed the laptop, leaving it where it was, and spared a glance for the dead man moldering in her apartment. She barely noticed Lamprey was there as she went through the dresser drawers above his body; it was like he was part of the furniture now. Although she didn't envy whoever found him if they left him too long to rot.

Ready to go, Cyra headed toward the hall and opened the closet, kneeling and pushing all the coats and other crap to the side, thinking about this version of herself. Who she became, or rather, who she finally embraced.

If she could feel regret, maybe Cyra would mourn what she did to Eli, but she didn't want to bring dead emotions back to life. Besides, even though he didn't kill Mira, Eli's actions helped lead to her death. Cyra was disappointed by her mistake, but that was all she could afford Eli.

Lamprey's words from when they first interacted outside the group rang in her head: *"You're not one of us. But I think you could be."*

Even then, he judged her wrong. He sensed a darkness, but he didn't know how far it had already spread.

The first thing Cyra pulled from the closet was the framed photo. Cyra looked at her own face captured in Mira's portrait—the fear, the anxiety, the desperation in her expression. She flipped the frame over, popped off the back, and grabbed the print, shoving it into the duffle bag, not caring if the edges got torn or crumpled. She would keep it as a reminder of who she could never be again. And a reminder of how Mira saw her.

Then Cyra dug past a pair of old rainboots and found it: the shoebox.

Slowly, reverently, she lifted the lid, peering inside. She shifted aside the plastic bag containing PJ's stained baseball hat, placing it gently on her knees to reveal the remaining contents.

There, at the bottom of the shoebox, was a ring.

It was big, ugly. From a hand that once pressed against her sister's throat.

Cyra ran a finger across the cold grooves of the ruby set in the band. Next to the ring was the other keepsake she slipped in the box a few months ago—a silver cuff link, shiny and new.

Cyra thought of Mockingbird; of the last thing he told her before disappearing. He said women killed for petty reasons, like revenge and heartbreak. Men killed for life, something he thought she could never understand.

He was wrong. She did understand. She understood that killing was not about ending a life, but preserving the beauty of those who got to keep breathing.

There were other bad people out there.

Killing them would give her air.

Cyra looked into the box and pulled something out from her pocket: the thin gold watch that used to encircle the wrist of Jason Weston. She dropped it in the shoebox. From her other pocket, she pulled out the library card she took from Eli's wallet before disposing of it and the golden earring from the floor of Izzie's apartment. Cyra paused for a moment, considering the library card. Eli wasn't like the others. Maybe he didn't belong in the box. She slipped the card back into her pocket and examined Izzie's earring instead. It was stained with a rusted red spot of dried blood. Cyra placed the earring in the shoebox next to the ring, the watch, and the cuff link, and she smiled.

Lamprey was right, she thought.

Perhaps she belonged in their group after all.

MISTLETOE

The rain splattered on Cyra Griffin's windshield as she drove down the darkening country road. It was dusk, the light blue and hazy from the clouds.

She went slowly, carefully. She was looking for someone.

After rounding the next bend, she spotted him. Finally.

Cyra saw Mira smiling at her phone the morning after Cyra confronted PJ for choking Mira out. Suspicious, she stole Mira's phone when she went to the bathroom and read the texts PJ was sending her, apologizing, begging for a second chance. Mira, still deep in the throes of gaslighting and abuse, would return to him. And he would keep hurting her until he killed her.

Cyra wouldn't let it happen.

She knew PJ worked at a local gas station after school twice a week. She knew he took the back roads home after his shift, biking to stay in shape. The weather was bad that day, so it was perfect—a plausible excuse for a tragic accident. A gift from the universe.

Cyra went looking for him.

PJ's baseball hat was plastered to his head by the rain as he pedaled furiously. He wasn't wearing a helmet. He never did. Young men thought they were invincible.

Cyra hit the gas, speeding up, gripping the wheel tightly, her heart hammering, swerving in front of PJ so that he yanked his handlebars, treads slipping on the slick pavement. Cyra slammed the brakes, putting the car in park as PJ toppled over, panting in the mud on the side of the road.

Cyra moved fast. She leapt from the car, leaving the door open, and ran over to her sister's boyfriend. He was groaning, face down in the weeds, starting to push into the ground and lift himself up.

Cyra grabbed a rock from the side of the road and slammed it against PJ's head, once. The sickening wet thump was echoed by PJ collapsing back to the ground. Blood was staining his baseball hat, and Cyra removed it. She would keep it, as a reminder she could do hard things for Mira.

Satisfied, Cyra carefully arranged the rock on the ground and turned PJ over on to his back, lifting his head up and letting it drop wetly against the stone, exactly where she hit him.

Cyra reached down, gently searching for his pulse. It was still.

Her shoulders dropped and her heartbeat slowed. Silence settled over her skin. Before she left, Cyra slipped PJ's class ring from his hand. She would keep that too. He didn't deserve it.

She drove off, PJ's bike's tires still spinning gently in the rearview mirror.

Five years later, Cyra waited for Arthur McCowen in his parking garage.

Mira told Cyra that Arthur always parked in the same spot, in the same garage, down the block from his office in SoHo. That was back when they were talking. Cyra was suffering through what felt like endless radio silence from Mira, so Cyra had been keeping herself entertained by blackmailing Arthur.

But it wasn't enough. He was the reason Mira was in pain, and worse, he was the reason the sisters weren't talking. Despite the growing heat for Arthur online as people began to notice Cyra's anonymous posts, Arthur wasn't personally responding to Cyra's threats, so it was time for a different tactic.

She hid behind a Range Rover and waited, glancing up at the useless camera affixed to the ceiling. She had checked it the day before while scoping out the garage—it wasn't wired up to anything. A camera for show only. The people parking here would be furious if they knew the truth, but it was perfect for Cyra's purposes.

Arthur's footsteps heralded his arrival, and Cyra's body quieted, became numb as she prepared to yet again protect her sister.

When she ran up behind him and pushed Arthur over the stone barrier on the sixth floor of the garage, her fingers snagged against his cuff link, ripping it off and sending it clattering to the concrete floor. Arthur was a shrimpy man with weak arms; it had been easy to activate her fighting strength to lift him up and over the wall using her own momentum.

She knelt and picked up the cuff link, slipping it into her jeans pocket, before peeking over the rail, spotting Arthur's twisted form on the sidewalk below. She heard someone scream, and quickly pulled her head back.

Arthur was facing public outrage for the Brush Culture article now. He was having his own little #MeToo moment. People wouldn't be shocked to hear he took his own life. Even if that wasn't the truth.

Cyra left the parking garage, humming to herself.

As she strolled down the bustling sidewalk, hearing the distant sirens as they careened toward Greene Street, Cyra thought about the future. Mira wasn't speaking to her now, but Cyra hoped she would forgive her soon.

Once they were back on good terms, she would tell Mira the truth, perhaps. About everything she did to keep her safe. Or maybe she should wait until they were old and gray and sipping iced teas on a porch somewhere upstate. Maybe at that point, Mira would find Cyra's actions admirable, a testament of Cyra's love. Or maybe it was better for Cyra to take these secrets to her grave, keeping any burden from her sister. After all, the whole point was to keep Mira away from pain. Keep her safe. And keep her close to Cyra. Forever.

Cyra's eyes landed on a set of twins on the sidewalk ahead of her. The girls were squabbling over a bag of kettle corn, their parents trailing behind them with the starry-eyed look some tourists got while walking around the city.

"You've had more than me, Mary!"

"No way! You're hogging it. Connie, share!"

The twins weren't identical, but they were dressed the same, wearing light blue rompers, their dark hair in pigtails. Cyra passed the girls, glancing back once over her shoulder to watch them go. The sisters, though bickering, were holding hands.

Cyra kept walking, not bothering to hide her smile.

ACKNOWLEDGMENTS

First, thank you, reader, for picking up this book and giving it a shot. Writing and publishing a novel is a long journey, and I greatly appreciate you being a part of it.

Lady Killers: Deadly Women Throughout History by Tori Telfer was instrumental in my research on female serial killers and in shaping some of the characters in this book—dangerous women are fascinating, and Telfer's research and analysis, especially in regard to our society's inherent sexism, was inspiring.

This novel would not have been possible without the guidance, passion, and expertise of my agent, Amy Giuffrida. Thank you, Amy, for your hard work, creative eye, and love for all things creepy.

Thank you to the entire Crooked Lane Books team, and especially to Terri Bischoff and Rebecca Nelson for seeing exactly what I was going for and helping to make this story stronger; to Thaisheemarie Fantauzzi Perez for all production and editorial assistance; to Dulce Botello, Mikaela Bender, and Cassidy Graham for their marketing efforts. Thank you to the subsidiary rights team, including Stephanie Manova and Megan Matti, and to the production and operations interns working behind the scenes.

To the A Team and all the other fantastic writers I met on social media along the way—thank you for cultivating an inclusive, positive, and honest community.

To Boozeless Book Club—I am so lucky to have such a supportive group of readers in my life. You are a truly special community. A big thanks to Nicki and Jennifer for reading an early version of this story, and thank you to everyone who read or reviewed an ARC.

To my friends and extended family who have been utterly amazing during every step of the process—I love you all dearly. Thank you for your warmth, kindness, and willingness to shout from the rooftops about my book. Each of you have a different skill or connection I was able to lean on, and I can't express my gratitude enough.

To Mark, for taking my headshots and immortalizing The Call (and all the emotional support thereafter). Good things happen when you're around.

To Bella—very grateful our relationship is nothing like Cyra's and Mira's. Although I would totally murder bad guys for you. Your wisdom and encouragement are unparalleled. I couldn't ask for a better sister to quote *The Office* and watch reality TV with.

To Mom and Dad—you loved me when I didn't deserve it; you believed in me when I couldn't; you made my books stronger and my writing better. I am here because of you (literally and metaphorically). From the bottom of my heart to the top of my heart, thank you.

And finally, two communities worked in tandem to help me get healthy and whole—thank you to everyone in the sobriety and climbing groups I was a part of who touched my life. I have no way to express how much that belonging meant to me. This is for all of you.